M J

## YOUR LIBRARY
### PERTH AND KINROSS

PERTH & KINROSS COUNCIL

Education & Children's Services

**Tel 01738 444949 • www.pkc.gov.uk/library**

Also by Barbara Cleverly

# BARBARA CLEVERLY

## Strange Images of Death

A Joe Sandilands Murder Mystery

| PERTH & KINROSS COUNCIL | |
|---|---|
| 05622823 | |
| Bertrams | 25/03/2010 |
| CLE | £18.99 |
| BREX | |

Constable • London

Constable & Robinson Ltd
3 The Lanchesters
162 Fulham Palace Road
London W6 9ER
www.constablerobinson.com

First published in the UK by Constable,
an imprint of Constable & Robinson, 2010

First US edition published by SohoConstable,
an imprint of Soho Press, 2010

Soho Press, Inc.
853 Broadway
New York, NY 10003
www.sohopress.com

A copy of the British Library Cataloguing in Publication
Data is available from the British Library

UK ISBN: 978-1-84901-118-1

US ISBN: 978-1-56947-632-1
US Library of Congress number: 2009049928

Printed and bound in the EU

1 3 5 7 9 10 8 6 4 2

**Mixed Sources**
Product group from well-managed
forests and other controlled sources
www.fsc.org Cert no. SA-COC-1565
© 1996 Forest Stewardship Council
FSC

# Prologue

*Provence, South of France, 1926*

He studied her sleeping face for the last time.

She was lying peacefully on her back, her fair hair spreading in ripples over the pillow. Warm-gold by day, the waves now gleamed pale silver, all colour bleached away by the moonlight. Her features also were drained and only the lips still showed a trace of emotion. They were slightly open and uptilted, perhaps in a suggestion of remembered and recent passion. He smothered the distasteful notion.

Such beauty!

He felt his resolve waver and was alarmed to acknowledge a moment of indecision. He reminded himself that this beauty was his – his to spare or to destroy – and a rush of exaltation swept away the slight uncertainty. It had been a wobble, no more than a weakness imposed on him by convention. Convention? Even at this moment of approaching ecstasy he paused to consider the word. From the Latin, of course. 'A coming together'. In agreement and common consent. Well, convention would never direct *him*. It was his nature to step away from the crowd, to walk in the opposite direction, to think his own rebellious thoughts and to translate those thoughts into action. He would be true to his nature. He would assert his birthright.

He leaned closer until his face was only inches above the still form. He had a fancy that, if he pressed his lips to hers, he might catch her dying breath. The thought revolted and fascinated him in equal measure and he lifted his head. He took a deliberate step backwards. He would not touch her. No part of his body would make contact with hers. To test his resolve he contemplated trailing a lascivious finger along her smooth throat as others had, of allowing that finger to ease over the left collar bone until it encountered the imperfection of a tiny mole half-hidden by a fold of her white gown. His hand remained safely in his pocket. He would look. Admire. Hate.

He stood for a moment, a shadow among shadows. The garment he'd put on had been carefully chosen: an old-fashioned hunting coat (English tailoring, he did believe), it had been abandoned on a hook by the door in the cloakroom by some visiting milord, years, possibly decades, ago. The thick grey tweed was a perfect camouflage – it even had a hood – and, essential for his purpose, not one but two concealed poacher's pockets. His fine nose was revolted by the smell of decay that lurked in the tweedy depths, still stained with the blood of long-dead creatures, but they accommodated the very special equipment he had needed to carry, covertly, along the corridors.

He played with the notion of taking out the heavy-duty military torch and lighting up her last moments, but an innate caution made him dismiss the idea. The moonlight was all the illumination he could wish for. A resplendent August moon shone through the uncurtained windows, coating the alabaster-fair features with an undeserved glaze of sanctity.

The Moon. Generous but demanding deity! He adored her. She was his friend, his accomplice. He welcomed the white peace and forgiveness she brought at the end of each day's red turmoil and sin. Like some sprite from a northern folk tale, he came to life in the dark hours. His eyes grew wide, his thoughts became as clear and cold as the moon herself. His senses were sharpened.

He listened. He turned abruptly as a distant owl

2

screeched and claimed its prey. A farm dog across the valley responded with a half-hearted warning howl and then fell silent, duty done. But from within the walls there was no sound. His stretched senses detected nothing though he could imagine the drunken snores, the unconscious mutterings, the hands groping blindly for a pitcher of cool water as his fellows slept, divided from him by several thick walls and a courtyard. He would be undisturbed.

The weight in his right pocket banged against his thigh and prompted his next move. He took out the heavy claw hammer and ran a hand over the blunt metal head; with the pads of his fingers he tested the sharpness of the up-curving, V-shaped nail-wrench that balanced it at the rear. He required the tool to perform well in both its capacities. It would smash with concentrated force and, with a twist of his hand, would lever and rip. It would be equal to the task. But there would be noise. He took a velvet scarf from his neck and wound it securely around the hammer head to muffle the blows.

He was being overcautious. No one would respond, even if the sounds cut through their wine-fuelled stupor. A strange light might possibly have excited curiosity and investigation by some inquisitive servant. No, he didn't discount a dutiful response from one of these domestics if he were careless enough to draw attention. The live-in staff were well chosen, adequately paid and highly trained. So, no wandering lights. But a few distant creaks and bangs in a crumbling old building went, like the dog's howl, unheeded by everyone.

He'd savoured the moment for too long. Enough of musing. Enough of gloating over her loveliness. Time to move on. Time to clear this filth from his path to make way for a worthier offering.

He took out the fencing mask he'd thought to bring with him and put it over his face. He wanted no tell-tale scratches raising eyebrows at the breakfast table. He pulled up the hood of the hunting coat to cover his hair. There would be no traces of this night's activity left clinging to his person, attracting the attention of that sharp-eyed girl who cleaned out his room.

He was ready.

As a last flourish, he muttered cynically an abbreviated prayer for a lost soul in Latin: '*Quaesumus, Domine, miserere famulae tuae, Alienorae, et a contagiis mortalitatis exutam, in aeternam salvationis partem restitue.* Have mercy on the soul of your maidservant, Aliénore, and free her from the defilement of her mortal flesh . . .'

As he murmured, his supple fingers ran with satisfaction along the smooth wooden handle of the ancient hammer. He'd used it often and knew its strength. The muscles of his arms were accommodated to its use as those of a tennis player to his racquet, and they responded now with familiar ease as he swung the weight upwards over his head and brought it crashing down into the centre of the delicate face.

# Chapter One

*France, August 1926*

'To wake or not to wake the pest?' was Joe's silent question.

Would she really welcome an elbow in the ribs only half an hour after sinking so ostentatiously into sleep? He glanced again at the suspiciously still form in the passenger seat next to him and the half of the face that was visible. The pure profile and slight smile were deceptively angelic, and he decided to leave her to her daydreams. But a road sign had just announced that they were a mere five kilometres north of the town of Valence. Here they were, booming on south at a speed the Morris Oxford cabriolet could never have reached, let alone sustained, on English roads. Joe Sandilands was no car-worshipper, but he could almost have persuaded himself that it (he refused to call this ingenious arrangement of metal 'she') was enjoying swallowing up the huge French distances.

The day was hot; the hood was down. Avenues of plane trees lined the route, offering, for mile after mile, a beneficent shade.

The girl in the passenger seat was fast asleep – or pretending to be. You could never tell with Dorcas. Joe was quite certain that she frequently rolled up her cardigan and pushed her head into it, facing away from him, the minute they got into the car, deliberately to avoid making polite conversation.

And that suited Joe.

Was she being considerate? Or was she bored out of her mind by him? He decided – bored. A seasoned police officer more than twice her age would never be an ideal companion for a fourteen-year-old English girl, however well travelled she might be. Lord! How old was he these days? Thirty-three! But at least no one had yet taken him for her father and Joe was thankful for that.

'My uncle Joseph Sandilands. Commander Sandilands of Scotland Yard,' was all the introduction Dorcas was prepared to supply when she felt their travelling arrangements called for clarification. But it was all the reassurance people seemed to need. The suggestion of a blood relationship and an impressive title put Joe beyond reproach or even question. Particularly when he hurried to add, allowing just the briefest flicker of martyrdom to flit across his agreeable features, that he was escorting his niece down to her father who was spending the summer at the Château du Diable – or whatever its pantomime name was – in Provence. Dropping her off as he himself flighted south to the delights of the Riviera. As he'd jokingly told his sister Lydia who'd engineered the unwelcome escort duty, he would be held up as an example from Calais to Cannes of self-sacrificing unclehood. And so, to his surprise, it had proved. The slight deceit, embarked on in the interests of an oversensitive English concern for the proprieties, had gone unchallenged and undiscovered.

*Uncle* Joseph! The word made him feel old. In his world, uncles were elderly and rather decrepit survivors of the war before the last. They sat in armchairs, smiling benignly at their descendants, muttering of Mafeking, their lower limbs rugged up in tartan. After a shifty glance to make certain Dorcas still had her eyes closed, Joe pushed his sun goggles on to his forehead, tilted his head and squinted critically into the useful mirror he'd had fixed to his windscreen in Lyon to keep an eye on traffic behind. They were all there on his face: the lines and the crow's feet sketched in by a tough life lived mostly outdoors. And undeniably

6

on the advance. But at least his grey eyes were taking on an interesting brilliance as his face grew darker in the southern sun. He narrowed his eyes, trying on an air of menace and mystery. All too easily achieved when the left side of your face was slightly distorted. He'd never found the time to have the battlefield surgery corrected and now it was too late – he'd grown into his shrapnel-scarred features. He wore the damage like a medal – with a silent and bitter pride.

'For goodness' sake, Joe! Book yourself into St Mary's and have that repaired,' his sister Lydia constantly urged. 'Surgeons are so much more skilled these days. They can rebuild whole faces – your little piece of mis-stitching would hardly begin to test them. You'd be in and out in no time and we'd have our handsome old Joe back again the moment the bandages came off.' She'd waggle a minatory finger at him and add: 'And never forget what they say! "The face is the mirror of the soul." A platitude, I agree, but a sentiment I've always put some store by. It's deceitful of you to present this distorted funfair reflection of yourself to the world.'

But he'd resisted. Quibbled. Procrastinated. In eight years of police work, he'd discovered the power of intimidation he could exert by presenting his battered left side to the suspects he was interrogating. It spoke of battles survived, pain endured, experience acquired. With a turn of the head, he could trump the villainy of any man he'd confronted across the interview table. 'You think you're tough?' he challenged silently. 'How tough? As tough as *this*?' Men who'd evaded the draft found themselves wrong-footed, fellow soldiers recognized an officer who'd clearly led from the front and accorded him a measure of silent respect.

Joe underlined the effect of the drama he was assessing in his rear-viewing mirror with the cruel grin and slanting flash of white teeth of a music-hall villain. Not quite Ramon Novarro in *Scaramouche* but, even so – not bad! Not bad at all! He could use that sardonic look at the casino or strolling along the promenade in Nice. He recalled, with a stir of excitement, the words his superior in the War Office had used when encouraging him, for Reasons of State, to undertake this journey to France: 'I'm sure I don't need to remind you, Sandilands, that female companionship – if that's what you're after – is available and of a superior style in France.' The Brigadier's remark was uncharacteristically indiscreet, unwittingly arousing. Joe had been surprised, amused and then dismissive but the titillating notion had stayed with him. His foot unconsciously increased its pressure on the accelerator. Yes, he was eager to be down there, sipping his first pastis under a blistering Riviera sun, eyeing pretty women parading about in tennis skirts and swimming costumes. And if they were enticing your ear with a French accent – so much the better.

'Ah! Bulldog Drummond races south, pistol in his hip pocket, ready for a shoot-out with Le Bossu Masqué,' commented a lazily teasing voice. Dorcas gave a showy yawn to indicate she was open to conversation. 'Only one thing wrong. Pulling a face like that, you really ought to be driving a Sports Bentley. You don't cut much of a dash in a Morris.'

'*Two* things wrong. My female companion – that's *you* – ought to be bound and gagged and wriggling helplessly on the back seat with her head in a bag.'

'Le Bossu's wicked accomplice whom you've taken hostage?'

'Very likely. Female of the species being what she is and all that . . .'

Dorcas looked about her. 'Oy! Didn't I ask you to be sure and tell me when we got to Valence?'

'I was just about to wake you, though I can't imagine why I should bother. It's not much of a place and we're driving straight by it.'

'Family tradition! Father always marks our passage through the town by shouting, "*A Valence, le Midi com-*

8

*mence!'* Though at the speed my family plods along in a horse-drawn caravan we have more time to enjoy the moment. Listen, Joe! In a minute or so, if you slow down a bit, you'll hear them. The cicadas. The sound of Provence.'

Joe smiled. She was right. In a strange way, everything behind them was of the north: green and quiet. The snow-clad Alps still funnelled their cold breath down the valley of the river the road was following. But the land ahead was tilted towards the sun. The atmosphere grew suddenly more brilliant, the rush of air warmer. The vegetation was changing and he welcomed the sight of the first outlying umbrella pines and the narrow dark fingers of cypress trees leaning gently before the wind, beckoning them on. Soon there would be olives fluttering the silvery underside of their leaves at him.

He took his foot off the accelerator and, hearing his first cicada, decided to stand in for her absent father, Orlando. The girl had little enough in the way of family life; the least he could do was reinforce the few happy memories she chose to share with him. *'Le Midi commence!'* he shouted. 'Here comes the South!'

Satisfied, the ritual complete, Dorcas breathed in the changing perfumes and asked for the umpteenth time: 'Are we nearly there, Joe?' to annoy him.

He decided to bore her back to sleep again with a recitation of distances, speeds and map references but a rush of good humour cut him short. 'No! Miles to go before bedtime. Big place, Provence. I was planning to spend the night in Avignon then set off into the hills straight after breakfast to track down your pa. Silmont? That's the place we have to find. Outskirts of the Lubéron hills. Olive-silvery Silmont?' he speculated. 'I wonder if there'll be vines growing there? And lavender. Honeysuckle. All those herbs ... wild thyme ... rosemary ... oregano,' he murmured. 'Dorcas?'

9

She was feigning sleep again. Botany also was a bore, clearly.

Joe fought down a spurt of irritation with the child's father. As a friend, Orlando Joliffe came in for a good measure of regard, even affection, from Joe. Joe found – and was surprised to find – that he admired his skills as an artist but he also enjoyed the man's company. He appreciated his intelligence and his worldly ways. When Joe made himself evaluate the relationship which would have been frowned on in his own staid professional circle, he came reluctantly to the conclusion that there was in Orlando a quality of raffish insouciance, a childlike delight in sensual indulgence that struck a chord in Joe's being, that spoke to something long buried under layers of Quaker respectability.

Yes, as a drinking companion there was none better but, judged as a father, Orlando failed on all counts to satisfy. He wasn't uncaring exactly but careless, ready to leave the upbringing of his four motherless children to anyone he could persuade or pay or blackmail into attending to their needs. When Joe's sister, in dire emergency, had shown neighbourly concern and rashly offered to take Dorcas under her wing, Orlando had accepted with shaming alacrity.

Lovely, good-hearted Lydia! Joe felt a pang of guilt whenever he thought of his sister's involvement with the wretched Orlando's family circus.

It had all been Joe's fault.

In a moment of concern for the family's situation, he'd handed over Lydia's telephone number. 'This here's my sister's number. You'll see she lives close by. She has children of her own and she's a trained nurse. You can depend on her. Give her a ring if there should be an immediate problem and you can't raise me.'

And Dorcas had taken him at his word. With life-changing results for several people, not least poor Lydia.

10

Appalled by the circumstances of the children's hand-to-mouth, bohemian existence Lydia had swept them all away to the safety of her own comfortable home. Dorcas had stayed on longer than the rest, and, with her uncivilized ways of going on, she'd become a project for Lydia, her upbringing a social duty. 'Give me that girl for two years and I'll have her fit to present to the Queen at a Buckingham Palace reception,' she'd been unwise enough to declare in Orlando's hearing. He'd hurried to take her up on the offer and Dorcas had become a fixture in the household. And Joe had acquired 'a niece'.

Months had passed but 'Auntie' Lydia was still a long way short of her target, Joe reckoned. As his brother-in-law commented, 'Buckingham Palace be blowed! I wouldn't trust that scallywag to behave herself at a Lyon's Corner Café.'

But then, on their journey through France, the child had surprised Joe. Lydia's training and preparation had not been in vain, it seemed. Dorcas had put on gloves and – alarmingly – silk stockings and behaved impeccably for the family at the Champagne Château Houdart where they'd stayed near Rheims. He glanced at the shiny dark head with its newly acquired and very fashionable fringed bob and smiled a smile that was both sad and tender. The wretched girl, he did believe, had fallen in love. With the highly suitable and totally admirable son of the house. Aged all of sixteen, Georges Houdart had seemed equally smitten and the two had been inseparable for the length of their stay.

It was all too premature, Joe feared. A scene from *Romeo and Juliet* in preparation? Joe grinned as he happily dismissed the thought. These two were old beyond their years; they'd both, in their different ways, grown up taking too much, too early, on young shoulders. But this too had happened on his watch. Perhaps he should have a word with Orlando when they finally tracked him down? Issue some sort of warning? Urge a belated paternal concern? 'Well, here's your daughter back, old man. No – no trouble at all ... In fact she's been most helpful. And here she is – delivered safe and sound in wind and limb, as you see, but – have a care – there may be unseen wounds in the region of the heart ...' No. Joe knew it would be a waste of time. He'd wait and report back to Lydia when he returned to Surrey. Lydia would know whether to speak out or be silent.

With her uncomfortable ability to intercept and respond to his thoughts, Dorcas, eyes still closed, was muttering: 'Do you think Orlando'll notice I've changed a bit? So many things to tell him when we get to him.'

'Yes, lots to tell Orlando,' Joe agreed. 'But I was wondering, Dorcas, when – if, indeed, *ever* – you were going to come clean with *me* and confess all. Would this be a good moment to tell me what you need to tell me?'

Her eyes popped open and he felt an undignified rush of triumph to see he'd surprised her.

'Whatever are you talking about? Confess? To you? You're a policeman not a priest!'

He grinned. 'I think it's entirely possible that you'll be needing me in *both* capacities before we go much farther. Do you want me to spell it out? Would it ease your confession if I were to say: *I know what you're up to!*'

Joe left a space for the inevitable outburst of denial to run its course but there was a long silence.

'When did you guess?' Her voice was suddenly uncertain.

'I don't guess. I work things out. It's what I do. But, to answer your question: it occurred to me before we left Surrey. All that nonsense about not wanting to go to Scotland with Lydia's family for the holidays? You were given every chance to come south with your father and his menagerie when he set off at the start of the summer but you refused. And I *had* noticed you'd been devouring Walter Scott's novels one after the other and you'd got together a whole collection of hill-walking clothes from

12

Lillywhite's – from boots to tam-o'-shanter and everything in between. You were looking forward to Scotland but the moment you discovered that – just for once – *I* wasn't going north with Lydia but motoring down to spend a month in Antibes with an old army mate, you changed your plans. You used every possible means of persuading my sister to talk me into bringing you along with me. Out went the woollies – sandals and shorts were chucked into a bag. Walter Scott was put back on the library shelves and Alphonse Daudet and something coyly entitled *So You're Going to Provence?* were done up with string and put out ready for the journey. Not one of my most challenging puzzles, Dorcas! For some reason, you wanted to be here with me in Provence. Am I getting this right? Say something!'

She nodded dumbly, unable to come up with a riposte. Joe paused, giving her time to make her own explanation.

She turned on him angrily. 'Crikey! You must be a difficult man to live with! Sneaking about looking in wardrobes . . . checking labels! Going through my books! You've a nerve!'

Again, he waited.

'Well, all right.' She took a moment to collect her thoughts, considering him through eyes narrowed in speculation. He knew the signs and prepared himself to hear one of her easy fabrications but her confession when it came was halting and clumsy, the pain in her voice undeniable. 'Yes. It seemed too good a chance to waste. I've been trying for years, Joe. Every time we've come south with my father, for as long as I can remember, I've tried. With no co-operation from Orlando. He doesn't want me to succeed. He really doesn't. I've searched and searched from Orange down to Les Saintes Maries on the coast. I've talked with gypsies and men of the road . . . I've checked every new grave in every cemetery. No luck. There's a limit to what a child can do even down here where there's more freedom to come and go and talk to anyone you meet.

Life's not so . . . so corseted . . . as it is in England. But even so, it's not easy. And now I'm getting older . . .' Dorcas looked uncomfortable for a moment, 'there will be places I can't go to, people I just can't interview without running a risk . . . I'm sure you can imagine. Gigolos and white slavers and bogeymen of that description. I know how the world works . . . I'm not stupid!'

'So you thought you'd latch on to a sympathetic chap who can go unchallenged into these dangerous and shady places and ask the right questions on your behalf –'

'A nosy fellow with a good right hook!' she interrupted. 'And one who speaks French of a sort? That's always useful.'

'Mmm . . . these valuable attributes come at a price.' Joe nodded sagely. 'I warn you there'll be a forfeit to pay. Agreed?'

'Agreed.' She accepted without thought, not bothering to ask what the fee would be. She knew he was just making pompous noises and he knew that she would break any agreement that proved not to suit her anyway.

He pushed on with his pretence: 'So long as you're hiring my detective services, I think I should insist on a clear client's instruction from you. I wouldn't want to discover you were expecting me to track down that silver bangle you dropped down a drain in Arles the year before last.'

Dorcas smiled. 'No. I want you to find something much more precious, Joe. Something I lost thirteen years ago. I want you to find my mother.'

# Chapter Two

'Well, according to the innkeeper, this village is indeed the one we're looking for – Silmont. He gave me a very old-fashioned look when I asked for directions to the château. Made verging-on-the-rude remarks about the acuity of my eyesight and brought my English common sense into question.' Joe waved a hand towards the end of the village street and grinned sheepishly. 'Can't say I blame him! It's obvious enough, wouldn't you say?'

'Like standing in the middle of Trafalgar Square and asking someone where Nelson's statue is. How embarrassing!'

'Is this what you were expecting, Dorcas?'

She was sitting in the passenger seat where he'd left her, parked outside the Hôtel de la Poste. Clearly she was taken aback, as he was himself. 'It's not what I'd pictured. No, not at all. But then . . . you never know with Pa.'

'All his geese are swans?'

'Yes. People *and* places. You know . . . every vagabond he meets round a campfire is really an undiscovered genius violin player, every pretty waitress in a café is the twin of Kiki de Montparnasse . . . any house in the country is a château. I've learned never to expect too much. But . . .'

'But *this*? What are we to make of *this*? If we've got the right place. It seems, for once, to be a true bill. The word "château" doesn't go far enough. It can, indeed, mean any grand house in the country but this is a *château-fort*, no less! A castle. With all its imposing bits and pieces in place. Impressive! I'm impressed. Overwhelmed might be nearer

15

the mark. Pass me the guidebook from the glove locker, will you? I think we should spend a minute or two getting this place in focus. Something so grand and ancient – it's bound to get a mention.'

They spent silent moments looking down at the guide and up at the outcrop of rock, a quarter of a mile distant at the end of the village street. The crag reared up in front of them, proudly bearing the weight of limestone masonry that grew imperceptibly from the rock itself to take the form of an imposing fortress.

'It's not a bit like the Château Houdart, is it?' Dorcas murmured. 'That was welcoming, lived-in, looked pretty on a wine label. This is a jolly scary place, Joe!'

'Machicolations, crenellations, canonniered arrow slits . . .' Joe muttered. 'Blimey! It's got the lot. Put your tin hat on, Dorcas! And hope they've not boiled the oil up yet. *A l'attaque!* Yes?'

He put the car in gear and moved off slowly.

'Is this the usual style of accommodation for one of your father's artistic jamborees?' he asked cheerfully to dispel her gathering gloom as they wound upwards under intimidating walls. Joe always tried to avoid speaking in a dismissive tone when discussing Orlando's activities. Privately, he considered it the height of indulgence, an embarrassing bohemian flourish, this habit of congregating together with a coven of fellow artists to spend the summer months daubing away in each other's company, stealing mistresses from one other, squabbling and boozing, conspiring to exchange one outrageous 'ism' for a newer one. Fauvism, Cubism, Dadaism, Futurism, and now, he heard, Surrealism was all the go. Well, that at least seemed to make sense.

'No. It *is* a bit grand. But his crowd will gather wherever some art-lover, some patron is kind enough – and rich enough – to offer them accommodation for a season.'

They looked up again at the château and Joe voiced the thought: 'Some accommodation! I do wonder who the generous host might be? Any information on *him*? I shall need to know to whom I should address my bread-and-butter note . . .'

Dorcas shook her head. 'No idea. You'll have to ask. But the artists always pay their rent! In kind, of course. You know – they leave some of their best work behind as a thank-you. They're very productive. And artists are very generous. Did you know that Van Gogh never *sold* a painting in his life? He gave away more than a thousand of them.' And, again, she hurried to defend her father and his chosen occupation: 'But some of Orlando's pals are getting quite well known in art circles. They're being offered really high prices for their work in the Paris salerooms. Fortunes have been made. If anyone offers you a canvas while you're here, Joe – don't refuse it, will you?'

He promised he would accept anything he might be offered by any of the inmates with a convincing show of pleasure. And pleasure might be just what he experienced, he corrected himself, remembering the one or two attractive and unusual pictures Dorcas had herself been given by her father's friends. He'd noted – and instantly coveted – one portrait of a dark-haired girl who could be no one but Dorcas, standing barefoot and windblown on a Mediterranean beach. The ugly scrawled signature at the bottom would have been unknown at the time of painting but Pablo Picasso was, these days, a name to be reckoned with in the saleroom.

After a noisy grind upwards in bottom gear, they arrived at a flat turning space in front of the entrance to the castle. Joe paused and put the handbrake on, reluctant at the last moment to commit himself to crossing the drawbridge.

The watcher at the summit of the north-east tower grunted in surprise. What was this? It could only be the brat arriving at last. In the company of the Englishman. But a *hesitant* Englishman? Circumspect and careful?

17

Lips curled in derision as the dark man jumped lithely from the car, bossily pointed a staying finger at his companion and proceeded to stroll over and subject the drawbridge to an unhurried examination. The underside was checked, the hauling mechanism inspected, the central planks stamped upon by a hefty English brogue and finally the man did what he should have done in the first place: he walked across and noted the presence in the courtyard of two vehicles heavier than his own tin-can conveyance.

'Get on with it, man!' the watcher yearned to cry out. 'You're already a week late and unwelcome at that! The way is clear before you – just deliver your package and get out. While you can.' But curiosity took the place of impatience. This was surely a display of untypical behaviour? One would have looked for an arrogant charge across the bridge followed by the squeal of brakes and an uninhibited: 'Halloooo the château! Anyone at home?'

The castle, over the centuries, had seen its share of English invaders and they'd never knocked politely. Roving gangs of masterless men for the most part, men for whom murdering, robbing and rape were a way of life. The dregs of crusading armies, they had deserted their cause to range unchallenged over a defenceless Europe.

Not quite defenceless.

The watcher smiled and looked to the west in the direction of the mighty Rhône. Distance, even from this vantage point, hid the gleaming towers of the fortress across the river from Avignon, but the image was easily and comfortingly conjured up: a white stronghold glowing against an ethereally blue sky, straight from the pages of a Book of Hours. And, farther yet, Tarascon, Les Baux, Carcassonne, Aigues Mortes. Defences against barbaric invasion.

And here was another northern barbarian at the gate, preparing to cross over.

There were more ways than one of defending a castle. The medieval architects had known their job. If you didn't want to have your drawbridge hacked down, your walls pounded into rubble, foundations undermined, you could always discreetly leave the way open, invite entry . . . Once inside the courtyard and completely surrounded, a small army could be – and on several occasions here *had* been – massacred by concealed defenders.

The watcher smiled. 'Come in! Come in! Test the warmth of our welcome!'

At last, the fastidious Englishman, apparently satisfied, had returned to his car.


'Well, if a Hispano-Suiza and a heavily laden gypsy cart can survive the trip over, I think we can do it in a Morris,' Joe announced. 'It's usually safe to take the road well-travelled.' He turned to Dorcas and grabbed her by the shoulder. Excited by the mention of the gypsy cart, she was already halfway out of the car, bare legs and sandalled feet sliding over the running board.

'Stop wriggling and listen!' He spoke to her in the guardian's voice he found he had developed over the past months. 'Look, Dorcas . . . last chance to say this . . . I've learned a thing or two about assessing new diggings from billeting officers. Security, hygiene and comfort. That's what you look for. In that order. Now, I think we can probably say of this handout – walls three yards thick: secure enough! From external assault at least. But the other two requirements? Do you suppose they have running water up here? Decent kitchens and proper ablutions? Flea-free mattresses? I won't leave you behind in dubious conditions. Aunt Lydia would have my guts for garters!'

Unusually, Dorcas did not pour scorn on his concern. She'd grown accustomed, he guessed, to the high level of cleanliness and comfort maintained in Surrey.

'Whatever your confidence,' he went on, 'always plan for retreat! We learned that much at Mons. I checked with the landlord back in the village that they had rooms to spare at the inn – and the telephone.'

19

'Ah! I thought you were taking your time in there.'

'I was making myself known to Monsieur Ferro and charming his good lady. I pointed you out and sketched for them the rough outline of your situation. Motherless child ... arty father ... concerned but distracted uncle. I even displayed my warrant card and gave poor old Inspector Bonnefoye's name as a referee ... you can imagine. The upshot is that they're prepared – and encouraged by a generous deposit! – to take you in at a moment's notice. Should you want to bale out at any time, you can cut along there and present yourself. And ring me in Antibes. You have my number.'

She didn't argue but sat back in her seat and thanked him quietly. Then, suddenly alarmed, she clutched his arm. 'Joe, you're not going straight off, are you? I thought you'd perhaps stay for a day or two. Meet Orlando's friends. You might find them interesting. Pablo might be here ... He usually turns up ... I know Henri Matisse is due to come up from Nice to put on a teaching session like the ones he used to give in Paris. There may be a poet ... a dancer or two. You can carouse with Orlando till the small hours ...' Her voice trailed away as she realized that none of her offers was likely to be attractive to a man with his sights on the Riviera.

'One night,' he conceded. 'I've brought my sleeping bag and if they can find me some hole or corner to bunk up in, I'll stay for one night. Long enough to make certain I'm not leaving you in a nest of robber barons, Left Bank lounge lizards or Portuguese pimps. And time enough to inspect the kitchens.'

This was not what Dorcas wanted to hear but her silence was witness to her acceptance of one further night's protective police presence. A stab of uncertainty, Joe decided. He was seeing the child's quite natural response to being catapulted back into her old life. She would soon acclimatize. By the end of the week, she'd be running around brown and barefoot, screeching at her father and herding the younger children, back to being the girl he remembered meeting in the spring.

He patted the hand still clinging to his sleeve. 'Don't worry, Dorcas. You took the Château Houdart by storm – this one will be easier. The occupants will all be friendly and you'll be back in the bosom of your family.' Feeling no relaxation of her grip, he added: 'I would never leave you in a bad situation, Dorcas. You know that.'

'Do you mean it?'

'Of course,' he said stoutly. 'Promise.'

She released his gear lever arm. 'Sorry, Joe! Nerves. Go on then. Advance!'


The motor car started up again.

The watcher in the airy space above changed position to follow the progress of the car from the vantage point of a narrow slit which widened at the base. A slim hand reached out to touch the cool limestone that an ancient mason had gouged out and rounded to accommodate the barrel of a musket. A trigger finger slid along the groove angled and channelled precisely to aim at the centre of the grassed courtyard and paused, targeting in imagination, one of the dark heads below.


Dorcas yelped with delight at the sight of the hooded gypsy cart parked in the centre of the courtyard as they passed through the narrow entrance. Joe eased over the cobbles and on to the grass to station his Morris alongside. The midday sun beating down on the open, treeless space was, in itself, a weapon deployed against invasion. The architecture surrounding them was so bristlingly military, Joe almost expected to hear the clang of the drawbridge descending behind them, the imperious challenge of a sentry, the rattle and swish of a sword being drawn. But no unfriendly sound reached his straining ears. The clang of a metal pail and the whinny of a horse came from some depth in the building, reassuring and domestic. No human greeting followed. He sat on, hands still clenched around the steering wheel.

'Joe? Are you all right? What's the matter?'

He began automatically to make reassuring noises but she interrupted him. 'Stop that! You're making me nervous! Something's wrong, isn't it? You've gone quite pale, you can't seem to let go of the wheel and your eyes are swivelling all over the place. Not a pretty sight! What have you seen? If I didn't know what a thug you are, I'd say you were in a blue funk . . . Joe?'

Joe made an effort to ease the constriction in his throat, released the wheel and shuddered. 'Sorry, Dorcas! Feet of clay, I'm afraid. All those years of soldiering . . . if you survive them, you never lose it, you know . . . But you're right. Blue funk it is! You're the only person ever to have caught me in one – or, rather, recognized it for what it is: fear. Soldier's best friend. Keeps you alive. It's the icicle-between-the-shoulder-blades feeling of a gun barrel sighting on you . . . the normally steady foot that hesitates and changes course a split second before treading down on something nasty. An instinct for survival.'

While he muttered on, his eyes were ranging round the tall curtain walls, taking in the dozens of windows and arrow slits from any one of which they could have been under surveillance. 'Officers were the favourite targets for snipers in the war and easily distinguishable at a distance. Peaked caps, side arms. High casualty rate. Lucky to have survived. For a moment I had a distinct and familiar feeling that someone was drawing a bead on me. Ridiculous! Going a bit barmy? But, of course – when you think about it – I was reacting just as the military architect intended. Freezing like a trapped rabbit! All these defences are carefully worked out and we seem to have parked ourselves right in the centre of an ancient killing ground. The earth under our tyres is probably steeped in blood! I wouldn't give much for the chances of any rough-tough army of medieval *routiers* with pillage in mind making it through to the keep from here, would you?'

'But you're not going mad, Joe. There *was* something moving up there,' Dorcas agreed slowly, staring upwards. He noticed that she didn't point and looked quickly away. 'I caught a flash of something white. Up there in that turret. North-eastern, would that be?'

Her voice changed from calming to startled and she gasped as, with a clatter and whoosh of wings, a flock of birds soared into the air. They eddied and swirled and with one mind descended on a different turret roof. Dorcas exclaimed with pleasure and relief. 'Well, you can come off watch now, Joe! But we weren't wrong, were we? The look-out turret *was* occupied. By peaceful white doves!'

Joe smiled. 'Yes, doves,' he agreed.

'And by whoever disturbed them,' he added silently. He kept the thought to himself. The suspicion that someone had been covertly observing their arrival was vaguely menacing and he wished he had not risked transmitting his fears to young Dorcas.

He needed to take action. He needed to assert himself and shake off the menacing influence of his surroundings. He gave two peremptory peeps on the hooter and got out of the car.

The response was shrieks and excited laughter. Half a dozen children appeared from a dark doorway and came tearing over the courtyard. Three of them, two boys and a small girl, hurled themselves at Dorcas, chattering in a mixture of French and English. The oldest boy Joe could just identify as her brother Peter who seemed to have grown over the summer to eye level with Dorcas.

The boy released his sister from a hug and went to stand shyly in front of Joe. 'Thank you, sir,' he began his pre-pared speech, 'for bringing her. We're all just sitting down to lunch in the hall. Will you come? No, no! Leave the

23

luggage. I'll get someone to help with it later. Now, you'll be wanting to wash your hands . . . But first . . .'

Well, things were looking up, Joe thought, noting young Peter's helpful manners. The lad was shooting up in size. Slim like his father and blessed with Orlando's distinctive thick auburn hair and fine features, he promised to become a handsome young man. In response to a sergeant major's glare from Peter, the others formed up in height order for presentation.

'Dicky, my brother, and Rosie, my sister, I believe you know, sir. The other three are . . . um . . . children of the household. All French.' Peter made the introductions in their language: '*Monsieur, je vous présente: Clothilde, René, et le petit Marius . . . Mon oncle, Joseph.*'

Joe shook a series of sticky hands and murmured the appropriate formulae.

As intrigued by the round-eyed French contingent as they were by him, he took the time to lean over and talk to each child in turn. He established that the fair-haired Clothilde, plump as a Fragonard cherub, was the daughter of one of the guests. She confided that she was seven and a half years old. The two boys, one eight and the other, *le petit* Marius, not quite certain of his age – or unwilling to confide it – were the sons of the cook. Joe rather thought, judging by the set of the jaw and the ugly glint in his eye, that Marius did not want it revealed that he was the youngest of this group and didn't press him.

But Joe quickly understood that he was not the star of the show. His questions answered, all eyes now slid past him, drawn by the glamour of a motor car. With a conspiratorial wink for Peter, Joe invited them to do what they had clearly been dying to do since they came into the courtyard. He lifted them all into the car and Peter organized a rota for sitting in the driver's seat and honking the horn. Distracted by the giggles and squabbles, Joe took some time to realize that Orlando had appeared and propped himself in the doorway, watching them with

24

amused indulgence. He called out Dorcas's name, held out his arms and she ran to him with a squeal of delight, hopping and chattering like a magpie.

'Now – lunch!' said Peter, remembering his lines. 'We've got a rabbit stew ... I hope you can eat rabbit, sir?' he announced and led the way back to the hall.

Dorcas stood aside and turned to Joe, allowing her father to greet his friend.

Tall, handsome, stagily framed in the archway, Orlando stood ready with his easy smile. He was wearing his usual gear of corduroy trousers tied up at the waist with string and a rough cotton shirt dramatically smudged with paint. A red scarf of Provençal pattern was knotted negligently at his throat. All carefully worked out, Joe always suspected. A *Punch* cartoon could not have more clearly signalled: 'bohemian artist at work'. But there was nothing studied about his welcome. The unmanly hug was rib-cracking in its enthusiasm.

'Where the blazes have you been?' Orlando wanted to know. 'We were looking for you last week! In Champagne? But why? What kept you up there? Was it the local brew or were you intoxicated by your hostess? What was the name of the enchantress? Calypso? Circe? ... Aline, eh? Well, come inside! Nothing fizzy to offer you, I'm afraid, but we do have a quite splendid red wine from the vineyard over the wall.' He grinned. 'And one or two seductive Sirens to divert the weary traveller.'

'I say – I hope we haven't fetched up here at an inconvenient time –' Joe began.

'No, not at all! This is really rather a good moment to drop anchor. We're all in the refectory. You'll find everyone at the table so you can get a look at the complete gallery. It's the one occasion in the day when you'll find them gathered together. Catch them between hangovers. And indiscretions. One or two stragglers yet to arrive but mostly they're into their second helping of stew by now.'

Joe's eye automatically sought out Dorcas as everyone began to troop into the building, and he enjoyed the sight of her picking up her little sister Rosie for a cuddle and carrying her on her back into the dark interior. Joe hung about ushering the others ahead and was the last to leave the courtyard. He turned and spent some moments staring with a residual unease at the summit of the watch tower silhouetted against a blindingly blue sky. On impulse, he sketched an insolent bow in its direction and went inside.

# Chapter Three

Joe entered the building with eyes still dazzled by his prolonged scanning of the midday sky and it was a second or two before he was aware of the figure coming towards him down the corridor. Dressed in black and moving on silent feet, the stranger made straight for him. Once within striking distance, the man grunted an exclamation and raised his hand, the chopping edge lined up on the centre of Joe's face.

Joe's reaction was swift and instinctive. He seized the outstretched arm by the wrist and tugged the man forward, jerking him on to his swiftly extended right foot. The unknown crashed to the stone-flagged floor, falling to his knees with a scream of pain. A second scream rang out as Joe yanked his arm up behind his back.

'What the hell? For Chrissakes, lemme go!' protested an American voice.

From the end of the corridor Orlando's voice rang out, reinforcing the suggestion: 'Joe! Let him up! Are you mad? What's going on?'

'Who's your friend?' Joe asked when Orlando joined them.

'That's Nathan! Nathan Jacoby. He's staying with us. He was only coming to say hello.'

'He has a strange way of introducing himself!' Joe grunted, his anger blocking any embarrassment or regret. He hauled the spluttering American to his feet and addressed him in a tone of false bonhomie: 'Look, mate, let

27

me explain: if you come at a London copper down a dark corridor dressed like a lascar thug and stick a fist in his face, you must expect to be lifted out of your socks. In polite circles we put out a hand at waist level. Like this.' Joe demonstrated. 'How do you do, Mr Jacoby ... I'm Joseph Sandilands ... And I'm pleased to meet you,' he added, remembering the American greeting.

'Well, I can't say I've been overjoyed to meet *you* – so far! But thanks for the advice. I'll be sure to hail a British bobby from a safe distance in future ... Like the width of the Atlantic. Shall we start over?'

Orlando gave a nervous burst of laughter. 'Nat, you twerp! You were doing that gesture again, I'll bet! That affected business with your hands. You'll have to forgive him, Joe – he gets carried away. Nat's one of those photographer chappies. He's incapable of looking at any new face or vista without framing it.' Orlando put up his hands, made a box shape and pretended to peer through it. 'Like this.'

'No, no, Orlando!' the American said in exasperation. 'You're just not seeing what *I'm* seeing. You haven't noticed it, have you? Perhaps you're too accustomed to the sight of this man's face?'

'Ugly brute to meet for the first time in a dark corridor, I agree,' said Orlando peering uncertainly at Joe. 'And perhaps I should have said something.'

The American sighed. 'Permit me, Sandilands?' He carefully put up the edge of his hand again, centring on Joe's nose, and turned it like a flap from side to side. 'I caught sight of you lit up in the doorway. See that, Orlando? This side you've got light, this other darkness. We've got ourselves a Janus ... a Lucifer in mid-fall ... an Oxymoron of War ... I'm assuming it *is* war we have to thank for this fascinating rearrangement of your physiognomy?'

'Oh, come on, Nat! He's just a bloke, you know,' Orlando protested. 'A bit battered but then so are thousands like him ... nothing out of the ordinary for an Englishman of his age. You'll pass a dozen in worse condition between the Ritz and Boodle's.'

The photographer raved on: 'If I put a high wattage bulb over him, up here –' an elegant hand indicated a spot to the right and above Joe's head – 'you can imagine the drama! No – a daguerrotype! Old-fashioned perhaps and a pain in the neck to perform but this face is worth the bother. Nothing like them for portraits, you know.'

'Do leave it for later, Nat!' Orlando pleaded and turned to Joe. 'He sees everything in black and white, don't you know. Only to be expected when he spends the hours of daylight squinting through a viewfinder and the hours of darkness closeted away in some garde-robe developing the stuff. I reckon all those chemicals he uses are softening his brain.' He grinned at the American, who grinned back cheerfully.

A face much more fascinating than his own, Joe decided now his eyes had readjusted. The smooth tanned oval was framed by an explosion of dark hair which curled in corkscrews, unrestrained by scissors, brilliantine or even a comb, Joe guessed. Startling enough and some preparation for the majesty of the nose which would not have disgraced an eagle owl or a Pathan warrior. But the first intimidating effect was countered by the warmth of the eyes. They disarmed. Deep-set and dark, they shone with humour and were fringed by lashes of an extravagance any cover girl would have envied.

What had Joe called him? 'A lascar thug'. He regretted the jibe. It was a common enough insult back home in the London docklands where these tough Eastern seamen had acquired a certain reputation for lawlessness and skill with the knife, but this man, by all appearances, could indeed have his origins in the Middle – or even farther – East.

'I say – do forgive me for implying . . .'

'I didn't take it personally. I'm not from Alaska,' came the easy response.

He waited for Joe's jaw to drop and added: 'But if your reference was to *Al Askar* and the ruffians who go by that name – well, I guess that's kind of flattering. It means "a soldier", they tell me. In Persian. Can't say I've ever been called a soldier before – in any language.'

So why, Joe wondered, was this intelligent and professional man parading about in his present costume? He glanced with some distaste at the baggy black cotton trousers, the chest-hugging, collarless shirt – also in black – and the black rope-soled espadrilles. All bought in the local market, Joe supposed, and more suited to one of the fishermen who lounged along the sea front at Collioure. Well, Orlando and his smart artist friends set a standard of flamboyant eccentricity a humble photographer might find hard to emulate. Tricking himself out as a devil-may-care cut-throat must be his way of keeping his end up. It was all a house-party game. Tedious stuff! Joe wondered briefly what gambit a humble policeman might use for the same purpose and resolved to annoy them all by simply changing his white shirt for an even crisper white shirt and polishing his already shiny shoes.

He smiled and, perfectly ready to offer himself to the assembled company as a source of derision or even a comic turn should that be what tickled their fancy, he straightened his Charvet cravat, smoothed down the pocket flaps of his linen jacket and moved off down the corridor. Joe Sandilands was used to singing for his supper.

# Chapter Four

It was lucky some sharp-eared child had heard the car
horn, Joe reckoned, as he made his way along several corridors, or they'd have wandered the maze like Theseus
without the benefit of a ball of wool. He noted, as they
passed, the contents of the one or two rooms whose doors
were open. Mainly they were used as storage for moulder-
ing sports equipment, artists' easels and encrusted palettes,
children's toys. One contained nothing but an array of
stuffed boars' heads and long-dead birds in glass cases.

At last they came out into what Orlando had called 'the
refectory'. A word that hardly did it justice, Joe considered.
This was the grand hall of a very grand castle. The intimidating space soared to a height of three storeys and was
lit by windows contrived at three levels from ground to
ceiling. Light was flooding in boldly through the topmost
rank of windows, the ancient, lead-paned glass filtering
and distorting it into ripples which moved along the stone
walls, washing them in southern warmth. The harshness of
the limestone was further softened by tapestries and hang-
ings quite ragged enough to be genuinely centuries old.

While the children trooped straight in followed by
Nathan, Orlando paused with Joe in the arched doorway
and watched his face, waiting for his reaction.

'Well, I never!' murmured Joe. 'Sorry! I'll think of
some more intelligent response when my brain's adjusted to all this grandeur.' And, feeling that a more
appreciative response was expected: 'Stunning! Simply

stunning! I say – these tapestries are certainly eye-catching. Could they possibly be . . .?'

'As ancient as they look and worth a fortune,' said Orlando. 'Thought you'd like them.'

Though threadbare in places and greying with age, the greens, the violets and the turquoise blues of Aubusson still told their stories. Joe's eye was caught and held by the small fierce eye of a wild boar cornered in a forest glade. Powerful and utterly fearless, the splendid animal was rounding on his tormentors. In the next tapestry, he was lying, spectacular in death, a prize at the feet of a lusty royal huntsman.

The scenes of venery were interspersed with scenes of courtly life: feasting, dancing, flirting and the playing of instruments most of which were unfamiliar to Joe. Hairy satyrs tootled roguishly on pipes making maidens swoon with delight. Maidens strummed on viols – if those pot-bellied instruments *were* viols – and youths fainted at their feet. The long-dead participants, apart from the satyrs, were universally young and handsome. Joe's impression was a blend of dark eyes, expressive hands, muscular thighs, winking jewels around swan necks, white coifs and rich attire.

'Wonderful, aren't they?' said Orlando. 'Woven especially for this château – for this very room in fact. I'll introduce you to the Shades of the Castle later. First you must meet the present incumbents. Not so aristocratic, I'm afraid – you'll be looking at *them* for a long time before you spot a tiara or a garter amongst them. And the standard of courtly manners is sadly eroded, you'll find. Still – you'll probably hold your end up . . . I say . . .' The normally urbane Orlando was disconcerted to be found speaking disparagingly of his fellows but he soldiered on apologetically: 'Not sure what you might be expecting but . . . they are a bit of a mixed crowd, you know. One thing they all have in common is – they know their mind and they speak it. Without fear or favour or regard for authority, if you know what I mean?'

'I talk all the time with people who have no respect for authority,' said Joe. 'Especially mine. A bunch of bolshie buggers, are you trying to say?'

Orlando grinned and waved a negligent hand towards the far end of the hall where a subdued crowd was at luncheon. 'Exactly that! And here they are.'

The guests, as many as twenty in number, Joe was surprised to see, were already seated on benches on either side of a very long oak table stretching across the room and positioned in front of an ornate fireplace. Though the day was hot, a fire of aromatic logs smouldered agreeably in the grate and Joe was glad of the homely scent in this intimidating space. But even a crowd this size was rendered insignificant by the size of the room. Noting the huddle, Joe's mind turned to defensive positions and famous last stands. Had some desperate voice, moments before he entered, called out: 'Circle the wagons!' 'Ten bullets each – make 'em all count!' 'Our swords? Come and get them!'?

The setting hardly favoured intimate or even comfortable dining, but this was the exact spot originally designated for it. There, at the far end, in splendour and state, the master of this place and his entourage would have feasted before a crowded and bustling hall from the day the castle was built. Joe guessed that it was the unchangeable proximity of the kitchens that had kept it in operation here over the centuries and he watched as two menservants came in through a door to the left of the table. One was carrying a basket of freshly baked bread, the other a large jug of wine. Both were soft-footed and swift, their every gesture correct.

He stood with Orlando at a polite distance from the table while Nathan, pausing to give him an encouraging slap between the shoulder blades, went to resume his place halfway along one of the benches. Joe looked for Dorcas and lighted on her already established at a smaller table set to one side. Clearly the children's table. Clearly too, Dorcas was, by general consent, already in charge. As he watched, she tapped one boy on the knuckles with a ladle and reproved him, grinned, then began to spoon out stew into bowls.

The murmuring stopped at their approach, forks were placed on plates, faces were raised in expectation to take in the newcomer. A bad moment. Joe fortified himself with the thought that they were strangers and, for him, likely to remain so. He prepared to smile blandly through a deluge of names, none of which he need commit to memory.

Orlando seemed to be of the same mind. He signalled to everyone that they were to remain seated and launched into a rough, joking presentation of Joe.

'Untraditional' was the most forgiving term Joe could think of to describe the introduction but he smiled affably through it, made a gracious, all-embracing bow and glanced along the ranks. Well, they earned his respect for the lively effort they were making to combat the medieval austerity. Colourful diaphanous clothing, floating scarves and gypsy colours made a gallant riposte to the aridity of the white spaces. Here and there, the garish glitter of a diamanté clasp caught his attention, a cascade of metal bangles tinkled distractingly down a slim brown arm. Joe thought for a moment he'd arrived in the middle of a mad fancy-dress party. Or had he crashed a rehearsal for an end-of-the-pier show? Make-up was certainly much in evidence – bold eyes dark with mascara were raised to his in speculation, reddened lips smiled invitingly. Small wonder that it was the women he was first aware of – scattered at random amongst the gathering, they seemed to make up almost half the number.

The men were dull in comparison: countryman's clothes mainly, corduroy jackets and badly tailored linen suits, with one or two stained smocks in evidence, proclaiming that the wearer was terminally forgetful, contemptuous of good manners or invoking the licence of artistic preoccupation. Stares directed at him were challenging, curious or welcoming. None was uninterested.

'Now, what shall we do with you? Where would you like to sit?' Orlando asked.

'The far side seems to be less densely packed,' said Joe. 'And it suits me to have my back against a solid wall with my sword-hand free to swish,' he added with an apologetic smile and a nod towards the left side.

'Coo er! Who's your swashbuckling friend, Orlando? D'Artagnan arrived, has he?' called a sarcastic voice. 'Pity he's come too late!'

'We'll make a place over here, next to me,' said Orlando quickly, ushering Joe to a seat at the end of the bench he'd picked out. 'Hey! Shove up a bit, all of you! Thanks! Far too many people to introduce all at once,' he announced bluntly. 'You'll not remember their names . . . never sure I can myself . . . Anyway, they know who *you* are now and if they want to get acquainted, they'll make overtures in their own good time.'

'Certainly will!' The voice was low, female and flirtatious. 'And now's as good as any. Bags I first in the queue for an audience!' it added, saucily.

A slim young woman got to her feet and extricated herself from the bench. She picked up her bowl and swayed around the table to squeeze herself between Joe and Orlando. 'Estelle,' she said and took his hand in hers. 'When I'm in France. Stella when I'm at home, which is – or used to be – London.'

Joe had already identified her accent as educated southern counties. 'My home too, these days,' he said. 'Joseph Sandilands,' delicately emphasizing his surname. 'Miss . . . er?'

'Ah, yes! Name, rank and number. One of the old school!' She managed to make the comment teasing rather than offensive. 'We all call each other by our first names here . . . It's Smeeth.'

35

'Excuse me – I didn't quite catch that . . .'

'Estelle Smeeth. That's S – M – double E – T – H.'

Joe's puzzlement turned into a hiccup of laughter. 'I see! When in France! And to which branch of the Smith family do you belong? Or is it – let me guess – an alias?'

'That's a secret between me and my passport. But *your* identity is no secret. Orlando's been trumpeting your arrival for a week now. We're all dying to meet the star of the Met! I've actually read about you in the papers – you came down on the guilty like Nemesis! The Garrotting at the Opera House, the Regent's Park Rapist . . . the Tory MP who was pushed in front of the 6.15 at Waterloo . . . Now, there's one I'd like to own up to myself.' She crashed through the flimsy hedge of Joe's mumbled disclaimer and cantered on: 'Orlando thought he'd better warn us that his daughter's chaperone was on The Force.' She flicked a glance towards Dorcas. 'Just in case any of us needed to search our conscience and prepare an alibi. Perhaps even make an excuse and leave in a hurry.'

'What? You're trying to tell me there are usually fifty of you here?' Joe asked lightly. 'Glad *you* felt brave – or innocent – enough not to flee before the Law, Estelle!'

He was teasing but he was sincere. The girl was charming and flattering. Too effusive for his comfort, perhaps. There was something in the warmth of her welcome that disturbed him. *Un peu surexcitée?* Yes. She was talking too fast, too loudly and with too many hand gestures. He reminded himself soberly that he was rubbing shoulders with young people of an artistic temperament, not nodding over a book in the London Library. And Estelle *was* exceptionally pretty. Her long fair hair was outrageously unfashionable and would have raised eyebrows in London but it flowed over her bare shoulders in waves a Pre-Raphaelite painter of the last century – or any red-blooded man of this – would have swooned at the sight of. Joe realized he was staring and tore his gaze away. Light brown eyes were emphasized by straight brows, her nose was

36

neat and her mouth rouged and generous. There was a highly strung, theatrical air about her and Joe decided she would have been convincing as one of the daughters of Boadicea in any village pageant. But instead of a Celtic cloak, she was wearing some kind of strapless sun dress in white linen, the better to indulge in the new craze of sunbathing, Joe guessed, noting peeling red patches on the creamy flesh.

'Here, let me help you to some *daube de lapin aux herbes de Provence*,' Estelle offered. 'It will be good. We have the services of a wonderful local cook. A woman. From the village. Poor lady! I don't think we're much of a challenge for her skills. In fact, I'm pretty certain she's had orders from on high to back-pedal on the menus. Keep it simple for the ignorant Anglo-Saxons. Stew one day, roast the next. At least we've never been offered boiled mutton and jam which is what they're all convinced we eat all the time back home. Though, occasionally, the cook forgets herself and does something seriously dreamy with asparagus. In England, it would get her a job at the Savoy!'

Estelle, he noticed, was saying appreciative things about the food but scarcely tasting her own portion, merely re-arranging the pieces on her plate. Too eager to chatter and make an impression, he thought.

'The staff would, indeed, appear to be impeccable. They are in the employ of . . .?'

'The owner of the château. The Lord of Silmont . . . can't remember all his titles. Count or Marquis? Something like that. We just call him "the lord". His name's Bertrand but no one would dream of using it. Even the seneschal calls him "sir" and he's a blood relative.'

'He has a seneschal, did you say?'

'Yes. That's his maître d'hôtel, you know. And I'm using the word "hôtel" in the original sense, of course –'

Smart town house?' interrupted Joe, piqued by the girl's condescending tone. 'And I shall think of the gentleman as "the steward". How very feudal! Tell me – are they here among us, this medieval pair? Do point them out so that I may direct a courtly bow in the right quarter or tug a forelock.'

She looked at him uncertainly. 'You have a very nice forelock. But don't tug it just yet. The lord isn't here at the moment. That's his place at the head of the table, the empty one, and no one ever sits there but him. He pops in occasionally, he *says* to practise his English with us, but as he speaks more elegant English than any one of us, I have to think he's actually checking on progress with the canvases.'

'Checking progress? What? Like some sort of overseer?'

'Yes. Exactly that. Keeping us all up to the mark. If you were imagining yourself joining some carefree house party – forget it! In fact it's a sort of assembly line. I can't call it a treadmill exactly – that would be too, too ungracious for words – but our host is a bit of a whip-cracker, Commander.' She waved a hand at the far end of the hall. 'Do you see the wall down there is doing service as a gallery?'

Joe noted that the tapestries and wall sconces had given way to three ranks of canvases, taking up the whole surface. Several more had been stacked against it.

'That's the week's output. Our patron has an eye to the main chance as well as an eye for a good painting. He's a collector and a connoisseur. And very well regarded in art circles. He has the critics in his pocket.'

'And his pockets are deep ones?'

'You bet! Nothing known for sure but I'd expect he knows exactly how to oil the wheels and grease the palms. The art-smart journalists and opinion-makers echo his views, kowtow to his prejudices, support his enthusiasms. He *sets* the fashion, having bought extensively into it, then he sells at vast profit to New York or London. He's made a fortune from his dealings.'

Joe looked around him. 'And these are his protégés?'

'His breeding ground. His worker bees. You identify

your talent, establish it in stimulating surroundings, satisfy all daily needs and you're in business.'

'You're very acerbic?'

'My sharp tongue! It keeps getting me the sack! But judge for yourself – our seigneur got rid of three painters he decided weren't worthy of support in the first week.'

'*Pour encourager les autres?*' Joe asked lightly.

She smiled. 'No. Because they failed to please. I told you – he knows his stuff. Right decision. He had a blazing row with a Cubist painter whose name – if I were indiscreet enough to mention it – you would certainly know.' Estelle affected a grumpy man's baritone: '"Looking at this stuff is like looking down a cracked kaleidoscope filled with rusty nails . . . undigested scraps of flesh . . . the dismembered leftovers of a crazed axe-man . . ." were some of the lord's polite descriptions of our artist's latest offerings.'

'Ouch! Poor chap!' said Joe.

'Save your sympathy! We all know that this particular artist – who does have a genuine talent, as far as I can judge – *agrees* with that view in private. After a second bottle, he's been heard to ask – in genuine mystification – how on earth the public can be taken in so easily by his artistic pretensions. But in an open exchange of views with the boss, he felt he had to stand up for himself and his art and he did. He's famously persuasive. And – he ended up by selling a dozen or so examples of his "dog's vomit" to our host, after prolonged haggling, before he flounced off in a well-timed huff.' She smiled in satisfaction.

'Followed by the cheers of the crowd?'

'Oh, ra*ther*! We're a mixed bunch but you'll find there's a certain group loyalty. We admire anyone spirited enough to put one over on the powers that be. When you *think* that those pictures are probably being snatched from the walls of a posh Parisian saleroom as we speak! For twenty times what the artist received! It's a hard equation to work out and one's never perfectly certain on which side one stands . . .'

'But when $x$ equals rather a lot of cash . . .?'

She grinned. 'That's right, Commander! Always keep your eye on the $x$! It's a new concept for many artists but they're learning.'

'I'm sad to hear you say so,' said Joe. 'I had hoped to fetch up in the company of high-minded creators of beauty . . . incorruptible visionaries . . .'

Estelle gave him a hard look and sighed. 'Another one of those who thinks you paint more effectively on an empty stomach? What nonsense! Would you detect more efficiently if they starved you for a week? Well, then!'

'And the steward?' Joe pressed on with his enquiries. 'Which one is he?'

'Go on – guess. You're the detective.'

Joe thought he had already spotted the man in charge. Sartorially, he was indistinguishable from the rest of the gathering in his casually tailored beige linen suit and open-necked shirt. A dark-haired, brown-eyed man in his late thirties, he was chatting amicably with the people about him and blended in with the group in all respects but one. He was the only man at the table who had monitored the comings and goings of the servants, with the discreet but all-seeing eye of a butler.

Joe took a moment to scan the company and then whispered in Estelle's ear: 'Got him! Do you see the man who's the spitting image of Albert Préjean? The film star?'

'Albert who . . .? Oh, yes, I know who you mean! He played the pilot in *Paris Qui Dort*, didn't he? Craggy good looks. A real heartbreaker. That's a more perceptive insight than I think you realize.'

'Yes, that's the one. And I'm guessing that the gentleman who so resembles him is the man who sits at the lord's right hand.'

Estelle giggled. 'He usually hovers behind his left shoulder. And you're quite right. Well done! I'll take you over to meet him after the meal. He'll expect it. Oh, and may I warn you? He shakes hands with his left. Right arm badly burned. He was with the Aviation Militaire in the war. One of the Cigognes Squadron. Meanwhile, although he's nattering away with Nathan in apparently complete absorption, he's actually giving *you* an ever-so-discreet once-over. Smile for the seneschal, my dear! He likes handsome men.'

Something in her tone alerted and annoyed Joe. He found he was torn between satisfying his curiosity and discouraging the girl's loose gossip. He chose the safer path of distracting her. 'Tell me two things, Estelle . . . what is the gentleman's name and was he late down to lunch today?'

'Late to lunch? What *is* this? My first interrogation?' she gurgled. 'How thrilling! I've no idea. I'm almost always the last to arrive so it's hard to say. I don't believe anyone came in after me . . . Let me think. Guy – that's his name: Monsieur Guy de Pacy – was already here. He came in through the kitchen door over there. I heard him shouting at one of the staff before the door banged shut. Then he fixed his suave smile on and entered stage left. Something on your mind, Commander?'

'Only the desperate hope there'll be enough of this delicious stuff left for second helpings,' he said. 'And why not call me Joe?'

'Here, have some bread to soak up the gravy, Joe. It's quite all right to do that over here.'

'Thank you, I shall. And thirdly I'm curious to know how *you* managed to get caught up with this stimulating company. Are you an artist?' he asked.

'Lord no! I'm an artist's model. I take my clothes off in cold studios and sit or lie for hours on end while some oaf at an easel turns me into something he's dreamed up – a stick insect, something on a butcher's slab or, at best, an odalisque in a silken turban and a bangle commissioned for some wealthy client's boudoir or bar. In the real world, Commander, you wouldn't know me. You might recognize my family name but *they* no longer recognize *me*, I'm afraid.' She shrugged a shoulder. 'I'm what's known back home as "a bad lot"! Kicked out of school, banned from darkening any paternal doors ever again. I've been adrift in Europe for the last five years. And I'm having a wonderful time!'

'And which of the company are you attached to – professionally, I mean?' Joe thought it wise to enquire.

'Nathan. The photographer. I came down from Paris with him. Nat's a sweetie-pie! He's not at all possessive and he's perfectly ready to lend me out to one of the others.' She nodded towards the gallery. 'You'll find two or three pictures where I'm just about recognizable . . . the girl and the unicorn on the beach . . . the concubine in red harem pants . . . the bride in Frederick's fresco . . . But I prefer sitting for Nathan. He makes me laugh and he doesn't . . . ogle. Not really possible, I suppose, when it's all over in – literally – a flash! And at least with a photographer I can be pretty certain that the results look like *me*.'

'They say the camera doesn't lie,' Joe offered.

'And that's another untruth! But it's more honest than any painting could ever be. I love the black and white clarity of it all. And it's quick. Click! The image is accurately caught for ever.'

'But you can have some fun with it,' Joe suggested with a smile. 'I remember admiring a shot of the luscious Kiki de Montparnasse, taken from behind. Someone had painted the curving sound-holes of a violin – or was it a cello? – on her bare back.'

'I know it! Wonderful! One of Man Ray's. I tried to persuade Nat to do something similar but he laughed and told me I hadn't got the waist and swelling hips for a cello. He suggested a flute might be more the thing.'

The arrival of fresh steaming bowls of *daube* coincided with a swirling unrest among the children.

Orlando leaned to Joe. 'That's good! It looks as though they've finished at the babies' table. They gobble down their food and get restive so I usually dismiss them.' He rose to his feet and selected a suitably paternal tone: 'You may get down now, chaps, and go out to play. You've all been very good so you're allowed sweets from the bowl in the pantry. Dorcas, my dear, you'd better supervise. They're allowed two – one for each hand. And don't get lost!' he shouted after their retreating backs. 'Chapel and ovens out of bounds, remember! Oh, and better make that Joe's car as well.'

Dorcas lingered behind, picking up discarded napkins and replacing used cutlery neatly on the dishes as she'd been taught. She directed an earnest stare in Joe's direction.

'Ovens?' Joe asked, intrigued.

'In the dungeons down below, where the children go to play hide and seek,' Estelle explained, 'there's a series of perfectly hideous hidey-holes with doors.' She shuddered. 'The kids will tell you that they're ovens where prisoners used to be shut in alive to cook to death. I think they're really called oubliettes. You know – tiny cells where prisoners could be put out of the way and forgotten.'

She caught Dorcas's eye over the table and spoke in a voice meant to be heard by all. 'So glad you've arrived at last, dear! It used to be my job to gather in the brood at the end of the day and do the roll-call. Never was dorm-prefect material, I'm afraid. Not the mother hen type, either! I'm delighted to see I can now hand it over to a competent youngster who will keep a closer eye on them.'

Dorcas gargled a gypsy oath and flung a knife down on to a dish with a clatter. Joe winced.

Everyone looked up and stared, sensing a drama. Even two very young girls with abundant dark hair who'd been fluting like finches in a mixture of Russian and French fell silent. The strikingly handsome gentleman sitting between the two beauties Joe had already marked down as possibly Russian, of intimidating aspect and out of place at that table. He was somewhat older than the rest of the company and more formally dressed. His linen jacket was uncrumpled and his silk cravat impeccably draped. Joe looked for a flaw in this ageing Adonis and decided that the hair, slicked back over a well-shaped skull, was suspiciously dark over the ears and, in a year or two's time, the jowls would have grown heavy.

The Russian broke off an intense conversation in accented French with Guy de Pacy to glower at Dorcas. He took a monocle from his shirt pocket, fixed it into his right eye-socket, and with all the menace of Beerbohm Tree playing Svengali at the Haymarket, he affected to seek out the source of the interruption. Not much liking what he saw, he glowered again.

Joe leaned behind Estelle and touched Orlando lightly on the shoulder. Orlando caught and responded to his enquiring look. 'Monsieur Petrovsky. Ballet-meister. Or so he bills himself,' he hissed.

Oblivious of the Russian disapproval, Dorcas began to speak. In a voice whose chilling hauteur brought back memories of the girl's formidable grandmother, she addressed her father. 'If you'll excuse me, Orlando, I won't take up any child-herding duties on a formal basis . . . I may not be staying long. The Commander and I are working on a project. We may have to come and go . . . leave early . . . get back late . . . Our schedule must remain elastic. And, anyway, it's a long time since I saw it as my job to go about extracting half-baked children from ovens at the end of the day.'

Someone exclaimed, all turned wondering eyes on Orlando, waiting for his reaction to this statement of rebellion. Waiting for him to discharge the musket of paternal authority over her head.

But the shot came from another quarter. Petrovsky's voice boomed out: 'Tell me, child, how old are you?'

Grudgingly Dorcas replied: 'I'm fourteen.'

'Fourteen? Indeed? May I recommend a few more years in bottle before you uncork your wisdom for the world?' The monocled eye swept the audience, gathering approval.

The finches tittered dutifully. Joe had the impression that

it wasn't the first time he'd delivered the line. Or the first time they'd heard it.

Orlando rose to his feet, distinguished and urbane. 'I take your point, Dorcas old thing,' he said calmly. 'But, I say, darling daughter of mine, may I ask you not to speak to your father in your grandmama's voice?' He gave a histrionic shudder. 'It gave me quite a turn! *One* termagant in a family is quite enough, thank you! Now, why don't you come on over to the grown-ups' table – where you ought to be – and we'll discuss our domestic arrangements more discreetly? We don't want to risk wearying the elderly with the frivolous concerns of youth.'

Dorcas grinned. She came stalking over to Joe's side and tapped Estelle on the shoulder. 'Dorcas Joliffe. How do you do? May I ask you to move along a little, madam? There are things I have to discuss with my uncle Joe.'

After a brief flare of surprise, Estelle shuffled peaceably along the bench and, as Dorcas inserted her skinny frame between them, Joe caught the model's brown eyes crinkling in amusement over the top of the girl's head. 'Understood!' said Estelle. 'Look – do you think we could do a deal, Dorcas Old Thing? One day on, one day off for as long as you stay? I'm sure Nunky JoJo wouldn't object. And considering half the junior contingent are Joliffes of one sort or another anyway, that's better than a fair offer. I'm not kidding when I say it's not my forte . . . All that "Cleaned your teeth? Washed your hands? Done your duty in the garde-robe?" They take no notice of me and it's so boring! At least share the boredom with me! Otherwise it won't get done at all.'

Dorcas extended a hand and took the one being offered her. 'Done!' she said with satisfaction. And, surprisingly: 'I'll take tonight's watch if you like? But you'll have to brief me. What time do they go down? Eight? Not until eight? Estelle, you spoil them!'

They dived into an easy domestic conversation, leaving Joe free to enjoy the apple tart and cheese and the

45

quantities of wine poured from cooling earthenware pitchers. Joe thought he could safely scratch the kitchen from his list of facilities to check on. He learned a few more names and listened carefully to a series of thumbnail sketches of the people around the table from Orlando.

'They'll bring coffee in a moment and then we'll break up into groups,' Orlando explained, looking at his wristwatch. 'We aim to be back at work by two – no siestas! But we like to circulate a bit. Exchange views and gossip, make plans for outings into the countryside by charabanc. You've no idea how inspiring it is to share and develop ideas. Gives you a certain confidence to know you're not alone. We usually settle on some of those piles of cushions and furs they keep about the place in lieu of proper furniture. This crowd seems to rather go for the informal approach,' he added apologetically.

'Suits me,' said Joe. 'I can lóunge like a sultan, given the chance. Just don't expect me to talk art and make any sense.'

There was a lull while the last of the dessert and cheese plates were carried off and one of the company took the opportunity to ask, 'Have you asked him, Orlando? What's he say?'

Orlando shook his head. He seemed embarrassed.

'Oh, come on, man! You said he wouldn't mind . . .'

'Me?' Joe asked warily, noticing he was the target of all eyes. 'What won't I mind?'

'They have some mad idea that you should be asked, although in transit and on vacation, to offer a little professional advice. I didn't want to impose but . . . oh, well, they're so uneasy about it, someone's bound to bring it up . . . Might as well be me. Fact is, Joe, we've got a little local difficulty.'

'Little local difficulty!' scoffed one of the women. 'You call an invasion and sacking by a band of Vandals a "difficulty"?' Her voice began to climb to a shriek. 'And when

46

they return? What words will you find to inform the police that we women have all been raped in our beds?'

'Beds, eh? At least we're to be violated in comfort,' muttered Estelle to Dorcas who, to Joe's dismay gave an appreciative giggle.

Estelle leaned across the table and caught the eye of the speaker, a woman whom Joe might have described as a statuesque redhead – if the statue in question were portraying an Amazon queen. The lady now quivering with anticipated terror appeared to be perfectly capable of repelling a squad of eager Vikings single-handed. And, indeed, dressed for repelling. Joe studied her outfit and tried to repress his subversive thoughts. She was wearing a pair of mannish dungarees, paint-splattered, and the top half flattened an over-generous bosom like a breastplate.

The elf-like Estelle squared up to her boldly. 'Put a sock in it, Cecily!' she said. 'You're spreading panic. It's unfair on Dorcas to greet her with such rubbish. And anyhow – when Orlando says "local" he's spot on! The drawbridge was up. No one could have got in here from outside after dark, you know that. It's one of *us* who's responsible. He's probably listening to your hysterical squawks right now and laughing at you. Or we could listen to Guy – it's most likely one of the live-in staff going on a drunken rampage. No more than that. I'm sure Guy will tell us when he's discovered his – or their – identity.'

'Orlando?' said Joe, faintly. 'Would you care to enlarge? I'm all ears.'

'Better tell him, Pa,' urged Dorcas. 'He wouldn't want to leave me anywhere Vandal-infested, you know.'

'Oh, all right,' said Orlando heavily. 'I do so hate a fuss but . . . it was really rather disquieting . . .'

Jeers, hisses and stamping feet urged him to recast his phrases. 'Very well – it was dashed upsetting! We're all agreed on that. Who was it who found her? Padraic? Padraic joined us last week on his way through Provence. Would you care to tell Joe what you discovered?'

A slender man got to his feet and the party fell silent. He had the Irish good looks to go with his name: black hair flopping over his forehead, misty blue eyes and an air of melancholy. The voice that accompanied this romantic outward appearance, though soft, had the resonance of a tenor bell and every word was clear.

'Padraic Connell, Commander. Writer, traveller, song-collector and, when I can no longer fight off the urge, second-rate poet.'

Good Lord! The man even had that self-disparaging, lop-sided smile that women fell for. Joe glanced sideways to check its effect on Estelle and saw that both she and Dorcas were caught on the hook of his charm. Wide-eyed, mouths ever-so-slightly open, they were eager to hear more. Even the finches at the far end had fallen silent.

'It was two days ago I made the heart-rending discovery.'

# Chapter Five

'I was going into the chapel to inspect the medieval fabric: the stones, the statues, the inscriptions – I'd been promised wonders. I've a fascination with the Courts of Love which were held in the castles hereabouts. You'll have heard of the Courts of Love, Commander?'

Joe didn't confide that he'd encountered the notion only two hours before in a guidebook. He nodded silently, not wishing to interrupt the man's flow.

'Well, I'm wandering through this blessed land of Provence in the tracks of these lords and ladies who presided over the birth of a concept so essentially a part of our humanity we are living by it today. I speak of Romantic Love.' He looked heavenwards for a second while he questioned himself. 'Now was it the *birth* or was it simply the acknowledgement of an ideal of love which already existed? An ideal which transcended the boredom and the distasteful duties of noble wedlock?

'*Wedlock!* The word itself snaps like manacles! In a time of arranged marriages and religious demands it pleased the ladies of the day to turn the phrase "God is Love" on its head. For many "Love is God" drew a warmer response.' His glance wafted lightly around the table, touching the women with a complicitous and forgiving unction. 'A wife was her husband's chattel but she could be queen of her lover's heart.'

Joe noted that the men in the audience – with one exception – were staring in disapproval or discomfort at their plates. The women were melting, intrigued. Even Dorcas seemed to be well adrift.

'All over this fair land of Provence, from citadel to citadel they reigned, these clever beauties, patronesses of the arts, spinners of the bright thread of romance which lives on and spells out their names in letters of gold: Stéphanette, Cécile, Blanchefleur, Aliénore, Elys . . .'

Having tasted the silver syllables, he surged into an explosion of the ancient Provençal tongue, its muscled certainty celebrating its stout Roman roots:

> '*Ah! Mounte soun le beu Troubaire*
> *Mestre d'amour!*

'Where is he, the handsome troubadour, past master of love? Where indeed may I find my troubadours, the wandering musicians who enchanted with music and song? I'm trailing them in the hope they will lead me to a queen. A queen of both England and France. A woman who was as clever as she was beautiful: Eleanor of Aquitaine. The wife of kings, the mother of kings, the daughter of a prince. I feel sure my heroine – for so she is, and I don't blush to declare it – must at one time have arrived here to preside over the revelries. Perhaps she even sat at this table, right there in the place which a beauty of our own day now graces.' He paused to lift his claret glass to toast a simpering blonde who dimpled and squirmed to find herself unexpectedly the centre of attention.

The Irishman was taking longer to come to the boil than Orlando, but Joe noted his audience had settled to listen to the hypnotic voice with the wide-eyed anticipation of children turning the last page of a favourite bedtime story. They knew the ending but were enjoying travelling with him towards it. And the whole performance was being put on for Joe's benefit after all. He assumed a more receptive expression.

'Here, at Silmont, I felt I was drawing closer, entering her world. I had a tryst in the chapel, not with Eleanor herself, but with one almost as well known – her contemporary and namesake: Aliénore. A noble lady whose legendary beauty had drawn me across the breadth of France.

'Aliénore . . . And there she was – or rather, there she had ceased to be.'

The handsome features creased in pain for a heartbeat.

'It's Keats who expresses the deepest emotions in the fewest words, don't you find? Knowing something of the lady I was about to see and afire with anticipation, my thoughts were captured by two lines of his:

'*Thou still unravished bride of quietness,*
*Thou foster-child of Silence and slow Time* . . .

'Well, that holy place was steeped in silence and the air was heavy with the slow passage of many centuries, but the *bride* . . .' The honeyed flow faltered and resumed, spiked with bitterness: 'Ah, the bride I was to find was no longer unravished, poor creature! She had been hacked to pieces by a barbarous hand.'

# Chapter Six

Joe had heard enough.

He was conscious that in the stillness that followed this sorrowful announcement all eyes had slid over to him, watching for his reaction. That most irritating of challenges – 'So there! What do you make of *that*, Mr Policeman?' – even when silently delivered, always drew an off-key response from Joe.

He leaned back and offered the Irishman a sympathetic grin. 'Commiserations, old chap! So you never got to fix a ceremonial smacker on those famous lips? I understand that's the tradition in these parts? My guidebook assures me,' he patted his pocket, 'that the carving in question is such a lifelike image and so remarkably lovely that no man can restrain himself from leaning over her and planting a kiss. Table-top tomb, I understand? A double effigy? The Lady Aliénore, dead as a doornail, toes turned up, alongside her crusading warrior lord? The question is: would *I* have had the temerity to wanton with his wife under the old boy's bristling gaze? I think I'd have had to drape a handkerchief over his face first. But many are less fastidious, I believe. To the extent that there was some concern over the erosion of the stone?'

His unemphatic question was heard with the sullen silence and offended stares that greet any child who has flippantly raised a doubt over the existence of Father Christmas.

'But now, if I get your drift, Padraic,' he went on,

unperturbed, 'you're telling me the statue has suffered more than the usual osculatory wear and tear? Smashed up, you say? How very disturbing! Has anyone checked the roof overhead and the remains below for a fallen corbel? I'm sorry I can't be of help . . . what you need is the name of a good stonemason or an architect specializing in ancient buildings. I'm sure Monsieur de Pacy has the details of both on his books. Good story though – we were all agog!' An appreciative nod to the Irishman marked the end of his turn in the spotlight.

Padraic looked about him uncertainly, opened his mouth, closed it and then sat down.

A pretty young woman with dark brown hair worn in a short bob fixed Joe with a scornful gaze from under her glossy fringe. 'Jane Makepeace, Commander. I'm a guest of Lord Silmont. From my reading and experience, I judge that you are missing the point by a mile. Calculatedly, I hope. I would not like to discover that the police force we depend on is not trained to pick up the underlying – and disturbing – implications of this event. I can only guess at your motivation – I assume you are wilfully ignoring the potential threat to us all in a public-spirited attempt to calm the rabble.'

'Jane's making a study of the science of psychology.' Orlando leaned to Joe and hissed a warning in his ear under cover of refilling his wineglass. 'Conserver of ancient artefacts with the British Museum and presently on loan to the lord for the summer. Worth hearing, Joe!'

'Miss Makepeace, you overestimate my sense of duty,' Joe replied jovially enough. 'My motivation in attempting to sweep the shards of this nasty business under the nearest carpet is a purely selfish one. By the morning I shall be gone. By the evening I shall be dining in Antibes. What I do is investigate crime – principally murder. Venting one's wrath on a stone effigy may not be in the best of taste but it does not constitute a capital offence. Wanton damage at the most. Deplorable. But surely there's a local gendarmerie who could interest themselves? I really don't think this affair would ever secure the attention of Commissaire Guillaume of the Brigade Criminelle, were you to approach him . . .'

Her next comment was delivered with an extra helping of scorn. 'Commander, you are being a very great disappointment. You really *haven't* seen the danger, have you?'

Joe didn't quite like to see the triumph in her eyes. Too late he recognized that his aversion to Padraic's plangent delivery had led him into too brisk a reaction. He'd oversteered and would have to correct his course. He sighed and conceded stiffly: 'You're referring to the probable repetition and escalation in the violence, of course?'

Jane Makepeace favoured him with an encouraging smile. She had a very nice smile, he was irritated to notice, and he corrected the balance of his approval with the observation that she was one of those over-tall gawky women, all wrists and elbows.

'It had occurred to me. Very well. I give you my thoughts: I dismiss the notion that we are dealing with the efforts of a disgruntled art critic. In six hundred years, the lady has attracted nothing but praise and admiration, after all. So what exactly has been attacked? Her beauty? Her sex? Her nobility? All of these? Perhaps we're contemplating a statement by some ugly misogynistic Bolshevik? Anyone here fit the description?'

Stifled laughter greeted this and a shout of 'Derek! He's got your number. Confess at once!'

Suddenly serious, Joe added: 'But we ought to consider that the lifeless image may well have been merely an unresisting substitute for a living, flesh and blood object of hatred. Could such a thing happen again? It's a valid question. And one we must ask.'

Nods of agreement broke out around the table and, in response to a further challenge from Jane Makepeace, Joe was led to make a further confidence: 'Yes, I have to say that your assumption is well founded, madam. I could reveal that, in my own studies of real-life criminals to whom I have access, I have noted that the worst, the most cruel, the craziest if you like, murderers have begun their bloody careers in petty and largely unremarked areas. Dolls disembowelled, domestic animals taken and tortured. And then smaller, weaker humans may follow: children or the mentally enfeebled. Family members may be attacked. And in his search for ever more satisfying outlets for his insane anger, the villain casts his net wider. Strangers are caught in it. And it's at that moment that he comes to our – and the public's – attention. Too late, you will say. He is already launched.'

Everyone was silent, appreciating Joe's candour.

'There! I told you all so!' crowed Cecily. 'The Commander agrees with me. There's a Jack the Ripper in the making prowling the corridors. A Beast! A sadistic killer! A lunatic!' Cecily had very blue, very large eyes and they were at this moment at their bluest and largest as they swept the table in triumph. They settled on Joe, and Cecily made a further dramatic point: 'Did you know that the moon was at the full on the night it happened, Commander?'

'I believe it was, madam,' said Joe curtly, not wishing to feed her fire.

'I don't think Herr Freud would give much weight to the phases of the moon in such a case.' Jane Makepeace's response was equally repressive, Joe guessed for the same reason.

'Huh! Only if the suspect were a woman, I bet,' chimed in Estelle. 'Then he'd have plenty to say about monthly madness. Now – have we got to the point where we shall have to go about the place suspecting everyone we rub shoulders with of being a weapon-wielding killer in embryo? *Bring me a jug of water, Marcel – and just leave the axe at the door, would you?*' she drawled. 'Are you happy now you've made your point, Jane?' she finished waspishly.

Joe looked steadily across at Jane Makepeace and raised an eyebrow, underlining the question. She flushed and murmured uncomfortably: 'No need to get carried away, Estelle. Crowd hysteria is something we should be on our guard against encouraging . . . In this much, at least, the Commander is quite right and we should listen to him. Though I maintain that ignorance is always a dangerous state. To *know* is to be able to arm oneself. If one chooses.'

'But can you tell me, Padraic?' Joe interrupted in his no-nonsense police voice, picking up the awkwardly expressed plea for calm. 'As no one will admit to a falling corbel – was there a tool still at the scene? Hammer? Axe? Pick?'

'No. None. But judging by the damage I saw, I'd say the attack could only have been carried out with a stone-mason's hammer or something of the kind.' Padraic appeared to welcome his return to the limelight and spoke in the voice of a thoughtful witness.

'What had been done with the remains?'

'The sculpture had been smashed into large pieces and then prised away from the rest of the display. Like this . . .' He instinctively mimed an action Joe had seen often enough: the swing of a man digging in the trenches, pounding, hacking, levering. 'Someone had gone to the trouble of hauling the bits off to a corner of the chapel. They're still sitting there in a pile if you'd like to inspect.' He shot a questioning glance at Guy de Pacy who nodded soberly and then got to his feet.

Was some careful servant keeping an eye on proceedings through the red baize door which dampened the sounds between the hall and the rear offices? Instantly, a footman appeared with a tray laden with coffee cups and a second followed with a steaming jug.

'Ah, we have coffee!' said de Pacy as though surprised. 'Interesting comments, Sandilands! Very interesting! And I intend to hear more. Right now! Why don't you help yourself to a cup and come over here where we might be more at ease to continue this conversation? Orlando? May we ask you to join us?' He spoke in English with the merest French lilt.

The rest of the company helped themselves to coffee and made off to the fringes of the room, moving cushions and rugs here and there to accommodate their gathering groups. Joe would have been intrigued to monitor the placings and affiliations but Guy de Pacy had something more serious in mind for him. Instead of going off to lounge, he set about clearing one end of the table himself before a man had a chance to scurry forward and take the dishes from his hands. Satisfied, he gestured to Joe and Orlando to join him there. In conference, Joe decided.

He embarked directly on the problem. 'Firstly: Sandilands, on no account are you to feel under any obligation to involve yourself in this mess. I hope I make that clear?'

Joe nodded. So far they were of one mind.

'I'm aware of your reputation and, being a racing man, I thought "horses for courses". This is an event for a sturdier breed than you! I insult neither you nor the good Sergeant Lafitte from the village when I say that this is definitely a task for the gendarmerie.'

'Well, thank God for that,' was Joe's silent thought.

'I entertained the theory that it might be young louts from the area sneaking in and having a bit of fun . . . Their great, great-grandfathers might well have done the same in the unpleasantness of the revolutionary times. I was confident that the Sergeant, once apprised of the situation, would nod wisely and advise me to leave it to him – a name or two came to mind . . .'

'You took steps to preserve the scene, of course?' Joe asked.

'Naturally. I went to investigate it myself the moment Padraic returned with his news. I took Jane with me. Miss Makepeace is an authority on medieval art – did you realize? – and a conserver. I thought she might well have insights . . . be in a position to advise on repair or reconstruction. I – we – judged that we were looking at an unnatural and disturbing occurrence.' He hesitated for a moment. 'I think I'm speaking to a soldier?'

'From Mons to Buzancy,' Joe said succinctly. 'And the four years of hell in between.'

De Pacy nodded. 'Aviation Militaire. I flew Spads.' He looked briefly at his motionless right arm. 'All wood and canvas. They go up like a match. They were lucky to get most of me out.'

The two men regarded each other quietly and, shibboleths exchanged, continued with more easy understanding.

'Inhuman acts of destruction were done in war, Sandilands. Even in sacred buildings. Things of beauty and worth were destroyed or stolen away. And in the frenzy, the overheated passion, the fear, all is possible. One understands . . . one does not forgive but one understands. The act of desecration we saw in the chapel would, in the war years, have been regarded as nothing more than some drunken private's revenge on the female sex . . . a howl of protest against a God in whom he can no longer believe. But the war is long behind us. No such excuse is available to us. I decided to treat it as a scene of crime because that is exactly the impression it made on me. We touched nothing. I immediately put the chapel out of bounds to everyone – adults as well as the children. *They* are, at all events, unable to gain access, even should they wish to, since the opening mechanism is a good four feet above the ground and far too heavy for them to operate.'

'No more than "out of bounds"?'

'It is never locked. It is the House of God and open to those who need to speak to Him,' he said solemnly and then smiled. 'And if there ever was a key it was lost many years ago. So, people are on their honour to do as I ask. Sergeant Lafitte was fetched. He inspected. He wondered. He surmised. He washed his hands of it. To my disappointment, he had no suitable candidate on his list. He gave me the telephone number of the police in Avignon and told me to contact them should worse occur.

'I wasn't prepared to wait for worse, Commander. I was left clutching at the theory you yourself propounded just now. I am not willing to risk the safety of any of the guests under this roof. I was eventually put through to – foisted off on to might be more accurate – the Police Judiciaire in Marseille. An inspector listened politely to my problem. His attention was not caught by the "crime" but the name and standing of the owner of the damaged statuary gave him pause for thought. *Quand même . . .*' he shrugged, 'we have to take our place in the queue for his services. With a gangland war, three murders and two robberies on his books, a beaten-up bit of alabaster has low priority. He informed me he could attend the scene in five days' time. In other words, he will arrive the day after tomorrow, Wednesday, at eleven o'clock.' He smiled. 'An hour's investigation of the crime scene will leave the officer well placed for lunch. He asked me to ensure the area was sealed off and left ready for his inspection.'

Joe was beginning to relax. He liked Guy de Pacy's brisk delivery. He nodded approval of his arrangements. And, with the élite Police Judiciaire, the respected equivalent of the London CID, in control of proceedings, a visiting English policeman was surplus to requirements. Joe could, with good conscience, bow himself off stage. He concluded he was, in the politest possible way, being excused from further participation.

'So, I was wondering, Sandilands, if we could persuade you to stay on for a couple of days to meet this policeman? To confer with him? You speak excellent French, Orlando tells me, and have used it in a military and diplomatic role during the war?' He smiled his genial smile again. 'A man who has the ability – and tact! – to deal with our French generals can safely be set to deal with a provincial police-man, I'm thinking. I would like you to use your knowledge of the profession to get inside his skull and discover his theories and his strategy for dealing with our problem. If, indeed, he has any. If he hasn't, I should very much like you to plant some in his head.'

He was silent for a moment before adding quietly: 'Some of the people gathered here under the castle roof are your friends, I understand, and a good number are your compatriots, Sandilands. This episode – an attack on beauty in a holy place – strikes me as being very un-French and coincides with the presence of a dozen foreigners of artistic temperament. There are undercurrents here I cannot account for in a public place over a cup of coffee to a stranger . . . But then again . . . it could well be that a clear-eyed stranger will see something obvious that has not manifested itself to me. It's a question of focus. I'll just say, I would be happy and relieved if you would accept to stay on and lend a hand.'

The furrows on the brow deepened, the dark eyes were earnest, conveying more than he had articulated. He waited again, taking the measure of Joe's silent indecision, then, finally: 'I'm not a man to run about squawking with panic, Sandilands. I do not easily ask for help. You hear me asking now. Will you stay on?'

'Of course, Monsieur de Pacy. I'd be delighted,' Joe heard himself saying.

# Chapter Seven

'Now. Before this crowd trails off back to its various occu-
pations, would you like me to detain any of them for you?
Any individual you'd like to speak to before I show you to
your quarters?' de Pacy offered.

'And instantly light the fuse of suspicion under some
poor bloke? No, thank you. Let them go about their
business. I'd like two things from you, Monsieur de Pacy.
The first, a list of everyone living or working in the
building over the past season, the second, blanket permission to go wherever I need to go about the building and
speak to guests or staff at will. I cannot function in any
other way.'

'But of course!' De Pacy spread his hands in an expans-
ive gesture.

'And I thought I'd start in the kitchens. No. No need to
escort me! I'm sure I can pick out the cook.'

'The cook?' De Pacy swallowed his surprise to mutter:
'You want to start with the *cook*? Not as straightforward as
you might imagine. Our *chef de cuisine* does not welcome
incursions by the guests. In fact they are expressly forbidden from passing through the red baize door.'

'Then you must introduce me as an employee. I have just
undertaken a commission for you, I think? With permission to rove about, did we agree?'

'Ah! A test! And I've stumbled at the first fence! At least
let me take you in ... *the staff*, after all, stand on some

ceremony ... even though Scotland Yard may have abandoned all decorum.'

He smiled as he got to his feet.


Followed by the mystified eyes of the gathering, they made their way through the swinging door covered in red baize and studded with brass-headed nails, along a short stone corridor and round a corner into a cavernous and apparently deserted kitchen. Joe passed a range the size of a Rolls-Royce rusting in neglect under a stone arch. He noted a row of brass taps dripping into a mottled sink which would have been quite large enough to wash a medium-sized corpse in. A dresser which had once been of the finest oak leaned goutily to one side, its matchboard backing seamed with the vertical cracking associated with wet rot.

'This is the *old* kitchen,' said Guy de Pacy. 'We don't use it any more.'

'I'm quite seriously glad of that,' said Joe and followed him into the further depths.

They passed below an archway into a stone-flagged, large, square space full of activity, the clashing of copper pans, laughter, exclamations and light.

'This is the new kitchen,' Guy announced unnecessarily. 'Our *chef de cuisine* moved in two years ago and insisted on dismantling the – er, Victorian, would you say? – facilities you have just passed and restoring the original and larger medieval space to its former grandeur. With certain modern additions, of course.'

'The refrigerator?' Joe asked, all admiration for the gleaming monster at the far end of the room. 'You're wired for . . .?'

'Yes. The lord installed a generator some years ago and we enjoy a reasonably effective electrical system. Our cook spent some time in the kitchens of the Splendide in Paris during the war years when it was easier for women to take up employment and she came away with notions of grandeur. And some fabulous receipts for iced-cream desserts. I must order up one of Madame Dalbert's *soufflés glacés aux framboises* as your reward before you leave! You'll be impressed. And there she is.'

A small dark woman, well rounded and much girt about with grey pinnies and the black skirts of a widow, was shrieking in what to Joe was a foreign language at a youth struggling to roll out a sheet of pastry. He watched as she snatched the rolling pin from the boy's hands, gave him a playful crack over the knuckles and demonstrated a lighter touch, wiry brown hands and wrists moving in practised gestures. The boy began again and she cooed and patted his head.

She came over to greet them and Joe realized that she had been aware of their intrusion from the moment they set foot in the room. She had chosen her own time to acknowledge their presence, marking out her territory and standing confidently within it. He would be respectful of the borders.

He reached for her floury hand and held it for a moment, smiling and listening to de Pacy's introduction.

'Well, there you are. Madame Dalbert, Commander Sandilands of Scotland Yard who has asked to speak to you, I'll leave you to . . . er . . . get acquainted.' De Pacy bowed and made for the door.

The woman took a step backwards, snatching away her hand on learning who he was, and Joe knew he'd made a clumsy mistake in coming here. There was no retreating so he advanced.

'First things first, madame,' said Joe briskly in French, eyeing the hostile face in front of him, 'in fact: two things. The compliments of an ignorant Englishman on French cooking. The main dish at luncheon was a countryman's dream! Honest meat from the *terroir*, simply cooked to perfection with local herbs. I so enjoyed it!'

'*Faites simple! Faites toujours simple, monsieur,*' she said. Her voice was low and strongly accented with the rugged

Languedoc accent. 'Escoffier knew what he was talking about. And your second comment?' She was uneasy in his presence, already glancing sideways at the young pastry chef, eager to be released to her duties.

'The tarte Tatin. There was something besides apples in there ... a trace of something red ... it enlivened the blandness of the apples and spiked the flavour of what can be a rather dull dish ...?'

She smiled and looked at him directly for the first time, her interest caught at last. 'I wondered whether anyone would notice. It's hard to tell sometimes. You have a spark of inspiration, try out a dish and your only clue that it's a success is the clean plates at the end of the meal. And that's not always a good indicator ...' Her sombre features lit up with a sudden flare of humour – or scorn. 'You English are taught from the nursery always to clear up your plates. Whatever the slop they contain. Rice pudding! Oat porridge! Pouah! ... *Figs*. It was figs. The first ones are just ready. They go well with the apples and a drop or two of fig liqueur helps.'

'It certainly did.' Joe began to make distancing movements and they parted company. Before he turned the corner, he caught her voice calling after him with a certain bold sarcasm: 'Let me know when you're leaving us and I'll prepare a *soufflé glacé*, monsieur!'

He bowed. 'It will sweeten a bitter moment, madame.'

He enjoyed the gust of girlish laughter that followed him down the dank corridor back to the hall.


De Pacy had waited for him by the baize door. 'How did you get on with the dragon of the castle?' he wanted to know.

'Dragon? I thought Madame Dalbert was perfectly charming. We exchanged recipes and planned menus. That sort of thing.'

De Pacy gave him a sideways look and changed the

subject. 'And next? Let me guess. You'd like me to look the other way while you sneak into the chapel to have a good poke about in the debris?'

'If that's an offer – how could I resist?' said Joe.

He walked off shoulder to shoulder with the steward back across the hall, amused to find they were unconsciously keeping step. They were followed by the speculative eyes and approving smiles of the guests who'd stayed behind to lounge at ease and chatter. Here were two decisive men in their prime, striding out together smiling and clearly already doing a lot of agreeing. The frisson which had interrupted their country idyll would soon be soothed away. This pair would stand no nonsense.

'Young Padraic gave a stirring account of the unpleasantness but he was assessing the scene with the eyes, ears and nose of a Celtic troubadour rather than a London policeman,' Joe commented.

De Pacy nodded. 'Whereas you'll sniff the air, not so much to detect the decaying glamour of centuries, as to pick out the . . . um . . .'

'. . . sweat, blood and hair oil of the last over-excited individual present at the scene,' Joe finished for him. 'At the Yard, they call me The Nose,' he joked. 'But however keen the old hooter, I'm afraid it's too late by days to detect anything so ephemeral as scent. But there may be other clues. People sometimes leave behind the strangest things in the heat of the moment. False teeth – still clamped around a beef sandwich . . . a whalebone corset redolent of Nuit d'Amour perfume . . . I've even had a hotel door key with its name and number on it . . . They leave traces of their presence quite unwittingly.'

'Wittingly too – if that's a word,' said de Pacy, suddenly serious. 'I don't want to anticipate your enquiry, Sandilands, but when I visited the scene I became aware of something that had clearly escaped the attention of the young Irish Romantic. Left behind intentionally, I do believe, by our hammer-wielding iconoclast.' He gave Joe a sharp look. 'You may find that nose of yours a mixed blessing!' he said with a bark of laughter. 'But I'm sure you'll see it and interpret the message. Well-travelled and well-educated man of the world that you are. And the Latin should be no problem.'

Joe recognized a manly challenge when it was thrown at his feet. Intrigued, he raised his brows and smiled his acceptance but didn't pursue the matter. In any case, he preferred to come at a crime scene with a mind uncluttered by other people's views.

He nodded goodbye to Guy de Pacy and stood for a moment before the great oak door trying to work out how on earth to operate the unfamiliar foreign latch.

'Turn the central knob and lift. It's heavy!' de Pacy called back over his shoulder.

Strangely, it was exactly the troubadour's soulful reactions that Joe found himself experiencing as the door clunked shut behind him and he was left alone.

The south-westerly sun angled through the stained glass windows, stencilling the paved floor with a pattern of rich colour. Vert, gules and azure – it was the heraldic names that sprang first into Joe's mind in this medieval setting. Green, red and blue. The fairy-tale colours illuminated the only thing that moved in this dim and quiet place – dust motes. Disturbed by the opening and closing of the door, they were eddying in the rays and rising to the sculpted roof above.

Joe observed their dance. A police scientist had told him once – and demonstrated with a high-powered Zeiss microscope in the CID laboratory – that 'dust' was not a simple substance. Perhaps Joe was even now watching flakes of human skin mingling in the air with minute shards of pounded stone. Perhaps if he made his way in further he would breathe in a blend of aggressor and victim? Good Lord! Joe shook away the fanciful thought. But he could see how a young man like Padraic might get carried away by this atmosphere.

He breathed in uncertainly. He doubted that 'thick' was a suitable word to describe a scent but it was the first one that came to mind. Centuries of devotion and incense clotted the air and there was something else. A base note. Joe's nostrils twitched in distaste. Rotting lilies. He glanced towards the altar but failed to spot the wilting blooms. But of course the flowers would not have been changed following the ban on entering. There were jugs of water and empty flower vases standing ready on a table. No flowers.

He began to make his way towards the object of everyone's concern. There it stood, built up with one long side abutting the north wall. The table-top tomb of Lord Hugues de Silmont, famous survivor of some crusade or other. Joe resolved to fill in the gaps of his knowledge. And, lying by his side, his even more famous wife, the Lady Aliénore.

Rendered widower in his lifetime by the early death of his young wife, the old boy was once more, after a sleep of six hundred years, bereft of her charming presence. There he lay all alone, calmly oblivious of the raw gap in the matrimonial bed. All vestige of the sweet girl had been hacked and broken away. At least, not quite all. Sir Hugues' feet rested on the body of a carved lion. A docile beast looking much more like a Pekinese dog, Joe thought. Still, rendering the heraldic beast small enough to slip under a man's size tens was an impossible task for any sculptor, Joe allowed. His wife's feet had rested on the shape of a sleek little greyhound. A whippet perhaps? Were they known in those days or had the sculptor scaled it down in size as he had the lion? The dog remained untouched. Its tail curled down cleverly over the tomb top and at the other end its nose was slightly tilted in adoration of its mistress. The poor creature now gazed with sad eyes at the empty extent of white marble on which she had reclined. So realistic was the carving, Joe almost expected to hear a throaty whine of distress. He patted the sleek haunches and murmured: 'I know – it's a bugger, old mate!'

He looked around him to spot the remains. And there she was as Padraic had described her. A pile of largish pieces placed in a careful pyramid in the corner between the north and west walls. Joe walked over to take a closer look. Two small slippered feet poked out from the bottom of the heap and from the top there extended vertically one slender white arm, its clenched, beringed hand appearing to offer a pathetic gesture of defiance.

He approached, eyes scanning the thick layer of dust on the floor. He grunted in disappointment to see two or three different shoe patterns, all so scuffed as to be indistinguishable from each other. He paused on the fringe of the disturbed area and scanned the remains.

On a red silk kneeling cushion carefully placed centrally at the bottom of the small cairn was Aliénore's head. The luxuriant gilded hair shorn by hammer blows, the nose smashed, the famous lips pounded into a gaping hole, none of her features remained intact. For a giddy moment Joe wrestled with a thought that had, he did believe, been seeded deliberately in him by the studied distribution of the remains. Celtic. The symbolism was connecting him with the head-hunting, head-worshipping Celts. But that was to do the Celts an injustice. The lopping off and triumphant display of an enemy's head, if distasteful to a civilized man, was at least comprehensible. This vaunting, unreasoning destruction was beyond the realms of human understanding.

Joe felt his limbs begin to twitch with disgust and rage. He could contemplate and draw evidence from the bodies of the recently dead and remain stolidly calm, so why this overreaction to a piece of old stone?

He was being manipulated and had felt the pull on his strings, the pressure on his back, the opening of a path from the moment he arrived in this frightful place. The thought that pushed all others aside was that here, amongst a group of people who would all declare themselves dedicated to the creation of beauty, was concealed a soul who could take an obscene pleasure in destroying something more lovely than anything their hands were capable of producing. Surely such a soul would stand out like a block of black iron amongst these tinkling, golden, ephemeral but well-meaning daubers? A hornet amongst the butterflies?

Unsettled, Joe breathed in cautiously and wondered. The stink here was strong. And he wasn't detecting lilies. Had the steward not been so firmly in control of his stomach as the experienced Joe and vomited in some dark corner? No. The man had survived four years of war. He would have recognized rotting flesh as easily as Joe and not been physically perturbed by it. But perhaps the flesh, wherever it was, had not yet begun to rot at the time de Pacy visited?

Joe followed his nose back to the tomb. His eye ran along the Latin engraving that encircled the three sides of the monument exposed to view. *Hic iacet Hugus Silmontis*, it read, under a swag of twining ivy, along the short west end facing the door, followed by *armiger honoratus Provinciae* along the long side. Four words completed the statement and acknowledged his wife: *et Alienora, uxor sua* was engraved across the short east end.

Dangling from a projecting curl of ivy was the source of the stench.

# Chapter Eight

Commissaire Francis Jacquemin of the Paris Police Judiciaire, lean, attractive and gallantly moustached, was enjoying a rare moment of unbuttoned ease. Two buttons to be precise. It was as far as decorum would allow. He had released his waistcoat to this extent under cover of the voluminous table napkin that defended his white shirt from the unctuous saffron-coloured sauce of the dish he was just finishing.

He ran a finger round his starched collar to release a surge of body heat created by the spices and sighed. 'Bliss! Utter bliss, my friend! Damned good idea to take ourselves off the hook and come out and celebrate. This is my first taste of bouillabaisse and – I'm sure you're right – the best in Marseille. Nothing like this to be had in Paris!' He took another sip of his chilled champagne.

'All the same, I think you're glad to be going back to the capital?' his companion said carefully.

The men grinned. Each was quite aware that the Parisian's departure was welcome on both sides. Inspector Audibert had been accommodating and polite when presented with the unrequested assistance of the big noise from the Paris PJ. Many would have objected. It was a fact that the authority of the Paris Brigade Criminelle ended with their geographical boundaries and technically Jacquemin had no jurisdiction whatsoever down here in

70

the south. Only the local force had the authority to slip on the handcuffs and haul the miscreants off to court.

The criminal fraternity knew this too.

In his clean-up of the Paris underworld, the Commissaire had torn through the gangs formed with the release of men after the war. Modelling themselves on the vicious 'Bande à Bonnot' they'd rampaged through the streets, robbing and murdering with a callousness and skill acquired in four years of killing.

In the end, virtually wiped out by Jacquemin's tenacity and his ruthless methods, they had succumbed. But one gang, more astute than the rest, had survived and moved on. Had moved south in fact. Had learned to steal fast motor cars and use them effectively to get away from the crime scene. And get to the next. They'd discovered that there were richer and easier pickings on the Riviera coast. After centuries of peace, the roving plunderers were back in business and based in Marseille.

Jacquemin the pitiless had pursued them.

Working under the aegis of the Marseille police, he had located, lured into a trap and confronted the gang in double quick time. He'd shot three of them dead and the rest had been scooped up by the Inspector's force. Neither officer spoiled the occasion by mentioning the assistance they'd had from a local underworld boss who'd infiltrated the newcomers' set-up and served them up on a plate.

The Commissaire and the Inspector were taking all the credit that was going and treating themselves to a celebratory lunch to close the case. The morning had been spent very agreeably dictating their experiences to a reporter from *Le Petit Journal* and offering their better profiles to his artist. A considerable triumph for both forces.

'So, what now, sir?' Inspector Audibert asked dutifully.

He received the answer he was hoping for from this smarty-pants intruder with his well-barbered hair, neat moustache, hand-made shoes and unfathomable grey stare: 'An earlier than expected departure! The train to

71

Paris tomorrow morning and two weeks' leave.' And then, with unexpected camaraderie, Jacquemin leaned across the table and confided: 'To be spent in Brittany with my wife's mother.'

'Ah? I find the northern seaside most uncongenial,' said the Inspector tactfully.

'I find my northern mother-in-law most uncongenial.'

They exchanged rueful smiles. Jacquemin's faded as he remembered that his current mistress also had plans for him – and Rachel's plans threatened to pull him in a different direction. He sighed. Rachel was beginning to behave more like a wife these days. Always a disappointment. And then there was that promising girl he'd taken to tea at the Ritz . . . That little vendeuse from the tie counter at the Printemps. Adèle? That was it! Adèle would be expecting a follow-up. And he wouldn't be averse to making a further move.

'Nothing much happening in Paris in August,' Jacquemin summarized lugubriously. 'Lost pugs, defaulting gigolos, false insurance claims . . . The silly season, you know. And you?'

The man from Marseille shrugged. 'I only wish I could say the same. You've seen my schedule. Up to my ears. I blame you! You've made it too tough for the villains up north. All your riff-raff comes down here to get into trouble. Our serious problems come from Parisians and wealthy foreigners – not so much home-grown crime around these days. Foreigners! Huh! I was feeling so elated at getting that gang of yours behind bars I did something really regrettable the other day . . .'

He reached under the table for the briefcase which never left his side and took out a notebook. 'Here we are . . . three murders, no – that's five after last night . . . several robberies on my plate and what did I hear myself expansively agreeing to do? Take a day off up in the Lubéron to investigate the hacking to bits of a young lady.'

He enjoyed the surprised lift of Jacquemin's expressive eyebrows and added: 'I deceive you! The lady is . . . was . . . of alabaster and not so young – six hundred years or thereabouts. Why did I agree to go?'

'Send one of your chaps. Any of them would welcome a drive into the country,' said Jacquemin comfortably. 'Why not reward one of the bold fellers who assisted the other night? What about the young lieutenant who risked life and limb when I was pinned down on that fire escape? He was impressive, I thought.'

'Martineau, you mean? Yes, he's keen. But it's not possible, I'm afraid. Big gun required to deal with the crew up there at the château. Here, look.' He opened his book at a page of pencilled notes and passed it over. 'For a start – note the address – it's the seat of some local bigwig – one who still clings to his aristocratic title. Recognize it? Yes, *that* Count! Known to you up there in Metropolitan circles, is he? I'm not surprised. Doesn't cut much ice with me but – they've all got friends in the real world, these musical-comedy types. Political mates in high places and they'll get you a kick up the bum or the sack if you upset them. And, to go on – half the people swanning about the place are foreigners. Half are artists. Some must be both!' He quivered with distaste.

'Silmont? Le Château du Diable, does this say?' Jacquemin pointed and gave a bark of scornful laughter. 'Aristide – they're having you on!'

'No, I checked. It's actually plain old Château de Silmont and the other rubbish is a nickname. A little local joke that stuck. I'm wary of jokes that stick – there's usually a good reason for it.'

'Romantic though? You have to say it has a certain allure.' The Commissaire smoothed down his moustache and placed his napkin on the table. His mind already moving ahead to Paris, he caught the eye of the waiter who came forward to clear away. 'I'm not surprised you agreed to go.'

'You could say romantic, I suppose. The château is full of summer guests according to the maître d'hôtel with whom I spoke . . .' He paused. 'Funny – the chap sounded quite capable of sorting out any nonsense himself without dragging in the Brigade . . . Army type, you'd say. Authoritative. Economical with his words. Used to getting his way. I can only imagine he's been put up to calling us in by all those foreign women he's got up there twisting his arm.'

'Foreign women?'

'It's some sort of artists' colony. Half the number are young ladies . . . models, mistresses, Russian dancers – posers of one sort or another. Intoxicating substances freely available, no doubt. You can imagine the squabbling and hair-tugging that goes on . . . the bed-hopping . . . Too much time on their hands and not enough clothes on their backs – you know the sort of thing.'

'Mmm . . . sounds interesting.' The Commissaire focused his iron gaze on the Inspector. 'Lucky old you!' He called for cigars. 'Tell me more about these Lubéron hills of yours. Rushing streams? Shady green forests full of game?' he mused.

'Sportsman?' asked the Inspector.

'You've seen me shoot! And I'm better with a shotgun than a pistol,' said Jacquemin with relish.

'Ah! I guessed as much,' muttered the Inspector. 'It has no charms for me, I'm afraid. *Homme du peuple* that I am, I wouldn't know which way up to hold a sporting rifle. I expect they've got whole shooting rooms equipped with the very best game guns from London – wouldn't you agree? Purdeys – would that be what they call them? Holland and Holland? Thought so. There's probably wild boar running around up there. I'm just surprised these idiots haven't taken to knocking each other off, out in the chestnut forest. Oh, yes, we get a dozen or so of those "accidents" every hunting season!'

He murmured on about the attractions and dangers to be experienced in the Provençal hills but Jacquemin was no longer listening.

'Aristide!' The Commissaire finally called a halt to the monologue. 'My friend, Aristide! You have been good to me . . . no, no! Hundreds would have resented my presence on their patch and attempted even to foul up the case. But you – you have been efficiency itself with nothing in view but the common cause. Look – you must let me, in some small way, repay you.' He brandished the notebook under the Inspector's nose and in one dramatic gesture tore out the pencilled sheet. 'I relieve you of this piece of idiocy! It's the least I can do. I'll attend and report back. This place is on my way north. Look – give me a car and a driver from the Brigade and we'll set off into the hinterland. There's bound to be a hostelry of some sort in the village – I don't mind slumming it. I'll poke about in the rubble, declare the destruction to be the result of a narrowly focused freak earthquake and send the driver straight back to you with a report when he's dropped me off at the railway station in Avignon. Let me ease your burden as you have eased mine, though to this very small degree.'

The men regarded each other dewy-eyed, exclaimed with mutual delight, protested and conceded and called for cognac.

The Commissaire's mind was already devising the wording of three telegrams. The phrases were grave and regretful: *unavoidably detained . . . case of international concern . . . reciprocity of fraternal assistance an imperative . . .* Monique (and her mother), Rachel, Adèle – they could all make what they liked of it.

The Inspector was asking himself how on earth he'd managed to pull it off so easily. Should he warn them up there at the château? No! Let the buggers find out for themselves!

# Chapter Nine

At the moment the two French policemen were settling their new-found agreement and their delicious fish lunch with a brandy, Joe, in the chapel, was working hard not to throw up his rabbit stew into some available urn.

The tiny body was hanging by the neck. Dead for some days, it was already being consumed by wriggling maggots of various kinds and giving off a revolting odour. Joe took a pencil from his pocket and poked at it. It gave signs of spongy resistance and was not yet dried out. A fly buzzed bad-temperedly from the throat and Joe swatted it away in disgust. Where in hell did they come from, these lousy flesh-eaters? He answered his own question: beetles and flies in the ancient woodwork aplenty no doubt. Some might well have been carried into the building in the animal's own fur.

And what was the significance? 'A message', de Pacy had hinted.

What was one dead creature dangling from a vandalized tomb trying to tell him? What had it said to de Pacy?

Joe was seized for a moment by a healthy rush of indignation and an urge to laugh at his ludicrous situation. His last case in London had involved multiple corpses, eviscerations, and disposal of limbs and heads in packing cases left at St Pancras station. It had involved the talents of the clever men who worked with test tubes, swabs, microscopes and Bunsen burners to establish blood groups and identify fingerprints. He heard himself gleefully recounting his exploits in France to his friend, Chief Inspector Ralph Cottingham, on his return to London: 'Equipped only with a pencil, I examined the entrails of a rabbit for a clue as to who'd smashed up a statue . . .' The story would grow in absurdity as he told it.

He remembered with a flash of guilt the statement he'd been provoked into making after lunch. 'They start with small animals . . . work their way up to children and weaker members of society' or some such guff he'd spouted.

And here was stage one, as predicted.

Or was it? Might it be no more than just – a message? De Pacy had clearly interpreted it as such. Joe couldn't leave the chapel and meet the steward's quizzical eye still unaware.

He stared on at the pathetic form willing it to speak. Hanging up in pairs outside a game butcher's shop, he'd have admired rabbits. He'd have known just which ones to choose. Served up to him in a dish with one of Madame Dalbert's wonderful sauces, he'd have scoffed the lot and dabbed up the juices with a hunk of bread. And complimented the cook. So why was he finding this one little corpse so sinister?

Sinister. There flashed into his mind a woodcut he'd studied with horror when he was a boy. He'd no idea what his age had been at the time but he had certainly been too young to be exposed to such a graphic image. Not exposed exactly! His own cunning and curiosity had led him to the discovery and he'd never confided it to anyone. Left alone with a head cold while on holiday with his London uncles one day, he'd gone along to the library to entertain himself and had straightaway headed for the section his uncles had banned him from approaching. He knew where the key was and in minutes had unlocked the bookcase and wedged the library door in case Simmons should come and thoughtfully offer him a glass of honey and lemon.

And there they were, to be pored over at his leisure: German, French and Italian publications with copious illustrations of naked ladies. And just the kind he liked. Large-breasted, long-legged beauties, sometimes goddesses, always smiling a welcome. He had imagined himself a Paris, Prince of Troy, in possession of a golden apple and, in order to give his illicit scrutiny a more acceptable motive, decided he was going to be the ultimate judge, making, in a classically acceptable manner, the award to the one who he decided was the most lovely. He unwrapped a disc of Sharpe's Toffee, popped it into his mouth and smoothed out the shiny gold wrapper. He folded it with his thumbnail into the shape of a crown and decided he'd leave it, as his prize, marking the page of the winner. So far Botticelli's Roman goddess Flora was in the lead. She had all her clothes on but he liked her naughty face. She looked straight out at him from the book, golden and lovely and about to tell him a joke or throw him a flower. But, strangely, he could never remember who had received the Sandilands Prize for Pulchritude.

It had been a drawing of the most revolting woman he had ever set eyes on that had stayed with him over the years. Lucky it didn't ruin him for life, he sometimes thought.

The book had been an Italian publication. Heavy red leather and gold lettering. The pages had a rich waxy feel to them as he turned them slowly. Italian beauties of the thirteenth century onwards had delighted him one after the other, until he came upon her. 'Luxuria' was her name. A drawing by Pisanello from the fifteenth century. She had everything that ought to have been alluring: youth, a smile, a distant expression of satisfied pleasure, an abundance of golden hair that waved its way like a cloak right down to her bottom. Her only jewellery was a chain about her left ankle. But she was skinny. Her flesh was wasted and her elbow bones poked through the skin. Her knee caps were prominent as was a bone on her right buttock. Joe had turned the book this way and that, using all his scant knowledge of female anatomy to decide huffily that the artist had never seen a naked woman before. Surely? Women didn't have bones in that place. And the breasts? A pair of small Scottish baps too widely spaced. The belly was all wrong too. Distended. The poor lady clearly had some kind of disease. He'd seen sheep out on the hill with the same symptoms.

Before turning on in disgust his eye had been caught by the animal crouching at Luxuria's right foot.

The painter reinstated himself somewhat in Joe's estimation by the quality of his portrayal of the rabbit. Joe knew about rabbits. He'd shot, skinned and jointed many a one ready for the pot and appreciated them in all their forms. So what was this witch-like hag doing alongside a perfectly drawn rabbit? Curiosity always won through with Joe and, sighing, he went to fetch an Italian dictionary to decipher the script that accompanied the strange picture. Half an hour later he had it.

The lady Luxuria was in fact Lust. One of the Vices. She was shown reclining in the manner of Venus but this was a parody. (A trip to the English dictionary eventually cleared up this notion.) So – a 'no better than she ought to be' lady. The commentator obligingly explained that her skeletal state was due to an overindulgence in the pleasures of the flesh. Joe decided to remain mystified by this. He was more intrigued to learn that the rabbit was known to be a 'harlot's familiar'. On account of its 'mating proclivities'. Joe took a guess at that one. Well, he understood that in fairy stories cats were the familiars of witches so the rabbit must play the same role for harlot women.

Poor creature. Round, sleek and furry, it would have made a beautiful pet. Unfair to give it to a bony frightening woman like the one in the picture. He decided suddenly that he was feeling hot and thirsty. A drink of honey and lemon would be very welcome. He'd replaced everything in order, locked up, removed the wedge,

79

placed *The Swiss Family Robinson* open on the library table and rung for Simmons.

Joe peered more closely at the dead animal. How dead? No sign of blood on the corpse or surrounding area. The man who'd brought it here had not, evidently, wanted to leave a messy trail to mark his passage. There was no sign that it had been killed on the spot. Broken neck? Most likely. Killed elsewhere and brought in, then strung up. He wondered whether there was any significance in the positioning of the string. Of course there was. The creature had been put to dangle over the words *et Alienora uxor sua*. The rabbit, the familiar of the whore. A comment on a woman so long dead? Why?

At least he'd have views to exchange with de Pacy when he returned. Even though what he had to say was largely unintelligible.

Joe looked up, suddenly uncomfortable. He didn't believe that emotions could leave an imprint on a scene beyond the dispersal time of sweat and other bodily fluids. He wasn't quite certain, in spite of all the evidence he'd gathered to the contrary, that Evil with a capital E existed. But he knew that if anyone had asked him at that moment to give an opinion he'd have said: 'This is a bloody oppressive place. Not good. There's something ancient and wicked here that the sanctity of centuries has done nothing to dispel. And it's chasing me out.'

The hairs on the back of his neck told him he was being watched. He stood up sharply, right hand going instinctively to the waistband where he usually carried his service revolver. Everywhere hidey-holes met his eye. Flounces of velvet drapery, carved wood ornament, pews and cupboards, even a confessional with a half-curtain pulled across. Places enough to hide a battalion. And then he saw the innocent cause of his concern. Innocent? Perhaps not entirely!

He exchanged glares with a trident-wielding devil that seemed to be taking an interest in him. Carved in dark wood and dulled by the candle-soot of ages, he was still clearly playing a robust part in a representation of the final judgement on the west wall. And keeping the visitor under surveillance. Joe gave him a cynical salute and left the chapel.

# Chapter Ten

*Château du Diable, Tuesday*

The morning began too early for Joe.

He lay still for a few moments collecting his thoughts and wondering where on earth he was. The lingering taste in his mouth of Havana cigars and the certainty that he'd drunk rather too much of 'the true, the blushful Hippocrene, with beaded bubbles winking at the brim', the night before brought back the memory.

Keats! He blamed the poet Keats for his condition. Now there was a minstrel who could stir up emotions and loosen inhibitions in a few superbly chosen words.

Joe considered Orlando Joliffe jointly charged. Just as the earthernware jugs of wine had been brought in at dinner, Orlando had risen to his feet, made a toast and given the company a verse of 'Ode to a Nightingale'. It ought to have been embarrassing. There should have been shuffling of feet and surreptitious glances exchanged. But the combination of Keats' sublime words and Orlando's confident light baritone swept all before them:

> 'O for a draught of vintage that hath been
> Cool'd a long age in the deep-delved earth,
> Tasting of Flora and the country green,
> Dance and Provençal song, and sunburnt mirth!'

Wine poured from a jug with a generous hand into clay

beakers of antique design couldn't possibly do much damage. This morning Joe discovered his mistake. It had been a pure incitement to drunkenness!

Clattering feet, banging doors and rattling water cisterns were followed a moment later by a peremptory tap on his door. The dashing figure of Nathan Jacoby entered at once, bearing a disarming grin and a cup of tea. Earl Grey by the scent.

'I come in peace!' he announced. 'Seven o'clock! Rise and shine! Orlando said this would be guaranteed to get your motor started. Urgh! Can you really drink this? I'll put it on the night stand. There's coffee brewing downstairs if you're interested. Fresh bread's come up from the village. All available in the refectory.'

He made his way over to the small high window and flung the shutters open, blinding Joe with daylight and a stream of fresh morning air. 'Come and take a look at this!'

Joe shrugged into his dressing gown and wandered over. He breathed in gratefully, enjoying the sound of a late cockerel crowing away in the distance and the sight of the hills rolling in a myriad of green interlocking spurs towards the horizon. 'Earth hath not anything to show more fair . . .' he commented and found that he meant it.

'Look, I'm going out with my camera today with young Frederick, one of the painters – the fresco bloke. We've hired a car. Plenty of space for you if you'd care to come along.'

'Ah, yes. I introduced myself. I went to watch him at work after lunch yesterday. Good-looking young bloke from London . . . preparing to express himself on several square metres of damp plaster. Intimidating! At which end do you start?'

'A dying art, he tells me. There's only a handful of artists in Europe who know how to do it. *I* can paint a bit,' Nathan admitted, '. . . the only reason some of the company are prepared to put up with me . . . but I'd never have the dash and sheer courage to embark on something like that. He's twisted my arm to take him out to the Val des Fées. Silly name for a spectacular sight. Outcrops of ochre – iron-stained rock and soil . . . colours ranging from creamy white to darkest blood red. Rather eerie and hellish to my mind . . . But it seems to have a fascination for young Fred. Back home we'd call it Death Creek or Bushwacker's Gulch or something like that. Here it's called the Valley of the Fairies! The village houses are mostly painted with the ochre they extract and – you might guess – painters go wild for the colours. The Mont Sainte Victoire at sunset – well, you just have to express it in the local pigments, don't you? Young Fred had the idea to chip bits off the rocks himself, pound and grind and prepare his own paints. Mmm . . . He ends up buying them ready prepared by Messrs Mathieu in the village *droguerie* like everyone else!'

'And uses them to wonderful effect! He showed me his sketchbook. I saw some terrific ideas for the finished painting. Expressing scenes from local history in colours straight out of the ground – it has a certain appeal. Though I can't immediately see what financial allure it might have for the lord? Fixed to the wall as it is – it must remain quite unsellable.'

'Even the lord makes his personal choices. There are several items I know of that'll never see the light of day outside this château. We're never given the tour of his own private collection but it's rumoured that he has one. Must be worth a fortune – he's been collecting for years. Look – why don't you come with us to the ochre valley? We're starting out straight after breakfast.'

Joe cheerfully told him he could resist the fairy charms for the moment. Duty called him to stay at home and get to know some of the other inhabitants.

'Thought you'd say that. But I also came to say – remember I have a camera. One or two in fact. For different uses. Not just for pleasure and art. And one of their uses is recording evidence, you know. The Ermanox will be perfect for the job. I was wondering if I might sneak into the chapel under a corner of your blanket permission to rove about. How about it? Shall we make a foray together into the forbidden chapel and take some shots of the depredations? If you think it's worth it? Word is that you went in there yesterday . . .'

'I was wondering how to ask!' said Joe. 'I found nothing very sinister, I'm afraid, but a record would be a useful thing to have.'

'That's great! Look – the light will have gone by the time I get back from the fairy realms . . . morning light is much better and that place has sensational east windows. How about an early start tomorrow morning, Wednesday, before the Inspector gets himself up here from Marseille? Present him with a fait accompli?'

'And yourself with an unusual photographic opportunity?'

Nat grinned. 'The thought had crossed my mind.'

'You're on!' said Joe. 'I'll look forward to it.'


Left alone, he stood at the window sipping his tea and reviewing his day.

'The lord sees that their everyday needs are catered for,' Estelle had told him.

Well, this was certainly to all appearances a happy colony of worker bees, Joe had to think. He'd made full use yesterday of his leave to snoop about the castle and, after his visit to the chapel, had reconnoitred unchallenged, to his heart's content. He'd leant over shoulders and admired half-finished works; he'd watched a lady sculptor pounding and chipping – 'No! No! The shape's in there . . . I just have to reveal it . . .'; he'd helped Frederick Ashwell to mix and apply a coat of plaster to a wall ready to receive the fresco the lord had commissioned. He'd been impressed by the boy's professionalism and had listened enthralled as he explained his techniques. Speed and forethought,

85

apparently, were the watchwords. Knowing exactly what you were doing. Impossible to have second thoughts. The preliminary designs complete, the final painting had to be done at the moment the plaster reached the perfection of dampness.

He'd decided on a tactful approach for today. He would wait until the guests were once again at lunch before he'd go, list in hand, to check on the sleeping quarters of each person Guy de Pacy had named. The only names that did not appear were those of the steward himself and his lordship. Orlando had indicated vaguely that the two men occupied rooms in two of the corner towers.

The single men seemed content with their dormitory arrangements, bunking down on camp beds set out, suitably enough, in the old guardroom. A similar area had been allocated to the women on the floor above. Scattered on both floors were small, cell-like spaces put to the use of married couples of whom there were two and, of the others, one had been awarded to Joe and another to the Russian gentleman. Joe had protested his readiness to muck in with the other men but de Pacy had insisted he avail himself of a measure of privacy – 'in case you need to interview someone – or I need to speak to you.'

His things had already been brought up and unpacked while he was at lunch on the first day so he'd conceded with good grace and settled to enjoy his solitary state.

Why in blazes was he staying on? He asked himself the question constantly and the same answers came back ever more strongly. Two answers.

There had been the surprise of discovering that one of the faces around the lunch table had been familiar to him from photographs and newspaper articles he'd seen some years ago in his early days at the Yard: *Earl's Daughter lets her hair down at the Savoy with Dancing Dreamboat . . . Every playgirl's favourite partner cuts a rug at Ciro's . . .* That sort of nonsense, he remembered. But Joe's professional antennae had quivered at the sight of this guest who he was reasonably sure had a darker side to him than the limelit, cocktail-fired image the press displayed. He was known to the Vice Squad back home in London. But Joe's hands were tied. There was no way he could make an accusation or even a discreet enquiry based on a piece of sketchily recalled Scotland Yard gossip.

And yet the man's reported proclivities were too objectionable for Joe to ignore in the circumstances. He had to ask himself whether it would be sensible at least to alert Orlando, and decided that it was more than sensible – it was essential.

And then – the most surprising part of his day – there'd been Estelle's strange behaviour.

The drinking and the yarning and the laughter had gone on until past midnight, he remembered, and the women had defiantly stayed on at the table. When the moment arrived, he'd looked questioningly at de Pacy and wondered which of the women would take it upon herself to rise and suggest that the ladies might like to withdraw. De Pacy had grinned and, in a marked manner, had launched into a conversation with Jane Makepeace, inviting her opinion on the mental state of Vincent Van Gogh at the moment he severed his own ear. Instead of the heavy psychological diatribe Joe had feared, her crisp answer had raised a shout of laughter around the table.

'Formidable woman,' he'd commented to Estelle.

'You don't say!' she'd drawled. 'Forget it, Joe! You'd need steel-lined underpants to tangle with that one! She wouldn't be interested in you.'

Estelle had offered to walk him back up to his room after dinner and taken his arm firmly in hers. And the flourish had not gone unremarked by the crowd remaining in the hall. She was wearing a fetching midnight blue gown in a silky fabric cut on the bias. The gown clung flatteringly to her slim figure and her slim figure clung flatteringly to him. Her hair brushing his shoulder smelled heavenly – Après l'Ondée, he thought, or something equally special.

She'd been scintillating and funny over dinner; a girl with further plans for her evening, he'd have said. But whom did her plans involve? She'd flirted openly with several of the men. And yet it was on Joe that her choice had fallen when she left.

Intrigued, excited but slightly alarmed, Joe began to try to estimate the quantity of wine he'd downed at dinner and could only conclude: too much. Should he say something ... issue a caution? Or hope for the best? They'd arrived at his stout oak door and he'd turned to her apologetically. 'I say, Estelle –' was as far as he got before she put a finger over his lips.

'Shush!' She'd made a pantomime of listening. Cheery sounds of the women settling down for the night came from their dormitory; a drunken chorus from *Iolanthe* rose up from the floor below and was quickly extinguished by yells of protest and possibly the application of a pillow. A child called out in its dreams and instantly fell silent.

Reassured by what she was hearing, Estelle whispered: 'Got a torch, Joe?'

He took one from his pocket. 'A torch? Never walk castle corridors without one. Er ... what do you have in mind? If you've found the bloodstained key to Bluebeard's lair, we'll have to come back in the daylight. Not at my sharpest at the moment, I'm afraid.'

'Can you at least stagger along to the end of this corridor? That's all you have to do.' She'd squeezed his arm reassuringly.

She led him along to the end of the corridor, eased open a window and let herself through on to a flat square of roof contrived between two dormers. Joe followed to find himself on a lookout platform with a low balustrade to ward off vertigo. From up here there was a clear view over the courtyard closed off at one end by the bulk of the chapel.

The cigarette butts underfoot explained the girl's interest in this private little space, he guessed. He shone his torch on to the roof tiles below, lighting up several packets' worth of mostly half-smoked ends. And a scattering of something else.

When Estelle turned to close the window behind them, he bent quickly and gathered up two pieces of screwed-up paper and slipped them into his pocket. Unwanted love-notes? He didn't think so. He managed in his torchlight to catch a glimpse of the name *Houbigant* printed on one of the flimsy pink sheets. Face powder papers? Discarded out here amongst the cigarette ends? An outlandish and unwelcome thought delayed for a moment his automatic offer of help with the window.

'Sometimes, when I've drunk too much or if Cecily's snoring, I can't sleep. Especially these hot nights. So I come out here, sit on the window sill and smoke. The others can't stand the smell of tobacco and I'm banned from doing it in the dorm. It's rather like being back at school! I was out here the night of the full moon. It was quite magical. The moon was over there.' She pointed behind her. 'A huge harvest moon shining down on the courtyard. It was almost as bright as day but of course the shadows were deeper. But then it all got a bit strange. I heard some dull thuds coming from the chapel and I stood up to have a look. There were no lights on so I sat down again. I thought it must be rocks settling, woodwork contracting after the day's heat . . . you know what old buildings are like. I've lived in some pretty decrepit places and nothing surprises me! About half an hour later I saw him.'

'Him?'

Estelle began to tremble and instinctively Joe threw a comforting arm around her shoulders and tucked her shawl more closely about her. The girl felt small-boned and about as substantial as gossamer in his arms but her voice when she replied was throaty and determinedly bold.

'Him? It? A ghost. At least that's what I thought I saw. Yes, really! That was my *first* thought.'

'Can you describe it?'

'Dark grey. Solid shape. It could have been male or female. I saw it very clearly. It was wearing a long hooded robe, just as you might expect, and moving along soundlessly. Coming from the chapel towards me. Like this . . . Head down, hands together in front . . .' She demonstrated. 'Not skulking or trying to hide. Floating along as though it did this every night. Perhaps it does . . .'

'Were you able to make out a face?'

Again Estelle quivered. 'It was hidden by the hood as it came towards me but, without breaking stride, it suddenly looked up in my direction. This is the sickening bit, Joe. It had no face. Where you'd expect to see features there was nothing but a white space. It was a faceless monk.'

'It looked up at you? Are you quite certain about that?'

'Yes. Almost as though I'd called out to him. I hadn't. I made no noise at all. I didn't move and he couldn't have seen me in the shadows. He had no eyes, in any case.'

'Listen, Estelle. I have to ask – could this . . . um . . . sighting have been a nightmare? Or a hallucination with a *physical* cause? Alcohol? Other stimulating and vision-inducing substances?'

He could hardly speak more plainly.

She answered in kind. 'Ah. Yes. Know what you mean! Was I squiffy? Sensible question and I'll tell you straight up – no! I couldn't have been more clear-headed,' she finished convincingly and then ruined her impression of unquestionable sobriety by adding: 'On that occasion.'

'And, having had time to mull it over, are you still thinking it was a ghost you saw?'

'Lord, no! I'm thinking it was something much more sinister. Something *human* was coming back indoors. He was one of us. And he felt it necessary to hide his identity. Has he put the cloak away in his wardrobe to use again later? Was he sitting there at the lunch table listening to Padraic's account of his exploits?'

'I'm wondering why you didn't speak publicly of this earlier?' Joe asked quietly, sure that he knew the answer.

'And be labelled some sort of crackpot? Spread panic? You saw for yourself how eager they all are to invent a bogeyman! There are children here, Joe. They're having the time of their lives, roaming about the place completely unafraid. I'm not going to be the one to take away their confidence, to give them nightmares. These innocent years pass too quickly. Mine came to a sudden end when I was seven.'

She dashed on, not wanting to hear a comment from him: 'And I've learned when it's best to keep quiet. I wanted you to talk to me first – before you heard my strange experience. To get to know me a little. I'm not a fanciful storyteller. I wanted to see you ankle-deep in my cigarette ends on the spot where I saw what I saw, so that you'd understand that I wasn't inventing anything.'

Joe peered over the edge, taking a measure of the distances involved. He glanced up at the pennant flying from the watchtower. Bending, he picked up a cigarette end, rubbed it between his fingers and sniffed. 'Untipped, heavy-duty stuff! French tobacco, if I'm not mistaken? Estelle – tell me – what sort of cigarettes are these?'

'Well, you're right. They're Gauloises. I like the strong taste. I started to smoke them because only *men* seemed to – defiance, you know. I like breaking down barriers. Shocking the prudes. And then I got to like them. Anything else seems insipid now.'

'And were you actually smoking a cigarette at the time? At the time of the sighting, I mean.'

Estelle had frowned in concentration. 'No. I'd just put one out. He couldn't have glimpsed a light. But I see why you're asking. Strong scent, too.' She gulped and turned large eyes on Joe. 'He's sniffed me out, our effigy smasher, hasn't he? He knows who I am. He knows I was watching him.'


All Joe could do was apologize for the obvious nature of his advice. She'd listened, amused, as he'd earnestly advised her not to be alone . . . to seek out the company of those she could trust.

'Exactly what I have in mind,' she'd said mysteriously. 'No! Thank you, Joe – you're a sweetheart! – but I really don't need an escort to cross the corridor!' She'd waved a hand towards the ladies' dormitory, whispered goodnight, kissed him on the cheek and left him at his own door, his head still reeling from the enticement of her perfume. A lure which had not been thrown on the water to catch *him*, he acknowledged.

He stood just inside his doorway listening to her scurrying feet which took her straight past the dormitory and on to the end of the corridor. From the click-clack of her heels, he guessed that she didn't much care if he heard, so eager was she to move on to her next assignation. He couldn't make out whether she'd gone up or down the staircase – nor decide whether he was relieved or disappointed.

In the end he had to admit that he was concerned. Not fearful. But definitely concerned. And his concern centred on the women and children. In a few quiet moments with Dorcas, he'd made clear his preference that she sleep in the small dorm with the little ones, just a door away from the single women's quarters. And across the corridor from his own cell. She'd listened quietly and told him that she understood. He thought it very likely that she understood quite as much as he did himself.

At least Dorcas seemed content and busy. Since her status had been publicly acknowledged on the first day, she'd thrown herself into doing exactly what she had made a play of despising and the children followed her every-where, delighted to have a gang-leader. She'd tapped on his door last evening just after eight as he was dressing for dinner and reported all well with the junior squad. They'd had early supper and Estelle had been informed that all were present, correct, clean and in pyjamas. The cook's children were spending the night here in the château instead of going back home to the village. When their mother stayed on, they generally stayed too, so including herself, the total was seven. And could she borrow his copy of *Kim*? There didn't seem to be much in the way of reading material about the place. Joe had reminded her that Orlando would be bound to know where the books were kept.

Orlando. Finishing his morning tea, Joe decided it was his duty to confide his fears and suspicions to him and let him make what he might of them. He realized he didn't know the man well enough to judge with any confidence how he would react. 'All his geese are swans,' Joe had agreed with Dorcas. And Joe was one of his geese. It wouldn't surprise him to hear Orlando proudly announcing to the crowd that in the space of a few hours his Scotland Yard friend had uncovered under their roof a tormentor of small animals, a drugs ring, a deflowerer of virgins, and the man who once shot at Queen Victoria.

There was no way around it. Joe would have to count on Orlando's common sense, though so far in their relationship it hadn't made much of an appearance.

Joe sat on after breakfast as the rest wandered off to their work, sharing the dregs of the third pot of coffee with his target. 'Come and help me find some children's books,' said Joe. 'I'm sure on the way in I passed a store room full of broken rocking horses, rickety dolls' houses and that sort of thing.'

Orlando looked a little surprised. 'I know the one you mean. Follow me.'

When they entered the room Joe shut the door and invited Orlando to take a seat on a gaudily painted pirate's chest. He pulled up a decaying nursery chair and tested it for strength and height before lowering himself on to it opposite and slightly higher than a puzzled Orlando. So far, so good. It never failed. Joe's over-close proximity, knee to knee with his interviewees, the stiff breeze of moral rectitude at his back and, for choice, the sun in their eyes, was too unnerving for any but the most innocent of victims.

Predictably, Orlando began to squirm with discomfort. 'Oh, goody!' he said, nervously. 'We're going to play Snakes and Ladders! No? Knucklebones then?'

'Shut up and listen to me, you clot!' Joe snapped. 'I need to put you on your honour and I'm a bit perplexed as to how to do that. Is there anything sacred you can be made to swear by? You don't believe in God and you'd cheerfully sell your mother to the devil. If I were to confide something disturbing – could I trust you to handle the information with discretion? How far *can* I trust you, Orlando?'

The ingratiating grin faded and Orlando looked back at Joe with a face suddenly unprotected by its usual mask of mocking self-awareness. 'You can trust me with your life. And any other burden you care to set on me. I thought you knew that?'

And, apparently regretting lowering his defences even for a moment, he reverted to his usual insouciance: 'Didn't realize I'd be made to swear a blood oath. I say, I hope you're not contemplating a little knife-work to seal this brotherhood ... Can't stand the sight of the old claret oozing from the veins, don't you know.' Then, into Joe's intimidating silence: 'So it's to be a round of Truth or Consequences, then? You tell the truth and I suffer the consequences?'

'Something very like that,' Joe agreed. 'A warning, Orlando. And here's the truth – this is not a safe place for the children. You must take them away from here.'

He waited for the automatic protests, the huffing and puffing to roll away. 'Yes, yes, I can see that. Oh, to be ten years old and free to roam in a pack about the Château de Silmont in summertime! With a dozen indulgent adults to take an interest. Twenty years ago I'd have thought I'd died and gone to heaven to be among them ... But listen – *it's gathering* ... I'm not sure what, but something dark. If there's anything more important to me than flushing out a villain who's committed a crime it's preventing that crime from ever happening in the first place. There's no glory in *that* for a policeman! No front page acclamations in the daily papers. And to hell with all that! Will you help me to take the necessary steps, Orlando?'

Joe waited for and got an understanding nod before he went on. 'There are one or two things you ought to be made aware of. Listen – I went to take a look at the mess in the chapel yesterday. All as described and disturbing enough, but there was an additional element . . . a small furry one . . .'

Orlando listened and, to Joe's relief, didn't make the all-too-easy Englishman's scoffing objections. 'Not much of a reader, I'm afraid, Joe, and I can't say I've ever opened a book by any of those psychologist chaps you go on about. From what I hear, it all sounds a bit like common sense and I can't see what the fuss is all about. Perhaps it sounds more impressive being expressed in German? But I can quite see why you – or anybody – would be on the alert. It rang a bell with me – what you had to say at luncheon yesterday – that stuff about progression.

'There was a girl in the village – yes, a girl – who was a bit queer in the head, you know. Started sticking pins in her dolls, chopping off their limbs . . . the family cat had kittens and they all mysteriously disappeared one by one. No one noticed.' Orlando breathed in and out slowly and shuffled his feet. 'Her baby brother, six months old, was found dead in his cradle one day. Suffocated, the doc said.'

Joe nodded. 'Classic case. I do hope . . .?'

'The doc is a clever man. He put two and two together and saw that the right thing was done.'

'I don't think your village gossip is going to be much help with the next problem. I have to ask – any dope-fiends in the neighbourhood?'

'Dope? Not as far as I know. People say there's a lot about these days. You can get anything you want in most Paris bars. You just go to the till with your cash. They even

95

have a slang word for the till: *la pharmacie*! And the Riviera coast is Paris-by-the-Sea at this time of year. Bloody awful stuff! I've watched friends of mine . . . well, never mind. I drink too much and, yes, I've sniffed a little this and that. Lost my nasal virginity at a young age but never got addicted. I don't think I'm the addictive type. Nothing clings to me and I cling to nothing. Everything and everybody rejects me in the end and moves on. Except for Dorcas. She'll drop a tear on my coffin.'

'So. Glad to hear you're conscious of the dangers.'

'I don't want the evil stuff or any rum bugger under the influence of it anywhere near the children. It's illegal here in France anyway. Throw your weight about, Joe. Lean on whoever it is you've flushed out and make them leave. Who? Give me a name!'

Joe took two screwed-up pieces of paper from his pocket. 'Let's examine the evidence first. What do you make of these?'

He handed one to Orlando.

Orlando took it and opened it up carefully. 'It claims to be face powder – shade, wild rose. My mama uses these. Dab, dab, dab on the cheekbones. Useful little things to slip into your handbag. They don't leak or spill. But this powder's *white*.' He licked a finger, ran it along the creases and popped it into his mouth. 'Definitely not cosmetic. It's cocaine,' he said.

'Thought so.'

'Some folk use a five-pound note for the purpose,' Orlando offered.

'All adds to the gaiety, I suppose.'

'Well, it could have been worse, you know.'

'What do you mean? Bad enough, I'd have thought.'

'There are more deadly concoctions about. Until recently, this stuff was sold openly over the counter as a tonic!'

'Here in France?'

'Yes. Never heard of Mariani Wine?'

96

'Of course. A tonic – as you say. One of my great-aunts swore by it. She imported it by the case.'

'I bet she did! But she was in good company. Other advocates of this infusion of coca leaves topped up with red Bordeaux wine included Edison – he of the electric light bulbs – Jules Verne, the Prince of Wales and His Holiness Pope Leo XIII. His Holiness actually awarded them a medal! At nine milligrams of the hard stuff per bottle, no wonder they were enthusiastic!'

Joe was entertained, as usual, by Orlando's worldly knowledge. 'Good Lord! I had no idea! Edison, eh? Isn't he the chap who said genius is one per cent inspiration and ninety-nine per cent perspiration?'

'He did. Failed to take the nine milligrams into his calculation, it seems.'

'But someone a lot closer to home is getting supplies of much more serious stuff. I should like to find out how.'

'If you'll open up and tell me *who*, perhaps I might have an answer as to *how*.'

'Estelle.'

Orlando spent a few moments absorbing this information before shaking his head sadly. 'Now you come to mention it . . . Yes, I can see there were signs there for those sharp enough to pick them up. The eyes! The mistimed gestures! The surges of jollity! Oh, Lord! What am I supposed to think now? I like the girl. So do the children. Why couldn't it have been that appalling pseudo-Russian? That impresario or whatever he is . . . Director of the Ballet Impérial de Lutèce – that's what he calls himself . . . Pretentious twerp! I'd have enjoyed watching you kick *him* out. I shall look forward to handing him the keys of his Hispano-Suiza and waving goodbye.'

'So that's *his* car? I had wondered. Well, on the subject of Monsieur Pederovsky –'

'I think it's Petrovsky.'

'Thank you. You may well yet have the pleasure of watching him depart in double-quick time. I'm sure his chiselled profile is known to the Vice back home. And if he's who I think he is, believe me, you wouldn't want him under the same roof as the children. But I make accusations without proof. I want you to come along with me to his quarters while he's at lunch and we'll look through his drawers.'

'Oh, I say! Poking about in a chap's privacy? Not sure I could do that.'

'You don't have to. Just stand in the doorway, and keep watch while the Law gets its hands dirty. I don't think we'll need to look further than his passport.'

'What colour *are* Russian passports? Do they have passports or do the poor blighters still just escape over the border and head for Paris?'

Joe groaned. 'Go back to your painting when we've finished here. At the lunch table, make sure that our ballet-loving friend is sitting there in best bib and tucker and then make a vague statement about regretting sending me off on a wild-goose chase somewhere about the place – I'll leave that to your invention – excuse yourself and come after me. We'll roll up, arm in arm, ten minutes later making apologies. Got that?'

'Got it!' Orlando tried to get to his feet in relief that his ordeal was over.

'Not so fast, blood brother!' Joe put his hands on his shoulders and pushed him down again. 'There's more I want from you. And you're not leaving until I get it! There's another little mystery I've been asked to clear up. I know you have the answers to my questions. There are just two of them. First: Who is – or was – Dorcas's mother? And second: Where is the lady now?'

# Chapter Eleven

'No good, I suppose, telling you the answer to both your questions is: "I don't know"? Thought not. And if I added: "None of your bloody business! Go away and leave me in peace, you nosy bugger . . ."'

Orlando got to his feet rebelliously and made for the door, to find that Joe was already blocking his way.

'Why don't we take a walk down to the stables, old man?' Joe said, unruffled. 'I'm sure I've heard horses somewhere in the distance. I'd like to take a look. You can always get the measure of a man by checking his horses – I've heard you say it. And, as the lord himself seems to be eluding me, it's the best I can do.' He knew that Orlando loved horses even more than art and would never raise an objection to strolling out to admire a selection. Orlando fell into step willingly enough. 'We can get a bit of fresh air before the day heats up,' Joe persisted cheerily. 'If you care to burble a few confidences into a sympathetic ear as we go, I can assure you of my utter discretion. And it *is* my business, I'm afraid. I've been engaged by Dorcas to find her mother. She seems very certain that she's to be found down here in Provence.'

Orlando sighed. 'And that's all the information you can count on. Why do you suppose I come down to this part of the world every summer? I'm still hoping to find her again. Laure. The love of my life. Well, the first love of my life.'

'Laure?'

'Yes. Like the name of the poet Petrarch's inamorata. We met in Avignon. Half the girls there are called Laure. The half that aren't are called Mireille. I'm not even sure that was her name. She was a bit of a storyteller. And secretive. Dorcas is very like her.' His smile was tender.

'Dorcas tells me all she knows is that her mother was a gypsy and a dancer and that she abandoned her at the age of one year and returned to France.'

'Village gossip. She wasn't a gypsy – just dark as the Provençaux are. Ancient Greek and Roman ancestry, of course, and it shows – the straight nose, the lustrous eyes, the black curling hair . . . But, of course, to the good Saxon folk of Surrey, dark equals gypsy. She was slim and lithe and looked like a dancer but she wasn't one. Not professionally. As far as I know. I found her in a state of destitution. On the street, sleeping in a doorway near the Pope's Palace. She'd fled her village and come to the big town looking for work.

'No honest work available for a homeless girl. She'd been earning a crust or two singing outside cafés. There was a sort of folklore festival on. Gypsies and other performers in town. People were more willing to open up their purses for a pretty girl singing the old tunes. But it was clearly not going to last. I was going through my Modigliani phase at the time and here was a girl my idol would have smacked his lips over. Thin, dramatic, enigmatic, beautiful . . .'

'Get on, Orlando!'

'She became my model and my mistress and I took her back home to England with me. I was very young myself . . . and the money soon ran out . . . By then, she was pregnant with Dorcas.'

Joe recalled the acid remarks, the hard slaps he'd seen meted out to Dorcas by her grandmother, and cringed. He could imagine the impression that flinty nature and unyieldingly aristocratic bearing would have made on a young and pregnant foreigner.

'A year? She survived a year under your mother's roof? A happy time was had by all, then?'

'You know my mama! I *have* tried to sell her to the Devil but he's having nothing! Hatred at first sight! She made Laure's life a misery. Tormented her, rejected the child when she was born. I did what I could. But, after a year, the moment the child was weaned, Laure disappeared. Left me a note asking me not to try to find her and to take care of Dorcas. I haven't even got a portrait of her. She burned all the canvases. Made a bonfire of them in the orchard while I was away in London. Not that you'd have recognized her from those pictures.' Orlando grimaced at the memory of his early work. 'And that's it. It was the year before the war broke out. For the next five years there was no possibility of travelling through France but every year since then, I've done my best.'

'And your other children?'

'All illegitimate like Dorcas,' he said cheerfully. 'Never married any of their mothers. Or rather *they* wouldn't have *me*. I told you – nothing and nobody ever sticks to the smooth surface of the life and character of Orlando Joliffe. Money, lovers, children, friends, they all lose their foothold in the end and they drift away, heaving sighs of relief. You will too . . .'

'Stupid, self-indulgent sod!' said Joe mildly. 'What about that angel, Nanny Tilling? That tower of strength, your groom, old Yallop? They've given their lives to you and your progeny. My sister Lydia is not unconcerned and it'll take more than a bit of self-deprecating hand-wringing to dislodge me, mate!'

'A good kick then? Will that work?'

'Not even. Would you like to hear what I'm planning?'

Orlando groaned. 'I don't want Dorcas to be hurt. And there's every chance that she might be if you go on with this ferreting. Hopes may be raised only to be dashed. Even worse – you may find her mother and discover that the woman herself has changed. Hadn't it occurred to you?

101

What do you think life will have been like for a fallen girl with no protector? She'll be something quite other after thirteen years. Dorcas has a picture in her mind of a young and lovely dancer. Laure might look by this time more like that raddled pouter-pigeon of a duenna that Petrovsky hauls about with him. Did you notice her at the dinner table?'

'Spanish-looking? Blue-black hair, wearing something purple and rather décolleté?'

'That's the one. Half a ton of gaudy stones cascading down the slopes of an ample bosom!' Orlando shuddered. 'Suppose my lovely Laure had turned into *her*! And she could have, you know! She's the right age. Doesn't bear thinking about. And, anyway, it's the last thing she would want – to be presented with a grown-up daughter and an ageing ne'er-do-well foreign lover she discarded in disgust before the war. Listen! If we're going to do this, and I see from that granite-jawed, mulish expression on your ugly mug that we are, there's a proviso. A sine qua bloody non!'

'Go on, I'm listening.'

'If *you* find her . . . I insist on being the first to be told. Before Dorcas has any inkling. I insist on the right to assess the woman she is now before you start making the introductions.'

'I understand. I too would place Dorcas's peace of mind above all else. Including yours.'

'Well, that's honest enough!' Orlando looked thoughtfully at Joe. 'The child knew what she was doing, I'm thinking, when she decided to sink her hooks into you. She saw Sir Lancelot riding over the hill, flashing warrant cards, clinking handcuffs and reading the Riot Act to her granny and thought, "That's for me!" Watch it, Joe . . . she's a manipulative rascal.'

'Don't I know it!' Joe agreed easily. 'Now, come on! The story! And I've never enjoyed the love duets from *La Bohème* much so spare me all the romantic rubbish. I want facts. Names. Locations. A village, you said? Near

Avignon? Which village? Think! In the Lubéron hills, is that all you know? Vast area. Did she mention her parents? Why had they thrown her out? Did she mention her school life? The name of a teacher? A best friend?'

'Crikey! Do leave off! I feel like a rat between the jaws of a terrier. You're shaking me to bits!'

'I've barely started. The girl was with you for two years, Orlando. She must have got a word or two in edgeways in your conversations. No one can talk without giving away something about themselves. Just one name or one fact remembered could give us the key. Life in village France is organized around the parish – the town hall, the school and the church. Let's start there. Was Laure religious?'

'Not very. Occasionally she'd ask me to take her into the local Catholic church for confession. She insisted on having Dorcas christened.'

'Then she was certainly a communicant. On somebody's parish records. Look – every French girl talks of her first communion – did she mention the name of her village church? We could check the rolls if we had a name.'

Orlando stopped walking abruptly. 'Good Lord! Sometimes I see why they call you a detective . . . It was the only photograph she had. I brought it with me . . . in case. I keep it here, in my wallet.'

He took a leather note-case from his inside pocket and produced a dog-eared sepia print. Joe had seen hundreds like it in every photographer's studio window. Four twelve-year-old girls were standing together in a row, wearing long white dresses and veils. Downcast eyes looking shyly in the direction of the camera, they were clutching a white book in one gloved hand and a small bouquet of flowers in the other. A communion group. And taken by a professional photographer in a studio, judging by the painted backcloth showing the inevitable ruined temple on a wooded hillside. Joe looked for the photographer's name and found to his annoyance that it had been scratched out.

He pointed to the defacement.

'I told you – she was determined I shouldn't know any-thing of her former life. I think she had something to hide.'

Joe was beginning to enjoy the challenge set so many years before by this unknown dark Provençal girl.

'Well, we could start by showing this to the photo-graphic establishments in the nearest big town which would be Avignon and asking if anyone recognized the scenery –' Joe began.

'I've done that. And the photographers of Arles and Aix and Marseille. You'd be surprised how many shut up shop in the war. The ones who struggled through didn't recognize it.'

'It's all we've got. There must be . . . Hang on! Only four girls! Four!'

'So what? Four friends. All the same age and size.'

'But not the same in looks. I'd say these two here on the left are twins. This beauty next to them rather fancies her-self as a dancer – do you see how she's standing – quite deliberately, I'd say – with her feet in the at-ease ballet position?'

Orlando peered over his shoulder. 'Oh, yes. Never noticed. And now I can't see anything else of course. The photographer must have been a bit miffed when he devel-oped it.'

'But she's not your Laure. I'm going to guess she's the one on the right.'

'You've got her!'

'It's a very small number for a communion class. That tells us it was a very small village. She was how old when you met her? . . . Seventeen? . . . In 1911? And she would have been twelve when this was taken. So we're looking for a village in the Lubéron which had in 1906 a tiny class of communicants. Every young girl remembers the priest who instructed her. Think, Orlando, did she ever mention the name of –'

'Ignace. Father Ignace.' The words fell, leaden, from Orlando's lips before Joe had finished his sentence. He

104

closed his eyes in a childlike effort to remember or squeeze back an unmanly tear. 'She once said, "Father Ignace would not approve." And I'm sure she was quite right,' he added with a haunted and melancholy smile. 'It was the first of many things she did that would have raised a priestly eyebrow!'

'May I keep this?'

Orlando began to splutter, clearly not keen to have the photograph leave his possession, but Joe was already sliding it away into his own wallet. As the last girl in the row, the small one at the end, the only one of the four not to have looked down in modesty, disappeared from sight, it seemed that she caught his eye and he knew he'd seen that look of mock innocence before.

# Chapter Twelve

'Opulent quarters provided for Monsieur Petrovsky! He may not impress *us* but he would seem to merit some consideration from the lord?'

They climbed the staircase of one of the round towers, possibly the most ancient part of the château. The house was perfectly silent, the full company at lunch in the great hall.

'Yes. He gets a set. It's said the lord has a considerable financial investment as well as aesthetic interest in Petrovsky's undertakings. Perhaps the rooms and hospitality are a quid pro quo of some kind. In here on the lower level, there's what it pleases him to call his *estude*. Do you want to sneak a look?'

And what a pleasant study it made, with southern light flooding in from the window on to the desk, bookshelves full of interesting volumes and comforting Turkey carpets on the floor. Joe took a moment to open each of the drawers of the desk with gloved hands. He inspected the neatly arranged documents on the desk top, turning over several envelopes to read the address of the sender on the reverse flap. He moved on to a drawing board, set up on an easel beyond the desk and tilted at an angle to catch the light. After a moment he began to make sense of the pencilled notes and watercoloured sketches.

'The man *designs* ballets too? As well as funding them? These are rather good. Outlines for scenery ... shorthand for some ballet steps ... He would appear to be planning an extravaganza by the name of *The Devil's Bride.* Do I have that right? Anything known?'

Orlando replied tersely, uneasy with his role. 'Yes. He may be some sort of fake but he knows his stuff. Some do say he was a dancer himself in his youth. Understudied for Nijinsky. Partnered Pavlova. That generation. And he's stayed pretty . . . er . . . lithe, wouldn't you say? Inherited money from his father some years ago just as his career was fading. "War money," people hiss out of the corner of their mouths, "dirty stuff!" Wherever it came from, it came in large quantities and launched our chap firmly into the higher realms of the ballet. Not sure "higher" is quite right . . . Anyway, he suddenly had the clout to start up his own company, to employ choreographers of a quality to rival Fokine, Massine and any of the other "ines" you like to mention. Funny that – in the ballet world you've got to have a French name to get on in choreography, Russian if you're dancing. Little Alice Marks of London found her career taking off when, overnight, she became Alicia Markova.'

'Ah, yes – those little girls he surrounds himself with like handmaidens are . . .?'

'Are indeed Russian. They flee to Paris from the Bolshoi and suchlike. The country produces them by the score. And now there are ballet schools springing up all over the place. A plethora of eager little girls showing off their pirouettes in every capital of Europe. Their mothers are desperate to get them noticed by such as Petrovsky. Some as young as twelve, if you can believe!'

'Oh, Lord! Baby ballerinas! Whatever next? I say, are they properly supervised?'

'Not always. Well, you saw their duenna last night – totally silent! Is she Spanish? Is she French? How would we know? Unaware and incurious. She's not there to inter-fere. She's there to turn a blind eye. It's usually the mothers who chaperone these girls. But they get distracted. Bored. Turn their attention to daughter number two or three, run off with gigolos. Have affairs with one of the dancers. Male or female. Having lived life through their offspring, they suddenly decide to enjoy the bright lights for themselves. Some, I suspect, are merely complacent and conniving. Everyone notes that the charmers who make the leap from corps de ballet to a cameo or even lead role tend to be those same girls who are allowed to keep close company with you know who. You see why I'm perfectly ready to think Petrovsky a villain of the worst kind.'

'Is he a fixture here?'

'Oh, no. Comes and goes. Seems to use the place as a country retreat. He's working – if you can call it that – in Avignon. The company's performing for the summer season on some of the more glamorous stages in Provence. Open-air stuff too. He's putting on extravaganzas in the Roman amphitheatres in Orange and Arles. Sylphs flitting about the ruins by moonlight . . . you can imagine.'

'And what reason does he give for bringing the girls with him?'

'He doesn't deign to. Drops hints in conversation that a day or two away from the theatre is a reward. For what, he leaves to our imagination. They don't stay long – have to get back to the barre and the rehearsal room. Can't allow their limbs to stiffen up, I suppose. The girls he brings are ever-changing. Practically indistinguishable one from the other, but then, the names are always different. The current pair are Natalia and Natasha.'

'Weren't you concerned about his proximity to Dorcas – knowing or suspecting all this?'

'Dorcas? Lord no! She can't dance a step and . . . well, you've seen her in action . . . tongue like a hedge-clipper and all the common sense in the world. She'd have Monsieur Petrovsky for breakfast!'

'I've seen enough here. Shall we move on upstairs?'

'If you must. This way.'

The door was standing open, which in a strange way eased the path for Joe's trespass. Orlando would not follow

108

but stood in the doorway and talked to Joe across the bedroom in a stage whisper. 'The girl's been in and done, you see.'

'The girl?'

'I mean the girl from the village. The lord doesn't trust a gang of artists to take good care of their surroundings and he has women in every day to keep our rooms in order. So there'll be nothing in the waste-basket for you to turn over.'

Joe slipped back on the one pair of gloves he'd thought to bring with him to France. Smart black leather but they'd have to do. His training would not allow him to search a room without protection, however superfluous it might appear. And the professional gesture seemed to appease Orlando.

The room was, indeed, perfectly ordered. A chintz cover in blue and white was spread over the made-up bed which seemed to Joe too large and sitting badly in this rounded room. A bunch of white roses graced the night stand. Toiletries were lined up with regimental rigidity ready for use. Penhaligon's Hammam Bouquet was his scent of choice. Joe removed the stopper and sniffed. Old-fashioned but mildly exotic by reputation. Rather sulphurous and odd, Joe decided.

A red silk dressing gown was draped neatly over the back of a chair. With practised gestures, Joe checked the pockets and found them empty. He looked at the label. Parisian. The contents of the wardrobe he next passed in review were equally expensive and well chosen. Well chosen if your life was lived flamboyantly in the public eye – on the stage or the dance floor or travelling between capital cities. With a smile, Joe calculated he would never have been able to afford even one of the cravats, had he had the dubious taste to want one.

'Turn away,' Joe shouted to Orlando. 'I'm about to be indiscreet!'

He began methodically to examine the contents of the chest of drawers by the bed, starting at the top.

'Well, that's one question answered,' he called into the corridor and, when Orlando turned, flourished a small dark blue book with gold lettering. 'British passport! Our bird is English and he's really . . . let me see now . . . Ah, he's really Spettisham Gregory Peters not Sergei Petrovsky.'

'*Spettisham*? Great heavens! What sort of cad is called after a sneeze? Man must be a lounge lizard. Kinder to think of him as Sergei!'

After a few more moments of stealthy inspection, Joe could not resist attracting Orlando's attention once more. He flourished a small box at him. 'Sexually active lizard, you'd have to say. And discreet with it! The very best prophylactic you-know-whats from a Parisian establishment.'

'*Quelquechose pour le weekend, monsieur?* Is that what you're saying?' Orlando was intrigued enough to take a step into the room to make a closer inspection.

'Quite. But no discernible evidence of a female presence in this love nest. I wonder . . .'

'No! Don't do what you're about to do!' said Orlando firmly. 'Leave the bed made up just as it is. He'd know if it had been disturbed. And the maids are well trained. All evidence of a delicate nature will have been removed anyway.'

Joe rather thought he spoke from experience and conceded the point. Orlando retreated and Joe started to follow him to the door. Doing everything by the book, he dutifully pulled it closed to check the inner side. Many a time he'd found interesting information in the pockets of a dressing gown hanging neglected on a hook. He was not disappointed. He stared for a moment, taking in the offering. Here on a hook was hanging a dressing gown so aged it reminded him of his father's moth-eaten old school gown. It even had a hood. Every large house had one such hanging about the place. Visitors who'd forgotten to pack one of their own occasionally shrugged gingerly into them in the middle of the night, preferring to risk possible exposure to skin rash rather than the certainty of the cold of the corridor leading to the bathroom.

Joe glanced back at the glamorous red silk number draped over the chair back and wondered.

The garment was of dark grey wool and so ordinary it might have escaped the attention of someone who had not heard Estelle's story the previous night. Joe patted it down like a suspect. Feeling a slight lump in the right-hand pocket, he took out his own handkerchief and used it in lieu of an evidence bag to receive the half-smoked cigar he extracted between finger and thumb. His eye, ranging over the fabric of the gown, was caught by a glint of gold low down near the hem and, cursing his lack of tweezers and magnifying glass, he managed with difficulty to pick out a tiny object which joined the cigar in the safety of his handkerchief.

All very fascinating and Joe would have liked to spend much longer studying the garment but Orlando was growing ever more restive.

And it was the incongruous item protruding from the left-hand pocket that seized Joe's attention. With that before his eyes, demanding his notice, he'd needed all his detective's discipline to first carry out his routine inspection of the dull gown itself.

It was artistically arranged, you'd have said. A pair of silken white ballet tights dangled seductively, crossed at the ankles, small feet pointing to the floor, clearly caught in the execution of what Joe believed to be called an entrechat.

# Chapter Thirteen

Joe reached out and hauled Orlando into the room.

'Look at this! What do you make of it?'

'Great heavens! What do you think I make of it! It's disgusting! The man's every bit as bad as we gave him credit for. I shall have to speak out.'

'No, no! Look. Just imagine a girl's legs in those.'

'I beg your pardon! What sort of perverted imagination am I to suspect you of, Joe? I had thought –'

'Clown! Look at them! They're dancing! The legs are dancing. Didn't your sister ever do ballet?'

'Lord, no! You knew Beatrice! Well, you didn't exactly . . . Missed her by a few minutes, I think. But you saw her even though she was dead at the time. Six foot tall with big feet! And not a musical bone in her body.'

'My sister did ballet.' Joe pulled a face. 'Made me lift her about the place and count time for her exercises. I know an entrechat when I see one. And here we have one. On its way up or down, who can tell? At any rate it starts and finishes in the same place – the fifth position.'

'Is that so?' Orlando peered more closely. 'Small size. You'd hardly get Dorcas into those.'

'They've been set out like that to attract attention . . . to make a comment . . . to cock a snook? But at whom?'

'We have to say – at us,' said Orlando heavily. 'You're saying we were expected?'

Both men jumped perceptibly to hear a rumbling voice calling in French from the bottom of the stairs.

'Sergei! Are you up there? Sergei?'

'And now we're caught!' whispered Orlando.

'Who is this? De Pacy?' muttered Joe.

'No. Much worse. Much, much worse! It's the lord himself.'

Surprising Joe, he straightened his shoulders, grinned and said lightly, 'Look – leave this to me. I'll do the talking. You just smile politely. Okay? Stay where you are. Put the door back against the wall and hide the fifth position. Oh, and take those gloves off!'

'Silmont! Is that you?' he bellowed back in confident French. 'We're up here. Looking for Sergei. The whole world's looking for Sergei this morning! Will you come up or shall we come down to you? Ah, here you are! Didn't see you at breakfast, sir – I was hoping to introduce my friend Joe Sandilands, who's doing the tour. I'll do it now. Come in, come in.'

With aplomb, Orlando made the introductions. He could have been standing in his own drawing room, Joe thought, confident and welcoming.

The lord was all charm. He was delighted to see Joe whom he had been hoping to catch at lunch and regretted that he would have so short a time with him. 'Just off to visit an old friend and neighbour for the day,' he apologized, indicating his riding breeches. 'Only ten miles distant – I usually ride over. Though I'm so enfeebled these days I never know when one of these rides is going to be my last. You get set in your ways once you reach fifty, you'll find. It becomes increasingly difficult to give up on anything. I look forward to spending one evening each week playing bridge with three old friends of my youth. This week it happens to be a Tuesday when we're all free. One of us being a doctor, we tend to follow his lead. Sounds depressing, no doubt, to a young man like you but our weeks turn agreeably around the event. I shall make a point of returning by lunch time tomorrow to do my duty! I feel I ought to exchange nods at least with this inspector of police we've been promised. I think cousin Guy allowed himself to be pressed into an overreaction by some of the shrill ladies we have on board at the present. What do you say, Sandilands?'

'In the same situation, sir, I would myself have called on the police – had I not been the police,' he finished with a smile. 'There is always the fear that it may be the prologue to a tragedy.'

'But as to the elusive Sergei, sir,' Orlando bustled on with his explanation, 'I'm afraid we can't help you. Someone said he'd eaten early and come back to his room. The fresco painter is looking for him also – trying to tempt him out to the Val des Fées. The *on dit* is that our Russian friend is, in fact, a watercolourist of some distinction in addition to his other talents, were you aware? . . . But of course . . . We'll continue our search and pass him a message should we find him before you do . . . What would you like us to say?'

While Orlando had flannelled himself through this one-sided conversation, Joe and the lord had been taking stock of each other. Joe decided he liked what he saw. Of medium height and slender with thinning brown hair and pale, angular features, their host did not at first sight live up to Joe's imagined aristocratic presence. Or to his fearsome reputation as art connoisseur. Here was one who had been a handsome man and an athletic man, but Joe had an uncomfortable illusion that he was seeing him, his essence diluted, his image reflected in a dust-filmed mirror.

He was wearing breeches and a tweed jacket and seemed to have called in on them – or Sergei, Joe corrected himself – on his way to the stables. He could have been any English country squire preparing to hack around his estate at the weekend. But he had a quality of blended awareness and ease that magnetized the space around him and drew the attention. Dark eyes seemed to gleam with increasing amusement at Orlando's performance and he risked an exchange of glances with Joe, politely suppressing a smile.

114

'The Val des Fées! Of course, you're quite right, Joliffe,' he returned smoothly, taking up the cue he was offered. 'Now I remember it being spoken of. Sergei is immensely interested in the colours and character of the neighbourhood – background for his new ballet, you know.' He turned to Joe. 'A local story of devilish horror which you must ask someone to recount to you. In the broad light of day for choice – not before retiring! Everyone's worst nightmare! He's seeking not only inspiration for the plot of the ballet but also an artist of some distinction who's capable of designing and painting the sets. Which must be stunning and fresh. He is unable to secure the attentions of Pablo Picasso or Henri Matisse who would have been his first choices because they are engaged elsewhere by rival companies. But I have introduced him to our young friend Frederick whom I have enlisted to paint a fresco in the north gallery. I have been greatly impressed by the boy's talent and I'm sure Sergei will be equally impressed. And if they have gone off together to the ochre landscape this is nothing but good news. My schemes would appear to be working!'

He smiled at Joe and confided: 'One of the pleasures of advancing years is that you have collected a wide acquaintance. You know many people and can move them around like chess pieces on a board. You can put them together – drive them apart should it be necessary – even wipe them from the board if they fail to please. It's a pity that you will be with us only for a day or two, Commander. I looked forward to watching you perform!'

'Not as a pawn, I hope?' said Joe with a smile calculated to veil rather than hide his irritation. 'I rather see myself as a knight, bounding gallantly about the board.'

'You are no bounder, Sandilands, unless I miss my mark. No. I picture you as the queen who bides her time, watches the play and swoops with deadly accuracy when the moment comes.'

He turned to Orlando. 'But carry on with the tour, Joliffe. I understand Guy has given carte blanche to the Commander to begin his swooping when and where he thinks fit.' An elegant hand flicked out, indicating the turret room. 'This would seem a strange place to start perhaps but,' he shrugged, 'the Commander knows best.' He edged to the doorway. 'Are you coming down? Then I shall accompany you and bore you with information about the building . . .

'This suite of rooms,' he began, affecting the tone of a guide, 'belonged in the thirteenth century to the mistress of the Lord Silmont of the day. Well, *one* of the mistresses. It's said that he had four in all, one in each corner turret. His bastard sons – of whom there were many – served him in the traditonal role of page boy or maître d'hôtel. Imagine the domestic disputes . . . the jostling for promotion . . . the back-stabbing . . . the shin-kicking! The sudden unexplained deaths in the struggle for the succession! Thank the Lord I have to face none of that.'

'You have sons, sir?' Joe asked as the lord seemed to have left a space for a response.

'Not so fortunate, I'm afraid. I have never been married. You're looking at the last survivor in a long chain of inheritance, Commander. The broken link, if you will. And we have Napoleon to blame for the destruction. The decay started with the introduction of the Code Napoléon. A disaster for the landed gentry! The law of primogeniture was swept aside and instead of passing down as one piece to the oldest son of the family, estates, small and great alike, were divided equally between the surviving children – however many of them there were. The inheritances grew ever smaller with each generation. But the families adapted. We always do. There was no longer a compulsion to produce large broods. One son became the preferred production. To be replaced as and when war and disease made it necessary.'

Uncertain as to how he was expected to respond, Joe murmured something that sounded like condolences.

'Oh, one ought not to set much store by a great name in these modern times. When I tell you that the aristocracy in France have flourished to such an extent since the Revolution that they number over two hundred thousand, you will hardly believe me! I know that you English assume we were all but extinguished . . . losing our heads to Madame Guillotine. It may surprise you to hear that a tiny percentage of the whole class – just over one thousand aristos – lost their heads. The huge majority kept theirs and either emigrated or lay low on their remote estates until better times arrived. All praise to Louis XVIII! Yes, Sandilands, we have a thousand times the number of gentlemen you have in England! Which might lead a sceptic – and I class myself as such – to say that the Silmont title is of little consequence. I shall leave it and my lands to my cousin Guy. Alas – he also is childless. And therefore, unless he pulls his socks up and remembers his familial obligations while he is yet young enough, the estate is destined, I'm afraid, to be bought up by aspiring neighbours. It will be absorbed by some marquisate or duchy. Or some rich nobody eager to avail himself of the noble particule. Monsieur *de* Silmont! Two letters, Sandilands! What extraordinary lengths people are prepared to go to in order to acquire them. Now, if you'd care to come this way . . .'

The cry went up at the most inconvenient moment. Somewhere deep in the castle a gong had announced it was time to think about assembling for drinks before dinner. Joe checked his watch and waited by the door of his room. Dorcas was late. Or Estelle was late. He found he could no longer remember who exactly was on herding duty this evening.

He heard the cry a second time and recognized Dorcas's voice. A moment later she shot up the stairs and into the children's dormitory. More shouts and yells and she came

117

dashing out again. Joe saw her take a deep breath and try to control her voice as she caught sight of him but she could not deceive him. The terror behind the calm words was very evident.

'I'm afraid there's one of us missing, Joe.'

# Chapter Fourteen

Joe listened on, hoping he'd misunderstood.

'It should be Estelle on duty tonight but nobody's seen her since teatime so I thought I'd better get on and do the rounding-up myself. I've counted six. There's me, Peter, Dicky, Rosie, Clothilde, René . . .' she recited, in her concern using her fingers to demonstrate. 'We're all here. It's the littlest boy who isn't. *Le petit* Marius. The cook's youngest. I sent everybody out again to hunt for him . . . they've not done their teeth yet . . . to look in all the usual places. Nothing. We've yelled his name all about the castle. We've looked in every oven and every cupboard he likes to hide in. He's just disappeared. I don't know what to do. And it'll be getting dark soon.'

'I'm sure it's all right, Dorcas. Look – if you like, I'll come in and have a word with the others. Perhaps they're playing a joke on *you*? Had you thought of that?'

'Of course. *First* thing I thought of! And I've told them what I'll do to them if they are. They aren't having me on. Besides, René, his older brother, is crying. He thinks he'll be blamed and he's upset. I can't make any sense of what he's saying.'

Joe went into the dormitory to find a huddle of murmuring children gathered together on one bed for consolation. Trying to keep his voice brisk and reassuring, he began to question them. Peter answered first as the oldest boy and confirmed that the last sighting of *le petit* Marius, who didn't know how old he was, had been just after tea,

119

before they'd started play again. Awkwardly Peter told Joe he might like at this point to question René.

Joe took the hint and turned to René. He knelt down and looked him in the eye. 'Tell me if he was sad or happy, your little brother, when you last spoke to him.'

'Sir, he was sad,' whispered René.

'Why – sad?'

'We'd had an argument. I'd just told him that he couldn't play with us in the game we were planning for after tea. He's too little for some things –'

'Don't be angry with René,' Dorcas interrupted. 'Marius can be a pain in the bum. He thinks he can do everything the others do but sometimes he just can't. And he always shouts the same thing: "I'm Marius! I'm a soldier!" I blame his mother for calling him after a Roman infantryman. Gives him ideas beyond his size.'

Joe smiled. 'What was the last thing he said to you, René? Can you remember?'

'Yes.' He hesitated then asked: 'You want me to say the exact words? They were rather rude. Well, he said, "Damn you, *crétin*! I don't want to play your stupid game anyway. I'm going down to Granny's!"'

Joe breathed deeply, the relief washing through him. 'Did that surprise you?'

'Well, no. He's done it before, stomping off in a rage. And telling tales. Granny always . . .' René's lips began to quiver and tears began to drip down his nose. Joe silently handed him a handkerchief and patted his head. 'Granny always takes his side. She always believes him and I get a smack for not looking after him properly. If he's gone home I'll be in trouble again after last time. He knows that. He wouldn't have landed me in it again, would he? He's a pest but he's not really bad. He's my brother . . . I was sure he'd be about the place just hiding to . . . to . . .'

'To pay you back? To make you feel guilty.'

René nodded.

'Look, all of you. Calm down. I'm sure this is going to

be all right. I want to see you with clean teeth when Dorcas and I get back up here. We're just going down to the kitchen to have a word with René's mother and see what she has to say. I think it's most probable that young Marius is, even as we speak, being tucked in and spoiled rotten by his grandma. But I like to be certain.'

'It's dinner time, sir,' René pointed out, his face creasing with anxiety. 'Maman doesn't let anyone into the kitchen at dinner time and guests never at all. She'll be cross!'

'Don't worry! She'll let *me* in. I shall know exactly what to say to her. And I tell no tales!'

Reassured by his calm and friendly voice, the children began to nod and smile and hunt about for their sponge bags. Normality returned.

'Sorry I bothered you, Joe,' said Dorcas as they made their way downstairs. 'There are things I don't understand yet about this set-up. I should have pressed him a bit harder and got the truth out of him. Do we have to disturb Madame Dalbert? She's a bit of a dragon, according to René.'

'And the steward! And me!' said Joe lightly. 'But come and take a look.'

'Well, if you're sure,' said Dorcas reluctantly. 'But – tell you what – let's not make an entrance through the great hall. There's a side door into the kitchen that they use for supplies. It leads in from the courtyard. The boys use it when they want to see their mother.'

Amongst dashing servers and hurrying kitchen hands they had difficulty in picking out the small figure of Madame Dalbert. Dorcas crept in behind on Joe's heels, apparently wishing herself a million miles away from this bustling scene. The cook stood rigidly watching him approach, confounded by his presence in this place at this time.

Joe plunged straight in: 'Madame, my apologies. I'm here to ask if you know where your son is at this moment.' He reached behind and pulled Dorcas forward. 'This here's Monsieur Joliffe's daughter and she's just turned the castle upside down searching for him. Unsuccessfully. He's disappeared. We can't find him.'

Joe was alarmed to see Madame Dalbert turn pale and sink down on to a stool, clutching her bosom. He hurried to counter the effect of his bald statement: 'I speak of the little one – Marius.There is some evidence that he got tired of the games and was heard to say he was going off home to stay with his grandmother. Is this likely, do you think?'

The cook found her voice again. 'Oh, thank God for that! Ouf! You gave me quite a turn! Yes, of course it's likely. Marius! He's done it before. He knows the way home blindfold. Everyone in the village knows him. He's always wandering about. He'll be all right. Now – if you'd said René had gone off, I'd really have been worried!' She got to her feet again and resumed her imperious stance. Back in control. 'Thank you for your concern, but I'm sure it's not necessary. Marius slipped in here to see me at about four o'clock. He was a bit grumpy. They quarrel a lot, the boys. I listened to him and gave him some bread and chocolate and a glass of milk and he cheered up. I told him he could go and see his granny if he wanted to. It's hard for him being the youngest and sometimes it's best for him to have some time to himself. No harm done. But thank you, sir . . . miss . . . for thinking of warning me. And miss –' she turned now towards Dorcas with a look that was very nearly tender, 'thank you especially for paying attention to them. Little Marius talks about you all the time since you got here.'

She wiped a hand on her pinny and tentatively held it out to Dorcas.

In one of the uninhibited rushes of emotion Joe had come to recognize and dread in Dorcas, the girl ignored the extended hand, stepped forward and wrapped her arms around the dusty little figure. They hugged each other in relief for a moment.

He walked back to the dormitory and distributed the illicit sweets he'd scooped up in the pantry as they passed through. 'All's well, chaps!' he announced. 'Marius's mother was aware of the situation. Marius has indeed gone to ground at Gran's. I'm giving my torch to Dorcas so if there's any problem in the night, you'll be able to shed some light on it. And I'm just across the corridor. See you all in the morning! Night night! Oh, just one word, Dorcas, if you wouldn't mind . . .'

She responded to his raised eyebrows correctly and came to join him in the corridor.

'Estelle,' he whispered. 'I'm very concerned for her. Would you mind awfully going into the women's dorm and asking if she's back yet? If not, see if you can find out where they think she might be.'

Dorcas groaned. 'Yes, I would mind. Awfully. I'm not going in there! They're all dressing for dinner – I'd be in the way. You've seen what they're like. And they're on their best behaviour when you're around. They'll rag me! Do I have to? . . . Oh, all right then . . . but if I have to kill one of those Russian girls it'll be all your fault.'

She went in, leaving the door open, and Joe skulked in some discomfort outside by the jamb. Judging by the noise, they were all still in there, quarrelling about stolen stockings and yelling at each other to be quiet in several languages. Dorcas ignored the cat calls and suggestions that she go straight back into the crèche and, cleverly, Joe thought, directed her question to the sensible Jane Makepeace.

'Miss Makepeace, can you help me?' he heard Dorcas say.

'Not really a good time, darling. I'm a bit behind . . . Look, pass me that stocking from the radiator, will you?

'I'm looking for Estelle. She's disappeared,' Dorcas persisted.

And Jane replied, 'Well, this here's her bed next to mine and, you see, she's not in it or on it or in the vicinity of it. Can't say I've seen her lately. Sorry, I'm not much help.'

'No, you aren't, are you?' Cecily's voice. 'Dorcas has been moved up to the top table now – I think we should give her credit for a little grown-up understanding, don't you? Listen, my dear – the truth is, Estelle doesn't often sleep in her own bed. She wasn't here last night either. She's most probably spent the afternoon with one of the chaps and she'll spend the night with him. If he has a room of his own. If he hasn't they'll find one somewhere without too much trouble. You could try her boyfriend Nathan – he's got a room to himself in the north tower where he messes about with his chemistry set.'

A lazy Russian voice drawled: 'Or, failing that, my darling, you could always ask your father.'

The response was a blend of titters and shocked protests.

'You'd do better,' Cecily went on, 'to check your *uncle* – if that's what he is. Oh, come on now! We all saw it! She was knocked sideways the moment he came in. Alley cat! She was on the prowl before he'd sat down to lunch! And I noticed – we all did – that she left the dining room on his arm last night. Wearing that little blue Worth number. She doesn't put *that* on for cocoa in the dorm with us! And none of the men have the sense to resist her. No, that's what I'd do – nip across the corridor and see what the Law's got in its long arms.'

'Cecily, you have a mind like a sewer!' Jane Makepeace again. 'Remind me to pass you the name of a good alienist in London. I really think you need the psychiatric equivalent of a flue-brush passed between your ears . . . or a good dose of liver salts. Why are you always so beastly to the girl? She means well.'

'I can't stand to breathe the same air as that tart!' Cecily's voice was vicious and uncontrolled. 'She's unhealthy! Goodness knows what we might catch from her!'

The room went silent, signalling that she'd gone too far.

The silence was broken by Dorcas. Stiff but polite, she spoke to the room: 'A child is missing. Commander Sandilands is in the kitchens at this moment interviewing the cook about the disappearance of her son. But thank you all for your help and advice. You've told me more than you know.'

'The cook's son? Well, why didn't you say?' Jane Makepeace exclaimed. 'I can tell you where they *both* were . . . oh, between tea and the children's supper time, if that's any use?'

'Please, I'd very much like to hear.'

'I'd gone down to take a look at Frederick dashing away at his fresco outside in the gallery. I heard Estelle call out and looked up. She was over by the gateway and she'd clearly just caught one of the children – the smallest one – by the hand. Rounding them up for their evening meal, I thought. In so far as I gave it any thought. It was just the usual routine. So it must have been just before six. You only have scurrilous things to say about Estelle, Cecily, but she does more than her bit with those little ones. Do any of us even know their names? I don't. So I can't name the boy she was with. Clogs. Green shirt. She was bending over, talking to him. Sensible girl, I thought. Checking up. If I had to speculate, I'd say the child was going home to the village. They do sometimes. Or perhaps he'd been *sent* home. Had he been naughty?'

'Did you see Estelle going out over the drawbridge?'

'No. But I expect she did. Well, where else would she go? When I looked up again, they'd disappeared. Good girl, I thought – she's gone down to the village with him. She was wearing that short red dress she had on at breakfast time and I don't see it hanging up. Oh, come to think of it – there *was* something strange about her . . . she was carrying that little brown attaché case of hers. No room in that for more than a change of knickers and a toothbrush so she wasn't going away for good. So, she's probably stayed on down there in town. There are places to stay, I think. They say the inn's pretty good.'

'Ah! Some village Romeo in the offing, do you suppose?' ventured someone.

'Just getting away from the rest of us for a bit,' suggested Jane. 'It's rather like being back at school living here. We all want to break out occasionally. Estelle is the one of us who has the courage to do it. I should take yourself off watch, Dorcas dear, and go to bed. Look – if she turns up again at dinner, I'll tell her to pop her head round the door and say goodnight, shall I?'

Murmuring her thanks, Dorcas excused herself and came out. She closed the door gently and Joe supported her slight form, quivering with rage, back into the safety of the children's dormitory.


Joe snapped awake in the dark hours, alert and listening. He went to his window and set about opening the shutters, surprised by the sudden force of the wind that almost snatched the iron locking bar from his hand. He stuck his head out and listened for a moment to the Mistral booming down the valley. With this northerly wind scouring the buildings, ancient woodwork would be creaking, unearthly howls would sound down narrow chimneys. He found the words of a prayer he'd not spoken since childhood were on his lips:

> In deepest dark no fear I show
> For Thou, O Lord, art here below.
> I feel as safe as in the light,
> Thy hand in mine throughout the night.

He crept silently into the corridor and went to stand by the door of the children's room, listening. Reassured by the silence, he went back to his bed, imagining Orlando's scathing comments if he'd been caught out in this show of sentimental vigilance.

# Chapter Fifteen

Wednesday morning dawned bright and clear. The wind had abated as suddenly as it had arisen, leaving a cool, combed and invigorated countryside behind it.

An equally cool, combed and invigorated Commissaire Jacquemin called for his coffee pot to be refilled and detained with a gesture the landlord of the Hôtel de la Poste who was personally waiting on his distinguished guest. 'Ferro – tell the Lieutenant over there ...' He nodded at the young man breakfasting by himself at the far end of the room, '... to join me at my table, would you? And bring another cup.'

The officer and the additional crockery arrived at Jacquemin's table at the same time. 'Ah! Coffee, Martineau? Sleep well? Good, good. Of course, being a native, you must be used to this confounded wind. Now tell me – the motor car – did you manage to get to the bottom of the problem with the ... transmission, I think you said? We weren't handed the cream of the collection for our little jaunt, I think? I want to arrive at the château snorting impressively not jangling like a bag of nails.'

'Yes. All in order, sir,' said the young man crisply. His broad brow, intense eyes and tight mouth gave the impression that here was a man incapable of saying or thinking anything but 'yes'. 'Snorting like a bull! There's a mechanic right here in the village who seems to know his business. He sorted it out in no time. All's ready for our assault on the Devil's Château.' He grinned dismissively.

'Ah, yes! This name ... I don't like to walk unprepared into strange scenes even of the comic opera type I suspect we're about to experience. A little local guidance is called for, I think.' He summoned the landlord again and invited him to seat himself. 'Monsieur Ferro, you know where we're headed this morning. Tell me – how did the Château de Silmont of venerable name ever acquire the sobriquet of du Diable?'

Monsieur Ferro was delighted to be of assistance. 'Because devilish things have happened there over the centuries. Oh, the usual murder and rapine, but this castle has always been associated with a particular kind of – I think you have to say, inhuman – evil. The kind that can only come from the Devil.'

'Monsieur Ferro will be able to point out to you the hill-top lair of the Marquis de Sade of evil repute, not many miles from here, sir,' the Lieutenant added helpfully. 'There are many such châteaux dotted about in the villages and each has a reputation worse than the last.'

'Ah, yes, but the Marquis de Sade was of flesh and blood. It's at Silmont that the supernatural makes its appearance most strongly through history,' insisted the landlord, realizing he was talking to a man of Provence. 'It started with the Devil's Bride. You must know that story?'

Jacquemin, mildly entertained, exchanged looks with Martineau and poured out more coffee. 'Do tell. The story hasn't reached Paris yet.'

It was only slightly encouraging but it was all the invitation Ferro needed.

'This happened long ago, in the days of the Counts of Provence, when Paris was a backwater and France just a neighbouring kingdom,' he said with pride. 'The young heir to Silmont was to be wed. To the lovely daughter of a rich marquis from a nearby estate. The château was *en fête* for the wedding celebrations. It must have looked like the setting for a fairy tale – guests had come from miles around, days of feasting were planned, there were acrobats and musicians by the score. The young bride – who came with a large dowry – was very taken with her new husband. She must have considered her father's outlay – some ten thousand crowns, it was said – well spent! The groom was somewhat older than she, in the custom of the times, but handsome and powerful and would inherit one day a splendid castle and lands. Ah! How were they to know . . .' He left a dramatic pause, rolled his eyes and sighed. '. . . know that the lord had a rival – a rival more powerful than himself? The girl already had a secret admirer. The Devil! None other!' Monsieur Ferro made the sign of the cross at the whispered name. 'Though she was unaware of his plans for her. After the ceremony, the bride, still dressed in her white wedding dress, insisted on playing a game with her friends and all the other little guests who'd been invited to keep her company. It was a game she loved to play. And she was, after all, still a very young thing. A game of hide and seek.

'She ran away and hid and everyone searched. And searched again. They called and called again. There was never an answer. Everyone feared for her. She did not know the château, her new home, at all. This was her first visit. The child did not reappear that day. And that night the château resounded with sighs and moans in every chimneypiece and no one slept.

'The search continued for the next day, the next week, the next month. The countryside was combed in the forlorn hope she had wandered off. Every gypsy tribe within a score of miles was questioned in case they'd snatched her away. But they found no sign. Not even a dropped kerchief. And they were never likely to find her. The Devil had made off with his chosen bride, it was said, from under the lord's nose. Her lord remarried. He came into his inheritance. The years passed. The first bride was forgotten. I cannot even tell you her name.'

'Is that it? That's all?'

Monsieur Ferro paused, shook his head and fixed the

129

men with the glazed eyes of a storyteller who is approaching his climax and resenting an interruption. 'And then, they say, a hundred years later, when they were rebuilding a part of the castle, they pulled the cover off an oubliette that no one knew was there. And, crouched in the bottom, was a small figure in white. The bride. As they tried to pull out the body, she and her dress crumbled to dust,' he finished with relish.

'Not a congenial place, it would seem, for young ladies of flesh and blood – or stone,' the Commissaire observed.

'People have so remarked over the years, sir. No one remembers the name of the missing child bride – as I said just now – but everyone knows the name of her successor. One of the young girls who'd played hide and seek on that fateful day was Lord Silmont's cousin – Aliénore. An impoverished branch of the family . . . she had no dowry but was famous for her beauty. They made a match of it – no one could deny him this comfort in his sorrow – and she produced a male heir within the year.

'But the lord had no luck with his wives. Aliénore died in her youth, it's said in childbirth, on her lord's return from the Crusade.' He sighed. 'Her husband was determined that she would be remembered for ever. He had the most splendid portrait effigy carved in alabaster and set up in the chapel. You must try to see it while you're up there, sir. It really is the loveliest thing. After all these years, you'd swear she was just sleeping.'

'How very fascinating. Now tell me, Ferro . . . I'm planning to stay for another night. May I confidently expect to encounter the smoked haunch of wild boar again on the menu this evening?'

Ferro, hearing dismissal in Jacquemin's voice, stood and tilted his head agreeably. 'But of course, Monsieur le Commissaire.'

The two men waited until Ferro was out of earshot before they laughed.

'Well, let's have it, Martineau! Your analysis, please!'

'I'd have had the cuffs on the young lord straight away, sir! I'd have sweated him to find out what he really thought of this annoying little twerp whose idea of the best way to spend a honeymoon was a game of hide and seek. I'd have wanted to know the size of his wife's dowry and whether it came to him on her death. I'd have asked about to find out if he had his eye on any other female in the neighbourhood. Someone whose name began with an A perhaps. And – if he was still at liberty after my attentions – watched with interest his further marital exploits.'

'Ah? I'm speaking to an admirer of the Perrault fairy tale? Do I hear echoes of the story of Bluebeard? Perhaps we should keep an eye out for bloodstained keys and locked cupboards full of dead wives while we're up there?'

Martineau acknowledged the Commissaire's sally with a smile. 'Always on the alert, sir. And I don't despise fairy tales. I slapped the cuffs on Bluebeard last year. In Marseille. The gentleman was going by quite a different name and he was certainly no lord. But the contents of his cupboards . . . well, I won't go into that so soon after breakfast, sir.'

Jacquemin nodded his approval. He liked a chap with the spirit to answer up for himself. And this sharp young officer, Martineau, had stepped in and saved his bacon in Marseille. Perhaps he could be encouraged to pursue his further career in Paris, conveniently in the orbit of the Commissaire? Jacquemin knew the value of a good man at his back. Another advantage to come out of this wild-goose chase? He looked at his wristwatch in great good humour. 'Bring the car round at ten thirty, will you, Lieutenant? If you're to work with me, you must understand that when I am not being punctual to the second, I am arriving ahead of time. Greeting suspects before they are quite prepared for you can be very informing and it puts them on the back foot – they are the ones caught burbling excuses. Let's see if we can surprise these pretentious buggers with their trousers down, shall we?'

# Chapter Sixteen

The company around the breakfast table at the château seemed equally enlivened and jolly. De Pacy gave out a gentle reminder that they could expect the presence of the Marseille constabulary at eleven and guests should hold themselves ready to welcome the Inspector at their lunch table. Joe interpreted this as a warning to dress suitably and put away any dubious substances.

As people began to disperse, he caught Nathan Jacoby's eye and both men rose and made their way out to the courtyard.

'You're sure about this?' asked Nathan. 'Nine o'clock now. We've got two hours before the police arrive. I estimate I'll take an hour at the outside.'

'You're on,' said Joe. 'At least I think so . . . Don't you need equipment? I don't see you hung about with the usual contraptions of the photographer's trade.'

'I left my things out here,' he said, picking up a small leather Gladstone bag. 'Travelling light. I'm going to use my Ermanox. There's such a splendid light pouring in through those east windows it should be a cinch. And this beauty has flash.'

They raised their heads and squinted up into the sun. Nathan sighed with satisfaction. 'Do you see the way this yard is striped with light and shade at this hour? And look at the pattern on that arched gallery over there where the children are playing! Wonderful!'

Joe took his bag from him and set off across the court-

yard, leaving him with two hands to frame his pictures
and point out his perceptions as they went. He was looking forward to seeing the chapel again with the benefit of
this man's insights and he was easy in his company. As
they approached the big oak door they looked at each other
in astonishment.

'Did you hear that?' said Nathan.

Joe was running to the door as the second dull thud
made itself heard. As he lifted the opening device and the
door began to creak open they heard a pitiful wail leak out.
Six inches was enough space for a small body to dash out,
flash between the men's legs and hare off, howling.

'What in hell was that?' said Nathan. 'Christ! That kid's
upset. What was he *doing* in there?' He made to run after
the child who was fleeing barefoot across the courtyard.

Joe held him back. 'Let him go. We'd frighten him further. He's on his way to find his mother in the kitchen. It's
the cook's son. The one who went missing last night.' He
watched on as Dorcas, drawn by the howls, emerged from
the gallery and raced across the courtyard to intercept him.
She seized the child's hand and ran on with him.

'It's all right. Dorcas has got him. He seems to be safe
enough. Now.'

'Good Lord! The poor little chap's been trapped in here
all that time? Overnight? In that wind?' said Nathan.
'That's one distressed kid!'

'And he could only have got in here if he'd been put
inside by an adult who opened the door,' said Joe grimly.
'Or sneaked inside while the door was open. Someone's
been in here. Are you ready for this?'

They entered carefully and waited for the door to swing
shut behind them.

The cool beauty of the space was unchanged at first sight
and Nathan stood still absorbing it, enchanted. But Joe was
looking for details. 'Look here! Poor child! He must have
been terrified out of his wits but he showed some style!
Little soldier indeed! He made himself a bivouac.' He bent

133

and examined the rough nest behind the door. 'Look – here's his bed.' A base of kneeling cushions had been assembled to form a mattress and an old velvet curtain had served as blanket. An inch of yellow fluid in the bottom of a nearby glass flower vase told its tale of night-time emergency. A discarded clog had been put to use to bang on the door and accounted for the dull thuds that had alerted them. Sick at heart, Joe thought of the child hammering through the night, the sounds masked by the infernal wind.

'Deserves a medal!' Nathan commented. 'But listen – if someone was here, he's not here any longer, would you say? Impressive place! Fourteenth-century?'

'Probably earlier. Twelfth, according to the guidebook. But with fourteenth-century additions and improvements. The Counts of Provence worshipped here when they were being entertained at the castle. It's said that the father of Eleanor of Aquitaine attended mass here. William of Touraine, gallant knight, poet and – they say – the first troubadour.' Joe's response was mechanical, all his thoughts centring on Marius and his ordeal, eager to be done with this inspection and go and get the boy's story from him.

'Can we take a look at Sir Hugues now?' Nathan asked, making his way over to the monument.

They stood in stricken silence staring at the table-top tomb.

There they were, two figures lying side by side, the lord and his lady.

The figure on the right, the armoured knight, his feet resting on the crouching lion, remained as impressive as at Joe's first sighting, but it was the pallid beauty of the figure at his side which seized and held the men's attention. Her delicate hands were peacefully folded below her breast, her slippered feet rested once again on her greyhound. The knight had lain here in this quiet place carved in white stone for over six hundred years. His lady was of flesh and blood and was newly dead.

The peaceful couple were framed by a canopy of sunlit stone. Hugues de Silmont lay in plate armour, gauntleted hands resting on his chest, helmeted head encircled by a jewelled wreath. At his left hip, on a richly sculpted baldric, was carved a slender dagger of Spanish design with an ornate gilded hilt. A misericord. His features were serene; as the sunlight slid across his face, he seemed almost to smile.

At first sight his lady appeared no less serene. Closed eyes, a dreaming face, her pallor a match for his alabaster. Her long fair hair had been arranged to frame her face before spilling in waves over the edge of the tomb. The white dress she was wearing had been carefully draped and folded.

The two onlookers could not take their eyes from the head of the dagger, sunk very slightly to the left and, very precisely, into the heart. The dagger at the knight's side and the dagger in the woman's heart were identical.

# Chapter Seventeen

Joe could feel his companion's shock through the hands that grasped his arm for support. After a few minutes of rigid stillness, Nathan's whole body began to tremble but he could not take his eyes away.

It was Nathan who spoke first. 'What *is* this? Some kind of sick joke? It's not real . . . Joe!' He turned an anguished face on him. 'Are you in on this? Is she dead or is she acting? Tell her – okay, okay! I'm sorry! And I'm knocked for six! She can get up now . . .'

Joe's pained silence swept away his attempt at self-delusion.

Joe placed a restraining hand on Nathan's shoulder and stepped forward himself towards the tomb. He went swiftly through the familiar gestures to establish that the girl was indeed lifeless and shook his head.

Nathan groaned. 'She *is* dead, isn't she? Do you see it? That dagger? Isn't that . . .?' A quivering finger pointed to the dagger in the woman's breast and moved on to point at the stone dagger in the knight's belt.

In a calming policeman's voice, Joe answered: 'You're right. It's the same thing. The carved one is a representation of a vicious stabbing blade, designed to penetrate plate armour with a short underhand stroke. A misericord. The word means compassion, pity. Such blades were often used on the battlefield to put dying soldiers out of their misery. What kind of sick trickery *is* this? The carved dagger and the wrought metal one in the heart are identical!'

'Sick is right,' Nathan murmured. 'She's on display. Some bugger's left her here to be ... viewed. Joe, we're being used! We're an invited audience. We've been set up to witness this horror.'

Nathan whirled about, hearing a sound Joe had not detected. His gaze searched the gloomy corners of the chapel, his slight frame crouched and hunted. 'He's here! Where's the devil hiding? Listen! He's in here with us, isn't he? Watching.'

His rising panic was catching. Joe spoke steadily to calm him. 'I don't think so. That creak you just heard? Would have been the woodwork expanding or righting itself after last night's buffeting. I think the murderer's long gone. They do sometimes return to the scene – that's true, in my experience – but I don't know of one who's waited several hours by the body expressly to enjoy the dismay and horror of the poor sods who discovered it. And she's been dead for some hours. We'd be looking at a seriously aberrant piece of behaviour. But, then, nothing surprises me any more.'

'Sheesh! How can you keep so calm? Face to face with a dead body like this? Someone you know?'

'I'm not calm! I'm as distressed as you are. I'm revolted and angry. It's just that it's my job to stare at corpses and make them talk back to me. And, if you'll be silent and use your keen eye for detail, Nat, she'll start talking to you as well. She would want us to hear what she has to say. Think of this as the last thing we can do for her.'

In an attempt to dampen the photographer's spiralling panic, Joe began to involve him in the scene by shooting a series of questions at him. 'Look at the wound. Focus on it. That's the idea! Do you see much blood? Come on! Answer me!'

Nathan focused on the spots of dried blood surrounding the blade. 'No. I'd have expected a gush, a trail ... Heart wound – you'd expect a fountain ... There's no more than a spot or two or five. All around the blade. Like a speared rose. And it's dark brown. She bled some time ago?'

'Right . . . "On her left breast A mole cinque-spotted, like the crimson drops I' the bottom of a cowslip,"' murmured Joe. 'That's the sleeping Imogen in *Cymbeline*. But this poor girl is beyond sleeping.'

'You can stand here, quoting bloody Shakespeare at a time like this?' Nathan's voice was strangled.

'I find myself responding to the killer's imperative – as *you* do. It's a scripted craziness. An Elizabethan melodrama we're being offered. Perhaps if we follow him in his descent to hell, we'll catch sight of his ugly features.

'Look again. What's he telling us? The wound was placed with precision, would you say? Nathan?'

'Anyone would. I'm sure I've never seen a heart wound before, not even a knife wound of any kind, but it does look sort of . . . meant . . . placed.'

'Expertly done, I think,' Joe confirmed. 'And what do you make of the hair, spread out like that? And the careful draping of the dress?'

'Lord knows! It's crazy! I can only say again – sickness.'

'Not crazy. I believe it's very deliberate. Have you seen this white dress before?'

Nathan shrugged and shook his head. 'It looks very old. Like something an ancestor might have worn. Hey! Where *is* the original wife?'

Joe pointed to the corner in which the cairn of remains still stood, the shattered head, as before, displayed on its red silk cushion.

It triggered in Nathan the same nauseated revulsion that Joe had felt the previous day. 'More madness! Anywhere around here a feller can be sick?' murmured Nathan.

'No, no! Stiff upper lip, old man!' advised Joe. 'Quite enough bodily fluids around here to keep the police busy. Don't add to them. Tell you what – if you need to pop out for a breath of air, why not go and pick up your bag? You put it down outside. Go and fetch your camera gear. Have you brought a flash?'

'You're not thinking . . .?'

'I certainly am! First thing we do these days. Photograph the scene. If you object, pass me the equipment and I'll do it myself. We can be quite certain that the man from Marseille won't have thought to bring a camera with him.'

'No! You unfeeling bugger! I won't do it!' Nathan protested angrily. 'I can't. You've no idea what you're asking. And I'm wondering just exactly when you're going to get up the courage to speak her name. Or are you waiting for me to say it? Don't you have to get a close friend to make the identification? I can see you're going to do everything by the book.'

Joe waited, uncertain whether the American intended ever to address another word to him. He had pushed Joe angrily into the background and his whole attention was focused on the pale features. Finally, he whispered: 'It's Estelle. My friend. She's been lying dead on a cold marble tomb this night when she should have been warm and safe in my bed.'

He turned aside and his body began to shake with dry sobs.

# Chapter Eighteen

Nathan was standing frozen and distant, marking his disapproval of the detective's schemes, when Joe returned with the bag of equipment.

Understanding his revulsion, Joe was almost ready to let the moment pass unrecorded. Professional concern, however, won out over emotion, and he firmly opened the case and took out the Ermanox camera. With relief, he noted that it was the same model as the one owned by his friend Cyril Tate. News photographer and society columnist, raffish Man-About-London, Cyril had nervously agreed to Joe's borrowing his precious camera for a weekend as a trade-off for information received.

New and very expensive. Joe sensed the same tension he'd provoked in Cyril in every line of Nathan's body. A true camera-fiend would rather see his lover in Joe's hands than his camera, he thought grumpily. He affected an air of confidence to reassure the trembling Nathan and was careful to first put the safety strap around his neck. He remembered to allow for the frontal weight of the enormous lens as he adjusted his hands to fit comfortably around the black leather-covered body, his fingers finding their place at once on the buttons and levers. Aware of Nathan's proprietorial eye on him, he set about his task. His first gesture was to remove the lens cap and automatically put it in Nathan's waiting hand.

'Widest aperture, slowest speed,' Nathan gritted. 'If you

must. You'll find an exposure meter and a flash attachment in the bag. First plate's in.'

Joe found what he needed and satisfied himself that the shots he was planning were possible. He silently made some adjustments. 'These will be no rival for *noire et blanche*,' he said awkwardly. 'The French police will take pictures but I'd like to have our own for reference. Do you have the means of developing these?'

'Anything. I've got a small laboratory next to my studio. The lord provides when he scents success. And he's interested. He knows a thing or two about photography and he's got a line to the illustrated journals. You're standing too far away!'

'For artistic perfection, perhaps,' said Joe easily. 'But for forensic reference, this is just about right. A locating shot. Close-ups will follow.'

As he spoke, he peered through the viewfinder and clicked the shutter. He took an overhead shot of the body and a close-up of the wound, working his way around the three sides of the tomb. At the far end, his foot caught on a solid object. He grunted and bent to examine it.

'Here's her attaché case,' he called to Nathan and, receiving no response, went on: 'It's got her red dress in it. The one she was wearing at breakfast yesterday. And here are her shoes. A pair of black espadrilles. She must have brought the change of outfit into the chapel in the case and slipped into Aliénore's gown and ballet shoes to enact this charade. Why in hell would she do that? Better leave this for the French Inspector to investigate.'

Nathan sighed and forced out words between his teeth. 'Posing? She was posing! It's what she did all the time. The outfit's straight out of the dressing-up chest. She was planning a joke on someone. I'd have guessed – me. Well, it would have worked. I thought for a moment she was going to spring up and laugh at me.'

'Did you tell her you were coming in to take some slides?'

'Yes. We talked about it at lunch time.'

'That may have given her the idea?'

'Could have. That's what we're looking at, Joe – a practical joke. The sort you English like to play on each other . . . "What a hoot! What a jape! I say, do let's!"'

Joe was disconcerted to hear in his accent echoes of Estelle's own very English voice. He ignored the man's rudeness, sensing his emotions were turning from shock and disbelief and hardening into acceptance and recrimination in a pattern familiar to Joe. Someone was to blame and quite often it was the unfortunate policeman, being on the spot, who was the one to get it in the neck. Joe was prepared for Nathan to demand next to know how he could have let such a thing happen. But he had underestimated the American. Nathan's mind was running on retribution directed at a deserving target.

'*Who*, Joe? Who traded on her sense of fun to lure her into this death trap? Someone she knew. Someone *we* both know! Has to be. You don't need to be a smart detective or a pathologist to see that she was stabbed while she was lying down there. I've got that right, haven't I?'

Joe nodded. 'The lack of vertical blood trail down the dress would indicate that you are correct. What blood there was has ponded in the chest area. If I could bring myself to do it, I'd lift her skirt and check for post-mortem discoloration. There's always gravitation of the blood to the lowest point of the body – it shows up as a reddish-blue bruising. She was, I think, killed right there where she now lies. But – again – I'm keeping my hands off what is the French Inspector's scene.'

'She knew him. Trusted him. You didn't know Estelle! I tell you she'd have fought like a hell cat if she'd thought she was in danger. Scratched him to pieces! Look at her hands . . . no, no . . . I understand. I won't get too close. No sign of fending off an attack, is there?'

'Not as far as I can make out. They'll need to take samples from under her fingernails.'

142

'He's over there, isn't he? In the hall, finishing his break-fast . . . Still in bed, exhausted after his night's activity? But what did he say to her?' Nathan blundered on, his voice rising to a shrill note of disbelief as he worked through the implications of the grisly scenario. 'To make her do this? Did he kill her somewhere else and arrange her up here for a laugh?'

Joe saw a flash of panic twist his features. 'Good God, Joe! You don't suppose . . .? Oh, no! I couldn't bear it!'

'No immediately obvious sign of a sexual attack – at least a physical one,' said Joe. 'But I have to tell you, Nat, I'm not going to pursue the possibility. Not now. That really must be left to the proper authority, properly equipped. I can just say – I think it highly unlikely. No. Whatever our perpetrator had in mind, I don't think it was rape.'

With a groan, Nathan moved forward at last to pull the camera clumsily from Joe's grasp. 'Let me have it. You're useless! I'll finish for you. And develop the plates. It's all I can do for her now, isn't it? You've got to find him, Joe. *We've* got to find the bastard.'


It was with difficulty that Joe persuaded Nathan to leave the chapel and return with him to the house. He explained that he was anxious to speak to the child Marius before too many well-meaning souls had put ideas of their own into his head. He was, if not the key to all this horror, at least the witness of it and they would advance faster and further towards catching Estelle's killer by getting his information. Joe was only surprised that the child had him-self escaped the murderous attentions. He'd been shut in here with a killer and his victim. He was small for his age, his neck could have been snapped like a chicken's and the sole witness removed in a second.

'How strong are you feeling, Nat?' Joe asked. 'Steady enough to go back into the hall and break the news?'

Nathan nodded.

'Look, I ought by rights to isolate you and make certain you don't spread this story around. But I don't think anyone's going to be able to keep the lid on for five minutes in the circumstances. And all things considered, if it's going to come out, I'd rather it came out straight. From you. You know what this bunch are like for speculation. Will you just say Estelle is dead and in the chapel which remains out of bounds to all? Can you manage to avoid going into details, do you think?'

Nathan agreed. 'What'll you do now, Joe? What *can* you do?'

Joe grimaced. 'Hands tied, I'm afraid! At home I'd ring for a squad, establish a scene of crime set-up, arrange interviews ... As it is, we'll just have to wait for the French spearhead to arrive, all unwitting.'


Joe made his way into the kitchen through the side door, not knowing what he should expect, certain only that it would be an unpleasant scene.

To his surprise, all was calm and orderly. All kitchen activity had been suspended and the staff were standing around, an attentive chorus backing up the main players. Dorcas was close by, he was relieved to note. Centrally placed on a chair that had been brought in from the dining room, Madame Dalbert sat holding her little son on her lap. Marius was no longer yelling. He was sitting, pink and vastly recovered from his ordeal, staring with fascination at the steward who had arrived to take charge.

De Pacy was on his knees in front of Marius. Joe almost looked for a gift of frankincense, myrrh or gold in his hand but he was holding out for the child's inspection a Limoges china bowl with a silver spoon standing up in it. The cherub was showing an interest in the contents. A kitchen boy thoughtfully came to take the bowl from de Pacy and held it steadily, allowing the steward to dig in with his good hand and tentatively offer up a spoonful of straw-berry ice-cream. Marius's eyes flicked in astonishment from the anxious face of the commanding officer on a level with his own and back to the silver spoon. Joe tensed. Would the child put back his head and howl or accept the offering? Marius made the right decision. He opened up his mouth like a baby cuckoo.

Joe approached quietly and watched the scene until the bowl was empty. De Pacy got up, grunted and tousled the boy's hair. 'Brave lad!' he murmured. 'He's a soldier like his father, Madame Dalbert.' He turned to Joe and spoke in English. 'I'm a bit lost. But I think *you* may be able to make some sense out of all this. All I can gather – and that mainly from Dorcas who came to fetch me – is that the poor lad spent the night trapped in the chapel and that you let him out just now. He's terrified. He hasn't told us anything. Doesn't seem to be able to speak – although I know he can! He has a fine way with words for one so young and swears like a trooper. He refuses to talk to *me*. Perhaps *you* could –'

'Why don't you both move away and let me speak to him?' said Dorcas. 'You're both big frightening men – he's been told to keep out of your way. He won't talk to you.'

They went to stand behind Madame Dalbert while Dorcas approached him and took hold of his hand. 'Awfully glad you're back, Marius! We missed you.' She spoke reassuringly in what Joe thought of as her 'Provençal voice'. 'We thought you'd gone to Granny's but we searched all over the place just in case. Never thought of looking in the chapel. However did you manage to get in?'

'It was all right. I was let in by a grown-up,' muttered Marius.

'Thought so. Which grown-up was that?'

'Estelle. She found me running to the gateway and stopped me. Said I shouldn't go down by myself, I'd be missed.'

'Well, she was certainly right. You *were* missed. And then what did you do?'

'She was a bit cross. I think I was in the way. She said she was meeting someone ... And I'd better just come along with her and keep quiet and she'd take me back to the hall for supper when she'd finished.'

'Was she carrying anything?' asked Dorcas, remembering the conversation in the dormitory.

'Yes. A brown case. A small one.'

'And then what did you do?'

'She opened the door and let me inside. She came in too. She looked at her watch. She told me she'd found the best ever hiding place and I could try it out. She put me in a sort of cupboard with a seat in it and a curtain hanging down.'

'Sounds like a good hidey-hole ...'

'It worked! He never saw me!'

'He? Who was that, Marius?'

'The man.'

'A man came in?'

'Yes.'

'Which man?'

'Don't know.'

'How did you know it was a man?'

Marius frowned. 'Trousers. Black trousers. And shoes.'

'Did this person know Estelle?'

'Yes. Estelle was laughing.'

'Who was the other person, Marius? Did you recognize the voice?'

Marius thought hard. 'No. They were whispering. And, anyway, I didn't know what they were saying.'

'You mean they were talking English – as I do sometimes?'

'That's it.'

'How long were they in there ... oh, you won't be able to say in minutes, I know that, but did it seem a short time, a medium time or a very boring long time?'

'I counted to a hundred,' said Marius proudly and, turning to the audience behind, added, 'I *can* count to a hundred! And I started again and got to twenty.'

Joe felt gooseflesh prick his arms as he listened to the innocent boast. The child owed his life to numbers. If he hadn't been able to count beyond ten or if he'd called out, '. . . ninety-nine, a hundred' and jumped out, he wouldn't have survived to be comforted with ice-cream.

'That was brilliant, Marius!' Dorcas gave him credit for his skill. 'So, after a hundred and twenty, Estelle and her friend went out and left you there by yourself. They'd forgotten you were there, you kept so still and quiet?'

'No! No! The *man* went out. Estelle stayed with me. She didn't leave me.' The boy seemed concerned that Estelle should bear no blame.

'She stayed in the chapel with you?' Dorcas made an effort to rein in her astonishment.

'Yes. All night. She'd put on her nightie and gone to bed. On the big stone bed. She didn't say goodnight. I think she'd forgotten me.'

Puzzled, Dorcas glanced up at Joe. He nodded slowly, indicating that she should plough on.

'So Estelle was there with you all night?'

'Yes. I was glad she was there even though she was asleep. I wasn't so frightened. I went and touched her hand and tried to wake her up but she wouldn't. When it started to get dark I made a bed for myself by the door and went to sleep. But the noise woke me up. The wind. I started banging on the door with my clog. I really wanted someone to come and let me out. I was crying,' he admitted. 'I had a wee and drank some water from a jug . . .' He pulled a face at the memory. 'And then I went back to sleep again. Until the morning. Then I banged again and someone came.'

He squirmed around and whispered to his mother, 'Am I in trouble, Maman?' with the certainty of one who knows he is definitely in the clear.

'I'm trying to persuade Madame Dalbert to take her sons home and have the rest of the day off,' said de Pacy.

'I think we should ask Marius what he'd like to do,' Joe suggested.

'Oh, he wants to stay here,' said Madame Dalbert. 'He's just longing to tell his story to René and the others! Aren't you, my little monkey?' She tickled him until he began to giggle.

Her stoic good humour and the laughter melted the tension in the assembled crowd and Joe felt a wave of relief wash over them.

'Then we should say three cheers for the hero of the hour,' announced de Pacy, correctly interpreting the mood. 'Hip, hip, hurrah!' He led the responses with an uninhibited flourish of his silver spoon. Marius chuckled.


'Excuse me? I'm looking for Monsieur de Pacy ... Would you by any chance be he?' enquired a chillingly polite voice as the last hurrah faded. 'We were directed to the kitchens. Which would seem to be the centre of activity. In a manner of speaking, you could say I had an appointment. Let me present myself: Commissaire Jacquemin of the Brigade Criminelle, Paris.' He allowed a moment for the import of this to sink in and then added: 'And this is my assistant, Lieutenant Martineau of the Marseilles police. I apologize – we arrive a few minutes early.'

He exchanged a knowing glance with his assistant.

'Not at all, Jacquemin,' said Joe, stepping forward to take the fire while de Pacy put his spoon away and regained his aplomb. 'You arrive, in fact,' he glanced briefly at his watch, 'sixteen hours too late.' He had been irritated by the Frenchman's supercilious manner. 'Monsieur de Pacy you have correctly identified. I am Commander Sandilands of Scotland Yard, London. But you must explain yourself. We had been promised a local inspector ... Isn't that what we understood, de Pacy?'

The steward was trying valiantly to disguise his bemusement and, like Joe, clearly resenting the cold stare of the

French policeman. 'Yes, indeed. An Inspector Audibert was so good as to offer his services. But we know the force is up to its ears in cases. We'll just have to accept the attentions of whatever officers they feel able to spare us,' he murmured, his smile taking the edge off his cynicism. 'Sandilands, I know you have familiarized yourself with the circumstances of our little lapidary calamity – perhaps you will conduct your confrères to the chapel and introduce them to what remains of the Lady Aliénore?'

He turned an anxious face to Joe and murmured: 'Find Estelle at once and have her sent to me. That young lady has some explaining to do.'

'Certainly I'd be glad to do that, but, de Pacy, before we proceed, there's something you absolutely have to hear . . .' Joe looked around at the alert faces, excited by the dramas they were witnessing and eager for more, and he decided on discretion. He spoke into de Pacy's ear. 'Regarding Estelle. Before you do anything else, I want you to have a word with Nathan in the hall. He was with me just now when we found Marius. Take Dorcas with you. I'll conduct the – Commissaire, did he say? – over to inspect the scene in the chapel. And we'll see you over there in a few minutes.'

He changed into English. 'Dorcas. There's something *you* need to be told also – but not in front of little ears – if you know what I mean. Go with Guy to the hall, listen to what Nathan has to say and do what you can for the children. Try not to frighten them – they've had enough disturbance for one day. Jacquemin . . . Martineau . . . follow me.'


They stood with Joe by the chapel door and, before entering, Jacquemin decided to establish a thing or two.

'Sandilands – this rank of yours . . . Commander? . . . I'm not familiar with it.'

A stickler for protocol, evidently.

Joe reckoned that at any Interpol conference table, the adjutant whose job it was to care about precedence would probably assign a commander a seat at least one notch higher than a commissaire. Whereas the regional French Brigades had at least eighty-five commissaires whom Joe would have ranked with 'superintendent', the Metropolitan Police of London boasted only two commanders and these came immediately above chief superintendent. Early in his police career, Joe had been made up to the extraordinary rank of third commander with special duties, duties resulting from the changes in policing following the war. Resulting also from the changes in the criminals themselves.

The humble bobby, and his not vastly less humble superior, was increasingly ill qualified to deal with the officer-class, battle-hardened men who had emerged from the war with an embittered view of society. They were wrong-footed by the country's intelligentsia, moving ever towards the left; they were speechless before the reasoned arguments and threats of direct physical action of the suffragettes; left puffing behind on their bicycles by the new motoring thieves. The Commissioner had looked about him for a man who could head a strike squad of fast-moving, socially confident and clever young men to plug these gaps in the service. Joseph Sandilands had come to his attention. Glittering war record, something of a linguist, the man had played a diplomatic role in his years in France and would have no difficulty liaising with Special Branch. Above all he was pronounced, by one of his supporters, to be, 'Quite the gentleman. Scottish, of course, but aren't they all these days.'

Far too young for the appointment, but he'd impressed the new and reforming Commissioner at interview. Sir Nevil had thought it wise to dub him, on acceptance of the offer, Commander. It had a certain naval ring to it that would fool some and impress others. A high rank indeed.

'I understand it to be equal with your own rank, Jacquemin, as far as it's possible to draw comparisons between our two so different forces,' Joe said diplomatically.

He knew that a man of Jacquemin's kidney would lose no time in checking this information and he would be nonplussed by Joe's response. But, for the moment, Joe wanted to get the best out of this peacock. Better not to set fire to his tail feathers.

'Indeed? And – tell me – are you a guest here or are you on official British business? Interpol or the like?' Jacquemin asked.

'No official capacity whatsoever. I am a guest.'

The response appeared to please the Commissaire. He did not go so far as to smile his pleasure but he smoothed down one side of his moustache in a quietly triumphant gesture.

'Good. Good. And the scene of the depredation is to be found in this building, are you saying? Then you may safely leave us to investigate.' He paused before the great door and Martineau set about opening it. 'I'm not seriously expecting many answers from a broken statue but I'm sure we'll arrive at a solution that will settle any remaining qualms. I'll hand you an official and calming line that you may safely give out to the ladies.'

He dismissed Joe with a curt nod.

'Commissaire, before you enter, there's something you should hear . . .' Joe began, putting out a staying hand, but, presented abruptly with the policeman's back, he shrugged his shoulders and watched the pair enter the chapel. He lit a cigarette and settled to wait for them to come out again.

Fifteen minutes and two cigarettes later they emerged, blinking into the sunlight, subdued and silent.

'Sandilands!' the Commissaire's voice rang out on seeing him. 'You've had your fun! Now bloody well get back in here and tell me what the hell's going on!'

# Chapter Nineteen

Joe had been startled to hear the big gun of the Paris Brigade Criminelle announcing himself. He had no idea what this hero was doing down here so far from his own bailiwick or why he was supplanting the Marseille Inspector but could have wished the man a thousand miles away. Reports of Jacquemin and his policing methods had spread across the Channel and had been received with a certain admiring incredulity by some in authority at the Met.

But not by Joe.

The 'shoot first and kick a confession out of them if they survive' method of crime-solving favoured by the Frenchman was not to his taste. But the unknown Lieutenant? A local man, clearly, with the bold dark look of a Provençal. His presence could prove useful. With a bit of luck and a nudge in the right direction, the Commissaire might decide their problems were all a bit below his status or out of his purlieu, say farewell after lunch and leave the whole thing in the hands of this Martineau and the local Prefecture of Police.

The scene in the chapel seemed unchanged when Joe entered. He looked around him suspiciously. You couldn't always count on police officers home-bred or foreign to restrain themselves from meddling with a crime scene but these men knew their business apparently. Joe was impressed to see they had left their shoes by the door and were padding about in their socks. Joe did likewise.

Without a word said, the three men went to stand by the tomb and bowed their heads in respect. Even in death, Estelle continued to weave her spell and draw the eye.

Jacquemin broke the silence. 'Your notes, Lieutenant, if you please.'

'Certainly, sir.' The officer flipped open his notebook. 'I summarize: Date, time, place and all that . . . Three victims noted.' He paused and offered: 'Oh – and two suspects.'

Joe intercepted a warning glance from Jacquemin and the young man, brought to heel, continued: 'In date order of commission of crime:

'First victim. Stone carving. Smashed by hammer or similar. Remains removed from original site and piled where shown on sketch. Provocatively displayed.

'Second victim. One rabbit. Death from a broken neck estimated to have occurred a week before inspection. Provocatively displayed where shown on sketch.

'Third victim. Young lady. Identity to be established. Fatal stab wound to heart. Weapon ancient dagger, still in wound. Estimated time of death – sixteen to twenty hours before time of inspection. Full rigor still evident. Body provocatively displayed.

'Noteworthy feature: signs near door of temporary occupation by intruder. Flower vase containing suspected urine bears traces of fingerprints. Tramp/wanderer of some sort seeking shelter or setting up an ambush position?'

'Thank you, Lieutenant. Now, Sandilands, perhaps you are in a position and of a mind to fill in some of our gaps . . . answer a few questions such as: Who? What? And why the bloody hell? We're listening!'


'She's English and her name's Estelle . . .' he began.

And concluded: 'Well, there you are, gentlemen. That's as much as I can tell you. You'll probably find more personal information if you locate her belongings. She had a place in the women's dormitory. Miss Makepeace will be

153

able to show you. There's clearly a meaning – a message –
here that strangers such as ourselves are not able to make
sense of at first sight. The element of display you've noted
I don't believe was intended for our eyes – transient visitors that we are.'

'Yes, visitors. I understand the place to be full of visitors.
Art school in progress or some such?'

Joe reached into his pocket and brought out a sheet of
paper. 'Here, take this. I've made a copy. It's a list of everyone who's spent time under the castle roof since the
beginning of the season. With a few details I've added
myself as they became known to me.'

'Thank you, Sandilands. Very useful.'

'It's incomplete. For more information you must refer to
the steward or the lord himself when he returns.'

'Returns? From where? How long's he been gone?'

'He left after lunch yesterday. He rode over to spend the
afternoon and the night with his friend some ten miles
away but declared he would be back in time to greet you.
Perhaps we should open the door and declare we're ready
for business?'

He opened the door and stepped out to catch sight of the
lord walking across the courtyard from the great hall
towards them, a motoring coat flung across his shoulders
like a cape.

He hailed Joe. 'Sandilands! I return not a moment too
soon! Guy tells me I must prepare myself for a pitiful and
distressing sight. Perhaps you'd show me? And introduce
me to our French policemen.' He took off the coat on entering the building and threw it over a chair. 'Jacquemin?
Martineau? Do I have that right? Welcome to Silmont.
Horse went lame. Had to leave him in Alphonse's stable
and accept a lift in his Delage. Now, gentlemen, what do
we have?'

He approached the tomb and began to falter as he took
in the unearthly scene. At that moment the sun shifted its
angle and a shaft of light, diffused through a pane of

coloured glass, dusted Estelle's cheeks with the rosy glow of life. The lord staggered, and for the second time that morning Joe found himself offering an arm in support. He did not brush it away but clung, trembling and panting. All animation drained from his features, his mouth tightened. In an automatic gesture, he put a steadying hand over his heart. He tried to speak but no word would come.

In one swift movement, Martineau produced from his pocket a small silver flask. He held it out tentatively to Silmont.

'A little cognac sometimes helps in these circumstances, sir,' he murmured.

Silmont accepted it with a grateful nod and downed a gulp, breathed heavily, and took another.

Joe was trying to identify the strong emotion that was racking the lord. Shock? Distress? Both elements were present but there was something more, it seemed to Joe, something bitter he was trying to repress. Anger, perhaps? He could not wrest his eyes from the form of Estelle. Finally, a little colour returned to his face and he found his voice. 'I'm sorry to show such weakness of spirit, gentlemen. I am physically not what I once was but that can be no excuse. I will just say that the shock of seeing a young girl who is . . . was . . . known to me in these circumstances is overwhelming. And the weapon! Do you see the dagger? It's mine. The bloody nerve of the man! She's been done to death with a misericord from my own collection. I have two on display in the armoury. We'll go over and take a look. I think we'll find there's only one remaining. You know – it's the element of parody that is ultimately distressing. None of you will have seen the original sculpture of my ancestress . . . This young woman has been done up to resemble the original.'

'Sir,' said Joe, 'in my pocket I have a guidebook to the region. It has an illustration of the carving as it was. Perhaps . . .?'

'Yes. By all means. Show it to the officers.'

'Great heavens!' Jacquemin was intrigued and offended. 'Someone's gone to quite a lot of trouble to make the girl look exactly like . . . what's her name? . . . Aliénore. Anyone can see there's a superficial similarity between the women but it takes more than a chance resemblance to trigger a man into going to all this bother, I'd have thought? All artistically arranged, you'd say. A crime of placement rather than passion? Is that what we're looking at? Something studied?'

'The shoes, the dress . . . the hair,' Joe agreed. 'Good Lord! I hope we're not being treated to an expression of the latest "-ism" . . . necroplasticism, perhaps?' he heard himself say and instantly regretted it. Jacquemin didn't strike him as being receptive to word-play or remarks of a fanciful nature. And now he would have him marked down as a facetious English lightweight.

The Commissaire turned his double-barrelled gaze on Joe for a moment. 'Wouldn't surprise me at all,' he said and then turned his attention back to the tomb top with its deathly offering. 'You should see what they get up to in Paris in the name of art! Necrophilia, necromontage, necroplasticism . . . could well be the latest thrill. I'll keep an eye out. And let's admit, Sandilands, to this extent, whoever this sensation-seeker is – he's succeeded! I, for one, am ready to admit I've spent rather longer transfixed by this display before us than I ever have by the Mona Lisa. Read what you like into that!'

'Don't you think, sir, it would take more than a flight of fancy and stage management to produce this?' Martineau dared to object. 'It would take a rush of energy . . . an outburst from a dam of pent-up hatred.'

'You're right, my boy,' said the lord. 'Look – let me show you something which may cast some light on what you've just said. A motive for murder which has remained alive and strong through the centuries. Will one of you give me a hand? I need to move this wooden superstructure, here on the side abutting the tomb.'

Martineau stepped forward and seized the wooden boards where the lord indicated and began to lever up the structure. Joe hurried to assist.

'I discovered this when I was a very young man. I had fallen completely in love with Aliénore – everyone did. A strange thing to say of a lifeless effigy but – she was deeply alluring.' He paused to cast a bleak look at the pile of rubble which had once been a glorious work of art. 'Throughout my guardianship I've kept her in excellent condition. The image was originally decorated, you know. The locks of hair were gilded, her shoulder cape painted blue – a formula we have never been able to recreate – the jewels, though paste, gleamed convincingly. Miss Makepeace has been studying and advising. And restoring. Beautifully. And all to end like this . . .'

He tore his eyes away from the stone shards and resumed: 'Aliénore's husband employed the very best talent to carve her likeness, I would say the work of an artist brought in from Italy. A man whose style makes the leap from Gothic to modern before his time. The workmanship was worthy of a man of the calibre of Giovanni Pisano, the Tuscan artist. If you ever looked on the stately beauty of his Madonnas you would see the same sweetness and humour, the same human individuality. I made myself an expert on medieval carving, the better to appreciate her quality. I can tell you that the second figure, that of Sir Hugues himself, was done by a different and less skilled hand. I am assuming that the lady was portrayed by someone who knew her well in life. Or possibly someone who was allowed to work for his initial sketches from the sight of her dead body.

'My yearning to know more about her led me to study the Latin inscription running around the three sides of the tomb. Here.' He pointed. All three men nodded.

'I was puzzled. I followed the words around and came up with *uxor sua* – his wife – and stopped, disappointed.

No date of death. No flattering phrase. Was there more hidden away around the back?

'Gentlemen, there was.

'I had the stone shelving, which sat awkwardly, like an afterthought, between the tomb and the wall, hacked away and, when I'd viewed and copied down the rest of the accursed lettering, unseen for centuries, I had this wooden structure built on to replace it and prevent anyone else from seeing the shameful truth.'

With a wave of his hand, he invited them to inspect the rear of the marble tomb. By leaning over in turn, at a neck-breaking angle, they could just make out the two remaining words of tribute from Sir Hugues to his wife.

'It says *et meretrix*, ' Joe, the last man to inspect, read out. 'And harlot. Aliénore, wife and harlot.'

'Harlot? What kind of man carves that word on his wife's tomb?' Jacquemin asked.

'A man betrayed by the woman he loved?' said Silmont. 'Once I had read the shocking word and accepted that the effigy I adored was flawed, other things began to fall into place.'

'Ah! The hair! I had wondered,' said Joe. 'My knowledge of medieval church sculpture – Provençal or otherwise – is sketchy but, from what I've seen, this hairdo strikes me as being a bit out of the ordinary. I've never seen a lady with her hair spread all about like this. Aren't they normally tightly coiffed . . . you know . . . every lock swept up into a headdress?'

'Quite right, young man!' said the lord. 'There are very few who remark on that. It's been forgotten over the years. In the Middle Ages, all married ladies wore their hair under a coiffe. It was the mark of a virtuous wife. Which would lead one to wonder what on earth the lady Aliénore is doing lying on display with her golden hair spread all about her pillow, looking for all the world like a Venetian woman of easy virtue.'

'It would seem a heartless sort of tribute to pay to your

dead wife, sir,' Joe commented since he seemed to be waiting for a response. 'And double-edged, since any onlooker of the day would have known exactly how to interpret it. Her husband was, thereby, shaming *himself* into the bargain. And it was uncomfortable to have the horns of the cuckold pinned on you by public opinion in those days.'

'The tomb would have been assembled here after his death. It's my theory that he no longer cared about his own reputation in his determination to ruin hers for ever more,' the lord suggested. 'Perhaps he left the whole image behind as an awful warning. To future generations. Here's the just reward for infidelity – an early death.'

'How did she die?' Jacquemin asked. 'Is it known?'

'Not for certain. It's said she died in childbirth. Nothing unusual in that, many women of the time did. But her husband was a crusader. Here history deserts us and we must speculate. If he returned from two or three years' absence in the Holy Land to find his wife in a delicate condition . . . Well, you can imagine. Neither she nor the child would have survived his wrath. And there would have been few to blame him. It was of paramount importance to keep the line of descent pure. A man could keep mistresses openly under his own roof and produce illegitimate children by the score but his wife had to be of proven virtue, her offspring undeniably those of her husband.'

He shrugged with sudden impatience. 'But this is very ancient history. What concerns me is the fate of this poor creature who has been persuaded? – inveigled? – forced? – into mocking the effigy of Aliénore and suffering her death. All over again . . . All over again,' he muttered. 'It never ends. Why would it? The poisoned chalice is constantly refilled and always overflowing. And always men are seduced by the gilded beauty of the container and swallow down the noxious contents with a smile of gratitude.'

Silmont began to breathe raggedly. Fatigue and dejection seemed to be overcoming his determination to be of assistance. He bit his lips, fighting a shaft of pain. He ran his right hand through his sparse hair and patted his forehead with a handkerchief. But it was to the trembling left hand that Joe's sharp eyes were drawn. The whole arm from shoulder to fingers was beginning to shake and Silmont made a clumsy attempt to push the offending hand into his pocket to keep it still. A palsy? Epilepsy? Or the warning sign of something more serious? He was showing all the symptoms of a heart condition.

It was Jacquemin who offered release. Suddenly alarmed, he clicked into action. He suggested that he should accompany the lord over to the main body of the castle, make a few telephone calls to alert the police in Avignon and have the morgue arrange for the corpse to be collected for post-mortem examination. Following these procedures, he would check the armoury for the missing dagger. He would leave Joe and Martineau to replace the wooden skirting around the tomb and take a further look at the scene in case something had been missed ... a fingerprint ... a footprint in the dust ...

'Look, Jacquemin,' said Joe apologetically, 'I'm hardly prepared for this. In London, I always have my murder bag with me ... gloves ... fingerprint kit ... I'm on holiday, halfway down south to the coast. I haven't –'

'Nor I! I'm halfway up north to Brittany,' snapped Jacquemin, uneasy at being caught out. 'Um ... Martineau?'

'Yes, sir. Of course, sir. I put one on the back seat. Never travel without, Commander. I think the contents will be familiar to you ... we use graphite powder and camel hair –'

Their professional murmurs were interrupted by an uncontrolled shriek.

'Get on with it, man!' screamed Silmont. 'Fools! Numbskulls!' he raved. 'While you're all on your knees in the mouse-droppings, playing with your fingerprint dust, the man behind this goes about his business laughing at you!

Can't you see beyond the dots and the brushstrokes? Get the whole picture in focus? This trollop spent some hours here, befouling the last resting place of my ancestor – but in whose bed did she spend her last night alive?'

He stood, shaking with rage, his charge of electric energy directed at Jacquemin.

To Joe's surprise, Jacquemin did not draw his gun or click his fingers for the handcuffs but returned a soft answer. 'Sir, you are unwell. Is there someone you would like me to summon?'

Silmont uttered a shout of mocking laughter. 'Yes. There is someone you could well bestir yourself to get hold of. If it's not too much trouble. My steward. Guy de Pacy.'


When the lord and Jacquemin had left, Joe took the other end of the woodwork and asked conversationally: 'Tell me, Martineau . . . when I came in, you mentioned that you had three victims but I think you also referred to two – was it two? – suspects?'

Martineau laughed. 'Oh, that was just a joke, sir, between me and the Commissaire. Didn't realize he has no sense of humour. Though I should have known from the stories the other lads put about! Did you know, sir – no, why would you – that the Commissaire is said to have a scale model of a guillotine on his desk in his Paris office? A working model! He uses it to chop the ends off his cigars. Dramatically – in front of men he's grilling for a capital offence."

'Good Lord!' said Joe faintly. He ought not to be listening to gossip of this nature but relished the thought of passing on this snippet to Superintendent Cottingham when he got back. Ralph was strongly against the death penalty and would be reduced to splutters of indignation at the idea.

'But I meant what I said – about the suspects, sir,' Martineau went on. 'We have two suspects right here in the

161

chapel.' He enjoyed Joe's puzzlement for a moment then explained: 'Suspects for a crime six hundred years old. The murder of Sir Hugues's *first* wife. Ah – you didn't know he had one? No tomb to *her* memory. No expensive Italian effigy. Name unknown. And – jointly charged in my book: Sir Hugues and his not so angelic wife Aliénore! You haven't heard the story?' The Commander's receptive features invited the young Frenchman to delve deeper into folklore. 'Oh, it's a corker! Let me tell you . . .'

The two men worked on together in complete harmony, their crime scene training meshing smoothly. At home, Joe would have insisted on an accompanying silence but here, in this sepulchral place, he found he was glad to hear Martineau's tale enlivening the routine business.

His story was drawing to a close and Joe was wondering just how much of the detail had been expanded or added by this natural storyteller when the door was flung open and Guy de Pacy stormed in. He left the door to crash shut behind him and strode to the tomb oblivious of Joe and Martineau who were on their knees logging footprints by the pile of debris.

Joe looked up and, for the third time that morning, watched a man's features working in acute distress at what he was seeing. But de Pacy did something in Estelle's presence that the other two had not attempted. He reached out a hand to touch her cheek.

Joe called out a warning, uncertain that the man was aware of their presence and at pains to avert for him the embarrassment of having someone witness emotion better concealed. 'Guy! We're over here! I say – would you mind awfully stepping back?'

'Rule one in the scene of crime handbook, sir,' explained Martineau, showing himself. 'Don't allow contamination of the corpse.'

They both started at the thunder of his voice. 'Contamination? Corpse?' His words were infused with a deadly energy. 'I'm not contaminating a corpse, you idiots! I'm saying farewell to a beautiful creature!'

They stood by helpless, unable to prevent him from bending over the body and brushing the cold forehead with his lips. He murmured a few indistinct words, made the sign of the cross over her twice and then looked up at the policemen, his face twisted with grief.

'I want him, Sandilands. I want his head; I want his guts. I want to see the light die in his eyes; I want to hear his last gasp. Find him!'

He walked away.

Reaching the door, he turned and called back over his shoulder: 'And you could start your search with my cousin. The Lord Bloody Silmont!'

# Chapter Twenty

'Did I say we had *two* suspects, sir?' whispered Martineau. 'Make that *four*, shall we? And two of 'em alive and kicking each other. Ouch! There goes another seriously disturbed gentleman. The steward, I think?'

'Yes. Guy de Pacy. The lord's cousin. You saw him in the kitchens attending to the child. Before he heard the news.'

'Does bad temper run in the family? What an outburst!'

'What was the phrase you served up to the lord earlier? The phrase he savoured? "An outpouring of pent-up hatred" or some such? That was an outpouring of emotion all right and it came from pretty deep but I wouldn't say *hatred* had much to do with it, would you, Lieutenant?'

Martineau shook his head in bafflement. 'No, sir. And I'll tell you what – he didn't care that we saw it. That was quite a performance!'

'Tell me, Lieutenant, have you ever seen a man make the sign of the cross twice over a body?'

'Can't say I have, sir. Once is usually sufficient.'

The throb of a six-cylinder engine greeted them as they moved out into the courtyard an hour later. The Hispano-Suiza was on the move. The motor car was advancing on them, as white, as silent and as stately as a swan on a mere. Packed into the rear seat were the duenna and the ballerinas and, at the wheel, just recognizable in cap, sun goggles, driving gloves, duster coat and white scarf, was Petrovsky.

'That man doesn't leave!' Joe snapped to Martineau and raced forward to stand, one hand raised, blocking his path to the drawbridge. The engine revved and the car gathered speed. Joe tried not to flinch as the car came inexorably on. As it surged towards him, his eyes were riveted by the aggressive emblem mounted on the bonnet. The Hispano's silver stork was flying at him, long neck extended, ready to impale him on its lance-like beak. He was conscious of Martineau lining up by his side as the car screeched and juddered to a halt inches from their toecaps.

Petrovsky chose to react in French: 'What the hell are you up to? Testing out my power-assisted brakes? As you see, they're damned efficient! Idiot! I could have killed you! Like to play this little scene again? I may succeed next time!' he snarled.

'Mr Toad, I presume? Good morning!' Joe said, oozing English affability. 'Mesdames!' He switched into French and doffed an imaginary hat. 'I must ask you to abandon whatever plans you have for the day and return to the great hall.'

'Are you barmy? We were leaving this morning anyway. Appointment in Avignon. And if you think we're going to stay on in this madhouse a moment longer, you're way off beam!' Petrovsky pushed up his goggles, the better to glower his disdain as he announced: 'Now hear *me*, Sandilands! We've all been made aware by that mous-tachioed French fop in there of this night's disastrous events. Events which *you* have signally failed to avert. As the Law seems to offer no protection, we must shift for our-selves. I have a duty of care to these ladies. I am not a man to expose them to the attentions of a murdering maniac. Now get out of my way!'

Joe replied again in French to be sure he was being understood by driver and passengers. 'Park your vehicle. Get out and escort your ladies back into the great hall.'

165

'Not on your life! You've no authority to stop me! You're not directing traffic in Piccadilly now, you know! This is France!'

Without a word said, Martineau drew his gun and trained it on Petrovsky. He bellowed back, echoing exactly Joe's words: 'Park your vehicle. Get out and . . .' And he added: 'In the name of the French Republic on whose soil you find yourself.'

'And *you* can bugger off, too,' said Petrovsky with suicidal boldness, Joe thought. He could almost admire the Englishman. He would never himself have risked snarling down the barrel of a Lebel pistol held on him by the practised hand of a Marseille policeman. 'I'm not French. You've no right to tell *me* what to do!'

'Oh, dear!' said Joe, turning to Martineau. 'The gentleman seems to be suffering from a little ethnic and geographic confusion. Is he awaiting the attentions of a *Russian* officer of the law, do you suppose? We could be here some time. Perhaps I should explain in his own language?' He addressed Petrovsky in formal copper's English: 'Spettisham Gregory Peters, of Maidenhead, Berkshire, subject of His Britannic Majesty, I am arresting you in English and French on behalf of the Metropolitan Police of London –'

'And the Police Judiciaire of Marseille,' Martineau inserted. 'For the offence of resisting arrest and attempting to flee the scene of a crime in a suspicious manner,' he added, enjoying his invention. He unhooked a pair of handcuffs from his belt and advanced on Petrovsky.

The engine roared into life again, the noise covering a string of oaths in mixed Russian and English. But it was a last flourish. Petrovsky engaged reverse gear and the stork, robbed of its prey, flapped off backwards. Petrovsky stormed away in the direction of the great hall, leaving Martineau to reach inside and switch off the engine and Joe to extend a hand to the ladies.

166

The Russian girls swore at him in Russian and hopped out, disdainfully ignoring his hand. The duenna caught Joe's eye and began to shake with giggles. With the grace of a prima ballerina she rested her fingers on his hand and floated down from the motor car. 'Thank you, sir,' she said. 'How good it is to encounter a gentleman at last in this uncivilized place.'

Joe was startled to hear that her accent was pure Provençal.

It is difficult to fill a room with panic when that room is three storeys high and large enough to accommodate hundreds, but the twenty or so people assembled were doing their best. Some, mainly the men, were sitting around the table in noisy conference, banging fists on the boards to underline the points they were making, spluttering denials and accusations, arguing and demanding. The women seemed to have gathered into two or three small groups, seated on cushions they had carried over nearer to the central table. Predictably the loudest and most hysterical voice was that of Cecily. Joe sighed wearily to hear the 'I told you all so . . . Well, if one *will* make oneself a target . . . Wouldn't it just be Estelle who gets herself murdered? Silly girl! And who's going to tell us the name of the next victim? He should allow the women to leave at once!' Joe rather thought she was repeating this for his benefit.

He looked about him, mentally calling the roll. He caught the sleeve of Mrs Tulliver, the lady sculptor, as she passed. 'Gillian – where are the children?'

'The French policeman sent them off into quarantine in the playroom and asked Jane Makepeace to stay with them. Have you heard? The Commissaire won't let anyone leave until he's made an arrest! We're all to bring down blankets and sleep here in the hall tonight. Can you imagine? All mucking in together! Sweating and snoring! Ugh! He says airily that it's no more than we would have done as a matter of course in the Middle Ages. It's all right for *him*! He's staying at the Hôtel de la Poste. But poor little Estelle – what a terrible, terrible thing. I, for one, shall sleep with my chisel under my pillow tonight.'

As he turned away, she called after him. 'Oh, Joe – the Frenchman's looking for you. He's set up shop in de Pacy's office – just commandeered it! He said anyone sighting you was to send you straight along there.'

Joe and Martineau presented themselves at the steward's office to find two footmen had been ordered to stand, in a state of some puzzlement, on either side of the doorway. Joe raised his shoulders and spread his hands in a comic gesture and, encountering no opposition, knocked and entered. He found Jacquemin comfortably installed. The large central table had been cleared and held only a telephone and the contents of Jacquemin's briefcase. Two chairs had been fetched and ranged on the side of the table facing the Commissaire.

'Come in – sit down! *You* took your time. Progress report! Avignon aware. Pathologist and medical conveyance on way. Also small back-up squad of gendarmerie. They're perfectly happy at the Préfecture to work with us and offer us access to their facilities. Fingerprinting, blood analysis and so on. They're all tooled up for that sort of thing. As they get about ten times more state funding to work with than the Police Judiciaire – so they ought!'

'The lord, sir?' asked Martineau. 'Is he . . .?'

'Safely confined to his apartment. Valet in attendance counting out his pills and mopping his forehead. I took it upon myself to order up a nurse from Avignon. She'll arrive with the squad. Now – anything more to report from the scene?' His question was put to Martineau.

'Prints, sir. On the tomb – we've marked the position on a sketch. Footprints likewise. In the dust near the remains of the statue. Oh – Monsieur de Pacy entered to pay his respects. We weren't quick enough to stop him. He may have left prints.'

'I'd expect to find that gentleman's dabs everywhere about the place. He's going to be the first to give me a sample. Now – got your kit, Lieutenant? We can get started on that lot out there. You print them and I'll interview.'

Jacquemin cleared his throat and turned his attention to Joe. 'Which brings me to a consideration of *your* position in all this, Sandilands. Two thirds of the cast list appear to be English. I shall need some professional help with the interpretation.'

It was reluctantly stated and his tone bordered on the ungracious. Joe's reply was succinct: 'I understand the circumstances and whatever linguistic, cultural or forensic skills I possess are, of course, available to the Police Judiciaire.'

'Good. That's settled then. I'll see that you're suitably deputized should it become necessary. And let's not forget –' his eyes became one degree less frosty – 'that technically we are both subordinate to the Lieutenant here.'

Joe and Martineau exchanged smiles.

'But first, Sandilands, I'm going to give you a résumé of the case as I see it. I expect you to add anything you feel necessary.

'We seem to have a classic case. We're looking for a man suffering from some form of . . . er . . . psychopathy.' He glanced at Joe to judge his reception of his modern view.

'*C'est un cinglé!*' Martineau ruined his effect.

'A nutcase!' It was what Joe's own sergeant would have said.

'Possibly a man who has suffered damage to the brain or emotions in the war,' Jacquemin said repressively. 'A misogynist at all events. That much is clear. We're looking at the work of a man with a deep dislike and murderous grudge against women. He announced himself with his first attack – I refer to the smashing of the effigy. A clear statement of intent. A known harlot gets her comeuppance. And just in case anyone's missed the point – here's a rabbit to underline it. As Sandilands has pointed out. And we

169

should listen to his view – Sandilands, after all, is familiar with this style of multiple killings. It was London, was it not, which gave the world Jacques l'Éventreur? And we have a gallery of Englishmen here on site from which to choose.'

He waved Joe's list.

'I fear you may be right,' Joe conceded. 'I see no end to this until he is caught. There will be further victims unless we can stop him.'

'So, the man we are looking for was (a) on the premises on the night of the attack on the statue ... date, Sandilands?'

'Friday the 20th of August.'

'Thank you; (b) he was possibly injured in the war; (c) as a hater of women, he is most likely unmarried; (d) he is able to come and go about the building without arousing suspicion – or a bedmate. Probably has a room to himself.'

'One character comes to mind straight away, sir,' commented Martineau. 'But he's not English.'

'Look, before you go putting the cuffs on de Pacy – consider this,' said Joe. 'Estelle was clearly attacked by someone she knew well. Someone she spoke to in English and laughed with. This much is known from the child's testimony, as I told you. Therefore there may have been a personal reason behind the killing. Someone wanted Estelle to die for a very particular reason. Because she was Estelle Smeeth, not just a stand-in for the female sex.'

'Could anyone have got in from outside?'

'Nothing easier. Anyone could have scaled the dip which we call a dry moat of sorts. All the children know the way. And you could stay out of sight of the rest of the castle by keeping the bulk of the chapel between you and it. We shall need to know more exactly when Estelle died but I was hazarding a guess at six o'clock.'

'Any sightings of the girl at about that time?'

'Yes. We have a sighting by Jane Makepeace of Estelle and the child by the bridge at about that time so that seems likely. Our dagger-wielder simply watches from the chapel door after the act – it's perfectly possible to stand in the shelter of the ornate door surround and be completely hidden from the rest of the castle. He nips over to the hall when he's sure the coast's clear.'

'You heard the child speak. Did he have a contribution to make?'

'Yes, he did.' Joe filled in as much as he could remember of the interview conducted by Dorcas and summarized: 'So, we have a dispatch by an apparent friend, with speed and without resistance on the part of the victim. We know that the aggressor spoke in English to Estelle – though everyone here speaks English, whatever their nationality – and he was wearing black trousers and shoes.'

'Now who wears that sort of outfit at six o'clock in the south of France?' the Commissaire wondered aloud.

'A priest?' Martineau suggested.

'Indeed,' said Joe. 'But also any of the Englishmen gathered under this roof. And their hosts. The French keep early hours in the country for dining but we English keep to our customs regardless. We dress for dinner. Drinks at six fifteen, first course served at seven. Every man would have scrambled into black trousers and dinner jacket by half past six at the latest, possibly before. I had done so myself. So, suitably attired, our chap strolls off into the hall for a drink when the gong sounds. Looking as though he's just drifted downstairs fresh from the hands of his valet.'

'Thank you for that. Very helpful. So – it's an intruder or a resident, a priest or not a priest, an Englishman or some other nationality we're looking for.' Jacquemin glowered.

'Afraid so! And here's something else to chew on,' said Joe, taking a handkerchief from his pocket. 'Evidence. Three pieces. Sorry – no useful little bags available at the time I made the discoveries.'

He opened it up on the table to show the contents. 'Now – this screw of paper was used by the victim. You

171

may like to check the powder.' The Frenchmen listened as he told of his time spent with Estelle on the roof platform.

'She saw the statue-smasher and he saw *her* watching him? That's another reason for getting rid of her, are we thinking? No, we're not! He was disguised. No reason to think she saw through it. Is there, Sandilands?'

'She certainly didn't seem to have made an identification.'

'And cocaine? Where was she getting it? Did she bring supplies from Paris? How long had she been here?'

'Since the beginning of the season. Three months. I believe she was a girl who was easily bored and would seek stimulation. Her mood swung while I was here in the castle. I think she was getting supplies. From someone with access to the exterior, clearly.'

'They'd get it in any city along the Rhône. Along the drug-smuggling route from the port of Marseille and up north to Paris. There are places . . . people in Avignon who would oblige. We must find out who's been making trips out into the world.'

'You'd need a vehicle, sir,' said Martineau thoughtfully. 'It's thirty kilometres to Avignon. Would you like me to take the Hispano-Suiza apart?' he offered with relish.

'It's not the only car around. There's a car available for hire by the day down at the village,' said Joe. 'A scheme run by the enterprising garage owner. And a charabanc for group outings – they're an adventurous lot and like to get about. And motorcycles. And even horses. Many of the guests make use of *them*. It's wonderful riding country. They go out all over the place, singly or in groups. We might make enquiries.'

'Still – the girl was a drug-fiend. So what? Not much of a reason to kill her, is it?' said the hard-boiled Parisian.

'Cocaine . . .' Joe mused. 'It's a sociable drug – where I come from. People sniff it up in company usually. At parties. In jazz club cloakrooms. To put themselves in a jolly mood.'

'Agreed. She's unlikely to have been sniffing the stuff all on her lonesome. So who was keeping her company?' Jacquemin pencilled a note in his book.

'And with the girl's contacts in mind, Commissaire, may I ask you, when the time comes to interview each of the denizens, to enquire which of them has a camera and what type it is? It may not be important but I should like to know.'

Jacquemin scratched in a further note. 'And what's this here?' he asked, poking at the sliver of gilded stone in the centre of the handkerchief with the end of his pencil.

'Ah yes! Pickings from the robe I think the perpetrator wore on the night he hammered Aliénore to bits. From low down near the hem. It could have brushed on during the attack and clung to the rough wool. It's a piece from the hair, judging by the gold paint. We brought a sample from the chapel for comparison.'

Martineau produced a white paper bag from his crime case and handed it over.

'Mmm . . . we'll get these put under a microscope – but clearly they're from the same source,' agreed Jacquemin. 'And what's this here?'

'The cigar end also comes from the robe. It was in the pocket. Orlando Joliffe and I found it hanging on the back of the door to a guest's room.'

'Guest? Which guest?'

'Petrovsky, the ballet-meister. Director of the Ballet Impériale at present performing in auditoriums all over Provence. Avignon this week.'

Jacquemin looked down his list. 'Personal guest of the lord. Frequent visitor. Accompanied by two dancers and a chaperone. Russian?'

'No, he's as British as I am. Name of Peters. Rich. Dilettante. Known to the Vice Squad. History (suspected only as far as I know) of keeping company with young girls.'

'Professional hazard in his line of work, I'd have thought,' said Jacquemin reasonably. 'Still – in possession of a vehicle . . . trips to Avignon . . . and all the arty-farty places where the sophisticated gather . . . We'll grill him. Now – tell me about this half-smoked El Rey del Mundo.'

'Is that what it is, sir?' Martineau peered with interest.

'So it declares itself,' said Jacquemin, pointing to the gold and red band it still carried. He picked it up, holding it by the smoked end, and squeezed gently. He sniffed the tobacco. 'Though I'd have known it without the hint. Very expensive. Smooth, light tobacco. The best Havana. I've only ever smoked three of them. Very expensive.' He turned to Martineau who was already rising from his chair. 'De Pacy. He'll know.'

In the Lieutenant's absence he went on studying the cigar. 'Carefully guillotined at the mouthpiece,' he observed. 'As you'd expect. A man who can afford these is hardly likely to bite the end off with his teeth!'

'Don't you take the band off in France?' Joe asked. 'We do in England. One tries to avoid flaunting one's taste.'

'Some do. Most, if they've any experience, puff away until the cigar has warmed through. It melts the glue on the band and you don't risk tearing it and the wrapper and looking a fool. And very useful for *us*! Men hold a cigar by the band. Between forefinger and thumb.' He demonstrated with an imaginary cigar. 'This'll have prints on it. If they're Petrovsky's we've got him! Any ash left at the first scene in the chapel, Sandilands?' he asked hopefully. 'Did he put his hammer down and pause to enjoy a soothing, post-climactic cigar?'

'Conveniently stuffing the unsmoked half away in his pocket? I don't think we're dealing with that kind of careless mind. No, what we've got is someone calculating, evil and yet . . . I search about and come up with the unsatisfactory word – playful. No, it's not as straightforward as it might appear,' Joe said thoughtfully. 'If he's gone to all that trouble staging the scene in the chapel, he's not going, casually, to leave his disguise on the back of his own bedroom door. For the English copper to find. They all knew

174

I had permission to roam about poking my nose into drawers and pockets. And besides – on display like something you'd find in the lingerie department at the Printemps store, there was another little item . . . rather surreal . . .'

'Surreal? Can't say I'm an habitué of the department you mention but I'd have said depraved,' was Jacquemin's response to Joe's account of the contents of the gown's pocket. 'Ballet tights doing an entrechat? What's his point?'

'I don't think Petrovsky *was* making a point. I think the whole little display was put on for my benefit. The man who really wore the cloak knew he'd been seen by Estelle and that he could no longer make use of the garment. So he abandons it, flamboyantly.'

'Hoping for what? To incriminate Petrovsky?'

'Yes, giving us the hint in case we hadn't already twigged: here's a man you wouldn't want anywhere near your daughters, he's saying. If we'd nabbed Petrovsky on various charges, I'm sure that would have been a very acceptable outcome – he clearly dislikes the chap – but I flatter myself he has more respect for my detective abilities!' Joe shrugged. 'He was *surrendering* the garment. No further use for it. And, almost as a joke, he left it where it would furnish evidence pointing the finger at our Russian friend. If I wasn't taken in by that here's another try – a very distinctive cigar end. A double bluff! The bloke who smoked that may be involved, he's suggesting. Another poor sod it entertains him to throw suspicion on? When we know the name of the smoker of the best Havanas we can put it down, second on the list of our perpetrator's denouncements. He's laughing at me or he's time-wasting.'

'And where is the cloak now?'

'It was impossible to make off with it at the time, under the scrutiny of Orlando Joliffe *and* his lordship, as I was! And I'm perfectly sure it will have been removed and destroyed many hours ago.'

Martineau entered smiling. 'Found him, sir. Yes, de Pacy knows who smokes those things. The chap leaves the stubs about all over the place in ashtrays. And, wouldn't you guess – it's Lord Silmont.'

'No surprise!' said Jacquemin. 'Second on our stool-pigeon's list, are you thinking?'

'And his first mistake,' said Joe. 'If we go haring off, following the second false trail laid by the cigar end, and arrest Lord Silmont, we're going to run into what I suspect is a cast-iron alibi. The villain we're dealing with could not have known that the lord was about to take the whole day off and spend it with his friends some ten miles away. It was an arrangement made just that morning. So our informant has chosen to set in the frame for murder an innocent chap who was playing cards ten miles away at the time.'

'Which indicates that he can't be in the inner circle, so to speak. Not privy to the lord's confidences and diary entries.' Jacquemin was thinking aloud. 'Someone recently arrived? Or on the fringes of the Silmont social scene?'

'Unless there's something wrong with the lord's alibi,' was Martineau's tentative offering. 'He's a clever bloke. That history lesson he gave us in the chapel! And all that guff about a horse going lame . . . how often do you hear about that happening these days?'

'Particularly to horses of the quality of those I saw in his stable,' said Joe. 'You could have ridden any one of them thirty miles before it laboured. The very best animals, in peak condition and several attentive grooms to check the state of their hooves and limbs before they set out . . . hmm . . . We have no sighting of his lordship between my own – when he appeared in riding gear and outlining his plans for the day . . . rather carefully, I now come to think . . . and his reappearance just before eleven this morning in a chauffeured Delage. I wonder what exactly the lord got up to in the last twenty-four hours . . . Perhaps he arrived late

176

for his bridge appointment? If he arrived at all? It would be interesting to find out . . .'

Jacquemin replied with the decisiveness Joe was coming to expect from him. 'Sandilands. Check his alibi. In depth. Take your car.'

Joe smiled to have got his own way. 'Delighted, Commissaire.'

# Chapter Twenty-One

'This is a wild-goose chase you're bringing me on!' Orlando grumbled as they drove out over the drawbridge. 'Why did you ask for me?'

'Because you told me you'd paid a visit. You know the way and your face will gain us entry.'

'I wouldn't bank on it. And anyway, I ought to be back there giving a hand with the children or assisting with the enquiry, not gallivanting with you about the countryside. Through the village and go left at the fork . . . I want to do what I can to catch the murdering sod who's killed Estelle. We all do. She was a wonderful girl and when I get my hands on whoever –'

'Shove it, Orlando, will you! I know you're upset but you'll have to join the queue of people who want to wreak revenge. And, at the moment, you're way behind me and Guy de Pacy.'

'And Dorcas,' Orlando said surprisingly. 'She'd got fond of her, you know. Estelle was like that – you liked her or loathed her at first sight. Mostly people liked her. Anyway – his days are numbered – the joker who did it. Dorcas has put a gypsy curse on him. And, believe me, you wouldn't want that! I know the old crone who taught it to her some summers ago in Surrey . . . The guilty party's probably shitting worms and spitting scorpions as we speak!'

'Tell me, Orlando – because I'm an inquisitive so and so, and I'll beat your brains out if you don't – about Estelle's love-life. I have reason to believe you have first-hand experience of it.'

Orlando, the pacifist, visibly struggled to prevent himself from tearing Joe's head off. He replied in a strangled voice: 'None of your bloody business! What *is* this unhealthy fascination with my love-life? I'm not a fellow who talks lightly about the women he's involved with. If I answer your impertinent question at all it is through gritted teeth and with the slim hope that you will use the evidence to bolster any detective powers that remain to you to bring this hideousness to a conclusion.'

After a little more harrumphing he added: 'I played a walk-on part only. Well, it was more of a walk-off part, when you come to think of it. Er . . . once only. Soon after we both arrived here. In June. She was, I would guess, an experienced player in the Ars Amatoria. She was kind enough to pose for me one day and the inevitable happened.'

'Inevitable?' Joe was angry enough to interrupt his flow. 'How can you say that? Do artists have some unchallengeable droit de seigneur over the girls who sit bored out of their brains before them, day in, day out?' He regretted his outburst instantly but consoled himself with the thought that Orlando would have suffered a much worse tirade from Lydia.

'No, you're right,' said Orlando mildly. 'You can't always depend on it. But it's not the out and out exploitation you suggest, Joe. You've never painted a woman, have you? You wouldn't understand the feeling that develops between artist and model. It's a very special one. Fraught with difficulties but rather intimate. It's more than just the clothes that come off. And it's not all one way! You can talk to each other while the painting's going on, you know. Pour out your troubles, air your fantasies. You'd pay five guineas an hour for the sympathetic ear of one of those psychiatric chappies in London. And *he* wouldn't be so easy on the eye.' Orlando pursed his lips, sighed and confided: 'She was a generous girl. Her emotions were not involved. Unless you count pity as an emotion. Is it? Anyway, her urge to compassion fulfilled, I think she quickly found someone else to occupy her time. Yes. I'm pretty sure there was someone else ... someone important to her. I can usually tell when a woman's in love ... And Estelle, I would say, was in love.'

'What were the signs?'

'A certain undirected euphoria. She smiled a lot. Of course, that could have been the cocaine ... but I don't think so. She dressed perkily, she chattered in an alluring and attention-seeking way at table, she went missing for long periods at a time, several times a week. Boring job – sitting about in the nude, not able even to read a book – who shall blame her for seeking a little excitement? But – and here's the odd thing – I haven't the slightest idea with whom she was involved! Why do you suppose she would keep something like that quiet? In a company like this – bohemian, I hear you sneer – who would care? It's a case of love and let love in this little world.'

Joe remembered the conversation he'd overheard in the ladies' dormitory. 'Some are more censorious than you'd allow, Orlando. They enjoy the idea of freedoms for themselves but still don't much like to see other, more attractive creatures, seizing their opportunities with both hands. Or their men! Perhaps the man involved was married? There are two married couples accorded the luxury of rooms of their own, I understand. The Whittlesfords and the Fentons? Jacquemin, when I left him, was putting them to the bottom of his list. Married couples tend to notice if one of them's donning a stinking old cloak, picking up a hammer and sneaking off for an hour in the middle of the night.'

'Returning, breathing heavily, in a state of excitement? Oh, I'm not so sure ... And anyway ... Mrs Whittlesford would have no idea what her other half was up to at night!

180

And you can bet your boots *Mr* Fenton was unobserved by *Mrs* Fenton!'

'What are you talking about?'

'Two rooms. Four people. Married couples, but not necessarily coupling within the marriage, if you take my meaning.'

'Good Lord!' said Joe.

He forced himself to pursue his enquiries since he'd got Orlando into a discursive mode. 'So – we don't know who Estelle was mooning over then, but was there anyone she disliked particularly?'

Orlando, feeling himself on firmer ground, was prepared to consider this. 'Not really. That's not Estelle. She tried to like everyone. Made an effort. Good manners, you know – early training shows through. There was no one she shied away from. She couldn't stand some of the women but then we've all wanted to strangle Cecily. Ghastly woman! Girls can be terrible bullies, you know. Cecily rather put the boot in from day one, I'm afraid.'

'Ah, yes. I thought I sensed a bit of bad blood between them.'

'All on Cecily's side. Upper-class twit of a girl, spoiled rotten, I suspect, by her doting daddy. No expense spared to launch her in her chosen career. Unfortunately for the rest of us, Cecily happens to have talent. I've always thought it unfair – the way talents like this are handed out by the Almighty. Great galumphing girl she may be but those road-mender's hands of hers have got a certain skill.' Orlando's lip curled. 'Of a marketable sort! A queasily romantic sort. Fantin-Latour would call for the smelling salts. But you'd be surprised how many Parisian and New York boudoirs are graced by one of her overblown Peony Portraits. This season she's unleashed her enthusiasm and loaded her palette to celebrate the Flora of Provence.'

'What about the other women?'

'Jane Makepeace terrifies us all and Phoebe Fenton has a laugh that would make anyone want to cut her throat.

181

Estelle really tried even with the ballet girls as they chasséed through. She always learned their names and made time to chat with them –'

'The men, Orlando, it's her relationship with men I'm interested in.'

'She was close to the photographer – Nathan. Met him in Paris. Obviously something going on or had been going on there . . . One doesn't ask. Then there's Frederick the fresco man.' He paused. 'Hard to say. She never spoke of him. Well-set-up young lad. Talented – he trained at the Slade with the best of the new crop. Good background. All the charm in the world. And the real thing – not like that three-coats-deep glaze the Irishman shows to the world. Estelle did some work for Fred a week or two ago. She sat for some of the preliminary sketches he was doing for *The Devil's Bride*. The two of them disappeared for days together. Hired a motorcycle from the village, had picnic baskets packed and off they went with Estelle on the flapper seat. "Location hunting," he told me when I enquired. "We're looking for the descent into hell. I think we may have found it!"'

'Why don't you go back and start at the top – with the lord,' suggested Joe. 'How did she get on with him?'

'The lord? Silmont?' Orlando gave a dismissive laugh. 'I don't think she had much time for him! But then, *he* doesn't have much time for *us*. She always went very silent when he was around, now I come to think of it. And I don't think she had much respect for his cousin, de Pacy, either.' Orlando furrowed his brow, remembering. 'I always had the feeling she had something on him . . . Knew something she shouldn't have known . . . Hard to recall at this stretch of time but there was some remark she made once. "Oh, if only you knew! That man's not what he appears . . ." That sort of comment. I would never suspect Estelle of the slightest malicious intent but she was a bit odd about de Pacy. She made the expected overtures when she arrived. Sailed in, all guns firing. The women all do, you know.

He's a good-looking man – war hero – and he has that authoritative air about him that the rest of us so envy.' Orlando sighed and glanced at Joe. 'You've got it, too. I say, you didn't . . .?'

'No such luck!' said Joe quickly.

'Well, she went through the motions but, experienced lass that she was, caught on rather more quickly than the other ladies who fancied their chances with him and sheered off.' Orlando paused, wondering quite how to proceed.

'She did confide – even warned me, you might say – that he is a man who likes handsome men,' Joe prompted, electing to use Estelle's own euphemism for a male condition not spoken of in company. He could not be certain of the extent to which the happily sexual Orlando was aware of inversion.

'Well, there you are, then! She found out quickly enough – and the hard way, no doubt. Can rock you on your heels, a rebuff of that sort. Leads to loss of self-esteem and insecurity if one is not hardened to rejection,' he replied with complete understanding and acceptance of Joe's suggestion. 'That would be the moment she started to avoid him. Oh – nothing done in a marked manner, you understand. She wouldn't deliver a set-down. Not her style. In fact, anyone less interested in the girl than I, wouldn't have noticed. Little things. She always managed to seat herself at the other end of the table, never joined him on his fur-pile –'

'On his what?'

'At the end of the meals – you know. At the moment the hall turns from *salle à manger* to *salon de compagnie*. You can tell an awful lot about relationships, friendships, involvements when people start to pull up those very medieval piles of furs and cushions and sit about in groups. Not so popular with the women,' he said with a twinkle of amusement. 'The ones who've only packed their short evening dresses. Much involuntary flashing of underwear on the way up and down! Those who brought their lounging pants or a long dress find themselves much more at ease. Take a close look next time – if ever – it happens again.'

Joe promised to give his close attention to the fur-pile friendships and, hesitatingly, asked: 'About Guy de Pacy's proclivities, Orlando . . . I'm a man . . . you're a good-looking chap, in the right light . . . have you any reason . . .'

'Good gad! No! Not the slightest!'

'Exactly. So why . . .?'

'Estelle could have got it wrong, you're thinking? Warning you off like that? And if the fellow did turn her down, one does rather wonder why? It's not every day a girl like her swims into your life, offering excitement and no strings attached. What could possibly . . .? Oh, I say . . . I'm having a terrible thought! He was a pilot, you know. Flew with the Storks. It's said he was badly injured in a crash landing towards the end of the war. No one has any idea – why would we? – of the extent of those injuries. Perhaps there's an unpalatable *physical* reason for the distance he keeps between himself and the women. I mean, apart from the arm.'

'He gets on well with Miss Makepeace?'

'Different sort of relationship there. She's trying to get into his head not his . . . Formidable woman. A scholar. You have to admire the way she does a man's job and no one questions her right to her position. They're good friends. A meeting of minds, I'd say. And good luck to him!'

The two men fell silent, too absorbed by their sombre thoughts and speculations to enjoy the beauty of the countryside they were driving through. Cool stands of oak trees crowding the lower slopes of the hills gave way to an airy upland where cherry orchards and vineyards and corduroy furrows of lavender vied with each other for prominence. In the distance a finger of ancient yellowed limestone rose like an exclamation mark, drawing the eye. It was echoed and softened by the slim, peremptory shapes of cypress trees.

'That's where we're headed,' said Orlando, suddenly conscious of the reason he'd been sent along for the ride. 'At least I think that's where the lord brought me. Wasn't really concentrating. I remember it was ten miles and he pointed out an Italianate campanile as the marker when we got within range. The house is right underneath it. Pretty place. Not at all grand. Gentilhommière of sorts. Nice man. You'll like Alphonse Lacroix.'

It had none of the grandeur of Silmont. An eighteenth-century *maison de plaisance,* the honey-coloured stone house was on a human scale and built, not for defence, but for a comfortable life. It had remained trim and symmetrical over the years, exactly as the architect had first rendered it, with not a trace of the haphazard organic growth of an English house of the same venerable age. A modest two storeys, from a long and emphatic centre, it extended wings forward in a welcome towards the approaching visitor. The rear of the house was protected from wintry blasts from the Alps to the north by a lift of hills, outliers of the Vaucluse, and its façade was carefully angled to miss the full glare of the afternoon sun. Pale grey wooden shutters were folded back revealing tall windows whose panes glittered in the sun's sloping angle. White curtains billowed, suggesting an airy interior. The central wide entrance door was clearly announced by a low flight of steps flanked by trimmed orange trees in tubs. The carriage sweep was freshly raked.

Joe parked the car a short way off in front of the house and turned off the engine. The noise of the cicadas flooded in, thrumming pleasantly and pierced, in the distance, by the excited whinny of a horse.

'Well, you could put your foot down here without fearing the blood of centuries will ooze up and ruin your Oxfords,' Joe commented. 'I can see why the lord escapes here for a day or two a week.'

Orlando grunted.

Joe tried again:

'*Là, tout n'est qu'ordre et beauté.*
*Luxe, calme et volupté* . . .

'And what do we find inside?'

'Gleaming furniture, polished by the years,' Orlando quoted back at him, paraphrasing Baudelaire. 'What else? Drives you mad after an hour. The measured order-liness . . . everything in its place . . . Not sure they'll be pleased to see untidy old *me* again. When I stayed here I indulged in a rebellious gesture. The precisely positioned gilt clock in the centre of the mantelpiece in the salon where we played cards had been annoying me. Too loud, too ornate, too gilded! And I didn't care for the look the goaty god Pan painted on the front had been giving me. I'll swear he smirked at every duff move I made. Before I left I sneaked in and turned its smug Sèvres porcelain face to the wall.'

'You *stayed* here? But why?'

'One of their bridge party is the local doctor. He was called out to a difficult case unexpectedly one day last month and Silmont invited me to ride over with him to make up a fourth. Yes, I do play. But on this occasion I played so badly they've never asked me back.'

'At least Lacroix will recognize your face. Look, Orlando, before we proceed . . . I'm not quite sure how best to play this scene . . .'

'We're playing a scene? I thought it was just a wheeze of yours to get out from under the jackbooted feet of that Commissaire?'

'Only partly. May I ask you, when we go in there, just to follow my lead? What I'm trying to achieve is very simple: to ascertain the time Silmont arrived here yesterday and whether he stayed for the duration. Establish the solidity of his alibi. That's all. Look – I'll come clean with you. It was de Pacy himself who told me – rather urgently – to enquire into his cousin's role in all this. He's not a man who will brook denial! And – there's something going on between those two that we have no inkling of.'

'You mean their intense dislike for each other? The rivalry? The uncomfortable fact that de Pacy is the only living relation Silmont has and he's eaten away by frustration and sorrow that, on his death, the estate will go to him because there's no one else in line?'

'Ah. Yes. That sort of inkling. Look, Orlando, I don't want this to look like a police enquiry. I don't want to barge in with notebook and pencil demanding to know where they all were at 6 p.m. yesterday. No direct questions will be asked. All *you* have to do is stand about affably grinning . . . burble a few inconsequential remarks . . . Can you manage that?'

'When did I ever do otherwise? Oh, come on! Let's get on with it!'

Orlando greeted the footman by name and was himself recognized. They were ushered into a spacious hallway and asked to wait. Monsieur Lacroix was in the summer *salon de compagnie* with the other gentlemen.

A moment later, Lacroix appeared, as smiling and friendly as his house. Slight and erect, he moved with the briskness of a military man and his welcome filled the room. 'Joliffe! How good to see you again! Somehow I thought it would be you who volunteered. And you bring a driver?' He looked enquiringly at Joe.

'This is a friend of mine and a fellow guest of Lord Silmont. May I present Commander Joseph Sandilands of . . .' Orlando recollected himself and added: 'of London. Joe, this is Monsieur Alphonse Lacroix.'

'An English Commander, eh? I should warn you that my great-grandfather died aboard the *Redoutable*!' The white moustache swept upwards with his smile in a rush of good humour. The bright blue eyes twinkled.

187

'Indeed!' said Joe, impressed. 'The first French ship to open fire on Lord Nelson! But, sir, I protest! I'm a Scotsman! I won't be held responsible for Trafalgar!'

'A Scotsman? Then you are doubly welcome. But come and meet my friends. We were just about to go out into the garden for lemonade.' He glanced down at their feet. 'But you come unprepared! I'll ask Fernand to go and make arrangements in the stables and, while he's at it, to look out a spare pair of boots. I'm sure we'll have a pair large enough for English feet,' he added dubiously, eyeing Orlando's size elevens. 'It will take them a while to saddle up, we've plenty of time for a chat. Tell me – have you ridden Mercure before, Joliffe?'

'Mercure? Ride him? But we thought the horse was lame . . .'

'Lame? Whatever gave you that idea? Young horse, in the pink of condition. Raring to go. Watch out – he can be a bit of a handful!'

# Chapter Twenty-Two

Two elderly gentlemen were talking together some distance away in the deep shade of an arbour. Joe located them and then looked about him with pleasure. From a sun-filled terrace behind the house a path struck off into what Joe's mother would have called 'a wilderness'. Here, the calm and luxury seemed to have been routed by Nature. Provence had asserted herself and thrown off the straight lines imposed by the Parisian architect. No shaven and decoratively distorted trees lined up here to salute them; instead, the thick shade of lustrous native foliage, a vine that swarmed unchecked over a wooden support, and scented curtains of honeysuckle, roses and jasmine crowded round for attention. The path itself gave way to a soft runner of close-growing herbs that gave up a delicious aroma under Joe's feet.

'There they are, lost in the gloom,' said Lacroix. 'This is what I still call "my wife's garden". She had an aversion to sun-baked symmetry. I allowed her to plant all this on sufferance! It was only after her death some ten years ago, I realized how right she had been. I often sit here after breakfast and tell her so. Come, let's get out of the sun and meet my dear friends, *le docteur* Philippe Simon and Monsieur Alfred Lesueur. Gentlemen, we have Joliffe with us again . . . Alfred, you will remember Joliffe – the Man Who Reverses Time? And, with him, he brings a gentleman from London – Commander Joseph Sandilands. No, don't get up – they're joining us out here for lemonade.'

Greetings exchanged, it was the doctor who spoke first. 'Have you enquired, Alphonse, about our friend?'

'No, Philippe, I thought I'd leave medical matters to you.'

'Then tell me, Joliffe – Bertrand, how did he appear, when he got back this morning?' The question was put with concern, in the expectation of a crisp answer.

'Not well,' replied Orlando with some reticence. 'Less than his usual self, I'd say. Somewhat tired.'

'Orlando is being discreet,' Joe broke in. 'You're talking to a medical man, Orlando. I think we can feel free to express our concerns. I'll be frank – he seemed ill, sir. Emotionally disturbed, of course – you will be au fait with the vandal attack to which his chapel has recently been subjected?'

They murmured their understanding. '. . . disgraceful affair . . . youth out of control these days . . . a six-month spell in my old regiment would . . .' From their reaction, Joe assessed that no message regarding the more serious crime had been sent to them. They were unaware of the murder.

'But *physically*, he struck me as being much diminished . . .'

'Yes? Go on.' The doctor was encouraging him to throw off his British reserve.

'In fact – jolly ill. From the way he clutches at his heart . . .' Joe mimed the gesture, 'it's apparent that he has some fears in that quarter. On his return, we noticed that his breathing was irregular and laboured, his face pale, almost blue. He was favouring his left arm. We were concerned.'

'There!' said Lesueur. 'We were quite right to ignore his tantrum and insist he went back in the car. He'd never have made it on that horse of his. Great, strong beast with a mind of its own! It'll kill him one of these days.'

'The ride over may well have done some damage . . .' said the doctor thoughtfully. 'Tell me, gentlemen – if you know – at what time did Bertrand leave home to come here yesterday? Precision would be appreciated.'

'We were with him when he set off to walk to the stable. At two o'clock, Orlando? Yes. Let's say he was mounted and off by two fifteen at the latest,' said Joe.

'And he arrived here at just after three!' announced the doctor. 'I knew it! He must have galloped most of the way to do the journey in that time!'

Orlando was desperately trying to repress a smirk and avoid catching Joe's eye.'It's not an easy ride,' he commented. 'Doubt if *I* could do it in an hour and I'm reckoned to be something of a centaur, back home.'

'It may be the one thing in life Bertrand still really enjoys, but my friend's right – it'll be the death of him. I sometimes think that's what he has in mind,' said Lacroix, weighing his words.

'Riding yourself to death?' said Joe, picking up his thought. 'Intriguing idea! Not a bad way to go if you know your time's measured. No guilt of suicide to bear if you're a religious man ... And if you can calculate it finely enough to collapse in the arms of your oldest friends and your doctor on arrival? A good end!'

'You understand me, Sandilands. It *could* kill him. You fellows all heard me ban him from strenuous exercise! And he flouts my good advice continually. Thinks he can fix it with the pills I hand out. *I'm* quite certain he can't.' The doctor looked seriously from Orlando to Joe. 'Your diagnosis is correct, Commander. Heart, you know. An established condition which has got much, much worse over the past few months. I speak of this to you in the hope that his young friends at the château will be able to exert a greater influence daily than his old friends who see him only one day a week. He must desist from exercise any more taxing than chopping the top off his morning egg.'

'Some chance of anyone exerting an influence over Bertrand de Silmont!' Lacroix shook his head. 'Pride, you know. And it gets stronger as he grows weaker. That's why he told these chaps his horse had gone lame. He doesn't want to be seen as a weakling who has to be driven about

the place by a chauffeur . . . who has to consider the possibility that it's time to give up the horses he adores.'

'We've heard and understood,' said Joe. 'We'll preserve
the illusion. And we'll do our best to urge restraint.
Though we risk having our ears torn off if we interfere, I'm
afraid,' he hazarded.

'Know what you mean!' sighed Lacroix. 'It's a pity
you've nothing in your medical kit for bad temper,
Philippe. Those rages of his! Practically foams at the
mouth – over nothing! He used never to be so touchy, you
know, Sandilands. Quite out of character. I'm sorry you've
been presented with this vision of our friend. Illness
reduces us all.'

'The stressful life he leads . . . One has to make allow-
ances. Jump in boldly and do what one can . . .' murmured
Joe. His invention was running into the sand.

They mumbled their agreement.

'But, gentlemen, allow me to reveal the *second* reason for
visiting you without ringing in advance.'

They exchanged puzzled glances but seemed ready –
even eager – for a change of subject and tone.

'We were just passing, returning to Silmont after an
unfruitful visit to the village.'

'Our village? Then it would be likely to be unfruitful! It's
very small – three farmers and their dogs. What business
could you have had there?'

'First, I must make a confession. Or is it rather – a clarification? The "Commander" of my title is not a naval one
but a police rank.'

'Police? What sort of police? Forgive me for asking
but, here in France, we have at least six different vari-
eties. There's the state police and the PJ and Clemenceau's
Tigers . . . or are they the same thing?' said Lacroix.

'And there are divisions of divisions,' put in Lesueur.
'There's Tax Evasion, Narcotics, Art Smuggling . . . er . . .'

'Pimping – that's one . . .' the doctor offered.

192

'And Wasting Police Time, you'll find, gentlemen!' Lacroix, eyes twinkling called a halt.

'I'm very simply with Criminal Investigation. If I say – Scotland Yard . . .?'

They had all heard of Scotland Yard.

'Joe's their crack sleuth,' Orlando offered. 'Criminal Investigation Department. And he liaises with that European lot in Lyon –'

'Interpol,' supplied Joe. 'It's in its infancy – birth throes might be more accurate – though it is intended to spread worldwide. But – don't be alarmed! I'm on leave at the moment. Not on official business. I'm actually on my way down to Antibes. I was cornered at a party in London before I left by a friend with a special plea.'

The doctor groaned. 'A cross we professionals all have to bear. Favours!' He put on an old duffer's voice: '"I say – you're a medical man of sorts, aren't you? I seem to have this lump behind my ear . . . this rash in an intimate area . . ." Pain in the rear, they mean! And then, having received a free diagnosis, they have the nerve to tell me they'll be sure to go and see their own doctor!' He levelled a sharp and humorous glance at Joe. 'As I expect you find, the ploy always works. I never have discovered the formula to deny anyone.'

'Exactly!' said Joe. 'The request I had was rather unusual. "I say, you're a detective, aren't you? Can you find a missing wife?" The worse for three cocktails at the time, I heard myself saying: "Not at all, old boy . . . rely on me."' He gave a shudder. 'And now I have to get on with it. Wonder if you could help? We called in on the off-chance. Long resident in the neighbourhood, pillars of your community – I thought you might be able to offer me the end of a ball of string. I've had no luck so far and the Riviera calls! My lost sheep is, of all things, a girl born and bred in these parts.'

'And her husband's in London?' asked Lacroix. 'Seems a bit unlikely.'

193

'He *was* in London. Recently dead, hence the hoo-ha. Yes. A pre-war, Belle Époque-style romance, don't you know.' Joe rolled his eyes. 'Young Englishman of good family, touring Europe, head full of Petrarch and Boccaccio, *La Bohème* as well for good measure probably, meets and falls in love with a very young Provençal girl. He marries her and carries her off to England. Not finding it to her taste, she flees back home and the war closes in. There wouldn't have been a problem, I believe, but there's a question of progeny and inheritance. It always comes down to cash.'

Heads nodded gravely.

'So, all other avenues of enquiry having failed, here I am, mewing with frustration and going through the motions.'

'Joe does himself less than justice,' Orlando backed up. 'Even after three cocktails he'll remember giving his word – and keep it. The man's a ferret. He'll find her. It'll just take time.' And then, slowly: 'Why don't you show them the evidence, Joe. You have it in your wallet.'

'Ah yes. I say – may I?' His query was more than a politeness and he waited for Orlando's nod before taking out his notecase.

He slipped the photograph from it and three heads bent, intrigued, over the faded sepia print.

'We've narrowed this down to 1906. And to a small village in the vicinity of Avignon. The girl in question is the one on the right, aged about twelve. We know that the name of the priest who conducted the communion classes was Father Ignace.'

'Our priest here is Father Pierre,' said Lacroix, intrigued. 'He's been here for decades. If anyone knows the whereabouts of the priesthood, he will. I don't know of one called Ignace ... You fellows?'

'No,' said the doctor. 'And I know every priest in the area. I can tell you with confidence that there is none such between here and Avignon. But look – 1906. I didn't take up my work here until after the war. I was based in Paris before that and moved down here to be close to my old academy friends.'

'And I was with my regiment in North Africa at that time,' said Lacroix.

'*I've* heard the name before,' said Lesueur. 'In a priestly context, I'm sure. Like the others, I've come and gone. These have not been settled times in France. But it does ring a bell.' He closed his eyes and concentrated. 'Getting old. Memory full of holes. I'll think about it. Let you know.'

Orlando went off to the stables looking rather chipper, Joe thought, when the message came that the horse was ready for him. Looking forward to the ride? Or happy to be getting shot of his police escort? Joe decided – both.

They agreed to meet in the great hall on their return. Orlando dashed off, Joe was quite certain, with the clear intention of getting home before him. He prepared himself to parry a few thrusts spiked with the word 'horsepower' when he got back.

He strolled out to his motor car, taking his time to give Orlando a head start and planning the rest of his afternoon. He found he was split between an eagerness to return to the château and a concern to give the Commissaire a run at the problem unencumbered by his presence. Joe decided to waste a little more time. There was one more step he could take in the mad pursuit of Orlando's Laure before he returned.

He was just climbing behind the wheel when he heard a thin voice calling after him. He turned to see Alfred Lesueur coming at a stately trot down the drive, waving his arms to attract his attention.

'So glad I caught you! Sorry – I nodded off! I came to with the answer in my head. The name Ignace. Well, *an* Ignace.' He frowned. 'I do hope it's not the one you're looking for . . . You wouldn't want to find *this* one. No, no! Terrible business! I'm not a religious man, Sandilands, but I have to say – with everyone else – shameful. If it's the affair I'm thinking of.'

He put up a hand to forestall Joe's question. 'No. I'll say no more. In case my memory serves me ill. It does play tricks ... You must find the evidence for yourself. Not difficult. It was in the newspaper. The local one. They'll have copies in the archives in Avignon.'

'Can you remember a date?' asked Joe without much hope.

'Before the war. I'm not certain of the year.'

'A season? That would be a help. If you could remember *where* you were reading at the time,' he prompted, 'you might remember *when*.'

'Oh yes. Let me think ... Now *I* take the daily national newspaper ... I was probably reading the local one at my aunt's house. The *Voix de la Méditerranée*. It comes out weekly. Yes! All the aunts were there, tut-tutting over it. The editor was much criticized for printing the article. My aunt Berthe had bought a copy to check the programme of events for the coming national holiday. So – there you have it,' he chortled. 'You'd be looking for the week before July 14th!'

'Well done!' said Joe, amused. 'You've saved me hours if not days of research!'

'Delighted to be of help, old chap. When you find the paper in question, you'll have to search with a fine-tooth comb because the story I recall, to everyone's disappointment, only made one appearance. I expect further reports were instantly suppressed by the powers of ... well, shall we just say – those with an interest. But even they couldn't censor the tittle-tattle!'


The priest's housekeeper showed Joe into Father Pierre's study. 'Commander Sandilands, Father,' she murmured and left them together.

'Good of you to see me, Father,' said Joe. 'I've just spent an hour with Alphonse Lacroix who gave me your name as one who might possibly be able to help me.'

'Sit down. Sit down. You're very welcome. But – help an English policeman?' He looked again at the card he held in his hand. 'A Scotland Yard Commander? Are you sure you want to see *me*?'

Joe assessed the age of the priest. The unlined, waxen features were difficult to read but he decided that he must be in late middle age and probably a contemporary of Lacroix and his friends. Joe repeated the half-truths he had given earlier to the bridge group with such success and concluded: 'So – I would be enormously grateful to hear where I might find this Father Ignace.'

'I'm sorry. I can't help you,' came the cold response. 'The man you seek does not exist.'

'I have it on very good authority that he does, or did, in the years before the war. If you are unable to give this matter your personal attention, could you at least direct me to the division of the Church which keeps records of the priesthood? I should like to look him up.'

'There is no record of such a man available to you, Commander. You will find his name on no church roll.'

To Joe's surprise, the priest got to his feet, walked to the door and opened it. 'You must excuse me, Commander. I recall that I have an engagement with a parishioner. My housekeeper will show you out. I suggest you waste no more of your time looking for a phantom priest. There is no Father Ignace.'

# Chapter Twenty-Three

It was five o'clock before Joe wearily parked his car between the Hispano-Suiza and a matched pair of Citroën police cars and presented himself again in the great hall. Someone must have been watching for him at the door. The cry went up at once: 'He's here!'

He was assailed without warning from all sides by distraught, angry and demanding voices. Hands tugged at his sleeves, someone trod on his foot. Joe hated mobs. Did twenty people constitute a mob? he wondered. Yes. If they were angry, vociferous and without a leader.

'It's a disgrace!'

'Someone must do something!'

'This'll show us what Scotland Yard's made of!' Joe thought he caught Petrovsky's subversive rumble.

The cacophony was quelled by a firm and totally reasonable plea delivered over their heads by Orlando to 'let the poor bloke have a cup of tea, for God's sake – before you tear him apart!'

A cup was instantly at his elbow, held out by Jane Makepeace. In a co-ordinated move with Orlando, she managed to cut Joe from the herd and settle him at one end of the table, sitting between them, next to the teapot. The crowd did not disperse but seethed about, looking likely to invade his peace at any moment. He guessed he was immune from them as long as he clutched his teacup in his hand.

'Am I hearing this aright?' Joe asked, unbelieving. 'That

lot are falling over themselves to tell me that an *arrest* has been made? Who's been arrested? And on what charge?'

'Much as I hate to echo the sentiments of the crowd,' gritted Jane, 'especially this crowd – Joe, you've got to do something!'

'They have a point,' added Orlando. 'Think of the fellow least likely to have done it, the one we all love the most – they've collared him for it!'

'They, and by that I mean the senior Frenchman – Jacquemin, is it? – have arrested Frederick Ashwell. Freddie! For the murder of Estelle. That's as much as we know. They've got him in there now – in Guy's . . . in the steward's office. That poor young boy! They've been grilling him for over an hour. It's ludicrous! Fred wouldn't swat a fly if it settled on his cream bun!'

'I've watched him catch a wasp that was being a nuisance and let it go in the lavender muttering "brother wasp"!' huffed Orlando.

'He's a baby – only just out of the Slade!' Jane's face was pink with indignation. Her dark eyes flashed with spirit and she tugged anxiously at a lock of silky hair. Joe wondered why he hadn't noticed at first sight what a very pretty woman she was.

'Is there anything you can do, Joe?'

He drained his cup of tea, set it down on the table and got to his feet. Time for Sir Lancelot to parade again. Joe steeled himself. Unflustered and commanding, he turned his battered side to the crowd and eyed them with what he hoped was a repressive glare. It worked a treat on new recruits and old stagers alike. It had signally failed with a tiger but it seemed to be working now with the excitable bunch in front of him. They fell silent.

'Don't worry! I'm sure there's something I can do, Jane.' His voice was directed over her head at the crowd. 'I'll go directly to Jacquemin and sort this out. I'm expecting to find we're hearing an unconfirmed rumour. What we need is *information*. When we have the *facts* we can take the appropriate *action*.'

Mutters of agreement started to go up on hearing his stressed words. Heads nodded support and they began to move aside, making a way through for him.

'Could you find Guy, tell him I'm back and ask him to attend with me? There may be useful evidence he can supply –' he started to say.

Jane replied lugubriously: 'He's tried! He's as angry as we are. But they wouldn't listen to him. The Commissaire threw Guy out of his own office! He's stormed off in a temper. I'll try to find him.'

The rebellious grumbles started up again at the mention of Jacquemin's overbearing behaviour to the steward. De Pacy was a popular man also in that company. Joe heard anti-French suggestions of an inventive nature being proposed by Ernest Fenton and seconded by Derek Whittlesford and thought the sooner he could bring young Frederick out of the office all in one piece or, for choice, selected body parts of the Commissaire in shreds, the better.

He approached de Pacy's office, nodding to left and right, feeling like a matador entering the ring. The door was, as before, flanked by two sentinels. The puzzled footmen had been replaced by two flint-eyed policemen from Avignon who seemed prepared to block his way. Joe showed his warrant card and informed them that he was expected. He knocked firmly once and walked straight inside.

He addressed the seated Commissaire from the doorway. 'Excellent news, Jacquemin! Lord Silmont's day passed exactly as advertised. No variation. No aberration. Three impeccable witnesses. I'll let you have my report this evening.'

'Good. Good. Always a pleasure to hear our lords and masters are in the clear,' he drawled. 'Now, what may I do for you?'

'Fill me in. Where've we got to? Have you found her passport? Contacted her next of kin?'

'Of course.' He pointed to a battered navy Vuitton suitcase behind the door. 'That's hers. We packed all her belongings in there. Nothing of interest or value. Mostly clothes. Her parents – named in her passport – were alerted by the force in Avignon and instructions sought. Some difficulties there,' he commented. 'Her father would appear to be some sort of dignitary in the Church with an address in Canterbury.'

He passed a scrap of paper over the desk to Joe. 'Anything known?'

Joe shook his head.

'They declined to travel down to view the body or pick up her things. We've been asked to dispose of them as we think fit.'

Joe grunted. 'There's parental affection for you! No more than Estelle would have expected, I think. Has her body been taken care of?'

'It's gone to Avignon, sir,' said Martineau, eager and deferential. 'Top priority! We'll hear back tomorrow –'

'That will be all, Lieutenant,' said Jacquemin frostily with a nod indicating the presence of an interviewee in the room.

Joe affected to notice for the first time the blond young man standing, hands cuffed behind his back and swaying slightly, opposite the Commissaire. 'Ah! Freddie, my boy!' he said jovially and went to pat him encouragingly on the back. 'Helping out the PJ, are you? Good boy! But don't stand on ceremony – have a seat, won't you?' Joe pulled a chair over and pushed Frederick on to it.

Frederick turned an anguished face to Joe. His long lashes were damp, his cheeks streaked with orange and green paint and trails of facial effluvia. Joe thought, with a stab of pity, that the young man looked like a pagan villager in *The Rite of Spring* a minute before the end of the last act, collapsing in a heap and dying of physical and emotional exhaustion. Embarrassed, Freddie twisted his neck and wiped his nose on his lapel.

'Strange fact I've discovered, Jacquemin, about artists,' said Joe conversationally. 'They never keep a clean handkerchief about them. Dishclouts of the most dubious provenance in every pocket but not a scrap of cotton to blow your nose on. Here, Freddie, have a good toot!' He held out his own cotton square and waited pointedly until Jacquemin nodded to Martineau to remove the handcuffs.

'Thank God you're here, Joe!' Freddie burst out. 'Estelle! She's dead! Murdered, they're saying. Why? And these fellows think I killed her! Me!' He dabbed at his eyes and blew his nose. 'Idiots!' he snarled, gaining courage from Joe's hand on his shoulder. And, losing all control: 'Arseholes! I loved her! I loved her!' he screamed again.

Jacquemin sighed. 'We all heard that, I think? Write it down, Martineau. In English and French. You'd be surprised how often that confession leads to the more serious one we're looking for. You've arrived, once again, Commander, at the *moment critique*. In at the kill, eh?'

'Explain yourself, Jacquemin.' Joe's tone was easy but menacing. He'd guessed from the Commissaire's failure to throw him out at once on his arrogant British bum that he had, during Joe's absence, made that essential phone call to establish Joe's bona fides and check on his rank. The Yard, if consulted, would have confirmed his high office in the force and most likely – since the enquiry came from France – would have mentioned the role he was playing in establishing Interpol, based in their own city of Lyon. A politically difficult moment. Jacquemin must by now know that he was outranked and outplayed by Commander Sandilands.

So why was he not hopping mad? Why wasn't he reminding Joe that, however elevated he might be back home, here he was without any authority? His equanimity was alarming.

'My colleague, Lieutenant Martineau of the local police force, was just about to inform this young person that, following his confession, he is to be taken away to Avignon, there to face the examining magistrate and answer a charge of murder.'

'I heard him just now confess that he loved Estelle. No more than that. If loving Estelle is a crime, man, you can slip the cuffs on at least five gentlemen baying for your blood out there. Six if you count yours truly.' Joe stuck out his hands cynically in the receptive position. 'She was a lovable girl. Her death has left us all distraught. We want to see the guilty man behind bars and soon. But a sacrificial goat shoved off a cliff satisfies no one. And makes the rest of the herd more difficult to handle.'

'We don't yet have Ashwell's confession in so many *words*,' said Jacquemin. 'But we do have it in *paint*.' He enjoyed Joe's puzzlement for a moment and went on: 'His crime is emblazoned on a wall. Painted two metres high in glorious colour and minute detail. And it's not merely a faithful portrayal of the crime *after* the event . . . oh, no . . . what we have is a statement of intent. We have a blue-print – an all-colours-of-the-rainbow print – for murder.' He chuckled. 'He's even signed and dated it! I invite you to come and have a look.'

He smiled wolfishly at Ashwell. 'And we'll take the great designer along with us to explain his theory and procedure, shall we? His modus operandi, I think we'd call it in the trade.'

# Chapter Twenty-Four

The small group left the office and headed off back through the hall towards the courtyard. The two French officers, with Frederick walking between them, followed by Joe and one of the gendarmes, raised a few questioning eyebrows but no one tried to bar their way. There was a moment of farce when Jacquemin was on the point of making the wrong turning and the prisoner had to tug the Commissaire by the sleeve and steer him on to the right path.

They emerged into warm late afternoon sunlight. Jacquemin had his bearings now and strode out for the north-facing cloister, a cool and airy spot, sheltered from wind and sun by its width and the arcaded aspect it presented to the courtyard.

'Outdoors?' the Commissaire mused. 'I have to ask: is this a sensible place to create a work of art?'

'It's not intended to be permanent,' said Frederick. 'I'm experimenting with what is rapidly becoming a lost skill. Lord Silmont, as you know, is an art lover in the true sense and I have found him very ready to support endeavours which may not seem immediately attractive to those who only view art in the saleroom. He understands the need for experimentation. I've changed the plaster formula and the schemes for the painting several times already.'

'What's all this mess?' Jacquemin wanted to know. He kicked with his foot at a slew of discarded crayons and scraps of paper that littered the paved floor.

'The children,' said Frederick. 'They gather here in the

shade and watch me work. They've been trying out their own ideas. They ran off in a hurry when little Marius burst out of the chapel.' He bent down and started to gather up the remains of his impromptu art school.

'Oh, leave it, for goodness sake! Now – starting on the left? Good. Explain this . . . this . . .'

'Delectable fresco?' supplied Joe kindly. 'It's stunning! Chagal would admire. But first, tell us, Fred, why is one of the four leaves – would you call them leaves, these sections? – covered over?'

'There's an illustration for each of the acts – they follow on each other like chapters in a story – and that's the last one. Act 4, you could say, the finale. I only finished yesterday. I do one section at a time. One a day. My *giornata*, it's called in the trade. Fresco means fresh. You've got to finish your picture while the stucco is still damp so that the paint you apply bonds with the plaster. No time for second thoughts or touching up. You have to go at it! In this weather I sprinkle my surfaces evening and morning with water and, to control the rate of drying, I drape a length of fabric over it when I've finished. I find it keeps the circulation of air to the minimum. I'm just feeling my way, you understand . . . using whatever seems to work. Guided by some useful instruction books the lord's lent me. In Italian. I say – anyone here know any Italian –'

'We start here,' Jacquemin interrupted.

'Ah yes. Now, this one here, the first, is, naturally, the scenery for the opening act of the ballet . . .'

Fred was getting into his stride, almost losing sight of the reason he was here. 'There's been a deplorable audience reaction to some modern ballets – *The Rite of Spring*, *Petroushka*, *Firebird*. Ignorant idiots who thought they were coming to swoon to a performance of *Nutcracker* or hum along with *The Yeomen of the Guard* were disappointed. Some hissed and walked out in a marked manner, some got into arguments with others more avant-garde. Fisticuffs broke out in the aisles. Right from the opening bars! In *The*

205

*Rite of Spring* a riot ensued. Police were called. Many customers took a dislike to the set. A brilliant design by Nicholas Roerich. The man's an archaeologist as well as a painter – he knew his stuff. But the design was lacking in the colour the audience wanted. From the title they were expecting yellows and greens and choruses of pink-cheeked virgins crowned with may-blossom. What they were presented with was sombre: shadowy purples and moss greens and glacier white, wonderfully evoking the awakening Steppes of Asia at the moment they begin to shake off winter. Bags of drama! But not comforting. Not the background for a jolly night out. What's more, the maidens were a disappointment. Clearly from rural Russia not Ruritania – grey-clad scarecrows with painted pagan faces –'

'I think the audience response may have had more to do with the musical score,' Jacquemin cut him short. 'It was the first notes of the bassoon, I understand, that got them on their feet. Monsieur Stravinsky can clear a concert hall faster than the fire brigade. Let us hope that the composer Petrovsky has in mind is more in tune with French ears. Now, guide us over your landscape will you, young man. By the shortest route.'

Frederick waved his arm and began to tell the story Joe had heard from Martineau in the chapel. The two men pulled surprised faces at each other behind Jacquemin's back.

*The Devil's Bride* was intended to intrigue an audience newly eager to rediscover and celebrate its roots, the painter told them. And what rich roots! The ancient Provençal tongue had been recently resurrected by the poet Mistral; folk tales going back to the Roman occupation and still being passed down by word of mouth in the villages had been discovered and preserved in print. In music too, discoveries had been made. Folk songs, shepherd's chants, gypsy tunes and love songs from the time of the troubadours had been coaxed from elderly inhabitants with long memories.

The story, the music, the setting, all were rooted in this soil, Frederick explained to the accompaniment of enthusiastic nods from Martineau, but the work would have an appeal for the whole world. If they could only find a costume designer with the genius of Léon Bakst, they would have a runaway success. There would be tours to America as well as the capitals of Europe.

'So, we lure the audiences in,' he explained. 'No discordant bassoons, no dull-coloured sets, no ragged costumes to scare them off. We appeal to the world!' He pointed to the first leaf of his painting.

In the background, a white castle thrust its pinnacles up into a vividly blue sky and on the grassy expanse at its feet all was prepared for a wedding. White birds flew; branches and garlands framed the scene which would be filled by colourfully clad dancers. Frederick had painted in a few figures, resplendent in a form of medieval dress. Joe peered more closely at these and wondered whether anyone else would notice that perhaps the genius costume designer had been found. But this was no idealized Sleeping Beauty castle. His eye searched for the discords. A second glance showed, sneaking in already amongst the springtime colours, a more sinister palette of dark red and grey. The splendid white château had its roots in a soil the colour of blood or embers.

'Explain the characters, would you. Be brief. I'm sure we're all familiar with the story,' Jacquemin invited.

Swallowing his offence, Frederick made the introductions. 'On your left, gentlemen, the ducal parents of the groom, splendidly attired. These will be elderly dancers who won't need to stretch their limbs or perform any vigorous steps so we can go to town on the costumes. On the right, the parents of the bride, likewise presented. The groom I have portrayed as a Nijinsky figure. Handsome with wonderful thighs. The central figure: the bride. We do not know her name. Dressed in white to conform to the old story and modern custom, though in medieval times I believe she would . . .' The frosty eye of the Commissaire nudged him back on course again. 'White. Yes. Clinging and simple. But glittering. Much frosting: silver and diamonds winking at her throat and wrists to indicate her wealth. And in this she is quite distinct from another girl over here in the half background, standing in the shadows – do you see her? The second female lead. The Odile to the bride's Odette, if you will. This is Aliénore, the penniless cousin who is secretly in love with the bridegroom. She is wearing a dark blue dress, the replica of the one the bride wears, but she has no jewels. The two girls do a pas de deux which reveals the girlish innocence of the one, the calculating jealousy of the other –'

'We'll imagine that. Carry on to the second act, will you?'

Their eyes followed Frederick's pointing finger. They noted the red fissure in the castle's foundations had increased in size. Ragged-edged, it oozed hellfire colours: thunderous purple, streaks of soot black, sparks of sulphurous yellow.

'And the audience will suddenly see movement here. On stage, I plan to stretch a diaphanous curtain over the crack, red-lit from above, and have dancers writhing behind it,' Frederick explained. 'And then, the bride having been left behind on stage while everyone goes off inside for the ceremony, she does a solo dance which turns into a pas de deux when a second character makes his entrance. Up from the roots of the castle comes the Devil. At this stage he's not terrifying but mesmerizing. Clad all in red, of course, handsome and charming. And – masked. Clearly he's fallen in love with the bride. He woos her. Nothing doing. She skips off into the castle and he does a dramatic solo full of power and rage. Not a creature to be thwarted!'

'And we can see what's going on here,' said Jacquemin, stepping on. 'The party's moved indoors. If I remember the story correctly, the bride encourages her friends to play a last game of childhood before she becomes a wife. A game of hide and seek. Which seems here to be going terribly wrong.' He looked closely at the third leaf. 'Looks exactly like the great hall we've just left. But decorated and *en fête*, of course.'

'A wide stage so that we can put on the formal wedding dances, performed to the traditional tunes, and then the wild scurrying of the young folk as they play their game. And, in the same stage set, the discovery that the girl is missing – with the resulting turmoil. The lighting dies and one part of the stage only is illuminated: over here.' Frederick moved aside and pointed to the bottom left-hand corner which they now saw to be the grey-painted outline of a dungeon. Two figures were standing hand in hand, in quiet menace. The bridegroom and his lover Aliénore were pitilessly watching the scene before them. Two further figures were dancing together, limbs entwined – amorously or in a frantic struggle – it was hard to tell. The Devil had the young bride by the waist and was wresting her from her hiding place to drag her down even deeper into the bowels of the château.

Martineau pointed an accusing finger at the groom and Aliénore. 'There they are – the guilty pair. In a moment, they'll spring to life, clang shut the door and nothing more will be heard of the bride for a hundred years. Death! The Devil is Death! But this devil has a face. Look! Can you see what I'm seeing?'

With his free hand the Devil was tugging the mask from his face.

'Good Lord! I hadn't noticed!' said Joe in surprise. 'But we know him! Isn't that . . .'

'Monsieur Guy de Pacy. Masquerading. Or not,' said Jacquemin with satisfaction. 'Interesting, and we look forward to hearing more from you on what prompted your choice of subject, Ashwell. But at last, here we are at the fourth and final setting. Will you unveil it, or shall I?'

Frederick shrugged truculently. 'I left it covered over because . . . well, in the circumstances . . . respect . . . sensibilities . . .' he mumbled and seemed unwilling to proceed. 'Not because I had anything to hide!'

209

Martineau moved forward to attend to the drapery.

'This is experimental, you understand. The ballet could well end with the third act. I've added this scene as the final chapter in the folk story. An awful warning – the wages of sin and all that.'

'And can you tell us at what precise time you put the last brushstroke to it? I'm assuming that the last flourish could well have been your signature?' Jacquemin leaned over and pretended to examine the scrawling black letters in the corner. 'It's always a puzzle to me – that men who have superb control over their fingers and their brushes seem to be incapable of forming their letters with any elegance. F. J. Ashwell, it says,' he reported unnecessarily. 'And it bears yesterday's date. I'm assuming that whatever time you give us will, of course, correspond to the time the laboratory comes up with when they examine the sample of plaster I've sent them.' He pointed to a gap six inches square chiselled from the bottom of the painting.

'All this has been reported also by Miss Jane Makepeace who observed Estelle Smeeth and the child Marius some yards away on the other side of the courtyard at the same time. Estelle – the young lady who had become, unwittingly, the subject of your last act. A piece devised and worked on for some hours before the young lady died. Completed, down to the signature, minutes before her death. Now, Sandilands, you see why I demand an explanation at the very least. Though a confession is, in fact, what we're looking at!'

Joe turned wondering eyes on the painter and then looked back at his vision of death on the wall before them.

The scene in the chapel was exactly as he remembered it. The table-top tomb was there bearing its grotesque burden. The crusading knight lay, unchanged, and at his side, his wife. But this figure was not Aliénore. The features were clearly those of Estelle. And the dagger in her heart was a faithful rendering of the misericord.

# Chapter Twenty-Five

'Easy enough to check whether the lad's telling the truth or not,' said Martineau when they returned to the office. 'Shall I go and collar his lordship, sir? That was as good a denunciation as I've ever heard! Shall I haul the blighter down and make him answer up?'

'It'll have to wait, I'm afraid,' Jacquemin replied. 'That valet of his . . .' He looked down at his notes. 'Léon something . . .'

'Bédoin,' supplied Joe. 'Old retainer type. Been looking after his master for decades.'

'Bossy old bugger! He's given the lord a stiff dose of something to send him to sleep. Without reference to me! Or to the hospital nurse I've sent up to keep an eye on things. The valet's uttering dire warnings of seizures to come. This fellow appears to be in charge of the pharmacopoeia. Which he keeps under lock and key in his own lair. He's got a room next door to the master's in his suite in the south tower.'

'You're saying you've –?' Joe began to ask.

'First thing I did. On the assumption that not a lot goes on under a roof of this sort without the knowledge of the owner, I stepped out and inspected his rooms. He raised no objection but I had to batter down the valet to gain admission.'

'Anything of note? I should particularly like to hear of what his medication consists. I was fortunate enough this afternoon to have a concerned discussion with his doctor.

He confirmed my suspicions regarding the lord's health. But it would be interesting to hear what the man is actually being prescribed.'

Jacquemin passed Joe a sheet of paper. 'Here you are. I took an inventory.'

Joe glanced down the list. 'Can you tell me why you've divided this into two distinct parts?'

'Because that's how we found them,' said Jacquemin. 'In two different cupboards and – this is extraordinary – with two different labels. The first group and the largest in number are the bottles and tins marked with the local doctor's details. The second, amounting to three or four items in all, bear the address of a Harley Street, London, medical establishment. With a name on the label we all recognize. Makepeace. Do you have a comment to make?' He looked keenly at Joe who had fallen into a silent perusal of the list.

'Er . . . not yet. I should like to take the time to check up on one or two of these items. I'm noticing that the London doctor and the local chap have one prescription in common. Both have decided to supply him with potassium iodide. Anything known?' he asked carefully.

'Heart and lungs. My predecessor swallowed them down like cachous,' said Jacquemin with satisfaction. 'Quite useless. It got him in the end.'

'May I borrow this? Take a copy and return it?'

'Certainly.'

'And, tell me Jacquemin, was there anything that took your attention in his quarters? What sort of set-up does he have there?'

Jacquemin pulled a sour face. 'Austere to the point of monkishness, I'd say. Fixtures and fittings and furnishings all of the very best but simple. Apart from some pretty fancy artwork on the bedroom walls.' He gave a knowing smile. 'Artwork which would surprise you, Sandilands. I expect it says a lot about the occupant of any room – the choice of pictures – if you think about it. A man can fill his public rooms with whatever he thinks will impress his

212

guests. That's the face he wants to show to the world but it's the image he chooses to rest his eyes on before he goes to sleep that tells you who he really is.'

Joe and Martineau were suddenly thoughtful.

'Passing in review your own walls, gentlemen?' Jacquemin grinned. 'Let me guess. The Lieutenant lives with his widowed mother. I'd expect a reproduction of a suitably pious religious scene – an Annunciation or something similar.' And, as Martineau coloured and shuffled his feet, added: 'With something more recreative under the bed, I'd guess. Now, Sandilands . . .'

Joe's annoyance at this invasion of his privacy bristled in his voice: 'Before you venture out on to another creaky limb, Jacquemin, I'll reveal the secrets of my bedchamber walls: horses and angels. Find fault with *them* if you can. I managed to acquire one of Alfred Munnings' paintings of the Canadian cavalry horses at war behind the front line before they were much collected. The angels – so buxom and bonny their gilded frame can scarcely contain them – are the subjects of an Italian renaissance drawing left to me by an uncle.'

Jacquemin's smile was self-congratulatory. 'Horses and women. One might have guessed.'

'Please, let us have no further confidences,' Joe begged. 'We'll let you off *your* round in the revelation game, Commissaire. Some things it's kinder not to ask, don't you agree, Martineau? Now, we're eager to hear what you made of Silmont's pictorial laudanum.'

'Ghastly taste! Simply ghastly! They tell us he's one of Europe's authorities on modern art – he could have his pick! And what does he choose to surround himself with? Medieval visions of hell!

'Right there on the wall, facing him as he lies in bed, there's a painting on wood, over two metres in height. He told me it's the right-hand panel of a pair commissioned to go over an altar. *The Descent into Hell.* Funny – from a distance you'd find the colours and composition intriguing

213

but when you focus on what's actually going on . . . well! Torture, rape and slaughter by the most inventive means is what's going on! All being perpetrated by devils equipped with tridents as well as more outré pieces of equipment, but, I can tell you – nothing like the dashing Devil in red that our young set designer envisioned.'

'I expect the church it was destined for refused to take delivery. You wouldn't want to expose a congregation to a sight like that for hours on end. Could give them unwelcome ideas,' Joe suggested. 'But the artist? Did he say who the artist was?'

'Some Dutchman with an unpronounceable name . . . Bosch!'

'Hieronymus Bosch?'

'You've got him! Strange thing – the other painting that took my eye – and crushed it – was by a Dutchman too. Vincent Van Gogh. A self-portrait painted, I was told, when he was an inmate in the lunatic asylum – quite near here – in St Rémy de Provence. Turned out dozens, apparently, and gave them all away.' Jacquemin shuddered. 'I know they're collected these days but I can tell you, I wouldn't say thank you for this one! I'll never forget it. It's a roughish painting – layers of livid colour slapped on, radiating outwards, and in the centre, a face. What a face! Green and yellow, emaciated flesh. You can tell the man was near death when he did it. Now, the sight of a corpse to me – and I suppose it's the same for you fellows – long since ceased to stir the emotions, but this was no piece of dead flesh awaiting the pathologist's attention. It was a living corpse. Sounds barmy, I know, but, if someone you knew had just died and you bent over him to murmur your farewell and he suddenly opened his eyes wide and stared at you . . . well . . . you can imagine the effect. Frightful! The eyes pin you to the wall! Dark, dull, blue-black, like a pair of ripe olives. They don't ask questions, they don't tell you anything, they don't accuse. They look at you but don't know you're there. And, of course, they wouldn't

214

know. The man was looking in a mirror when he painted it. You're standing in the way of a man who's interrogating himself, judging himself, and finding himself guilty of some appalling sin. A man full of self-hatred and on the edge of death.'

A forceful painting, Joe thought, to have aroused such feelings in the apparently unemotional Commissaire.

'Those eyes burn with pain,' Jacquemin added, still enjoying his subject. 'No wonder he has trouble sleeping. A nice Corot or two – that's what I'd prescribe for his walls. Much more effective than the laudanum-based sleeping draught – item number six on the list I've given you.'

'Books? What about books? I've inspected the lord's library but it would be interesting to hear what he has by him.'

'The usual line-up of novels. Hugo ... Dumas ... Tolstoy. Nothing more recent than Proust whom he seems to have read. A lot of poetry ... classics ... history ... much local history ... everything Mistral's ever written about Provence. A history of the château, privately printed. Numerous photographs of the building including some of the chapel and tomb. I have to say, there's no element we couldn't accept in the lad Frederick's story. He was definitely put up to it,' his voice curdled with suspicion, 'whatever *it* was, by his lordship. The books Ashwell showed us – the blueprint for his designs – were pressed on him by Silmont. The gaps were still to be seen on the shelves between Perrault's fairy tales and the Almanach de Provence. Martineau measured them.'

'So, just as Ashwell claims, he was handed his subject, his scene and his model – her services paid for in advance, on the house so to speak. All complete, on a palette, by the man commissioning the work,' Martineau summarized. 'And it was the lord who first put into his head the similarity between the statue and the live model, Miss Smeeth. The lord who gave him the keys to the armoury and invited him to study the daggers. The lord who, jokingly, suggested he paint the Devil with his cousin's features. And – wouldn't you know it? – who was known to be ten miles away himself at the time of the killing? His lordship! What's going on, sir? Murder by some sort of hypnotic influence? By proxy? By witchcraft?' He pursed his lips, uncomfortable with his suggestion. 'Do you suppose money changed hands?'

'Ah! Now you're being fanciful, Lieutenant,' sneered Jacquemin. 'The English are known to be unbribable. But it will be entertaining to hear the lord's version of events when he comes to the surface again. Meanwhile . . .' He shuffled his papers and invited the two men to pull their chairs closer. 'Just in case any further murders by suggestion are being planned, it will be sensible to reduce the number of potential victims. Can we take blonde young females as his preferred prey? I think we must. It's the only pattern we've got – if two attacks constitute a pattern. Taking the smashing of the alabaster image as a statement of intent, it seems reasonable. Accordingly, I'm getting the remaining two possible victims out from under our feet. That little strawberry bonbon . . . what's her name?'

'Clothilde?'

'Her and her Parisian mother. Blonde woman. Artist. Paints Madonnas and suchlike. I've ordered up a taxi to take them into Avignon and from there they can get a train back to Paris. Both very ready to go. I thought we'd take a chance on the redhead. What was she now? . . . Flower portraitist, she calls herself.' His lip curled. 'Big and overblown, like her subjects.'

Joe thought he recognized Cecily. 'Jacquemin – the other children. I believe Marius Dalbert to be in some danger. When word gets out – and it most likely has by now – that he was hidden in the chapel with a murderer on the loose, steps might be taken to silence him.'

'Already thought of, Sandilands. The older boy also. I'm sending the pair of them down to the village to the safety of their grandmother's house in the high street. I'll post one of the gendarmes they've sent us to stand guard at night.' He glanced at his watch. 'They're due to start off after their tea. In about half an hour. Miss Makepeace has volunteered to escort them down and their mother is very agreeable. Nothing much I can do about the Joliffe children. Father Joliffe insists they'll be safe enough in his orbit. He's promised to keep them on a tight rein. I'm not letting *him* leave. Reported to have had a certain relationship with the deceased. He's on my list.

'Now, here you are.' He passed a sheet of paper to Joe. 'You asked for the names of all those in the castle who have cameras, I believe. Didn't take long to compile.'

Joe looked at the Commissaire in surprise. 'I say – I'm impressed. And thank you for taking the trouble. I don't think you'll have wasted your time.'

He began to read out: 'The lord – a two-year-old German one. Zeiss-Tessar lens, quarter plate reflex.'

'Good but barely used, his valet tells me,' said Jacquemin. 'He keeps it to record works of art he's interested in. Not one for filling the family album. His cousin borrows it occasionally.'

'Nathan Jacoby. Great heavens! Can the man really own so much photographic gear? Three plate cameras and the Ermanox?'

'I haven't had time to check his version yet. A visit to his dark room is called for, I think. And soon. Those powders and chemicals may not be all they're said to be.'

'Petrovsky. A large plate camera.'

'He takes shots of the ballet sets, portraits of the ballerinas for release to the press as well as for his own records. He last used it to photograph Ashwell's set paintings.'

'Two Kodak pocket front-folders. One belonging to the Whittlesfords, the other to the Fentons.'

'Each with an exposed film inside. I've asked Jacoby to develop them.'

'Cecily Somerset. Ah! Sweet Cecily has a brand new

Leica. One of those tiny 35 millimetre, thirty-six exposure jobs. Goodness, how smart!'

'And not much of an idea how to use it. She hardly knows which way up to point the thing. Martineau, who's sensitive to mechanical devices, had to take it out of her hands to stop her wrecking it. I asked her nicely to remove the film for our inspection and she was nonplussed. No idea where the lever was. "Oh, but I always get a man to do that sort of thing," she said and batted her eyelashes. "I was going to wait until I got back to London to do that. And Daddy wouldn't be best pleased if he knew you were opening it up. It was a birthday present." And then she noticed, in all this argy-bargy, that her lens cap was missing. Flew into a temper and accused me of losing it. "You've dropped it! Yes, you have! You were fiddling with it!" Made us both check our turn-ups! What was that English name you called the woman just now? *Sweet Cecily?*'

'I was being sarcastic. It's a shy wayside flower in England. Smells delicately of aniseed.'

Jacquemin chortled with laughter. 'Nothing delicate about this specimen! We had to take the camera from her hands. But it was worth the effort – it had the bonus of a part-used film in it. With Jacoby's assistance – he's as good as a laboratory – we got it wound back and he's busy developing it. Are you going to tell me why you want to have this information?'

'Not just yet. Call it an unformed thought. Look – call them all in, will you? These cameras. The whole lot.'

Jacquemin smirked. 'In the box!' He gestured towards a large cardboard filing box on the floor, standing next to Estelle's attaché case. 'All of 'em except Jacoby's lot. I let him keep all his equipment in what he calls his laboratory. Too messy and bulky to cart downstairs.'

A tap on the door preceded the appearance of one of the guards. 'A lady to speak with the Commissaire.'

Jane Makepeace strode in. 'Jacquemin, the Dalbert children are lined up ready to go down to their granny's. Shall we set off now?'

Jacquemin gave his permission for the squad to move off and thanked her for her consideration. Joe excused himself and followed her from the room.

'That's a kind gesture, Jane. I'll just watch you start off. I must say, the fewer children there are around the place, the happier I am.'

She smiled back at him. 'Not entirely altruistic. I'm glad to get out of this place even for a few minutes. And there they are – your efficient niece has rounded them up.'

The two boys were standing with Dorcas in the courtyard. Joe bent to say goodbye and thank them for being such a help and so calm at a difficult time. They smiled and nodded, eager, he thought, to be off.

'And here's Miss Makepeace who's going to walk you down,' Joe added.

He was embarrassed by their reaction. One on either side of Dorcas, they reached for a hand and backed away behind her.

'But we thought Dorcas was going to come with us and spend the night, sir,' said René. 'You *did* say, Dorcas! You were going to finish that story . . .'

Jane Makepeace laughed, instantly identifying and defusing an awkward situation. 'You see how children react to me! Unfortunately, I have the same effect on dogs and men! That's fine, René, old fruit! In fact, it's a splendid idea that Dorcas should stay the night. But the Commander will have to give permission. None of us may move around, brush our teeth or blow our noses without some policeman giving us leave. Boys – you're well out of it!'

'You're sure you want to do this, Dorcas?' Joe asked.

She held the boys' hands protectively. 'Yes. I want to stay with them.'

'Then hang on a tick . . .' Joe gave a sharp whistle and summoned one of the gendarmes on duty at the gate. He spoke to him quietly for a moment. 'That's all right then,' he said. 'This is Corporal Lenoir who's detailed to stand guard tonight anyway. He may as well set off a bit early and go along with you. Behave yourselves, now!'

As they started back towards the château, Jane stopped and turned to confront Joe. 'At last! I've got you by yourself! You've been avoiding speaking to me since you arrived, Commander. I meant what I said about dogs and men, by the way, so I'm not surprised. Though I don't always understand why I have this repellent effect.'

'Well, I can't answer for the dogs but I'll tell you about the men,' said Joe cheerfully. 'It's because they're generally ugly or stupid, frequently both. Confronted by a woman as pretty and clever as you are, they feel at a loss. Diminished in some way, their manhood challenged.'

'And do I diminish *you*, Commander?' From any other woman the question would have had a flirtatious tone.

'Lord no! I'm not stupid and I grew up surrounded by women all cleverer than I am, so, for me, an intelligent woman who speaks her mind is par for the course. If it's credentials you're looking for – I march regularly with the suffragettes around London and I'm invited every year to attend one of Mrs Pankhurst's little soirées. It gets me into quite a lot of hot water with my department. Now, why don't we take a stroll around the courtyard and you can tell me what's on your mind.'

'Murder – what else? I think I know who did this awful thing. I think I can work out why. And I'm pretty sure you've reached the same conclusion.'

# Chapter Twenty-Six

'And you're right. I do look for credentials. Probity, honour, a useful role in life – these are all important to me. I choose to confide in you because I understand from others and I observe for myself that you possess all three in generous measure.'

She spiked this Victorian flattery with a mocking smile and passed her arm through his. 'Why don't we go along to my workshop for a few private moments? It's not far. Just to the left down here. In the old stables. When the lord had his spacious new building put up for his horses he converted the old one into a studio. It's lavishly equipped – no expense spared. Better than we can boast at the BM!'

The words were confident but the arm trembled slightly in his and she turned to take a swift glance over her shoulder. They started out together, two friends deep in conversation.

'I offer reciprocal assurances, Joe. I hope you'll find that you can trust me. On such a short acquaintance – why should you? But in dire circumstances, I believe honest souls recognize each other and it's *you* I've chosen to burden with my foul suspicions. I can no longer keep them to myself. If there were to be another killing . . .' Her words trailed away and then she started again, more firmly: 'I have my faults – indeed my sole virtue I sometimes think is the ability to acknowledge this – but the fault people find most annoying in me is that I don't suffer fools gladly.

"Intolerant and intemperate girl!" I remember my father calling me when I was quite small. "You will never marry," he raged some years later, "because the man has not been born who would come up to your expectations." And here I am, Joe, thirty-one next month and still single.'

Joe was disarmed by her disclosure and saddened by her stout-hearted acceptance of her situation. And how on earth, he wondered, was a man supposed to respond when a woman revealed her age so baldly? 'Perhaps he *was* born, this hero, but died in the carnage, destined never to meet his equal?'

She looked at him, wide-eyed. 'Do they know, at Scotland Yard, Commander, that they are harbouring a Romantic in their brass-buttoned bosom?'

He cleared his throat. 'I believe they have an inkling. Tell me, then, did you never set eyes on him – your *beau idéal*?'

He received another surprised stare. 'Well, yes, as a matter of fact, I did find him. A man I could love. A man – strangely – imperfect in every way. How Pa would have laughed! But, you know, it's been my father and my brother who have been much in my mind lately and pressing me to confide in you.'

At last she was coming to her point. Joe could only imagine that this preamble signalled a subject of some importance.

'Doctors both,' she explained. 'My father is an eminent psychiatric practitioner . . .'

'With a practice in Harley Street? Yes, he is well known in London.' And now known to the police from a name on a label, he did not add.

'And my brother intends to follow him after his medical formation. From family conversations and my own studies, I have acquired, over the years, some understanding of the diseases of the mind. Some have a psychological origin but others have a purely physical cause. I've learned to recognize the symptoms of a peculiarly distressing, badly understood and little talked-of disease. It's one my father has been closely concerned with. His patient list reads like selected pages from Debrett and the Almanach de Gotha. Sufferers from this disease tend to seek treatment discreetly, abroad in a foreign capital, and he has many distinguished Europeans – men and women – on his books. Treating, but, sadly – and he would be the first to admit this – failing to cure.'

Finally, she came to her point. 'Commander, I believe we are in the close company of a man who is in the throes of the third – and deadly – stage of this illness.'

They had reached her studio and entered to find an enchanting space, full of colour and activity. Jane spoke to the girl in maid's uniform who was busy planing down a length of wood clamped in a vice, telling her to pack up and consider herself dismissed for the day. She moved two pieces of embroidery from a pair of Louis XVI armchairs and invited Joe to sit. He looked about him, intrigued. He was aware of an Aladdin's cave of antique and lovely objects lined up, propped up or sitting in boxes on tables awaiting the attention of the latest scientific equipment. A German microscope, Bunsen burners, glass phials and a range of chemicals in jars spoke of a serious attempt to test, understand and repair the decaying contents of the château.

'Tea?' Jane invited. 'I always keep a kettle going on the stove and I have some deliciously strong Assam. Would that suit?'

'It certainly would. If you will serve it in a stout white porcelain mug. I wouldn't want to risk one of those delicate china confections I see you have over there.'

'The Limoges? Not even the lord is allowed to use those,' she said. 'Far too delicate. They're here for repair.'

Joe watched her movements about the room with pleasure. He had at first sight wrongly assumed gawkiness in those long limbs. Her every gesture was neat and

223

controlled. The cracked china cups would benefit from a passage through her capable hands.

'If what I see about me are the sick men of the castle's contents, I must concentrate and track down the real treasures. They must be quite an eyeful! Are they all Silmont heirlooms or have they been collected over the years?'

She answered him as she busied herself with the tea things. 'Almost all authentic. Some very ancient indeed. But you know what these feudal castles are – "chivalric receptacles for stolen goods" I once heard them called! The aristocracy – and the priesthood – were allowed the luxury of a bit of banditry and got away with it for centuries. They were always above the law. It doesn't make the objects themselves less admirable. Here's your tea. I noticed you don't take sugar. Oh, thank you, Louise, I'll see you tomorrow after breakfast,' she called to the girl, who bobbed by the door and left them together.

'Louise,' she explained, 'has the makings of an excellent craftsman. I'm training her up. She's quite wasted on bedmaking and dusting.' She looked about her with more than satisfaction – with love. 'I have the delightful job of cataloguing the precious contents, Joe, as well as repairing the dicky ones – that is the ones I have the competence to tackle. I know my limits and the Aubusson tapestries I've sent to their factory for repair. They still have the skills. I have nothing to do with his art collection which I haven't the knowledge to evaluate. Beyond anyone's estimation I do believe!'

'Guy de Pacy is a lucky man – heir to all this and his cousin breaking up fast on the rocks.' Joe commented, a slight question in his tone.

'If he is indeed the heir, I can only approve. He is a fine man and I can think of no one who would value it more,' said Jane stoutly. 'Always excepting myself and about six other aficionados at the Museum. It will be in safe hands at last.'

They sipped their tea companionably for a moment then: 'You did some restoration on the effigy of Aliénore, I understand?'

'Yes. That was entirely in my compass. I was horrified to see the damage. Guy took me in to examine it. I'd just regilded her hair! Hours . . . days of work lost, but that's as nothing compared with the loss of the artwork. It really was exceptional, you know. Carved with love.'

She glanced at Joe. Trying to judge how receptive he might be to one of her theories, he decided. His alert and friendly grin clearly did the trick as she plunged into a confidence. 'Do you know, I found something quite extraordinary under a fold of her dress – just under the neckline. It would only have been perceptible to someone peering very closely at it from an odd angle, as I did. I thought at first it was a flaw in the stone and ran a finger over it. No, it was smooth and intentional. It was a mole, Joe. A little brown disfigurement invisible to any onlooker during her life or after her death, in stone. It was a very personal touch.'

'The artist had an intimate knowledge of the lady's body, are you saying?'

'Perhaps so intimate that their relationship was the cause of her death.'

'And her husband, with a cruel turn of the screw, made her lover carve her effigy after death?' Joe shuddered at his thought.

'Yes. But the artist made his own secret farewell. He carved into her likeness a sign of his very special intimate knowledge. So special and heartbreaking that, here we are, Joe, six centuries later, understanding him.' She leaned closer, emphasizing her point. 'Just you and I. I never did speak of it to Lord Silmont. The knowledge would have inflamed his rage, I think.'

Knowledge to which Joe considered he himself had no right, outsider that he was. He saw in Jane's earnest face the desire, often unconscious, certainly never acknowledged, of the expert for the objects in his or her care. 'Was it yours to withhold, Jane, this discovery?'

She blushed. 'No! You're right, of course. A romantic whim of mine . . . I wanted to keep the lovers' secret from him. I shouldn't have. Not my place. I'm just a jobbing craftsman around here, after all.'

'But a moving story,' Joe murmured. 'I wonder what happened to the artist.'

'I'd guess that he didn't long survive the completion of his work. The lords of the day were vindictive, possessive and cruel. And – believe me – they still are!'

'You were about to speak of the present Lord Silmont and his problems, I think.'

Jane fell silent. The moment she had been working towards had come, an opportunity for free speaking to a receptive ear presented itself, and yet she hesitated.

'It's syphilis,' Joe said bluntly to bump her over her hesitation. 'Extraordinary how one hesitates to say the word. The French Disease, the Italian Swelling, the Scotch Fiddle, the Spanish Gout: the dose of nastiness we say we catch from whatever people we perceive to be our enemy at the time. The "great pox" is a term anyone would understand. All words for one ghastly, incurable scourge. And one may go about one's daily life, suffering from it for years . . . decades.'

She nodded. 'And it frequently goes undeclared or undetected. Even medical men are deceived into diagnosing a weak heart, high blood pressure, epilepsy, poor digestion. Indeed, it mimics all those ailments brilliantly. My father has been consulted by men regarding the mental damage they were experiencing, men who did not associate it with their "other complaints". But in the end it shows itself in all its hideousness. The spirochetal bacterium that causes it may take thirty years to climb the spine and reach the brain but eventually the parasite will settle there and destroy whatever cells govern our personality. Mild-mannered men become demons overnight. They storm and rage and then become calm again. The end may not come quickly. There are recorded cases of men who have lingered for years, on the brink of death one moment and enjoying a normal life the next. Frequently, towards the end, the fury gives way to periods of intense creativity – artists, musicians, writers – all have revealed this.'

'It's extraordinary,' Joe agreed, 'that the heights of human artistic achievement may be reached only to be countered moments later by a plunge to the depths of human behaviour. Jekyll and Hyde? Oscar Wilde's portrait of Dorian Grey? Are these an allegory? A warning?'

'Beethoven's last works, those of Schubert ... Guy de Maupassant ... Baudelaire ... Oscar Wilde perhaps, and Van Gogh's late canvases. Those last, completed in a frenzy of inspiration within the madhouse itself.'

In spite of himself, Joe found his voice dropping to a whisper as he revealed: 'He has in his room – were you aware? – a self-portrait of Van Gogh. Three-quarter profile with a stare deadly enough to terrify the Commissaire.'

'Has Jacquemin worked it out?'

'No, not yet. In spite of compiling a list of the medicaments he found in his cupboards. Amongst the laxatives and painkillers and milk of magnesia tablets, I saw listed potassium iodide. The Commissaire understands this to be a prescription for heart disease.'

'And so it can be.'

'But, prescribed along with – salvarsan?'

'Ah, yes. And there's your proof – an arsenic compound that's been in use for the past few years. Much trumpeted as a certain cure for syphilis. My father has reservations. And, I think you'll agree, it doesn't appear to be doing much good in this case. Shall we say, Joe, what even we have been tiptoeing around? Shall we say that the manic rages, the decay in personality and the delusions are symptoms of the tertiary stage of syphilis and, under its influence, Lord Silmont has launched himself on a mad course of destruction and murder?'

'Jane, whilst I must agree with the first of your assertions – that the lord is in the throes of this disease – I cannot agree with the second. I spent the afternoon with his friends and his doctor, splendid men all three, and can tell you that the lord was in their company at the time Estelle was murdered. He has the soundest alibi I've ever encountered. Ill he may be in mind and body, deluded and certifiably insane, but he is not guilty of murder.'

She made a small noise in her throat. Dissent? Surprise? Disappointment? It was not relief.

'You're perfectly sure of that?'

'Perfectly.'

She shook her head in embarrassment.'Oh, dear! I have made a mess of that, haven't I?' she said. 'Spreading doubt of the worst kind! You must think very badly of me.'

'I've learned never to come up with a theory and stretch the facts to fit it,' he said, smiling. 'It's taken years but I've got to the point where I can let evidence, impressions and sound advice from well-meaning friends – such as I've just had from you – swirl about until the moment comes when they settle into a convincing pattern.'

'And for you they're still swirling?'

'Yes. Perhaps the pieces will begin to fall together tomorrow when Estelle has spoken to us.'

'Estelle has spoken?'

'I'm going to Avignon to see the pathologist. A task Jacquemin seems willing to delegate to me. By then there may be other indications. If I were at all fanciful, I'd say that the dead sometimes try to pass on a message. They stand about on the fringes of perception, unable to influence the living agents involved with their corpse but urging us on.' Joe didn't quite like the way her lip curled in disbelief so he pressed on: 'You'd be surprised how often I've watched a pathologist put down his instruments and declare the job finished only to pause, uneasy, think a bit and say, almost to himself: "Hang on a minute . . . there's something else I could look at . . ."'

Jane sighed and this he identified clearly as a blend of derision and impatience.

'And now I see in your eye what your father saw all those years ago! "Intolerant and intemperate girl!" I shall shout. And possibly stamp my foot. But I shall know that I've deserved your scorn.'

She smiled and the hard expression melted away. Jane Makepeace was, indeed, a very pretty girl, Joe considered. But her father had known his own daughter.

Becoming the dry detective again, Joe wondered aloud what – had the lord had the means and opportunity to commit the crime (which he hadn't) – could possibly be his motive. What on earth would prompt him to attack first his own much-prized effigy and follow this with the murder of a strikingly similar victim? Could they ascribe this to complete, unreasoning dementia? It seemed to him that there was rather too much of a pattern to dismiss it as motiveless violence.

'Come now, Joe!' she said annoyingly. 'You've thought this through, as have I. Of course there's a pattern. And a motive too – a crazy one which might spring from a diseased mind. It comes down to blood.'

'Blood? There was little or no blood spilled,' he ventured.

'You're wilfully misunderstanding. I mean blood line. Descent. Silmont has never married – and now I think we can guess why – and therefore has no children. He has to deal with the problem of his imminent death and the inheritance of all this. It's not quite like the English tradition where the name and position are inherited along with the property. A man of a different name, finding himself the owner of the estate, could call himself "de Silmont" and there you have it – yet another member of the aristocracy. Ten a penny but they still set some store by it. The writer, Voltaire, was a plain Monsieur Arouet until he bought the Voltaire estate. After a few years he was Monsieur de Voltaire and had quietly dropped his own family name. What's the betting that Monsieur de Pacy will seamlessly become Silmont?'

'Sounds like a good solution to me,' Joe said.

'Not if there is bad blood between the two men.'

'Blood again? Did you use that term intentionally?'

'Yes. You will have heard that the men are cousins. This is a polite acceptance. They are not. They are, in fact, half-brothers. Some sort of cousin as well, if you can be bothered to work it out, I suppose. Guy was born somewhat illegitimate.'

'Somewhat?'

'It's not straightforward. He was brought up by Vincent de Pacy and his wife in their household, their acknowledged son. And why not – de Pacy was indeed his father. The man had quite a reputation locally for philandering apparently. But Guy's mother? Well! Prepare yourself for a surprise. She was, in fact, Ariane, the wife of the Lord Silmont of the day, Bertrand's own mother.'

'Ah, here she is again – the Unfaithful Wife!'

She shrugged her shoulders. 'It was the nineties. La Belle Époque. There were many liaisons of that nature. But are you seeing a pattern? The Lord Silmont already had a son in Bertrand and had no use for another who wasn't his own. He compelled his wife to hand the baby over to its father, de Pacy. Everything was hushed up and given a veneer of propriety as is the custom but I can only imagine what effect it must have had on both boys.'

'And both women!' said Joe, aghast. 'I'm surprised there wasn't murder done! I had no idea.'

'And I trust you to keep it to yourself. Guy is a survivor, something of a stoic, and he's adjusted to his circumstances. A man to be respected. But he would not be pleased . . . I feel I've betrayed a man who has befriended me. I have said too much.'

'Not if it has a bearing on this case. But how did *you* manage to dig so deep?'

She laughed. 'Me? Bad-tempered, angular, unsympathetic me? I have acquired a certain skill, Joe, over the years. I have learned the techniques of the psychiatrist's couch. I know when to be silent. I know which phrases will provoke a response. And I know how to interpret those responses.'

'I suppose I must resign myself to being read by you?'

'Not at all, Joe. I take you for a clear rock pool. The sunlight and clarity I see on the surface goes all the way down to the white pebbles on the bottom.'

He didn't believe her but made no denial or affirmation of her challenge, spotting her outrageous comment for the trigger it was. If he'd been lounging on a tapestried couch instead of perched rather gingerly on an ancient chair with a rickety leg he might well have given way to the temptation of sinking into an indulgent bout of self-analysis. Steered by Jane Makepeace in the direction of her choosing. He helped himself to another cup of tea from the pot.

'So why the frenzied attack on womankind?' he asked, wondering whether she had reached the same conclusion as himself.

'Brought up with medieval notions of inheritance, the fascination for the treacherous wife, Aliénore, whom he adores and loathes in equal measure, he finds at an impressionable age that the family tradition continues. His own mother he discovers to be a strumpet – in his vocabulary. I despise the word and seek unsuccessfully for the male equivalent. At any event – a woman who has been unfaithful and given away the product of her unfaithfulness. His own brother. A heartbreaking loss? Or relief that a cuckoo has been pushed out of the nest?'

'Your father would have a field day with all this,' said Joe, bemused.

'And then, we must assume somewhere in his early twenties – that is the most usual time, I understand, for young men to go off the rails, usually with an infected prostitute – he finds through the appearance of a chancre in the groin, and probably a fever, that he has been infected with the most hideous disease known to man. It is incurable. It is unbearably painful. It is transferable. No one is sure of the period of contagion but he knows that if he marries, he risks infecting his wife. And the disease may be passed from a mother to her child. She will bring into the world an infant covered in black pustules and condemned to a life of pain. Silmont does the honourable thing and forbids himself ever to marry.'

'Which leaves him with a certain resentment against women,' said Joe. 'Unfaithful, diseased and dangerous creatures!'

'The anger and bitterness grow over the years like the tumours. And now he's reached the third stage and his diseased brain is no longer capable of exercising restraint or reason. He sees the statue of the ancient whore as the seed bed of vice and his own illness as destruction visited on him by an unclean woman. I think the arrival of Estelle with her incredible looks and her licentious reputation burst the boil of his venom. She was fated to pay the price. The moment she stepped over the drawbridge she –'

Joe was anxious to discourage Jane's doom-laden tone. He detected a trace of lip-smacking jubilation and, though he could understand, he could not sympathize.

'Which was exactly when? Her arrival?' he interrupted brusquely.

'Let me think . . . I was already here. My six months' secondment started in May. It would have been at the beginning of June. She came down with Nathan the photographer.' Jane's eyes narrowed. 'I remember clearly the effect she had on the men that first day.' She fell silent and let her remark hang in the air between them. She had taken her reprimand and this was her riposte: if Joe wanted to hear gossip, he was going to have to ask nicely.

'Any man in particular seem smitten?' he enquired because he needed to know. He was reluctant to hear an account seen through the prism of Jane Makepeace's critical faculty but it would be interesting to compare her version with the one he already had from Orlando.

'You want individual profiles – a barometer of lust? Let me see. Freddie was an obvious victim from the first moment. The mercury rose to danger level in seconds. Storm warnings hoisted. She treated him kindly, I think. He was her devoted swain, you could say. Poor chap! He was much ragged for it. Derek and Ernest were sat on hard by each other's respective wife. Bubbling under, I'd say. Petrovsky? There was a blip from him until he discovered that she despised him and his level fell. Such a man thrives only on adulation. And his hands were rather full at the time, anyway. Nathan Jacoby watched all these fools manoeuvring from the sidelines, cynical and indulgent. But concerned. Definitely concerned. Your friend Orlando? Now, there's a lovely man!' she said surprisingly. 'A pacifist and a reformer. And a fine artist. Far too good for her. He registered a certain warm interest and I thought at one point they might make a go of it. Wouldn't have blamed her for trying – he's easy and funny. Perfect man to spend a summer with.'

Joe hid a smile. He wondered whether he should warn Orlando that he had a secret admirer.

'And the Frenchmen? You're saving them till last?'

'I appreciate a crescendo. Guy de Pacy . . . Handsome, competent, stand-offish Guy. He was amused, I'd say, by the reactions of the other men. But she was the type who *would* go for the unattainable. He was much too old for her. Too experienced. Too choosy. She tried hard – to everyone's embarrassment. It didn't take long for her to get the message and she stopped pursuing him. Very abruptly. One day she was all over him, the next she was glowering from the other end of the table. Something emphatic happened to make her change her mind.'

Jane seemed genuinely puzzled and not fishing for a reply from him. Could it be that this modern, so well-informed young woman had no knowledge of the possibility of male inversion? He decided not to raise the subject.

'This message that Estelle got? Any idea of what it consisted?'

'Lord no! I'm on good terms with Guy but he doesn't *confide*. He's not approachable in that way – you must have noticed. Not a gossip. But it might not have been Guy who spoke to her. Had you thought of that?'

'Not Guy?'

'The Lord Silmont. If he noticed her interest, he would have taken steps to discourage it.'

'Steps?'

'Yes. Here my theory begins to crumble.' Jane frowned and looked to Joe for help, her confident assertions suddenly faltering.

'Because he could just have sent her away, couldn't he? A hanger-on, a potential trouble-maker, a girl who represented everything he despised, why wasn't she on the next train back to Paris?' Joe wondered.

'You're right. Young, unconnected and foreign, you could add. He's unpredictable. I've seen him dismiss a servant for squinting at him. But he kept Estelle on.'

'Could he have been fascinated himself?'

Jane nodded slowly. 'Not obviously so. His visits to the dining room didn't increase with her arrival. He didn't seek her company. But when they were in the same room he watched her. Hardly a word exchanged but he was always . . . *conscious* of her, I'd say.'

'Jealous of Guy?'

'Probably. Well, you would be, wouldn't you? Younger man, attractive, healthy, and being besieged by the girl you've a fancy of some sort for yourself? Yes. It could have been the lord who warned her off. Another reason for him to want to get rid of her permanently. Had it occurred to you, Joe, that the table-top tomb looks very like an altar? He could have cleared the stone strumpet away to make space for a flesh and blood victim. Sacrificing her symbolically – all in the throes of his diseased urges, of course.'

They had come around full circle. 'But I told you, Jane, he could not have stuck the dagger in Estelle yesterday.'

'You haven't quite got there, have you?' she said, annoyingly. 'Well, I leave you to work it out for yourself. I don't intend to put ideas into your head. I have no concrete evidence to present yet to back up my suspicions but I'll let you have it the moment I uncover it.'

Joe very much doubted that she had. Miss Makepeace, he thought, had shot her bolt, exhausted her evidence. But he was mistaken.

'I'll leave you with another thought,' she said, as one turning in the saddle to fire off a last Parthian arrow. 'You only ask me about her relationships with the *men* in the party. She was not popular with the women in the dorm, you know. They're mostly quite open-minded – as females go – but when they're cooped up together! Well! They can behave no better than schoolboys . . . or hens . . . The most awful bullies! They choose one of their number to be the sacrificial one, the poor specimen all agree to peck at. They chose Estelle. She was easy to despise and a threat. Cecily, in particular, could get into a froth of rage at the mention of her name. There was bad blood between those two. Cecily tormented her. The second night Estelle was with us, I caught the appalling Cecily making an apple-pie bed to trap her. Reverting to schoolgirl behaviour.'

'What did *you* do, Jane?' Joe asked, trying not to smile.

'It's not funny, Commander! Girls, even hard-boiled ones like Estelle, can be psychologically damaged by such evidence of rejection by their peers, you know . . . I told her if she didn't undo it at once and be nice, someone might think of putting a snake in hers.'

'That was telling her,' said Joe.

'If it was, she wasn't listening. Cecily did it anyway as soon as my back was turned.'

Joe swallowed uneasily. 'And . . .?'

235

'There's a nest of adders on the fringes of the woodland.' Jane grinned. 'We've had no trouble with Cecily since.'

'I sincerely hope the snake suffered no psychological damage,' said Joe faintly. 'An enforced appearance in Cecily's bed could leave its mark on man or beast.' He instantly regretted his startled aside.

Jane considered him through narrowed eyes. 'I say again, Commander – it's not funny.' She waggled a finger at him in joking reprimand. 'Interview over, I think.'

She began to collect up the teacups in a marked manner and added: 'But I was forgetting – when it comes to gathering information, Joe, you hardly need to listen to *me*. You're on the inside of the bend! Estelle's cold lips may yet whisper into your attentive ear. I'm sure you'll listen to *her*.'

Jacquemin would not appreciate a second female corpse appearing on his patch, Joe judged, so he decided to put off strangling Jane Makepeace for the moment. Really, he'd rather listen to the dead Estelle than the very much alive and unfortunately named Miss Makepeace.

# Chapter Twenty-Seven

Estelle was a silent sheeted figure, conveying nothing when Joe was shown into the room of the *institut médico-légal* where her body lay on a channelled marble slab. The pathologist had accepted the handwritten note of introduction from Jacquemin with a surprised and slightly amused lift of the eyebrow.

The hand he extended to Joe was rough and warm, the eyes friendly, as he introduced himself. Lemaître was an ex-army doctor, middle-aged, confident and direct. The perfect antidote to his gloomy and dripping surroundings.

'Ah! The Entente Cordiale at work at last,' he said. 'I wondered if we would ever see such a thing.'

'Well, it's not much of an *entente* and I would hardly call it *cordiale*,' said Joe with a rueful grin.

'No. We Frenchmen are fond of the sea. We particularly appreciate the bit that separates us from Albion.' The doctor returned his grin. 'And I've worked with Commissaire Jacquemin,' he added and was content not to embroider on his comment.

'First things first.' The doctor took a bulky paper bag from a locker and handed it to Joe. 'The Commissaire asked us to return to you everything we found on her body for his further inspection instead of putting it into storage here. You'll find everything in there. All the items found were removed, catalogued and put away by my assistant before the autopsy. He's meticulous. They've been finger-printed, combed and swabbed, as appropriate. Make what you will of it.'

He drew the sheet down to uncover Estelle's face. 'Well, here she is. All done. I've even got the report typed out. I had my secretary come in at six this morning. I had the impression that there was some urgency?'

'There may be danger of a repeat performance,' said Joe.

'Ah? The English crime? Multiple slayings? Slaughter on the streets? I wouldn't be so sure. Your bloke is no Jack the Ripper! I've never seen a neater, more effective wound. If anyone back there needs to know – she didn't suffer. Was probably hardly aware of what was happening to her. What you *haven't* got here is a maniacal sex-driven dis-embowelling and mutilation. But tell me, detective – served up on an altar tomb top? How can that have come about?'

'We have some theories which I won't expound in case what you have to tell me subsequently makes them sound ridiculous,' said Joe. 'You go first! And perhaps we could well start with how she got there. Was she was stabbed in the place and position in which she was discovered?'

'No doubt about that. The blood had sunk down and found its level.' He delicately turned the sheet down further and pointed. 'Gravitational discoloration. You see the dark blue tide line? The lividity shows the body had not been moved after death. She died where you found her. And the estimated time of death Jacquemin gave me is as exact as is possible to give. He rightly calculated that she died in the late afternoon or early evening of the day before. I was informed of the ambient temperature of the chapel and took that into consideration. It's all in my report. Calculations and all. Do I need to mouth the usual caveats?'

'No. Not at all. Bodies cool in the same way in London. At annoyingly variable rates.' Joe smiled. 'And the wound itself? Anything of interest?'

'As I say – neat. Strong wrist on him, whoever it was. Though perhaps I should stress the precision? We should remember that her flesh offered little resistance – rather a skinny girl – and the nightdress she was wearing was old and fragile. The blade, being some eight inches long, wasn't engaged to the hilt. Just the right length of steel used. All the same – we have a transfixing wound. In the region of the right ventricle. Death within seconds, possibly hastened by cardiac tamponade.

'But now you're here you can tell me: on which side of what we will call "her husband" was she lying?'

Joe explained that she was on the warrior's right side and that the girl's right lay next to the aisle of the chapel. He demonstrated.

'I see. Then we can add – precise *right* wrist. I'm assuming the killer stood in the aisle and leaned over her prone body – up to you to find out why she kept still and let him – and dealt the blow like this.' The doctor mimed. He transferred an imaginary dagger to his left hand and tried again. 'Awkward. Unnatural. And you'd expect a corresponding change in the orientation of the blade. East–west instead of north–south. A left-hander could have approached from behind, I suppose . . .' He changed position and repeated the killing stroke over Estelle's head. 'It seems very unnatural to me. But then, sticking a blade into a lovely girl like this from any angle seems unnatural to me.'

'Could the blow have been delivered two-handedly, like this?' Joe asked.

'Yes. Entirely possible. The handle is quite long and stout, you see, with a good grip on it. To allow for use by a gauntleted hand. But I was assuming that your bloke would need to keep one hand free to control the victim and stab with the other. Why would the girl just lie there and watch a blade descending on her ? She'd have rolled away. She'd have tried to defend herself. You noticed there were no scratches or cuts on her hands and arms?'

He took the murder weapon from a tray under the table and handed it to Joe. 'Take it. It's clean. The print chaps have finished with it. Nothing apparent – rubbed clean, they say. It's not as old as you might have thought, by the way. These things came into use in the 1300s but this is a copy. Probably Italian work, 1600 or so.'

'Yes, it falls naturally and comfortably into one's hand,' said Joe. 'Excellent quality.'

'Had to be. Those things were in the hands of butchers. Battlefield executioners who'd spend hours despatching the enemy wounded. Delivering the *coup de grâce*.' The pathologist smiled. 'But I'm not telling you anything you haven't worked out for yourself yet, am I? Never mind. I'll plough on with the reassuring thought that I have at least one surprise for you . . .

'Death came within seconds. The aorta was penetrated with precision. Sketches and copious Latin references on page 10 of the report, you'll find. Whoever it was seems to have had all the time in the world to focus on his spot and line up his blade. He knew what he was about . . . He had a knowledge of anatomy and a certain strength of arm. That's as much as I can say.'

From the cause of death the doctor moved on to general comments on the state of the body. He confirmed that toxicology tests had revealed the victim to have no traces of drugs or poisons in her system.

'No cocaine?'

'That's right. None. She was fit and healthy and completely compos mentis at the time of her death. And you will need to know that there was no trace of sexual attack. There *had* been sexual activity some hours before, we can assume the previous night, but nothing unnatural. No sign of violence.'

Joe sensed they were coming to the end of the interview. 'Anything else?' he asked.

'Yes. It occurred to me there was something else I perhaps ought to look at . . .'

Joe smiled to hear the casual warning. Pathologists, in his experience, liked to do this. The few words added as an 'oh, by the way,' at the end of a discussion so often shredded his theories or set him off on a completely different tack.

'She was pregnant. Ah! *That* you didn't know! Yes. Undetectable to the eye of the general public, but there was a foetus. Two months . . . nine weeks . . . thereabouts.'

'Sounds a bit ridiculous but – would she have been aware?' said Joe.

'Oh, yes. I think we could bet on that! She was no ingénue. She'd know the symptoms, I'm sure. And she would have missed two monthly indications. She'd probably gone off her food. There was very little in her stomach . . .'

Joe stood in silence, dumfounded and deep in thought.

Dr Lemaître was clearly used to such behaviour from policemen on receipt of his devastating remarks and fell into a companionable study of the body. The clock on the wall of the morgue ticked loudly twenty times before one of the men moved.

Joe went to stand by Estelle's head. Silently, he moved a wisp of damp hair from her forehead, yearning for a last waft of her perfume to rise and torment him. He smelled nothing but carbolic. Lightly he touched her cold cheek with his hand. He leaned over and, not caring whether he was overheard, whispered: 'I've heard you, Miss Smeeth. Loud and clear. I know why you were killed. I think I know how. I just need now to find out which one of three men you trusted, hated you enough to plunge a dagger into that generous heart. And I *will* find him. Soon.'

# Chapter Twenty-Eight

Joe left his car at the commissariat and walked in towards the centre of the small city. This morning he was going to try to ignore its beauty and its tempting cafés; he was going to ignore the warnings of a stomach that had missed breakfast and was rumbling at every waft of coffee-roasting and bread-baking from the shop fronts he passed along the boulevard.

He struck out with the river Rhône on his left, heading for the tight swirl of medieval buildings still standing inside the city walls. He steered by the white towers of the Pope's Palace rising, with a careless disregard for sym-metry, to lord it over the huddle of pink-tiled roofs. This was the point of his day. The visit to the morgue, though it had in the end proved more fruitful than he could have expected, was a cover for his next assignation.

He found what he was looking for in a back street near the Place de l'Horloge and entered the double-fronted premises to the sound of a jangling bell over his head through a door marked 'For Public Access'. The offices of *La Voix de la Méditerranée* were not exactly buzzing. He reminded himself that this was August and the middle of the holiday season. The papers were still being produced but probably working with a skeleton staff. On the high mahogany counter a printed notice told members of the public that this was the place to present your news (at any time), your personal advertisements (before twelve noon), or request to consult the archive (between ten and eleven, Wednesday to Saturday). Clearly browsing was not encouraged.

Joe checked his watch. He was five minutes into the narrow time slot. He rang the counter bell for attention.

This came two minutes and three rings of increasing volume later and was offered by a distracted and peaky-looking youth in a long green apron. Joe sighed. The skeleton staff. After the exchange of greetings he announced cordially: 'I'd like to consult your archive, please.' He presented his credentials. 'This is a police request for access to certain of your back numbers.'

'Year, please?' The boy had barely glanced at his warrant card.

'Between 1906 and 1911 . . .'

'Sorry, sir. You'll have to be more precise.' The unhelpfulness turned to truculence. 'I can't bring all that lot out. They're down in the cellar! And they're bound, you know. By the month. That's . . . that's . . .'

'Seventy-two bound volumes,' said Joe. 'At least it would be if I wanted every month. But let me finish. I want to see the papers printed for the second week of the month of July. That's six folders only. And look – I'd like some advice from one of your editorial staff – someone over the age of forty for choice.'

'Not possible, I'm afraid. There's only Monsieur Rozier in and he won't come. He's busy.'

Joe leaned across the counter. He took from his inside pocket the letter of introduction from Jacquemin. With his thumb carefully placed over the 'Dear Dr Lemaître', he passed it under the eyes of the clerk. The impressive letter heading and the swirling signature brought a spark of interest.

Joe heaped kindling on the spark. 'Recognize this signature? Well, why would you? But you'll recognize the man who scrawled it next week when his heroic features appear on the front cover of *Le Petit Journal*. Commissaire Jacquemin is in town, my lad. Yes, The Implacable One himself! And he's flushing out the villains and personally filling them full of lead. Three dead in Marseille over the weekend. You'll read about it. He requires co-operation.'

The boy hurried away with a mumbled 'Leave it with me, sir . . . I'll see what I can do . . .'

Rozier took less time to appear than the counter clerk. The bespectacled, moustached man in shirt-sleeves came bustling in, mild annoyance losing the fight with extreme curiosity. He examined Joe's warrant card, talking as he did so. 'Rozier. Deputy editor. I'm forty-four. Hair's going grey but I still have my teeth. Good enough for you? What's all this shit about Jacquemin? And what's an English police-man doing in Avignon running errands for that pitiless old prick?'

'Long story. A peek at some of your papers, accompanied by some insights from a man who knows the local area, would help me to solve a fifteen-year-old mystery, reunite a pair of young lovers driven apart by the war and restore a lost child to its mother.'

'Is that all? You drag me from my fat heifer sales report for this?'

The hard eyes gleamed and Joe decided that, though the man showed no sign of having a heart, at least he had a sense of humour. It was a start.

'Michel says 1906 to 1911, week two of July,' Rozier went on briskly. 'I've asked him to haul them up and wheel them in. If you'd like to take a seat at the reading table over there I'll come round and scan them with you. Know what you're looking for, or are we just browsing?'

'I know exactly. A name. The name of a village.' Joe pre-sented his problem as an enquiry for a missing person. He added his invention of the question of an inheritance which seemed to go down well with listeners.

'A girl from one of our villages . . . Hmm . . .'

Joe had gently stressed the local aspect of his problem and embroidered on the aspect of mystery.

'Hang on a minute, I'll call for coffee. How do you take yours? Croissant with that? I usually have one at this time of the morning.' He yelled into the back quarters: 'Dorine! Nip next door and tell them to make it two servings of *café complet*, will you? Priority!'

The coffee arrived before the volumes and was served in heavy green china from the local café. A basket of croissants was a blissful sight to a man who'd not yet had time for breakfast and Joe helped himself with pleasure.

When the six bound copies of *La Voix* appeared on a trolley, Rozier handed the 1906 volume to Joe and himself took the 1911 one, sitting next to him at the table. 'Twice as fast this way. We'll start at opposite ends. If you can keep up a reasonable speed, we should meet up in July 1908. Now tell me what I'm supposed to be looking for.'

'I'm interested in a news item for a very particular area. Somewhere between here and Apt.'

'Shouldn't be too difficult. It's not Chicago! The inhabitants tend to lead God-fearing, well-ordered, excruciatingly dull lives. Try the centre pages first. "News from the Villages" section.'

Joe leafed swiftly through his volume and grimaced. 'See what you mean! Pig-rustling and chicken-snatching would appear to be the crimes of the month. We're looking for the week announcing the programme for the Bastille Day jollifications, remember. I've finished with this one. Pass me the next lot, will you?'

Rozier was working more slowly, constantly distracted by news items that rang a bell with him. 'Good God! So that's how the turd got started! You'd never credit what heights this chap's risen to! Député now ... Before my time, of course ... Ah! Storms over the area – that's what buggered up the vintage ...' His comments were salted with a vocabulary Joe hadn't heard since the trenches.

And then: 'Well, here's the programme for 1911. July 7th. Opera and plays on at the theatre ... folklore extravaganza on the Rocher des Doms, gypsy bands, dancing –

wouldn't you guess? – on the Pont Bénézet. Grand parade on the day itself. Now what are we *really* looking for?'

'Any reference to a priest by the name of Father Ignace. I need to know in which village he had his cure of souls.'

'Is that it? Couldn't you just have looked him up in whatever lists the Church keeps? They must know where their blokes are.'

'Well, apart from the fact that I have very little time available to me and you know with what speed the wheels of the Church turn when they're determined not to be helpful, I don't think my enquiries would get anywhere. Bit of an obstacle been raised . . .' he said conspiratorially. 'Whoever he was or is, this priest has been effaced from the records.'

'Oh, ho! One of those! No. Sorry. You won't find any record of him in here either then,' he said firmly, but Joe noticed that he was continuing to lick one long bony finger and scan the pages as he turned them. 'Catholic city, you know. The new Vatican in the new Rome from the fourteenth century when the popes took up residence here. The Palace has always been the heart of the city, a mighty and controlling presence. Anything disrespectful about the clergy just wouldn't get through on to the pages. A curé could go berserk, slaughter half his parishioners and rape the rest and you wouldn't read about it. Now, a bad olive harvest . . . Oh, Good Lord! Look here!'

The long finger was pointing to the centre of page 35.

'"Mysterious disappearance of priest from village",' he read. 'That's the headline.'

The much-loved curé of the church of St Vincent-les-Eaux, near Avignon, has disappeared in mysterious circumstances. Villagers report they had no warning of his departure and his superiors are unable to state what has happened to him or where he has gone.

It is understood that no steps had been taken to replace him or redeploy him.

246

His distraught housekeeper claims that the young priest, 29-year-old Father Ignace, who is as good as a son to her, had packed none of his things and had not called for his suitcase to be made ready.

Father Ignace, a renowned scholar and musician of note, is a lively and popular member of his village community and will be sadly missed, in particular by the young people to whom he was especially close.

'Heavens!' said Joe. 'Rozier, you replace one question with a dozen others! But I have what I was seeking – the name of the village. Now I can find traces of the young girl who was in his confirmation class in 1906. A certain Laure of St Vincent-les-Eaux! She's firming up. I'm getting close now.'

The editor snorted, reading the article again. 'Now how in hell did the old bugger get this one through?'

'I beg your pardon?'

'The pre-war editor, old Goutière. He took some risks! Must have stirred up a hornets' nest. He was in his last year here when I signed on. A raging red! Communist sympathies, you know. Anti-monarchist, anti-Church. You name it – he was against it. But especially the Church. He hated the authorities. Always scrapping with them. Getting back at them by inserting bits of innuendo like this one.'

'Innuendo?' said Joe. 'What am I not seeing?'

'Look at the last bit: "lively ... popular ... missed by the young ... especially close ..." Shorthand for taking advantage – sexually no doubt – of the young things under his influence. It had to be hand-under-the-skirt-stuff – I doubt fiddling with their minds would have got old Goutière excited. Everybody in the area would know how to interpret this but – clever old sod – there's nothing there that could trigger a legal challenge.'

'But the Church must have put the boot in,' said Joe, 'since this is the one and only reference to the priest. No follow-up, I'm told. Though it's not all that damaging. I'm surprised they got so hot under their collars.'

The editor had fallen silent, distracted. The finger pointed to a further column, level with, but at one remove from, the article about Father Ignace.

'What did you say the girl's name was?' he asked.

'Laure.'

'Ah. Not the same one then. But all the same, this is interesting. And may be exactly what upset the Church!' He grinned. 'Cheeky bugger! Do you see what he's done? On the same page! Look at the headline! "Mysterious disappearance of young girl from village". And – wouldn't you know – it's the same village! The depopulation of St Vincent-les-Eaux? Is that what we're looking at? Anyway, it's not your girl. It's plain Marie-Jeanne Durand who shows a clean pair of heels. Anxious parents call in the police, reporting the disappearance of their daughter. Ah – now she *had* packed a case. Her friends claim Marie-Jeanne gave them no reason to believe she was about to abscond.

'. . . Watch being kept at railway stations . . . Public asked to be on the alert for a five-foot-three-inch, slim, dark-haired, dark-eyed, seventeen-year-old. Well, that narrows the field to about ten thousand! And – here it is! – Marie-Jeanne was a member of the church and had been prepared for her communion by the village priest, Father Ignace, to whom she was thought to be very close. If she'd had something on her mind, she would certainly have confessed her problems to him. Father Ignace was unavailable for comment on the disappearance of his young parishioner.'

'Due to his own mysterious disappearance.'

'And the fact that he was himself most likely her problem.' Rozier sighed gustily. 'Bloody hell! It's Abélard and Héloïse all over again. Young girl falls for unattainable man. They *will* do it!' He shook his head in despair. 'I expect *he's* joined the Foreign Legion and *she's* a worn-out tart plying her trade on the streets of Paris by now. Have you got what you want?'

'More than I want,' said Joe, grasping the editor's hand. 'Sadly, much more. Monsieur Rozier, let me thank you for your excellent coffee, your life-saving croissants, your welcome and your invaluable help. I think you could just have ruined at least three lives.'

# Chapter Twenty-Nine

Orlando was loitering in the courtyard, kicking up the gravel on the path, when Joe drove up. He hurried forward to open the car door and started to speak the moment Joe turned off the engine of his Morris.

'I seem to have been appointed your sheepdog,' he grumbled. 'Jacquemin posted me here to warn you . . . alert you . . . It's the lord! He's come round from his morning sedative, according to his valet, and he's asking to speak to you. Jacquemin wants you to go straight up before it's too late. He's reported to be sinking fast. If you ask me, the Commissaire is a bit miffed that he hasn't been asked along to hear the last words himself.'

'I'll just dump this lot on Jacquemin's desk first,' said Joe. He leaned behind and picked up the file of notes from the hospital and the bag of Estelle's belongings. 'The lord'll stay afloat for a few minutes more. Possibly much longer than most of us expect and some of us want! And, don't worry, Orlando, whatever else he has to convey, I'm not expecting a confession to murder. I think a priest is what's called for. Has anyone thought to . . .?'

'Of course! There's one on his way. The Commissaire sent a car, would you believe! Glad to see you're so relaxed about it. The Commissaire's climbing up the curtains! Oh . . . by the way . . . thinking of priests . . . your expedition into Avignon . . . Anything interesting to report?' He rearranged the gravel nervously with the toe of his boot.

'Oh yes! Indeed! But no urgency to reveal all, I think. Not to a man who's been in possession of all the pieces of the jigsaw but one all along. Did you think I couldn't count to thirty-eight? I'll hear *your* confession later, Orlando!'

He hurried towards the steward's office, smilingly brushing aside anxious people trying to waylay him in the great hall. He noticed as he passed through that it was looking quite medieval in its noisy, colourful disorder. A gendarme was standing posted at the doorway, arms folded, watching the scene with an expression of disbelief.

Piles of bedding and cushions were littering the floor, easels had been set up under windows, children were playing a noisy game that involved racing around the pillars and screaming. Battling away at the far end of the space, Mrs Fenton was thumping away at a piano which had been dragged in from somewhere. A jolly English tune – *Country Gardens*, he thought he recognized – was being played in strict rhythm for the benefit of the two ballet girls. These two, lost in their activity, were exercising. Barefoot and clad in an improvised costume of rolled-up pyjama bottoms and shirts, they yet managed to be impressive. Joe paused for a moment to admire their lissom movements.

Loud-voiced and authoritative, the duenna was pacing about in front of them, banging occasionally on the floor with a stout walking stick. As Joe marvelled, she shrieked for a stop, railed at Natalia and demonstrated a position herself on light, precise feet. The bulky, insignificant lady was transformed. The girls listened and nodded and copied.

'I say . . .' the wail went up from Mrs Fenton. 'I adore Percy Grainger as much as the next man but that's eleven times I've played that piece! What about a little *Nutcracker*? *Sugar Plum Fairy*, anyone?'

'It's the siege of Lucknow without the bloodshed,' Orlando muttered.

'Where's de Pacy?' Joe asked.

'Still in a sulk, I'd guess. He won't come out of his quarters. He's had a huge bust-up with his cousin. At least that's what Jane says has sent him into a tail-spin. The servants have clearly not been directed to tidy up the mess. They're playing cards in the old pantry. It looked worse an hour ago. Then Jane came in and gave everyone a pep talk. Pulling together, keeping calm, putting on a good face for the French ... you can imagine the sort of thing. Ah! Here she comes.'

Joe hurried off down the corridor to the office.


'Here's the pathologist's report and here are the things they took from her body.' Joe placed the bag and the file on the desk and sat down opposite the Commissaire.

'Good man, your Lemaître,' Joe said. 'With interesting things to say. I'll tell you now – the most significant thing he had to report was that our girl was between two and three months pregnant. She would have been aware. And she had no drugs whatsoever in her system.'

Jacquemin seized the file and began at once to leaf through it. 'So, she was clear-headed when she went and laid herself down on that stone altar?' he muttered. 'How in hell did he ...? Hypnosis? What about mesmerism? Isn't that all the go at the moment in the music halls? Did the doc have any suggestions? They're worth hearing, you know.'

'He was as puzzled as we were ... are,' he corrected himself.

Jacquemin gave him a cold stare. 'You can leave this with me, Sandilands. Your presence is requested by the lord. Thinks he's dying.' He rolled his eyes. 'Again. His valet claims he's been doing this every month for the last year. And then he springs back again, hale and hearty, and asking why he sees nothing but long faces about him. But we'll humour him. You're to go up to his apartment at once. Try to get up there before the priest arrives and

252

forgives him for everything he's done ... makes him change his mind. And come straight back down here and report to me. Got your notebook? I shall want to hear every word of his confession to murder.'

Joe shook his head. 'That's the last thing I expect to hear from his lordship.' He checked his pockets for his notebook, helped himself to a pencil from a pot on the desk and went out.


'Bédoin!' Joe remembered the valet's name and greeted him with a serious face when the man opened the door to the lord's quarters. 'A sad business. I hear Lord Silmont wants to see me.'

'Indeed, sir,' murmured the valet. 'He wishes to make a full confession to you before he sees the priest.'

'Ah ...' said Joe. 'Am I to take it his lordship is experiencing a period of ... shall we say ... lucidity?'

'Complete lucidity. He's as sharp as a pin and feeling no pain for once. You arrive at a good moment. If all goes according to past form, he will present his normal self, though he's a little sleepy as yet. As the last of the soothing dose I gave him wears off he will become somewhat euphoric. And his behaviour less predictable. May I advise you to summon help and withdraw should you be overtaken by circumstances, sir? He is in no way restrained and experience indicates that it would not be wise to attempt to sit out the storm.' He put a small bell in Joe's hand. 'I will be next door. Summon me at once should his lordship become difficult.'

The lord was sitting up in bed, pale but cheerful and leafing through a copy of a Parisian colour magazine.

'At last! Sandilands swoops in! Glad you could come. Your sensation-seeking Parisian colleague was not best pleased by my request to unburden myself to you. But I can't say I fancied confessing all to that sour-faced, publicity-seeking Commissaire. He'd have me on the front of one of these rags before you could say knife!' The lord threw down the magazine in disgust. 'Gentleman that you are, I think you'll understand a gentleman's problems. We'll do this in French, if you don't mind? There may be nuances I couldn't convey in English.'

The walls of the spartan room were, as Jacquemin had told them, adorned by two of the world's artistic master-pieces and Joe deliberately kept his gaze from them, knowing that, once he looked, he would see nothing else. The lord must have his full attention. He turned his head resolutely away.

But his slight movement had not gone unnoticed.

'No! Do look! You'll never see another one so wonder-ful,' Silmont said, gesturing to the Van Gogh. 'You are aware of my problem?'

Joe nodded. 'You're suffering from the great pox.' He thought the old-fashioned name would be more acceptable than the modern clinical term.

'Then you'll know what I mean when I tell you that, should a man make an effort to understand the devastation of this disease, he could either spend weeks reading eminent physicians' writings on patients' symptoms or, Sandilands, he could spend one minute looking into that tormented face. I have done both. Believe me – the face has it!'

Accepting the invitation, Joe turned at last and stared into the wild, doomed, self-knowing eyes of the painting.

'He was at the asylum not many miles from here – you knew that? And there he produced some of his most mar-vellous works. I have been lucky enough to acquire a few of them. But this one . . . He gave it away, you know. To one of the warders . . . nurses . . . whatever you like to call them. The man didn't appreciate what he had and it spent many years in his attic, unregarded. I bought it from his daughter for a very modest sum. Sandilands, I could be looking into a mirror!'

'And the delusions which are symptomatic of the foul scourge you have suffered have directed your behaviour of late? You have contemplated – even carried out – acts which have been contrary to your nature? Acts which you must now confess to your priest?' Joe asked delicately. How much easier it would have been for him to accuse an out-and-out villain of his premeditated crimes and slap on the handcuffs. And here he found himself treading on eggshells around this damaged penitent, whom, despite his assurances, he could not truly understand.

'And to you. And I trust you to convey my confession to the Commissaire.'

'I'm listening. Would you like to start with the destruction of the effigy of Aliénore, sir?'

'It was Lady Moon who suggested it.'

Joe pursed his lips, uncomfortable with this contribution. 'Lady Moon, sir?'

'It's quite all right, she's not speaking to me at the moment.' Silmont's voice was all reassurance and reason. 'She's not even in the room. But when she does come and whisper in my ear, there's no denying her. She was at her most regal that night. Glowing, powerful. I could only obey. She had asked for a sacrifice. And what more suitable spot, Sandilands? The offering was to be carefully timed for the moment when the moon's beams illuminated the tomb top. I had to clear it of the original strumpet to place a choicer creature in her place. I knew the moment she arrived that the girl Estelle was the chosen one. And she was even there that night watching me as I crossed the courtyard. There was a moment of epiphany when I looked up and saw her. Her hair was lit up from behind, turned to a silver halo by the moon. My goddess had marked her out for me.'

'Estelle didn't identify you that night,' said Joe, in a matter-of-fact tone. 'Your mask – fencing mask, was it? from the box in the sports room? – and your cloak – which you so thoughtfully surrendered to me – did a good job.'

255

'Surrendered? To you? My cloak? What are you talking about? It's in my cupboard. Take it. I expect you'll want to examine it for evidence.' He seemed annoyed at the interruption and muttered on: 'Immaterial. She was the one. The harlot was taunting me – attacking me in the centre of my being, threatening the things I still hold dear – my position ... my family name ... my possessions. This promiscuous woman had to be got rid of before she could get her filthy fingers on my life's work. Before she brought down the curse of bad blood once again on the family.'

He looked anxiously at the door and his voice dropped as he made his accusation: 'She was conspiring with my cousin to be rid of me. He's not here with you, is he? Guy? You didn't let him up?' His voice was rising to a shriek. 'He's always treading on my heels, tripping me up, pushing me downstairs. No? You're sure?'

Joe hurried to reassure him that he'd come alone.

Jane Makepeace would have had a word for this display of the further disintegration of the lord's character. Tertiary stage neurosyphilitic paranoia or some such. Joe acknowledged he was going to have his work cut out to distinguish truth from vindictive imaginings.

'I decided to remove her,' the lord said more calmly. 'I always expected to be found out but – why care? I am dying. I would be dead before they could sharpen up the guillotine.'

'With a house full of policemen, sir, it was just a matter of time,' said Joe easily.

'It's close now, Sandilands. This may be my last lucid interval ... they grow shorter ... and why risk any false accusations lodged against me? The dead cannot defend themselves. So – I say now: the crime I committed, I was entirely free to commit. It was my statue to do with as I wished. And I wished to smash it into dust. But the girl? Much though I longed to plunge a dagger into her pullulating entrails, I was robbed of the opportunity.'

His voice began to rise alarmingly, his face was suffusing with rage. 'Who was it, Sandilands? My cousin declares he didn't kill the girl. And I must believe him – if he had, I know he would delight in telling me so. He's always gone faster and farther, climbed higher, ridden harder, had more women . . . He's the one who has the glittering war record, the respect and loyalty of the servants. If not Guy – then who?' he shouted again, struggling for control. 'Who first stole my scheme to kill, took my dagger, and snatched from me the satisfaction of forcing her dying breath out through her lying lips? You know, don't you? Tell me! I insist on knowing!'

The door opened slightly and Joe heard the valet cough a warning.

'Your priest is coming up the stairs,' Joe improvised. 'I must leave. But yes, I do know. Now. And I will tell you. By the end of the day. Do we have until the end of the day?' he asked, suddenly uncertain.

The lord favoured him with a beaming smile which chilled Joe to the bone. 'It's time for you to make your move, Sandilands,' he said. 'Bring me the name before the moon rises.'


How easy was it going to be to convince Jacquemin that the lord was innocent of any crime he could arrest him for? Joe thought – not very. Before he returned to face him, he decided to take a detour.

Not being quite certain where exactly in the building Guy de Pacy had his rooms, he greeted an approaching footman and asked him to take him to the steward's quarters. The man showed no surprise at the request and Joe had a clear impression that he was expected and this escort had been thoughtfully provided.

The man led him to a tower Joe had noted but not yet explored. The one diametrically opposite to the lord's. It was spacious. It rose to three floors, commanding a good view of the courtyard and the door giving access to the great hall. An excellent military choice for what was, Joe guessed, the command post of the château.

The manservant led him through the ground floor which had been left as an open space, largely plain and unfurnished, though the stone floor had been covered agreeably with a softening carpet of local weave. One boot-rack stacked with highly polished riding boots stood by the door and, at the far end of the room, a mahogany table held a cargo of two heavy wooden church candlesticks in which fat wax candles had been very recently lit and a matched pair of silver vases filled with bunches of white lilies. The scent in the enclosed space was overpowering.

A winding staircase led to a first-floor office with a stout oak door, the twin of the one in Petrovsky's apartment. The manservant knocked gently and entered. Joe hung back and heard him say: 'Excuse me, sir. I've got that Englishman with me. The policeman.'

And the gruff response: 'Tell him I'll see him. Just give me a minute, will you, Félix.'

There was the sound of furniture creaking, foot-stamping and nose-blowing, and Guy de Pacy appeared in the doorway, rubbing an unshaven face. 'Thank you, Félix. That'll be all.' Even red-eyed and black-bristled, he cut an impressive figure, Joe thought.

Joe went in and took the chair being pointed out to him. 'Forgive the squalor,' mumbled de Pacy, making a careless gesture around the room..

Joe looked for the squalor and saw that it consisted of one jacket flung around a chair back. Everything else was neat and comfortable, a working room supplied with arm-chairs and bookshelves. A phonograph standing in a corner was giving out a moody piece of Mahler that Joe thought he recognized. *Kindertotenlieder.* De Pacy hurried to lift the needle arm and turn the record off.

'Now – where in hell did *you* get to this morning?' de Pacy said, beginning to stride about the room. 'I was

258

looking to you to exercise some control over your fellow countrymen. Have you walked through the great hall? I peered in this morning and decided to leave them to it. Jacquemin thought it would be a good idea to keep the lot of them herded in together. Mad notion! He'll find he's got more corpses on his hands than he knows what to do with. By the end of the day, we'll be looking at the Black Hole of Calcutta! And I'm quite sure I don't care a button!'

The steward was talking in his bluff tone to fill a gap and distract Joe from an examination of his emotion-racked face.

Joe decided to have none of his nonsense.

'I was in Avignon,' he said. 'At the morgue. She didn't suffer, Guy, the pathologist assures me. She could hardly have been aware of what was happening to her. She looked very peaceful. I paid my last respects to Estelle and her baby.'

De Pacy uttered a strangled cry and went to collapse on the other chair, turning his face from Joe.

'How the hell . . .?'

'It's not usual to make the sign of the cross twice over a body. Not unless, perhaps, you understand a second tiny life to have been lost also.'

'My child,' said de Pacy. 'And I was only aware of his existence for one day. I say *his* because Estelle was quite certain that we would have a son. It might well have been a girl. Would they have been able to tell?'

The naive question wrung Joe's heart and made him feel uneasy. Responding with kindness to the man's grief: 'It's thought you would have had a son,' he lied. Somehow he judged the devious answer would bring comfort to this military man.

The vision of Estelle in her blue Worth dinner gown came back to Joe with a memory of her perfume and the elation he'd sensed in her. Elation not chemically achieved as he'd thought, by cocaine, but by love. Orlando had had it right. She was in love. And Joe was looking at the

259

object of her affections. Dishevelled and sniffling, de Pacy slumped in his chair and it was suddenly hard to see in this man the hero Estelle had clearly fallen for.

'She loved you very much, Guy,' Joe said quietly.

'How do you know?' The drooping head shot up. Far from distressing him further as Joe had feared, it seemed he'd triggered in de Pacy an eagerness to hear his reassurances.

'I was with her on that last night. The night she wore her blue gown. She took me on to the roof . . . No! In all innocence, I assure you, old man! To give evidence. To tell me what she'd observed from up there on the night of the statue-smashing. She had an assignation – with you, I think – and she dashed off to keep it. But not before I'd got the clear impression that here was a woman in love. Not a sight I've had any *personal* experience of, I confess. Something similar but not like this. Once seen, never forgotten. You have been a fortunate man, Guy, to have known such affection.'

A watery smile rewarded his insights. 'That was the last night we spent together. It was the night she told me. That she was having a child and that it was mine. You won't understand the feeling, Joe. News like that turns your life around. It can be devastating . . . It can be elevating. It made me twice the man I was. I was damn nearly destroyed by the war . . .'

To Joe's dismay, he began to peel away the grey kid glove from his right hand to show a twisted claw from which the skin had been burned away. The two men looked at it silently. De Pacy with revulsion, Joe with politely concealed embarrassment. In his tight London world, men did not go about revealing their war wounds. And, he suspected, in de Pacy's world also. He was being granted a sight of the depths of despair to which the man had sunk over the past two days and he steeled himself for further revelations.

'This isn't pretty but, by God, it's nothing compared with the state of my soul or whatever you like to call that inner spark.' De Pacy gave a bitter smile. 'I'm not a religious man, Sandilands, but I find myself using their vocabulary. I'm talking about that bit of us that is truly who we are. Is that the soul? Mine was atrophied like this claw. And then, one night, Estelle kissed my hand and burst into tears over it. And suddenly, what had been a bit of an unexpected fling for me became something far more serious. I knew I loved her. I asked her to marry me and she agreed. The future was suddenly in focus.' He looked about him wildly. 'I was ready to leave this suffocating place behind us, the years of servitude and subordination, and take off with her wherever she wanted to go. I'd even have gone with her to England. I have resources of my own. We'd have managed.'

He looked Joe in the eye. 'How did he find out, Joe? How in hell did my cousin know? We were so careful. It started out as a flirtation and then an indulgence and, before we'd realized it, we were in it up to our necks and there was no going back. At my age! But then they say that love, like the measles, catches you harder the older you are. And I had a bad case! I knew he'd disapprove. Send her away. Find a way to hurt her. We decided to affect a cooling off and put on a show of dislike for the audience. We'd spend our days staring coldly at each other and our nights in each other's arms. Estelle flirted with the other men – even you came in for a little attention – to put everyone on the wrong track and I pretended I didn't mind. I was sure Bertrand was fooled.'

'You were so afraid of your cousin finding out?'

'Yes. Bloody mad Silmont! He hated her, discovered what we had become to each other and killed her because of it. Why did he have to kill her? She didn't want any of this . . . his possessions . . . not any of it.' He waved his arms around. 'But I am his heir. He wouldn't risk her presence, her influence over me contaminating the estate. If I'd married her, I'd have been – in his eyes – bringing back an infection into the family.'

'You say you are his heir. Tell me, de Pacy – it may all be different in France – but what's to prevent him, on a whim, changing his will and leaving his worldly goods else-where? In England, cats' homes and donkey sanctuaries are known to thrive on last-minute changes of mind by vindictive old maniacs.'

De Pacy glanced briefly at a file on a top shelf and smiled. 'Don't be concerned. All arrangements are made and will be executed according to the law. And should there be any awkwardness about possessions I could call on the testimony of a specialist in Paris whom I insisted my cousin consult some time ago. The demented have no more legal powers than they have in your country. He knows this. He knows Silmont will be mine. He couldn't bear the thought that a golden-haired, foreign and – I admit it – promiscuous girl, the image of Aliénore, should share it with me. That *her* son might inherit one day.

'I'm warning you, Sandilands – he's not going to get away with it! If you don't take his rotting carcase away from here, I'll finish him off myself. But – don't be con-cerned! I'll kill him cleverly . . . neatly. You won't be called on to arrest me.'

'No need for that, Guy. No need for violence of any kind. Calm down! Your cousin didn't murder Estelle. I have myself confirmed his alibi. He it was who smashed the statue as a prelude, indeed, to offering up Estelle as some mad sacrifice to the full moon. But he was thwarted. His plans went awry. He was in a paroxysm of fury when he returned from his bridge-playing session to find someone had beaten him to it. And using the very method he'd planned himself.'

'You're sure of this, Sandilands?'

'Completely.'

'Then, if I am to accept this . . . and I suppose I must . . . what are we to understand? That someone in this household has been aware of everything from the beginning?'

'Yes,' said Joe quietly. 'You're right. Someone here has been close enough to Silmont to wriggle inside his diseased brain and follow his sick thoughts to their conclusion. There's some human spirochete about – someone in our company who's as mad as he is.'

'Hideous thought, indeed, Sandilands.'

Joe got to his feet and prepared to leave. He gestured to the phonograph. 'I'll leave you in peace with your grief,' he said. '"Wenn dein Mütterlein", wasn't it, the song I interrupted? . . . *Oh, light of your father's life – a joy lost too soon.* I don't have that quite right – but near enough, I think. My condolences, de Pacy.'

De Pacy looked uncomfortable as he murmured his thanks. 'You know who it is, don't you?' he persisted, walking to the door with Joe.

'I'm almost certain. But I do nothing without firm proof. And this I hope to have in my possession,' he smiled and continued, 'before nightfall. Or I risk the grave displeasure of Lady Moon and her devoted acolyte!'

De Pacy groaned. 'Much longer in this madhouse, Sandilands, and you'll be as barmy as the rest of us. Hang on to what's left of your wits, man!'

Joe walked swiftly down the stairs to the reception room where the manservant was standing waiting by the door.

'Thank you, Félix, I'll find my own way back.' And he added, in a spirit of mischief: 'I think you may extinguish the candles now. And – leave the door open for a blast of air, would you? One could choke on the funereal fug in here.'

Joe stepped outside into the sunshine, seized on his sanity with both hands and breathed in a deep, clean lungful of the breeze blowing from the pine-clad hills.

# Chapter Thirty

Joe stood for a moment, trying to shake off his bleak mood, and was surprisingly uplifted to spot a familiar figure in a red-striped dress striding over the drawbridge and heading towards him.

'Dorcas!' he shouted and went to meet her. On impulse he seized her and swung her round his head like an infant. 'You arrive in time to save my sanity, child!'

'Gracious, Joe,' she said, wriggling to the ground. 'What's got into *you*?'

'Other people's madness is what! I'm reeling from a double dose. And your fresh face is just the antidote I need. Shall we fire up the old Morris, climb aboard and leave them all behind to kill each other off? I think it might be a kindness in the long run.'

'Oh, I see! No arrests yet, then? I was hoping you'd have someone in a dungeon by now and be sounding the all-clear for the boys to come back.'

'Not yet. But I do know who planned and carried out Estelle's murder. My hands are tied in the matter. I can only report my suspicions to Jacquemin and leave the heavy stuff to him. But, tell me, miss – what are you doing up here? Have you deserted your charges?'

Dorcas smiled. 'That officer who's been asked to guard us all was an inspired choice! He's a country boy and he's set himself to chopping logs, repairing the out-house roof, feeding the chickens. The boys follow him everywhere, adoring. They have no father, you know, though they remember him. And their grandmother's a widow too.'

'And how are you getting along with the old girl?'

A broader smile greeted the question. 'She's wonderful – compared with the granny fate dealt *me*! She's their father's mother and took them all in when Monsieur Dalbert died – belatedly – of wounds he got during the war, three years ago. She's well able to keep the boys safe and entertained. It's a small house and I thought I might be in the way but I think I made myself useful.'

As they spoke, they were making their way over to the great hall. 'Look, Dorcas,' Joe said hurriedly. 'I've been busy but not so busy I've forgotten about your ... er ... commission. In fact I was in Avignon this morning in pursuit of your instruction, searching the archives of the local paper.'

'With any success?'

'Yes. Great progress! I have your mother's name. I know the name of her village. It's just a few miles down the valley. I thought I'd go and make some enquiries this afternoon if Jacquemin can spare me. We're close, Dorcas. Very close.'

Dorcas stopped, turned and looked him straight in the eye. This honest gaze, he'd discovered, was usually followed by a whopping lie and he prepared himself to hear one. 'Listen, Joe. For once, I'm going to say something sensible. Something you'll want to hear. I've been thinking. You have far too much on your plate. Truly important things. It would be selfish of me to expect you to go on searching on my behalf and I want you to stop now. That's really what I've come up for ... to tell you this.'

Joe listened on, waiting for an explanation.

'I want you to forget what I told you and that I ever asked you to find my mother. I've thought about it some more and I've come to a conclusion – that if I did find her, it would all be a mess. She mightn't want to see me. After all, she *did* go off and leave me to be brought up by Nanny

Tilling, didn't she? She almost certainly wouldn't want to see Orlando again. I expect his annoying ways were what drove her away in the first place.'

'You're not telling me everything, are you, Dorcas?'

She began to find the toes of his shoes especially interesting and was no longer able to meet his eye. Was she about to tell the truth or sink to a lower level of fibbing? 'I think I don't want to find her, after all. Seeing the boys – the Dalbert family – close up . . . well, it made me think a bit. These villages – they're all much the same. If we found her perhaps I'd have to spend some time with her and whatever family she has. It would only be polite, wouldn't it? I mean – "Hello, I'm the daughter you left behind thirteen years ago . . . Well, I could just stay a few minutes to get reacquainted . . ." It wouldn't do. Would you think me a spoilt little twerp, Joe, if I said my heart would sink at the thought of living here? It's not my place. It seemed to me that I had two choices and each ruled out the other one. I can't have two lives in two different countries. And I'd die if I didn't have Orlando and my brothers and Rosie and Aunt Lydia. And, before you say it – why didn't I think of this before?

'Well, I did. Of course I did. But staying here – it's changed the balance somehow. And I think I've done a bit of growing up. There are other people in this equation with me, Joe, and I can't cancel out their thoughts and feelings. They're every bit as important as mine. I'm selfish but I've seen the error of my ways. I'm sorry I've wasted your time.'

'They do say you should be careful what you wish for . . .' he replied. 'It's not my place to offer advice or tell you what to do. I was enjoying the chase, I must admit, but I abide by your wishes. And don't worry about the time. No charge! Consider instructions revoked. Sandilands off watch. Now go and find your family. The children are driving poor Orlando round the twist!'

She heaved a sigh of relief and started to skip away.

266

Oddly, she hadn't even asked him to tell her what her mother's name was.

He hoped his quick compliance with her wishes at least hadn't raised her suspicions.

He called her back: 'Dorcas! I forgot to say – it's good to have my assistant back. I've been missing you!'

She turned a suspicious face on him. 'What do you want, Joe?'

'Well, if you're offering, there is one small thing. Could you, before you get involved with the circus you'll find in the great hall, just sneak upstairs? There'll be no one about. There's something I want you to check for me . . .'


Jacquemin was all smiles and efficiency when Joe returned. He patted the neat pile of pathologist's notes in front of him on the desk with satisfaction.

'Well! All just as we expected. And the bonus of a motive for murder. Blackmail. It's a blackmail attempt that turned sour. Someone didn't want to be revealed as the father of this child. Or to pay Miss Smeeth to keep her mouth shut. A child conceived – let's say – at the beginning to the middle of June. Eight weeks gone out of a forty-week pregnancy.'

'Oh, you have forty weeks in a French pregnancy?' Joe enquired, smiling. 'In England it's generally reckoned to be thirty-eight.'

'Whatever it is, we're thinking that the perpetrator had to be one of the men – or menservants . . . there are some very well-set-up young fellows amongst the ranks, had you noticed? – who were in residence here in the fortnight or so after her arrival. I've compiled a list. The Lord Silmont heads the list of runners and riders, as you see. Though *physically* he carries quite a handicap. Can you imagine –'

'Let's not try,' Joe interrupted.

'Well, let me have your guesses. Go on – tell me which bloke your money's on, Sandilands.'

267

Joe took the list from him, picked up a pencil and circled a name.

'Guy de Pacy? Bugger me! What makes you say that?'

'I don't say that – *he* does. Pin your ears back, Jacquemin, and hear the confidences and confessions I've just had thrust at me by these two warring gentlemen. You're going to enjoy this!'

After twenty minutes of question, answer, speculation and reference to Jacquemin's copious notes, Joe caught the Commissaire's eye over the littered desk and risked a sly smile. The smile was reciprocated. At least the moustache twitched briefly in a not unfriendly manner. An acknowledgement, finally, that the two men were working together. At different rhythms and with different methods but working satisfyingly towards the same objective.

'We're nearly there, Sandilands,' the Commissaire said. 'It's a jigsaw and we're looking for the last piece. Where to look?'

'I usually find it down the back of the sofa or under the table,' said Joe. 'You have the notes on interviews with the inmates? Did you have time to get through them all? There are two witnesses in particular I'd like to hear from.'

Jacquemin indicated a box packed with notebooks and papers. 'Yes, everyone. Ready to be typed up at HQ. I thought we'd keep them here in case we need to check something. We've got sketches of the crime scene – Martineau has a flair for that sort of thing – everybody's fingerprints have been taken and rushed off to Avignon. Photographs also have gone to the laboratory. Everything done by the book. The answer's in there.' He sighed. 'We're just going to have to grind through it again.'

'Did you check the contents of the brown attaché case?' Joe asked. 'What have you done with it? Nathan Jacoby and I didn't disturb the contents when we found it at the scene. Left it for you. I just noted that it contained the red dress and espadrilles she'd taken off in the chapel. I presumed she'd smuggled the white nightdress and satin slippers in that way. Jane said she'd seen Estelle carrying it minutes before she disappeared – she remarked that the girl looked as though she was taking off for the weekend, case in hand. Too much to hope for a note in the dress pocket – *Meet me at six in the chapel, your lover, Pierre-Auguste, head stable-lad*, or some such?'

Jacquemin scrabbled about under the table, picked it up and passed it to Joe. 'Here, check for yourself. We found nothing.'

Joe eased the shoes and the folded dress out of the case and examined it. It smelled delicately of her perfume. The rest of the case contained no surprises. He replaced it on the floor next to the package he'd brought back from the hospital.

'I say – did you have time . . .?'

'No. Not yet,' said Jacquemin. 'Shall we do that now?'

He cleared a space on the table top and carefully upended the bag. Out spilled the white garment, folded to show its bloodstained section on top, and a pair of knickers. The garments were accompanied by a sheet of paper and a brown envelope. The brief note, typed by the pathologist's assistant, listed three items. Jacquemin read it swiftly: 'One: dress . . . Two: undergarment (one piece only) . . . and Three . . .' He froze and looked across at Joe.

'Open up the envelope,' he snapped. 'Something odd going on here!'

Joe tore open the flap, tipped out the contents and stared. 'That's it!' he muttered. 'The missing piece. It was under the table, Jacquemin. Let's hear what the good doctor has to tell us, shall we?'

Jacquemin began to read out the accompanying notes. 'He starts with an assurance that we may handle the object – it's been tested for fingerprints, revealing three different subjects. These are being compared with records of prints they've been promised from the force at the château and they'll send word when they have a result. It was found grasped in the victim's left hand. Unremarked by the officers discovering and transporting the body because rigor had preserved it clenched in her palm. It fell to the floor when the period of rigor relaxed her limbs on the pathologist's table. Well, bugger me! Remind me, Sandilands. How were her arms placed when you found her?'

'Like this.' Joe demonstrated. They were crossed over each other just underneath her bosom, exactly imitating the statue. He picked up the small round object in his left hand and crossed his arms again, left under right. 'Well tucked up, you see. Quite invisible.'

'It wasn't hypnosis or mesmerism that got her on to the slab, lying perfectly still, eyes closed, smiling gently, was it?' said Jacquemin. 'It was something much more simple. All the killer had to do was ask nicely.'

'Nathan Jacoby had it right, you know,' said Joe thoughtfully. 'While we were standing looking at her, he said Estelle would do anything for a joke. He sneered at her English voice . . . *Oh, do let's! What a cracking jape!* or something like that. And that's the only impulse that would have led her to offer herself up without resistance. She was all co-operation! Imagine – someone suggests to you what a laugh it would be to make use of the cleared space on the altar top to stage such a scene. A beautiful girl lying in exact imitation of the alabaster lady, next to the six-hundred-year-old knight. But this one, recognizably someone known to whoever their chosen audience was to be – someone still very much alive . . . at least at the moment the shutter clicked – that *would* be entertaining. Because that's what it was all about. A sick English joke.

'It's just the sort of nonsense you see printed in the society magazines every week back home. It's all the rage to have yourself photographed in some surreal pose in fancy dress. Inside a mummy case, on top of a gatepost . . . Cartier-Bresson, Man Ray – they wouldn't have been able to resist either. So, laughing together, Estelle and the would-be photographer meet in the chapel.'

'Just as the child reported,' said Jacquemin.

'Yes, indeed. Inconveniently, Estelle spots the child Marius in some distress and takes the time to haul him in, with a view to sorting him out when the little photographic session is over. Thinking his presence may not be entirely appropriate to the occasion – what with the disrobing that's about to occur – she hides the small person in the confessional and proceeds with the lark. She changes into her white costume, clambers up and assumes the recumbent position.'

'She took her clothes off, right there in front of her killer?' Jacquemin wondered.

'Again – there's the aspect of *intimacy* in all this. I don't think Estelle would have stripped off so readily in front of someone unfamiliar. And the photograper armed with camera . . . and concealed knife . . . encourages: *That's just perfect. Hair spread. Dress folded just so. Feet on the greyhound. Eyes closed. We're ready. Oh, drat! Could you just hold my lens cap for me? Thanks, darling.*

'The moment her eyes are shut and she's keeping rigidly still, the camera is put down, the dagger picked up. If Estelle is conscious of her companion leaning over her, manoeuvring, arranging, breathing deeply perhaps – well, that's photographers for you. And that's a photographer's model for you! She spent her days keeping still in strange poses. The killer can take as long as necessary to position the point exactly where it will do its swift job, Estelle won't move, because she trusts her killer absolutely. She's smiling, enjoying the joke, possibly even muttering: "Oh, do get on with it!"

'A second later it's over. She probably died instantly, according to the pathologist.'

'And in the excitement of the moment, and the urge to make a swift exit from the scene, the lens cap clutched in her left hand is forgotten,' Jacquemin muttered. 'But why ask the victim to hold it in the first place?'

'Do you take photographs?' Joe asked.

'Never. I get someone to take them for me.'

271

'I can tell you – lens caps are a damned nuisance. They have to come off at the last moment and be put straight back on again. And is there ever a safe place to park them? Leave them lying about and they get lost or trodden on. There was no flat surface available at the tomb if you remember it. And the appearance of a lens cap in the shot would have ruined the gruesome medieval flavour somewhat. No – the thing to do is what I always do – put it into the nearest available hand. They always remember to return it.'

'Unless they've died clutching it. Hmm . . .' Jacquemin poked at the insignificant object on the table with a pencil. 'Well, Sweet Cecily Somerset! I told you I'd find your wretched lens cap! I'll take pleasure in returning it. You won't thank me for the arrest warrant for murder that accompanies it, though.'

Joe frowned. 'We know *how* it was done. But before we say who did it, we need to find out why, Jacquemin. Why. There has to be a desperately strong motive for plunging a dagger into someone's chest. Cecily? I very much doubt that –'

He was interrupted by a tap on the door. Martineau came swiftly in, his face flushed with excitement. 'Sir! Commander! You're wanted at once up in Jacoby's studio! He's got the prints of that film you gave him to develop. The one we took out of Cecily what's-her-name's camera.'

# Chapter Thirty-One

The handwritten notice on the door – 'No admittance. This includes you, Jacquemin' – was greeted by a harrumph of outrage and a pounding with a fist by the Commissaire. Nathan opened the door after what he considered a suitable interval and the three policemen stepped tentatively into the work room.

It was hot and dark and stank of chemicals. Every dimly discerned working surface was crowded with bottles, jars and trays. Strips of celluloid dangled from the ceiling and the whole room was lit by an unnatural red light. Seen so illuminated from above, Nathan's mischievous features would have given Frederick inspiration for Beelzebub, Joe thought. He was playing with them, of course. The red light was switched on merely to establish his alchemical credentials, his mastery of the space.

They had interrupted no photographical procedure and Nathan replaced the red with the white room lights the moment he judged the intruders had been sufficiently impressed. He seemed pleased with himself.

'Don't touch anything and mind where you put your heads and feet,' he warned. 'All developments a success. I've made prints from the negatives in the two Kodaks, from the slides of my Ermanox and Miss Somerset's Leica. Right! First in the programme – overture and beginners. The pocket Kodaks, gentlemen.'

He set out two rows of photographs on the bench in front of them.

'I've forgotten which is whose but I think they're inter-changeable,' he said.

'Café terrace ... that's in Aix ... le Mont Sainte Victoire ... the Dentelles ...' said Jacquemin. 'Landscapes. Some, I see, with added figures.' He peered more closely. 'What is going on here, Sandilands?'

Joe peered alongside. 'Picnicking? Would that cover it?'

'Mmm ... *le déjeuner sur l'herbe* seems to be a popular theme with you English.'

'Well, you know the slogan: *A friend, a memory and a pastime – a Kodak,*' said Joe, smiling. 'Next exhibit, Nathan?'

'Now the Ermanox. My camera. See here: I want you to take a careful look at these. First the pictures taken in the chapel on discovery of the body yesterday.'

He spread out on the counter in front of them the eight reproductions of the Ermanox slides. They were numbered one to eight.

'Well? What can you see?'

'I'd no idea you'd got these,' grumbled Jacquemin. 'Why didn't you tell me? That's withholding evidence. Chalk another one up, Martineau. Oh, and I'm taking these away with me. Very handy. It'll be some time before we get ours back from the labs. What are we supposed to be seeing? Come on, man, it's no time for a guessing game.'

Joe saw at once. 'We're meant to look at the *quality* rather than the subject, I think.'

A quick nod from Nathan confirmed this.

'The first four were taken by a keen amateur,' Joe said with amused self-mockery, 'and they'll just about serve – as a record. But the second four were taken by a profes-sional hand and, if the subject were not so lugubrious, could take their place in the pages of *Vogue* magazine. I see I must get in closer next time, Nathan, and focus up more precisely.'

Jacquemin peered again. 'It was you two clowns! Now, I can see that. Get on.'

'Just preparing you for the next lot. Now – I want you to

keep in mind what you've just seen,' said Nathan with the encouraging tone of a stage conjuror.

He removed the prints of Estelle's death scene and began to place on the counter another and clearly inferior set, one by one.

'This is the film from the Leica belonging to Cecily Somerset. Number one, crossing the Channel. Rough day? Impossible to keep the camera steady at any rate. Number two. Arrival in France. Water calm but we still have the shakes. The strip of grey matter along the top half-inch is the French coastline. The other five and a half inches are the sea. Number three: jolly group of friends posing at the front door of the Hôtel Ambassadeur in Paris. Pity about the passing cycle. Numbers four and five: a selection of the guests at Silmont. You'll recognize yours truly, well, half of yours truly, far left on the second one. Cecily herself does not appear. Behind the camera, evidently ... And still shaking and still trying to find the f-stop ring.

'Change of subject for six to twelve. Flowers. They all seem to be roses.'

'*Rosa gallica, Rosa mundi, Rosa damascena* ...' Jacquemin pointed out the ones he could identify. 'My grandmother's dining room was lined with Redouté's best. I spent many a boring Sunday lunch memorizing the names.'

'And here's one I know,' said Martineau. 'Hard to tell in black and white but I think that's the white rose of Provence.'

'She made an excursion to a Cistercian abbey near here. It has a collection of old roses,' said Nathan.

Jacquemin was beginning to paw the ground with impatience.

'There were six more exposures,' said Nathan, suddenly serious. He snapped them out one at a time in a row. Again, each print had a number in the corner.

'Great heavens!' Martineau broke the stunned silence. 'Shall I go and bring her in, sir?'

\* \* \*

275

'Wait! Wait! I think our friend Jacoby has something more he wishes to impart? Go, on, man, we're listening.'

'Number thirteen is a shot of the chapel. Taken from the side nearest the dry moat – the east. Probably taken from a balanced position halfway down the far slope. An unusual perspective but out of sight of the rest of the castle. And, looking at the shadows, you can see that the sun is in the south-west and getting low. What we have here is an – accidental? experimental? – essay in *contre jour*. I think, gentlemen, if you go and scramble about in the moat on the far side of the chapel at just before six this afternoon, you'll see exactly the same shadow lines.

'Number fourteen is interesting for its detail. The camera has now moved a few yards on towards the corner and is pointing across the south side of the chapel and over the courtyard. If you look carefully you can just get a glimpse of the stable clock in the distance, between two roof lines. I wonder if this was intended?'

Martineau selected a magnifying glass from a tray on the counter and handed it to the Commissaire.

'It's saying six o'clock, near as dammit,' confirmed Jacquemin.

'Next up is number fifteen. An unfussy view of the great door. Clearly we go through it and here we have, at number sixteen, a shot of the table-top tomb.'

'We're being taken for a walk,' Martineau observed.

'Let's hope it's not a ride,' muttered Joe.

'And the tomb, you'll see, has only one occupant which dates and times the photographs quite narrowly. Sir Hugues is lying there by himself next to the rough patch of stone where his wife had previously lain. But it's numbers seventeen and eighteen that are the clinchers, I think you'll agree?'

'Good God!' breathed Martineau. 'Are they the same? Have you done two prints from one exposure, Jacoby?'

'No, he hasn't. They're different. Very slightly,' said Jacquemin with benefit of magnifying glass. 'A whisker of a difference in angle. And again, Jacoby, we must ask – intentional? I'd say they're separated by a second or two. No more . . . Very similar to the Ermanox set we've just seen. Look at the blood pattern. She's not play-acting. She's definitely dead. Can you enlarge the wound area, Jacoby? From such a film?'

Nathan produced further reproductions of the last two shots. 'I thought you might need these.'

Martineau peered again. 'Ah, yes! I thought I could just make out . . . The blood . . . Here, Sandilands, take a look. There's a greater quantity on the second of these shots. Not much but enough to make it out. And unless our friend here has been working some of his magic . . .?'

Nathan looked aggrieved and shook his head vehemently.

'It's caught a highlight. The blood's still shining. These shots were taken moments, seconds, after the girl was stabbed. While the heart was pumping its last. While she was still expiring.'

A silence fell and, in the hot room, three men shivered.

Martineau spoke first in a deadly voice: 'Now shall I go and get her, sir?'

'In a moment. We'll definitely have a few questions to put to Sweet Cecily but, if I'm not mistaken, Mr Jacoby has a further point to make?'

Joe was sure that Jacquemin had seen the truth as quickly as he had himself and was, with unexpected generosity, allowing Nathan to take the stage again to give his expert opinion. Or to check his own conclusion.

'The first set I showed you – Joe's efforts followed by mine – made it quite clear that the hand holding the camera, the eye behind the lens, is always individual. I can see the differences in style as clearly as one artist can identify another by his brush strokes. It's like handwriting. But it only works when you're familiar with the photographers, of course. Here, I'm working in the dark. I assume the first five to have been taken by Cecily. Careless, expecting the camera to do all the work. Jolly snaps for the album. Really – she'd have been better off with a five guinea Kodak. The next group, the flowers, showed an improvement. Learning had occurred. Perhaps she finds it easier to get the measure of inanimate objects? But the last six –'

'Were taken by someone different!' exclaimed Martineau. 'Even I can see that! They're not perfect . . . I mean, they're not a professional job like Mr Jacoby's but they're well focused up and framed and . . . well . . . not arty, but sort of businesslike. By someone used to holding a camera and the right sort of brain to operate it.'

'And the cool nerve of a sniper,' Joe added.

'Are we thinking: Cecily Somerset? Most probably not. Ask the lady politely to meet me in the office in ten minutes, will you, Martineau? And tell her nothing of this. I'm sure we'll all be interested to hear her answer when I ask her to whom she lent her apparatus on the day of the murder,' said Jacquemin.

# Chapter Thirty-Two

Cecily stood in front of the desk, facing up to the Commissaire and Joe, while Martineau sat in an opposite corner of the room taking notes.

In a swift discussion on the way down, the two officers had come to an agreement on technique. The Commissaire was to be obviously in charge of the interrogation, directing his English *confrère*. He made it clear to Joe that he wished to appear remote, implacable, dangerously foreign. Joe's: 'Oh, I say – are you sure you can you pull that off?' had received the frozen stare.

The interview was to be conducted by Joe in English. The Commissaire's knowledge of the language was perfectly adequate for an understanding but he shied away from the notion of speaking it himself. 'We must catch every nuance,' he declared. 'And Miss Somerset's French is worse than my English. We will see how we get on.'

'Yes, Sandilands, I can identify that camera as mine,' stated Cecily, pointing to the Leica on the desk in front of her. '*Again*! It can tell you itself – look at the name on the strap. Come off it, Commander! I've done all this already. For that Frenchman.' She glared at Jacquemin. 'Is he deaf? Or just being French? Shall I shout louder?'

'Just a formality, Miss Somerset,' Joe said mildly. 'Imagine you're in Scotland Yard, will you? Helping the police with a very tricky enquiry. Lieutenant, a chair for the lady, please.'

Cecily lowered her dungareed bulk on to the chair with

a suspicious glower that was meant to tell Joe she'd got his number and that English smarm was as unwelcome as French froideur.

'And this is how you can help us.'

He laid out the first twelve shots from her camera and invited her to inspect them.

A few moments of: 'Good gracious, I never thought you'd be able to do it! Develop them right here on the spot. I was going to take the camera back to London with me and have them done properly. I say, I won't pay for these, you know ... Oh, the roses came out well, didn't they? However did you manage ...?'

'We had a bit of luck. Nathan Jacoby spent some weeks working in the Leica laboratory in Germany,' Joe improvised. 'It was a piece of cake for him.'

'But I hadn't finished up the exposures,' protested Cecily. 'I'd only taken about half. Now what shall I do for the rest of the hol? I can't afford to waste half a film just like that, you know!'

Joe smiled. 'Well, why don't you come to some arrangement with your friend – the one you lent the camera to and who finished off the rest of the cassette?'

Her face lost its calculating expression, her voice its querulous edge as she replied after a long moment: 'Friend? What friend? Finished off ... I've no idea what you're talking about.'

'The second half of your film was used by someone else, Cecily. And we'd like to know to whom you gave permission to borrow the camera.'

'Borrow my camera! Never! Nobody! I wouldn't ... I didn't!' she protested. 'What's going on?'

Joe produced the shots of the exterior of the chapel and the door. 'These are the next three from your roll of film. Did you take them?'

'I've told you! No!' She turned to the Commissaire and said rudely: '*Non! Non!*'

Looking back at the photographs, she commented:

'What's the point of these, there's no people in them. And no flowers, which was the whole reason for bringing it. Why would I want to take a picture of a door? I didn't take these.'

'And yet they are there on your negative. We must assume someone helped himself or herself to your camera without your knowledge.'

'I'll have their guts for garters!' said Cecily, swelling with rage. 'Everyone knows my possessions are off limits! I made that quite clear when one of those Russians tried to make off with my nail scissors.'

'Tell me – where did you keep your camera?'

'In the general ladies' dorm. You know where that is. We each have our own chest of drawers. My camera was in the bottom drawer.'

'So anyone could have entered and taken it away for a few hours, replaced it, and you wouldn't have noticed it had gone missing?'

'Yes,' she admitted. 'I hadn't used it for at least a month . . . six weeks . . . too busy . . . and I can't say I've ever got into that silly habit of snapping everything in sight all the time. So common!' She thought for a bit and, encouraged by Joe's silent attention, ventured to say: 'Anyone could have helped themselves, you know. The maids are in and out in the morning and, as if that's not enough, they let a manservant come in to check that the maids have done their duty . . . at least that's what they say . . . And the steward checks on the menservants. It's like Piccadilly Circus. You yourself, Commander, are well placed to nip in and take it. Your room is just opposite. Or those children next door. Why don't you ask your niece Dorcas? It's the sort of thing she might do. And any one of those women I share with could have taken it. They all knew where it was.'

'Was any one of these ladies more likely than the rest to take it?'

'Oh, I'll say so! But you're going to have some trouble interrogating *her*! Estelle Smeeth. The dear departed. She hated me.'

'The reason for this hatred was . . .?'

'She couldn't take a bit of teasing, that's why.' Cecily's features took on an unpleasant truculence. 'She irritated me from the moment she arrived. I made a mess of her bed on her second night. Nothing much – just the usual dorm foolery. But Miss Smeeth didn't seem to have the background to understand or appreciate that sort of thing and – my! – did she ever overreact!'

'Are you saying she retaliated? She got her own back?'

'With knobs on!' Snorting with outrage, Cecily confided: 'She put a snake in my bed!'

'A moment . . . you're quite certain it was *Estelle* who did this dirty deed?'

'Well, who else? She'd never admit it. Tried to blame Jane Makepeace. But it was *her* bed I'd messed up. *She* was the one with a certain close association with the under-forester . . . that raffish, curly-haired one who delivers the rabbits. I noticed he always made an appearance whenever there was a sight of Estelle in the offing. And who else would be able to catch one and chop its head off? The snake, I mean. A completely overworked reaction, I think you'll agree, Commander?' she finished primly.

'Head? Off?' asked Joe faintly. He had a sudden sick feeling that the interview was spiralling out of his grasp.

Jacquemin shot a meaningful look at Martineau who was already scratching a note in his book.

'The maids were not best pleased to be called up to deal with it,' Cecily said frostily.

Having listened with a commendably inexpressive face to this embarrassing catalogue of English eccentricity, the Commissaire suddenly lost patience and leaned forward. 'Miss Somerset,' he purred in his heavily accented English, 'a Frenchman always keeps his word to the fair sex. I told you I would find and return to you your lens cap. And here it is.' He took it from his pocket and placed it in front of her.

Cecily picked it up and examined it. 'Oh, I say! Thanks so much. Yes, that's mine. Wherever did you find it?'

'Clutched in the dead hand of your friend Estelle,' he said in a doom-laden tone.

Cecily dropped it with a clink on to the floor and squealed.

'Interview over.' Jacquemin smiled. 'For now. I must ask you to hold yourself available, Miss Somerset, for our further entertainment.'


'I had thought better of the English, Sandilands! A nation that has given the world the Whitechapel Ripper, the Brides in the Bath Smith, the Royston Disemboweller, the Brighton Poisoner, should be ashamed to now offer us the hair-tugging and wrist-slapping exploits of a gaggle of overgrown schoolgirls!'

Joe looked at the cynical face and understood his opposite number. 'You're no more fooled by all this flummery than I am, Jacquemin. That was uncomfortable but it had to be gone through. And now, I think we could say we're moving in for the kill ourselves. The Silmont Slayer is within our grasp,' he added fancifully.

'A clever business,' commented Jacquemin. 'A blend of careful forward planning and on-the-spot reaction to favourable circumstances.'

'The qualities of the best generals,' Joe said. 'I've known a few such. Two of them were even French.'

'I can see when, how and who,' said Jacquemin. 'And certainly that will be thought to be enough to make an arrest. But I cannot yet see *why* it was done. And that concerns me. Where is the profit in it? Where the satisfaction?'

'I think I've got there,' said Joe. 'And I can tell you, the profit is great – and material: the satisfaction, twisted up as it is with thick strands of envy and vengeance, enormous. Bad blood, Jacquemin. It's a case of bad blood.'

# Chapter Thirty-Three

'Not now, Orlando. Things to do. Can't it wait?'

Orlando seized him by the arm as Joe, leaving the office, tried to push past him.

'No, it damned well can't! This is something you started and when you've heard me you'll perhaps have the good grace to say thank you. You may even admit that what I have to say will make your life easier.'

'Walk with me, then. I'm just going to the great hall to check that someone I'm interested in is still there in plain sight, obeying the rules. I shouldn't have asked Dorcas to go ferreting about the castle by herself.'

He quickened his step.

'No, you shouldn't! And, yes, this is about Dorcas. I managed to exchange a few words with her before she beetled off running your errands. I tried to countermand your order and told her to stay in the hall but she went off anyway. I begin to think, Sandilands, that she's too much under your thumb.'

'Is that it? I don't agree. That girl is under no one's thumb – not even yours. But I understand, sympathize, concur . . . whatever you want me to say. You're her father. Will you tell the child her position of Sorcerer's Apprentice has been terminated or shall I?'

'No, that's not it! That was a by-the-way remark. What I want to say – after due consultation with my daughter – is that we both, she and I, want you to desist.'

'Desist from what, precisely?'

'You know damn well what. I'm telling you to stop looking for her mother, Laure. She's lost and, after much thought, we've both decided that it would lead only to trouble and disturbance if you managed to find her. Go no further, Joe. Clear?'

'Clear. Look, mate, I'm inviting you to waste a few further minutes of my time and step into this room with me so that I can give you a dressing down without disturbing the castle.'

Joe pushed him though the open door of a games room and closed the door after them. 'You wouldn't want anyone to overhear what we have to say to each other, I think. There are chairs over there by the snooker table. Let's sit for a moment. And last time we sat knee to knee you looked me in the eye and told me less than the whole truth. You've been stringing me along ... To say nothing of Dorcas. Leaving us both to stumble about in a darkness *you* could have illuminated. That stops here and now. Imagine yourself in the confessional. There's nothing you can say to me that will shock or amaze me. Okay?'

'Okay. It was your snotty remark about thirty-eight weeks that got me thinking. The duration of a pregnancy. I was surprised to hear a bachelor knew that,' Orlando said resentfully.

'Part of the job. In fact it was exactly the puzzle of poor Estelle's similar condition that put me in mind of it. Yes – she was pregnant. Over two months gone. And, no, we can't be certain who the father was. With *your* known proclivities, Orlando, I should keep my head down and stay off the firing step until the guns fall silent. You'd be surprised how often a week or two either side of the critical day can lead to mayhem. Though in France I believe they grant themselves a little leeway and count to forty.'

'Yes, well, whichever it is, you've worked it out, haven't you?' Orlando said unhappily. 'I ought to have come clean.'

'I can see why you didn't. In your position, I do believe I'd have done the same,' Joe admitted. 'And *I'd* have been a bit more forcefully obstructive if a nosy Scotland Yard bugger had been hassling *me* with impertinent questions. So, all things considered, old mate, you come out of this, in my estimation, covered in glory.'

Orlando looked doubtful. 'Not much glory in this for anyone, I'd have thought.'

'But there is. I'm seeing a young, idealistic, carefree Englishman who on 14th July 1911 or thereabouts stumbles on an outcast girl, little more than a child, and takes her under his wing. Feeds her up, shelters her, paints her picture . . . gets fond of her.'

'You make her sound like a starving hedgehog. She wasn't a bit like that,' Orlando objected.

'But here's the bit that impresses me: the Englishman knows, because she tells him, or it's becoming obvious, that she's pregnant. And he takes her home with him regardless and cares for her. And the unknown man's child.'

Orlando stirred uncomfortably, then nodded.

'I know this child was born – because she's been so obliging as to write it in my birthday book – in January 1912. So, her mother got pregnant in May or June at the latest of the previous year. She must have been aware of her condition by the time she met you, and, indeed, this was most likely the reason for her being thrown out of the family home.'

'You have it right,' said Orlando dully. 'Dorcas is not my natural daughter. I have no idea who her father was – some village boy, I expect, or a sweet-talking travelling salesman – isn't that whom they always blame? But it makes no difference. No difference at all. She's my daughter. I love her more than most fathers can be bothered to love their daughters. And, I'll tell you something, Joe – if you ever breathe a word of this to her, I'll . . . I'll make your life hell! I'm not a vengeful man but I really think I might kill anyone who threatened my relationship with my children. Any one of them. And Dorcas is my eldest. Got that?'

'I have indeed. Understood. I could never think of her as anything else. But, Orlando, I work faster and dig deeper than you give me credit for. Look, old man, and tell me at once if you want to shut down this conversation, I think I do know who the father was. If you want to hear – it's up to you . . .'

Orlando considered for a moment then nodded. 'It might help. Not knowing is always worse than knowing.'

'Well, he lived in the village as you might expect but he wasn't the "village boy" you have supposed. He was young, handsome, intelligent, educated and something of a musician.'

'All that?' said Orlando. 'Well, no wonder *I* failed to impress!'

'He was also – a priest.'

'Good God! Not . . . not . . .?'

'Yes. Father Ignace who sounds as old as the hills was, in fact, only twenty-nine on the day he disappeared from the village. The same day Laure went missing. Except that she's really Marie-Jeanne Durand.'

'Oh, my poor, poor girl!' Orlando shook his head in sorrow. 'No wonder she could never tell me. The shame! She was genuinely a religious person, you know, from a devout family. It must have broken her heart and wrecked several lives. And I was always second best. She never quite managed to love me. She would never want to see me again.'

There was an uncomfortable moment as Orlando pondered and then he repeated: 'Please, Joe – no further. Promise? For Dorcas. She lost her mother years ago. I don't want her now to lose her father. Me, I mean. You know what she's like! If she knew the truth, she might take it into her head to skip off and go hunting down this mystery man. I couldn't bear to lose her. She must never be told.'

'I understand perfectly. Her uncle Joe wouldn't want to lose her either,' he said more cheerfully, getting to his feet. 'No further action on this front, eh?'

The two men shook hands solemnly.

Joe found his step was sprightlier, his breathing freer, a load of responsibility off his back, as he continued his interrupted path to the hall.

He needed all his new-found buoyancy to confront the mob.

He was greeted by a crashing wave of outrage. Suitcases had been packed, wristwatches were being ostentatiously consulted. Deadlines were being delivered.

'No right to keep us here!' Padraic Connell was standing by the door lamenting, ready for the off, pack on back. 'I'm expected at the abbey.'

'No right at all! The British consul must be informed!' boomed Petrovsky. 'I demand the return of our passports!'

'We're leaving this afternoon for Avignon,' announced Mrs Whittlesford, slipping on her gloves to underline her message.

'We sent a servant into the village with a note.' Derek's voice was triumphant. 'We've hired the charabanc. Anyone who wants to can climb aboard. It'll be here in two hours.'

'Stupid bugger!' said Fenton. 'You shouldn't have told him. He's hand in glove with the frogs! Now he'll ring and cancel it.'

'If Jacquemin needs to know anything more he's going to have to ask quickly. We've all suffered enough.'

'Dashed if we're spending another night under this roof!'

'Just waiting to be picked off! First it was Freddie, then it was Cecily. She's in a frightful state.'

'She has no cause to be,' Joe said. 'She's not been arrested. She was merely helping by giving information. I'll have a word with her.'

Someone pointed to a gesticulating figure enjoying the attention of a small audience. He made his way over and, smiling, asked her to step aside with him.

'Better for all, I think, Miss Somerset, if you stop stirring up dissent in the ranks. It's an arrestable offence in France.'

Caught in the act, Cecily hurried to comply.

'Now, can you tell me if Dorcas is here? Or Jane Makepeace – she'll do. I'd like to have a word with either of them.'

'I haven't seen Dorcas since yesterday and Jane . . .' She looked about her. '*She* seems to have been accorded special permission to come and go as she pleases. She's appointed herself go-between for the guests and de Pacy. She *was* here before you called me in for interrogation. Can't see her now.'

Joe cursed under his breath and began to look about him wildly.

'Oh! Speak of the devil – here they come,' said Cecily pointing to the door. 'Your two birds together! I wonder what they're hatching.'

Joe turned on his heel and hurried towards them. 'Miss Makepeace,' he said pleasantly, 'I was looking for you. Hoping you can do something for me. Could you possibly establish a little calm around here? It's all getting out of hand. Perhaps if you were to announce that everyone must stay here in the hall and be ready to hear a statement from the French police concerning their plans for departure, they might settle down.'

Jane smiled her understanding and began to clap her hands for attention.

'Dorcas, with me. Outside,' Joe muttered, pushing her back though the door.

'Well? Did you get what I sent you for?'

'No. It wasn't there.' She spoke quietly as they hurried along the corridor back to the office. 'I looked carefully but I knew it was a waste of time. I mean, this killer isn't going to leave evidence like that just lying about. Luckily for you

I'd guessed why you wanted it so badly and how it had been disposed of. I was caught in the act though! Jane Makepeace came in while I was standing in the middle of the dormitory wondering what to do next.'

'What did you do, Dorcas?'

'What I always do. Made up a story. I pretended I was just beginning my search not ending it and asked her if she could point out Estelle's drawers. I wanted to return a bracelet she'd lent me and didn't quite know where to put it. I took it off my arm as I spoke. She recognized it. It actually *was* Estelle's, you know.' Dorcas produced a slim rope of coral beads on a string from her pocket. 'I think it was convincing. Jane showed me Estelle's empty drawers. The police, she said, had been in and taken all her things away. They'd been packed up in her suitcase for sending back to England. And then she told me – very kindly, I thought – that the beads were supposed to be a good luck charm. Estelle had clearly given her good luck away with the bracelet and she thought Estelle would want me to keep it. Don't go bothering the Commissaire with a little thing like that, was her advice.'

Dorcas slipped the bracelet back around her wrist. 'Just in case,' she said. 'But that certainly tells us where the thing you're looking for fetched up, doesn't it?'

'Tell this to Jacquemin, will you?' said Joe grimly.


'Discipline's completely broken down, Jacquemin. You really can't keep them all here much longer. In fact they've given us a deadline. Four o'clock. Rather less generous than the lord, who specifies moonrise! The charabanc arrives then to take them to Avignon in time for the night sleeper to Paris. Orlando and his brood aren't hurrying off – they're planning a more leisurely take-off in the caravan. And Jane Makepeace refuses to abandon Guy de Pacy and the lord in their hour of need.'

'I ought to make an arrest before the bus arrives,' grumbled Jacquemin. 'We're not ready for this. We await the evidence of fingerprints from the lens cover and that's about all we've got. They may not send it until tomorrow.' He tore a clump of grey hairs from his moustache. 'It's no good – I can't proceed without a confession.'

'I can understand that,' said Joe. 'So – let's extract one, shall we? No guns, no thumbscrews, I think you'll agree? Lacking the scientific evidence, the only thing we have left in our repertoire is low cunning and deceit. I think we can manage that between us! But first, Dorcas has something to tell you.'

'Look, do we have to have this child in the incident room? Send her away, Sandilands.'

'No. You must listen to what she has to say.'


'You're asking me to unpack that lot?' said Jacquemin, glaring at Estelle's suitcase.

'Sir, Forestier packed everything while I made an inventory,' said Martineau, shuffling through a pile of papers. 'I don't recall any such item . . . Ah! . . . Here – look – items seven to nine in the clothing department. Brown skirt, black skirt, red print skirt. Any good?'

He dragged the case into the centre of the room and began the business of removing the strap and unlocking the fasteners. The packing was carefully done and halfway down he found what he was looking for. He held the garment up for inspection.

'Folded up neatly in the middle of the pile with her skirts. Black trousers. Soiled on seat and trouser bottoms with dust and plant matter, sir. Lady's.'

'Tall lady's,' said Dorcas. 'Here, let me show you.' She held them up in front of her. 'You see? You're looking for someone at least six inches bigger than I am. And Estelle was quite small. Only one inch taller than me, I'd say. This pair did not belong to her.'

291

'And how do you safely and discreetly dispose of an incriminating item in a building swarming with people . . . observant domestics . . . and the police expected any minute? You're not going to start a bonfire or put them in a rubbish bin. No. You slip them off as though changing for dinner, kick them away casually under the bed, and you put them away later in the drawer of someone who is in no position to deny ownership and whose belongings are being shipped straight out back to England,' Joe said. 'Here, let me have a closer look, Martineau.' He took the garment to the window and held it this way and that. He checked the label inside the waistband; he scratched at the fabric with a fingernail. Finally, he smiled and said: 'Leave them available on the desk, will you? That's going to be the first of my pressure points. The second . . . where did you put the lens cap?'

The Commissaire produced it in its envelope.

'Fine. Now pass me that sheet of headed paper I brought back from the lab with me, will you? A clean envelope? Large one?'

Joe sealed the lens cap and the sheet of paper inside the envelope and asked Martineau to write the Commissaire's name on the front in large, curlicued French handwriting. Satisfied with the look of his package, he handed it to Martineau. 'This is where you'll have to disappear for a bit, Lieutenant. Drive one of the police cars out of the court-yard and turn around. Dramatic crunch of running feet on gravel, please, and then, moments later, you bustle in waving this envelope. We'll take it from there.'

Martineau grinned and went out, checking that the corridor was clear.

After a few more minutes' consultation, Jacquemin stepped to the door and handed a chit to the two attendant coppers. 'Your instructions, Corporal. At once, please, and to be carried out in that order. Straight into my pres-ence, mind! No wandering off to be permitted on any

292

pretext. Assume imminent arrest and take appropriate precautions.'

One of them was back, rapping on the door in three minutes.

Jacquemin opened it himself, all gracious smiles. 'Ah! There you are, Miss Somerset. So sorry to have to haul you back in again so soon.'

# Chapter Thirty-Four

'He's lying!' Cecily shouted, pointing a finger at Joe. 'I haven't been inciting to riot! They were already rioting and if –'

'Calm down, please, Cecily,' Joe said agreeably. 'We just want some advice. We want to tap into your expertise if you'd be so good as to grant us a minute of your time. I've heard you spoken of as something of a botanist. You *are* an expert on the flora of Provence, I understand?'

'Oh, well, I wouldn't say –'

'I'm thinking now of the wild flowers, grasses, herbs – that sort of thing. Have I come to the right shop?'

His crisp and friendly tone found a response in her reply. 'Ask me. I'll try. Have you got a sample for me to identify? Is that it?'

'Not exactly. I just need an impressive-sounding name. Any low-growing, sun-loving wild plant particular to this part of Provence will do. The rarer the better. I want to impress someone with my knowledge.'

'Well, you'll be wanting a Latin name then or – how about a Provençal one? You could consider . . . um . . . well, my favourite name is the one they have for thyme. *Le farigoule* they call it around here. Creeping thyme – *Thymus serpyllum* – but that's not at all rare. Better still . . . Yes! Woolly thyme is the rather splendidly named *Thymus pseudolanuginosus.*'

'Perfect! Thank you very much. That's all. Now, will you go along with the corporal, Cecily? He's just going to ask you to step into the room next door with him to fill in a few details – forwarding address and suchlike. You'll be wanting us to send on your film when we've done with it. He'll only keep you a few minutes.'

Long enough to keep Cecily from view while the second officer appeared at the door with the second interviewee, he calculated.

A sharp tap and Jane Makepeace came in. She greeted them pleasantly. 'Commander. Commissaire. Well, it's eeny, meeny, miney, mo, this afternoon, isn't it? I wondered when it would be my turn to hear the clink of the cuffs.' And, catching sight of Dorcas seated behind the door: 'Oh, we meet again, Dorcas! Have they put you to sit in the corner? What have you been up to?'

'Miss Joliffe is here as a witness,' said Jacquemin.

'Sounds serious! What on earth have you witnessed, Dorcas, dear?'

'Nothing as yet,' said Joe. 'But she will witness an event in the coming minutes. She will have the dubious privilege, along with me and the Commissaire, of witnessing your confession to the murder of Estelle Smeeth.'


The spontaneous burst of laughter was disarming. It was not scornful, not nervous, not threatening. Yes, Joe admitted to himself, Miss Makepeace had a very nice laugh.

Jacquemin caught his eye and shrugged the responsibility for the interview over to Joe.

'Lord Joe! What's next on your script? I know – you're going to say: "The game's up!"'

'Do you agree to confess with no further ado to this crime or will you insist on hearing a full account of your movements and deeds on the day in question?' Joe asked.

'Neither. I have nothing to confess and I certainly haven't time to sit here and listen to the next instalment in your increasingly desperate flights of fancy. Busy woman, Joe! I have things to do. Objects and people to stick together, you know . . .' Her eyes flashed a warm and conspiratorial message to him. 'You'll have to try this out on whoever's next on your list. That'll be number four,' she said helpfully and made to turn for the door.

'Sit, mademoiselle!' Jacquemin bellowed. His right hand went dramatically to his pistol holster and hovered there just long enough to make Jane Makepeace swallow, glare and decide to take the seat offered.

'Joe, this goes too far,' she advised him. 'Enough's enough! You must call this attack hound to heel. Who does he think he is? Who does he take me for?'

'Miss Makepeace, we both take you for a killer. The killer of Estelle Smeeth. We're waiting to hear your confession.'

'I will say not a word further until I have my father's lawyer at my side, to offer counsel,' she announced.

'Well, you'd better tell him to attend you in the women's prison in Avignon,' said Joe. 'In about a month's time. They do things differently in France.' He had no idea what the rules were himself and was reasonably sure that Jane Makepeace knew even less than he did of the French legal system. Jacquemin backed him up with a sententious nod.

'The first thing the examining magistrate, after reading your confession (which we will note down), will want to know is *why* you killed Miss Smeeth,' Joe said. 'Would you care to rehearse it with us first?'

The answer came patiently: 'I've told you – I didn't. I liked her. I was her friend. Why would I kill her?'

'On the contrary, you loathed her and were jealous of her. But these feelings in themselves were not sufficient to incite you to murder. Your motive went beyond personal dislike. Miss Smeeth's death was a cold and clinical event, a step on your ladder to the goal you had set yourself.'

Jane appeared puzzled. 'Goal? And what do you imagine that to have been? To get myself arrested by the Police Judiciaire? For that is the only result I can see ensuing. I could have bumped off . . . um . . . Cecily or yourself with much less fuss, had I wished to provoke a pantomime of this nature.'

'It was a step in your progression. A death to fulfil the desire of a black and pitiless heart.'

Her lip curled. 'I never read penny dreadfuls and I don't want to sit here and listen to you regurgitating one.'

'I see I shall have to tell a convincing tale, Miss Makepeace, in blunt policeman's language. Not to satisfy you particularly – but a French judge. Where to begin?'

Joe had already decided on his beginning. 'With the clever, choosy and disillusioned woman who met last year an interesting guest at her father's dinner table. A French aristocrat. Lord Silmont. September, was it, Jacquemin, when the lord paid his visit to Harley Street? The stamps on his passport bear witness as do the labels on the medicine bottles in his cabinet. Do feel free, Miss Makepeace, to step in and correct me at any point. The talented daughter finds she has much to talk about with her father's elderly art-loving patient. He is impressed with her. He is a man who, by his own admission, enjoys collecting people as well as objects. He invites her back to work on his collection of antique possessions. Eager to escape the dim bowels of the British Museum with its masculine environment, its scramble for promotion, its petty jealousies, and spread her wings, she accepts.

'She's good at her job. She settles in and finds her surroundings congenial. More than congenial – she falls in love with the château and all it contains. The lord, aware that she understands his physical condition, trusts her doubly. But it is not the lord who intrigues her. It is his younger cousin. She becomes deeply attached to the future owner of the household she has already fallen for.

'She grows ever closer to Guy de Pacy, content to take her time and make herself indispensable to him. And she monitors the lord's advancing sickness. But then her idyll is disturbed by the annual irruption into the house of the summer colony of artists from whose efforts the lord

297

derives all manner of benefit. And one of their number, a pretty young model, sets her cap at the steward. Though skilled in the art of fending off female attention – Guy has his own demons to contend with – such is the allure of this girl that he finds himself swept off his feet and in the middle of an affair with the much younger woman.

'It has to be stopped. Our London lady – shall we call her Jane? – has a word in the ear of the lord. We must imagine the poison she drips in – "promiscuous, manipulative whore," may well have featured. The family name is threatened once more. Guy must be made aware. Brought back to his senses.

'Her ploy seems to be successful. A cooling-off ensues. Perhaps certain threats regarding testamentary dispositions were made? At any rate the two lovers are, from now on, left casting hard glances at each other across the table. Estelle, broken-hearted, flirts rather desperately with the other men to rekindle his interest but only makes things worse by doing so. Jane monitors the success of her tactics by becoming close to Estelle. The girl begins to trust her – Jane, after all, has some skill in drawing people out – and, with no one else to confide in, Estelle tells her new friend more than is wise.

'Meanwhile Jane is establishing her position in this little society. How often I've heard it since I arrived – "Oh, you'd better ask Jane . . . Jane will know . . . That's Jane's preserve – tell her." You asserted your authority,' said Joe, turning at last to confront her directly, 'in the dormitory in the matter of Cecily and her schoolgirl activities. And the snake it was that died. By your hand. Or your instruction. The under-forester's evidence is yet to be heard. I dare say you had no more bad feeling for the creature than you had for Estelle. Its death was necessary and its body useful to you. It established your precedence. Dorm prefect first, school captain next, add a dash of matron. All very useful but what you really wanted was the châtelaine's keys. You wanted Guy de Pacy and you wanted Silmont.

'And then your ambition suffered a kick in the teeth. Estelle discovered that she was pregnant. She seems to have been quite clear that de Pacy was the father. Who knows? She went to tell him. What can have been his reaction? You could probably tell us, Jane, because I suspect he unwittingly asked your advice. You probably heard Estelle's version of events after lights out? Whatever you said – it doesn't appear to have damped down the incandescent reaction. I was here that evening Estelle had her rendezvous with Guy. I believe she was genuinely in love. I'm guessing that he was fond of her. I'm further guessing that, in the flood of feeling that came with the notion that he was to be a father, he was telling the truth when he said he proposed marriage to her that night and she accepted him.'

Jane's face had grown pale and her mouth was set in a tight line as he pressed on.

'One or other of them confided in you the next morning. And you sprang into action. You decided to kill two birds with one stone. If you removed Estelle, there yet remained the obstacle of the lord. You were alarmed to note his stretches of normality between the fits of madness and pain. Wills may be altered at such times. And you knew from your father's experience that patients can linger for inconveniently long periods. You were aware of Guy's hatred for his cousin and his impatience to take the reins. The lord's own behaviour presented you with an irresistible opportunity.

'In a fit of moon-fuelled rage last Friday evening he had cleared the table tomb of its stone cargo. Anyone making serious enquiries would come rapidly to the conclusion that *he* was guilty of the vandalism and if the conclusion was not being arrived at rapidly enough, there you were, ready to whisper gravely of psychological disturbance and fearful disease. Ready to deliver up his cloak with a cigar end conveniently in the pocket to intrigue any bumbling bobbies. If, subsequently, a flesh-and-blood offering appeared in the same spot, the inference would be clear. The maniac had struck again. And that, I'm sure, is what you were expecting. Both crimes would be laid at the door of the mad lord. He would be arrested, executed or locked up in an asylum for the insane for the rest of his days. Two lives for the price of taking one.

'But how to persuade Estelle to make a victim of herself? Nothing easier. She is happy once more and in high good spirits. Her sense of fun leads her to agree to playing a silly joke on Cecily. "Imagine the scene – when she gets back home and Daddy has the film developed! What a souvenir! What a laugh!" You borrow the camera and arrange to meet Estelle at the chapel. But you gild the lily. You plan to have a fall-back position if things go wrong. The lord is to take the blame but he is a man with influence. You can't be perfectly certain that he won't come up with some defence you hadn't anticipated. So Cecily is a reserve suspect.

'A wise precaution, it must have seemed! Things did go wrong for you at first. It was your bad luck to find the crime being investigated by two competing detectives, one, at least, the star in his force's firmament. But worse – the lord was inconveniently and unexpectedly away from the scene at the moment of the murder. And then the diligent police discover for themselves the contents of Cecily's camera. You had decided these officers, since you'd been landed with them, could be of great use to you. A little nudge here, a dig of the spur there, and you'd have them moving wherever you wanted them to go. You didn't have much respect for their detective abilities but you feared the possibilities of the new forensic sciences and took precautions. Fingerprints were . . .' He paused and went on, 'mostly . . . rubbed away. Pity. It is fingerprints we rely on for a conviction. More reliable than a confession, we find in England. Were you aware – I think you must have been – that a single print is enough to clinch a case? Juries adore them! They take the weight of responsibility from their shoulders. A scientifically arrived at conclusion is always

300

more acceptable than a moral judgement to twelve good men and true. Circumstantial evidence, deduction, are as nothing compared with the cold scientific condemnation of a single print.'

He broke off tantalizingly, leaving Jane Makepeace to wonder exactly where she had carelessly left a print.

'The trousers you wore for their convenience in scrambling about in the moat were – just in case – stashed away amongst Estelle's skirts, ready to be packed off and sent abroad unremarked. But . . .' Deep in thought, Joe strolled to the window and flung it open, fanning his face.

Jacquemin reached down and produced the black trousers. He handed them to Joe. Jane's eyes followed them but still she did not break her silence.

Joe now faced playing his two last cards.

'You slid down a south-facing slope to get the incriminating shots you wanted. Leaving fragments of earth and plant matter on the fabric. These have been studied under the microscope in the laboratory and identified.'

'Oh, really! I've heard enough! One: those are not my trousers. And two: Cecily who owns them is always crawling around in the undergrowth. Ask her where she's been lately.'

'I can tell you exactly where the trousers went on their last outing. There's a tiny Provençal plant growing on the south side of the moat where we found boot scrapes. It is very rare. *Thymus pseudolanuginosus*. Are you familiar with it? It is vestiges of this plant that we were able to comb from your trousers,' he lied convincingly.

Jane Makepeace was convinced. But unimpressed. 'I think you cannot have heard me clearly. Those are Cecily's trousers. She wears the uncouth garments all the time. You must have noticed.'

Such was her bored confidence that Joe was silent for a moment. He picked up the trousers, examining them once again. He looked up to see Dorcas mouthing a number at him, and went straight back on the attack. 'Miss Somerset's waist size is a generous thirty inches, I'm told. These are twenty-four inches. Exactly the same as yours. In any case, not difficult – merely time-consuming – to check sales receipts from Harrods.'

A slight flicker of emotion across her face told him that she understood the seriousness of her position but she still refused him the satisfaction of a comment.

A car screeched noisily up to the window and a door slammed. At an annoyed glance from Jacquemin, Joe got up and closed the window again. They listened as feet pounded down the corridor. There was a rap on the door and Martineau came straight in.

'Yes, Lieutenant?' Jacquemin greeted him.

'It's here, sir. They've just driven it over from Avignon. Urgent, the sergeant said.'

He handed over an envelope to the Commissaire.

'Ah! At last!' Jacquemin exchanged meaningful glances with Joe and slit open the envelope. 'From the laboratory.' He studied a sheet of paper with an expressionless face, stared at Jane Makepeace for a moment and passed the sheet to Joe, ensuring that Miss Makepeace caught a clear glimpse of the police letterhead.

'Now what have we?' Joe began to mutter. He summarized for his audience: 'The fingerprints lifted from the enclosed object were clear. Photographs reveal, apart from smudged prints – possibly those of the owner – one thumb and one first finger. The thumb provides fifteen distinct points of agreement with that of one of the people whose prints were sent in from the château. Fifteen! Remind me, Jacquemin, how many you require in France for a conviction. Twelve, you say. Will you show Miss Makepeace the object on which her fingerprints were so clearly evident?'

Jacquemin opened the smaller envelope and placed the lens cap on the desk.

'You gave it to Estelle to hold. She still had it clutched in her dead hand on the pathologist's slab. I told you the dead could speak, Jane.'

302

# Chapter Thirty-Five

Joe held his breath. If this was not Jane Makepeace's breaking point, she didn't have one.

The room fell silent, all eyes turned on her.

Pale with stress or anger, she rose to her feet and, ignoring Joe, spoke to Jacquemin in clear French. 'This cap is the bit that comes at the front of the camera that Cecily's so proud of. She didn't exactly pass it around for the appreciation of the crowd – she is rather possessive and secretive about it. But I managed to get my hands on it on one occasion. If you've developed the film, you'll have noticed a picture of a group of us posing in the courtyard. I'm on the front row. Cecily asked me to hold the lens cap for her while she took the photograph . . . she didn't want to put it down on the gravel . . . always treading on it, she said. You can ask any one of the others who were there at the time. They'll tell you. Of course my prints are on that thing! I'm always the one who gets asked to hold things, find things, sort things out! And now I'm being expected to bear the responsibility for this nonsense? Not on your life, Commissaire!'

Enjoying Jacquemin's consternation, she drew herself up to her full height and with the cool, amused expression of a Greek Kore added: 'And now I'm leaving to go about my lawful business. I suggest you get on with yours.'

Joe and Jacquemin looked at each other, unable to conceal a flash of dismay. Each understood that the case against her was so weak as to be laughed out of court in

France or in England. Jacquemin had been right – a confession was essential. It was clear that nothing less would bring her to justice. It was equally clear that she would never deliver one.

'No! Make her stay, Joe!' A shrieking, stamping Fury dashed forward and blocked her path. Dorcas delivered to her face a torrent of cursing in Romany, as far as Joe could follow a word. 'You're a murdering, hard-hearted witch! And why,' she turned to Joe, 'do you keep saying she took *one* life? Doesn't Estelle's baby count for anything? Two!' she yelled at Jane. 'They were brought in as an offering – like a cat's kill in the night. "There, see what a loving cat I've been. Blood on the carpet? You should be grateful. I did it for you ... Pat my head and tell me how clever I am ..." She can't just walk out of here ... Joe? Commissaire?'

Before they could speak she was rattling on: 'Give her a choice. She can either make an oral confession here, at once in front of us, and then get straight into a police car to take her to Avignon or –' her tone chilled and she spoke emphatically – 'we make her face a much more terrible authority.'

Joe was mystified. 'You're calling on God?' he asked.

'No! Divine retribution takes far too long. And the thunderbolts never land where you'd like them to land. Not God – Guy! You could summon Guy de Pacy to have an interview with her. Here in this room. When you've told him exactly what she's done – leave them alone together. Let *him* ask the difficult questions: Why did you kill the woman I loved? Why did you kill the child I would have loved? Why did you think I would spend the rest of my days with a conscienceless killer?'

'No! No!' Joe protested. And, seeing his way through: 'Impossible! Guy is wounded to the heart and suffering dreadfully. The words he delivered over the corpse of Estelle constantly come back to me: "I want this killer, Sandilands," he said. "I want his guts. I want to see the

304

light die in his eyes; I want to hear his last gasp." He has a filthy temper. And – let's remind ourselves – he's something of a killer himself. We couldn't leave her alone with him, the woman who murdered his child.' Joe shuddered. 'Out of the question! I won't be held responsible! This woman's ruined his life. In the grip of a red rage he would throttle her!'

Jacquemin picked up his cue. 'It would be a *crime passionnel*, Sandilands. Crimes of passion! I am aware that we French are generally condemned for our too ready understanding and forgiveness of such uncontrollable flare-ups!'

He pursed his lips, shook his head and came to a decision.

'Martineau, go and fetch de Pacy.'

# Chapter Thirty-Six

Joe settled down at the table in the deserted hall with a cup of tea brought to him by Nathan Jacoby and, in return for the kindness, launched again into an account of the confession and arrest of Jane Makepeace.

Nathan's reaction of: 'Good Lord! I don't believe it! But she was kind to Estelle! None of the others were. A fine woman, I'd have said,' was completely at odds with the rest of the reactions he'd listened to. Everyone else, on hearing the news, suddenly put on an expression of omniscience. Of course, they'd always had their suspicions. She was just too good to be true, wasn't she? Oiling her way into the lord's confidence like that. And what a way to treat poor Guy who'd been so good to her . . .

'A fine woman,' Nathan had insisted. 'Are you quite sure, Joe?'

'She admitted her crime to the Commissaire rather than face Guy de Pacy and account for her foul act,' said Joe.

'But why?'

'She loved him. As far as that woman is capable of finer feeling, I truly believe she did. For the first time – and quite late – in her life, she found a man she could admire. But I don't think he would have come in for such close attention had he not been on the brink of inheriting all this.' Joe waved an arm around. 'She really fell with a bang for Silmont. And for the wonderful things it contained. For their own sake, I'm sure. Greed of a monetary kind was not, I think, a spur to murder. She handled the silver, the

306

china, the tapestries every day . . . knew them better than their owner possibly. She wanted them for her own. Quite desperately. And was ready to sacrifice three lives she considered worthless to have them.'

'Glad to hear you're counting correctly, Joe.'

He turned to find Dorcas had come up silently behind them.

'But it was very nearly four, you know,' she pointed out. 'Marius?'

'Yes. When she found out he'd caught a glimpse of her in the chapel, she decided to get rid of him too, didn't she?'

'She certainly volunteered to walk the boys down to their grandmother's house. And perhaps that was out of character.'

'It certainly was! The boys can't stand her. She could just have intended to question Marius on the way down and check that he hadn't remembered anything incriminating. She was safe from suspicion as long as he held to the story he was telling everyone that it was a man who'd come into the chapel. In his village world, women just don't wear trousers. And, being a tall woman, her feet are larger than the average woman's. But had he heard her voice? She couldn't be certain and had to find out.'

'We'll never know exactly what her intentions were. But what I do know is that you stepped between them, Dorcas, and put a stop to it. I begin to think you have a more insightful knowledge of the human mind than the psychiatrist's daughter!'


Joe had waved goodbye to the charabanc party with disguised elation. He was staying on for a day, he told them, to catch up with his notes and help Commissaire Jacquemin. Orlando and his mob would be on their way to Aix when he'd finished a painting sometime in the next few days. Petrovsky and his merry band were staying the night also, held over not through duty but necessity. The diligent Martineau had taken it upon himself to crack open the boot of his grand car and discovered there many items of interest to the local PJ. Cocaine, rude pictures, even a rude ciné film in which certain faces at least were clearly recognizable. He and his party were being detained until the morning when he could give a full statement of his activities to the Avignon police.

And Joe had settled to closing down the murder case for any of those guests who wished to speak of it.

'I'm hoping, Nathan, you'll fetch up in London one of these days,' said Joe. 'Let me give you my card. We'll spend a boozy evening remembering Estelle.'

He took out his note-case to find a card and the photograph of Laure and her friends slipped out. Nathan seized on it at once and began to identify and criticize the unknown photographer's equipment and technique. The men were startled to hear a gurgling exclamation of surprise and amusement behind them.

A hand reached out over Nathan's shoulder and took the photograph from him. 'But how on earth, Mr Jacoby, did you come by this? I last saw one of these ten years ago on my mother's mantelpiece. I hardly recognize myself!'

Joe turned to find Petrovsky's duenna laughing down at them. 'Nathan found it in an old postcard sale in Avignon,' he invented.

'That's right. The fair in front of the Pope's Palace,' Nathan added, puzzled but gallantly decorating Joe's lie. 'I collect old photographs.'

'Anyone you know on this, Madame . . . er?' Joe asked with a show of polite interest.

'Carla is my name. I know everyone! Gracious! How dreadful to be a collectable item! It's my confirmation class. Can you guess which one is me?' she asked with a touch of flirtation in her voice.

'Easy,' said Joe. 'I'd recognize those handsome features anywhere. But it's the feet that are the real give-away!'

'I got a ticking-off from the other girls, I can tell you! Showing off and spoiling the line like that. And they were right – I *was* showing off. My parents could afford the ballet lessons, you see.'

'And do you remember the names of the others?'

'Of course! There's the twins Babette and Berthe on the left. They married neighbouring farmers and I still see them from time to time. And my best friend, Marie-Jeanne Durand, on the right. Poor Marie-Jeanne. She got into a spot of bother and we none of us spoke to her for years. Unkind. But after the War to end War, a little thing like a romance that turned sour seemed not so dreadful . . . water under the bridge. She's fine now and I always make a point of coming up here to see her again when the company's in the neighbourhood. I'd never volunteer for this tedious duty otherwise!'

Joe cleared his throat. 'She's still here in the region, are you saying, your friend?' he asked in a strangled voice.

'Of course. Like me, she's much changed. Married – to a veteran of Verdun, widowed, two children . . . life leaves its mark. But she's right here. And happy now. Come with me and meet her, show her the photograph. She'd be very interested . . .'

'No, no! Thank you.' Joe's refusal was more brusque than he would have wished. 'Water under the bridge, as you say,' he murmured. 'Kinder to let it flow away.'

A footman appeared and looked about him in surprise. No lord, no steward, no Miss Makepeace. His eye lighted on Joe.

'Sir. The kitchen would like to know the numbers for dinner tonight. Have you any idea . . .?'

'Make that eight adults and three children. That would be safe. What have we on the menu, Marcel?'

'There's *boeuf gardiane*. Oh, and cook told me to tell you, sir – she's made a *soufflé glacé à la framboise* for dessert. "A bitter-sweet send off", she said I was to say. If that makes any sense?'

'Tell Marie-Jeanne it makes a good deal of sense, will you? Thank you, Marcel.'

309

# Chapter Thirty-Seven

*Surrey, England, late September 1926*

'Lord! Rotten Bramley time again!' said Joe, trampling over the windfall apples in the grass. 'What are you doing, Dorcas, mooning about down here in a damp orchard? You ought to be indoors packing your trunk. Socks to be counted, pencils to be sharpened. Look – I've brought you the geometry set I promised. Aren't you in the least little bit excited at the prospect before you?'

'Of course! I'm terrified but looking forward more than I'm scared. Just. I was saying goodbye to my youth. It's the right season for it, isn't it? Every leaf that plops on to the ground reminds me. Four years of school to come. Intensive years. I've got a lot to make up before matriculation. If I want to get into Imperial College I shall have to work through every holiday as well.' She turned a determined face to Joe. 'I shan't see you again for . . .'

'Four plus three is seven,' he supplied cheerily. 'Seven years. I shall be in my dotage by then and you'll be the one bringing *me* gifts. You know – knee rugs and mint imperials in a two ounce bag. How's Orlando? I haven't seen him since I got back.'

'He's well. Productive and hard at it. He's got a show on in a London gallery in December.'

'How lovely! You must get me an invitation.'

They stared at each other, their minds not engaged by the trivialities they were uttering.

'There's something I must ask you, Joe, before Lydia calls us in for supper.'

'Fire away.'

'You didn't ever tell him, did you? That you'd found my mother? It's important.'

Joe was silent for a moment. 'No. I haven't spoken of her since he asked me to stop my search. But how on earth . . .?'

'She told me herself.'

'What!'

'I got to know her pretty well. She told me her friend Carla had unwittingly given her away to you.'

'But how did *you* ever put two and two together?'

Dorcas grinned. 'I found out the truth in five minutes. I felt very guilty, knowing that you were blowing a gasket, working on the problem. But I asked you to stop as soon as I could.'

'Five minutes? What can you mean by that?'

'That first night I spent at Madame Dalbert's house, looking after the boys, they were a bit upset . . . you know . . . ripples from an adult world disturbing them. When they'd cleaned their teeth I offered to read them a story and sing a song or two. That's always calming. The little one, Marius, bragged that he could sing in English. He knew a special going-to-bed song, he said. He started to sing.'

Dorcas shivered and Joe put his warm scarf around her shoulders. 'I was devastated! He sang words to the tune of "Golden Slumbers". Do you know it? It's rather a dirge but an easy tune for children to carry.'

In her clear voice she launched into the old song:

'Golden slumbers kiss your eyes,
Breakfast awakes you when you rise.
Sleep, Nanny's dumpling,
Do not cry,
And I will sing a lullaby.'

'Dorcas, those aren't the right words. Surely it's "Smi-iles awake you" and "Sleep, little darling", isn't it?'

'That's right! You've met Nanny Tilling who brought me up? Well, you'll know what I mean when I say she's a bit eccentric. Over-bright to be a nanny, Orlando says. She was brought back out of retirement to help my mother look after me the first year of my life, before she ran away. Nanny was easily bored by stories and songs and used to invent her own happy endings and change the words to songs to make more sense. Those words were Nanny Tilling's version of what she thought was a boring piece of nonsense. My mother learned the English song from hearing her sing it and she passed it on to her French children. Her second brood. Marius and René are my half-brothers.'

'And there I was, chasing about, offending village priests, arm-wrestling news editors, and you knew all the time.'

'I'm sorry. And, before you ask – I know about my father. My real father. She told me that too. I think she knew she'd never see me again so she made a clean breast of everything. And she was very concerned that I should know the truth about her leaving me squalling in my cradle. You've probably guessed – my grandmother! Orlando's mother. God rot her! The moment I was weaned, she ordered my mother to leave. She chose a moment when Orlando was away from home, being treated for his lungs in a London clinic. If my mother refused to go, Grandma was going to tell the police that she'd stolen a necklace of hers. And with the attitude of the law being what it is concerning gypsies, she'd spend the next few years doing hard labour in Holloway. Either way, she was going to have to leave her baby in Orlando's care since her son was unaccountably fond of it. Granny gave her a hundred pounds and told her to take the train out in the morning. My mother was alone, despised, friendless and very, very angry. She decided to go home to France and try to come back for me later. At least, that's what she told me, but she could just have been saying that, couldn't she?'

The slight appeal in her voice left Joe speechless and searching for an answer she could believe in.

But before he could flounder into a comforting formula, Dorcas rallied and decided to take a positive line: 'Anyway, my mother showed a bit of spirit and –' she gurgled – 'having been accused of the theft of Granny's best pearls anyway – she took them! Made off with them and sold them in Paris. The money tided her over until she found employment in a hotel kitchen.

'After the war, she went back to her home and was taken in again by her parents. She married a man, a local man who'd been wounded in the war, and they had two sons before he died. Her cooking skills were well regarded and when she was widowed and penniless again, the lord gave her a job in the kitchens at Silmont.'

'She must have been mortified to catch sight of Orlando on the other side of the red baize door!' said Joe.

'Yes. That's why she was so insistent no one should ever pass through it. And when *you* burst in regardless and announced you were an English copper – well, you can imagine the turmoil! She still expects a hand on her shoulder demanding the return of those pearls!'

'Poor Marie-Jeanne! And I shocked her a second time, turning up with you in the kitchens. She was so overcome – now I realize at the sight of you, Dorcas – she collapsed. But she managed to recover herself pretty quickly. It must have been a trying time for the poor woman. Still, I think we came to an understanding, Marie-Jeanne and I.'

'I think she rather liked you ... Now listen, Joe! I'm telling you all this so you'll see how important it is to me that you don't get drunk and reveal all to Orlando. He's as dear to me as any real father. I don't want to distress him. And it would curdle things, cause mistrust, if he suspected I thought of him as anything other than my father. He'd be forever thinking I was about to run off on another wild-goose chase, looking for my own flesh and blood. Well, I'm not! I've decided flesh and blood's overrated. Look at the trouble it caused at Silmont! I love the Dalberts but I knew when it was time to come home. To Orlando, Nanny Tilling, Yallop, Auntie Lydia. To the people I've *chosen* to love and who care for me. I think a child's character is formed by the people around her, the loving faces she sees every day. She inherits their morals, their language, their physical gestures.'

'There are scientists who would take a different view,' Joe objected mildly.

She smiled. 'I know. Nature versus Nurture. Which is more important? It's going to be fun, Joe, acquiring the skills to answer such questions. Ask me again in seven years' time and I may have a different tale to tell. But you do promise you won't say a word to Orlando?'

'I haven't and I never will. Your secrets and everything about you are safe with me, Dorcas.'